Don Juan in Lourdes

For the children of my friend John –

from Henry 9/12/01

By the same author

CARNIVAL OF ANGELS

CLODIA

THE SATYR

THE DECLINE AND FALL OF AMERICA

TO BE A KING

BLOWOUT

OUTBREAK

THE EMPRESS

SECRET PLACES

A PASSION FOR POWER

SONS AND BROTHERS

STONE OF DESTINY

Don Juan in Lourdes

ROBERT DEMARIA

Vineyard Press
Port Jefferson, NY

Copyright by Robert DeMaria, 1966
Originally published by
St Martin's Press, New York, 1966
Library of Congress Catalog Card Number 66-15327.
Published in Canada by
The Macmillan Company of Canada Limited
70 Bond Street, Toronto 2

Vineyard Press edition, 1999
106 Vineyard Place
Port Jefferson, NY 11777
ISBN 0-9673334-0-7

All Rights Reserved

Don Juan in Lourdes

1

WILLIAM SAT DOWN next to Alex on the bed. He looked at his watch and then around the tiny hotel room and then out the single small window. 'London again,' he mumbled. 'London in the fall.'

'I don't believe it,' said Alex.

'You don't believe what?'

'That I'm in another country. I mean it doesn't feel like another country. There are walls and floors and rugs and all that. The people even speak English. The whole idea of being here makes me feel giddy.' He turned over on his back and propped himself up on the pillow. 'How long have we been here now?'

'About six hours,' said William.

'And when is my guided tour going to begin?' said Alex. 'You know this town. You lived here for a year and a half. What do we do now?'

'Well, we unpack our luggage and then head for the nearest pub and order an enormous whisky before it shuts down at three.'

'Professor, you're a genius, a man of action. None of this waiting for Godot, like what do we do now and what do we do now, and after that and then what.'

And after that and after that became a stuttering echo in William's mind. He mocked himself when he wrote, asking always *and what happened after that*, *and then what happened.* And always he argued that it did not matter what happened. All that mattered was how people felt. But no, that wasn't right either. All that mattered was . . . He shook his head imperceptibly. *And after that and after that.* The trouble was that he did not know what mattered. After two unsuccessful novels and one unsuccessful marriage and six years of unsuccessful teaching and indifferent scholarship, he did not know what mattered. *But what do we do now?* We have an enormous whisky. *And then what?* We have another. *And then what?* We write some pages; we tell a story. *And then what?* We find a woman and get laid. Perhaps she's sitting in a café. Perhaps she is in the kitchen in a bathrobe, frying eggs. Perhaps she is even your own wife. But one must find her. *And then what?* Then you smoke a cigarette of course. One always smokes a cigarette after making love. One looks at the ceiling and smokes and tries not to think of what is coming next. *And then what?* And then you say I love you and go to the bathroom.

'It's ten minutes after two,' said Alex. 'Let's go down into the grey and smoky town. It takes me a long time to see things through this keyhole of an eye of mine, and I want to get my fill before some bastard stuffs the hole with cotton.'

'What have they given you this time?' said William.

'Six months to a year. For five years now they have been giving me six months to a year and still nothing happens. It doesn't get better and it doesn't get worse. I went through the whole damn thing again before we left New York.'

'You never told me what they said.'

'What's the difference what they say? They really don't know any more than I do. They keep telling me that I'm slowly going blind, as if that were news to me. But they don't know why. There's no visible cause.' He laughed at his own pun.

'Maybe it's a curse and not a disease after all,' said William.

'Did you ever rape anyone or look the wrong way at your mother?'

'Not that I know of.' Alex adjusted his tie. He was a lean, muscular man of forty with very short black hair and dark, hard features, which came, he insisted, from the Indian blood in his father's line. It was the perfect face for an eye-patch. In fact, he looked like a very civilized pirate, an effect he relished, especially since his last name was Morgan—Alexander Morgan, American, self-made, contractor, speculator, pirate, drunkard, Roman Catholic, father of nine children, autocrat, proletarian gadfly, electrician, commoner by birth, aristocrat by choice, weeping lover, and organ player.

William was taller than his friend, and broader. He looked uncomfortable in his clothes, as though nothing quite fitted him. But under the excess weight and the puffiness of his face one could still distinguish the handsome athlete, the Ivy League halfback who once won the Curtis Memorial Trophy, 'a hunk of plated tin' as he called it, which he later gave to an incidental girl friend in a fit of drunken bravado and generosity.

William turned the key in the old door and they almost tiptoed down the noisy wooden steps, three flights to the lobby with its high-backed chairs and outdated magazines. Behind the reception desk sat a pretty young girl. 'She wasn't there when we checked in,' said William. 'There was an old broomstick full of broken arteries. I'd better give the lovely the key. One never knows.'

'Don't start anything now, Doc, it's almost closing time at the pub. Later.'

William went to the desk and handed the girl the key. They exchanged smiles and a few words. Alex watched them patiently.

William came back grinning. 'Her name is Lucy Gordon,' he said. 'She's got the biggest, juiciest lips I've ever seen and she and her girl friend are having dinner with us tonight.'

Alex shook his head and laughed and they went out into the dull but shocking sunlight.

At the End-of-the-Wall pub William the guide and his near-blind friend Alexander Morgan had two double whiskies each.

'My first pub,' said Alex in his best boyish manner. 'After all these years, after all the books, after rolling that delicious word around in my mouth a thousand times.' He waited for his piece of an eye to adjust to the cosy, dark room. The shapes grew clearer. The faces that at first had been blank now developed noses and eyes. 'There's a rug on the floor,' he said. 'And a lot of dark woodwork. It smells warm and friendly, like a private living-room.'

'It's the names I like best,' said William, waiting over his Scotch for Alex to make his slow transition to the world of colour and form. He was impatient sometimes with his old friend's ailment. He wanted him to see everything. He wanted to share his own experience, his glimpses and revelations, with this innocent, playful boy of forty. They had little in common except this wonderful ability to sense, with equal swiftness, the humour or sadness or strangeness in a situation or a given moment. William was a writer and a teacher. Alex downed his booze in the local gin-mills with carpenters and labourers and drifters, and was, indeed, one of them. His world was made up of wrenches and electric wires and black tape and paint, not of books and typewriters and quiet intelligent conversations about Smollett or Melville or Virginia Woolf over polite cups of coffee in faculty lounges, or sherry at Dr. Woodside's house between five and seven.

'There's the Bag of Nails and the Blue Goat and the Crack-in-the-Floor and the Golden Bird,' said William.

Alex laughed. 'How about the Purple Heart, the Blue Ball, the Bard and the Bawd, the Stick in the Mud, the Fly in the Soup?'

'Stop! Enough! Show a little respect for a fine old institution.'

They raised their glasses and drank again. They listened to the babble of the half-dozen voices in the muffled room.

Then Alex said, 'Don't fool around with the sweet young thing at Woodbury Court. She's probably just out of high school with hot pants and high hopes.'

'Well, that gives us something in common, then,' said William. 'I mean I'm just out of a job and in the same condition.'

'I don't mind the old voluptuaries and the sophisticated career girls, but I hate to see you spoil the young ones.'

'Only because you have daughters and feel very fatherly and protective. But not all the girls in the world are your little girls.'

'If I could get away with it I would turn them all into a harem of wives for myself, just to keep them away from bastards like you.'

William looked away, and then glanced at his watch. 'It's closing time. Let's get out into the fresh air. I'll show you Soho, if you want. You'll enjoy it.'

They walked through Wardour Street and Old Compton Street and Greek Street. Alex held his friend's arm and William guided him, though he felt somewhat self-conscious. They passed the shops, the restaurants, the strip-tease joints. A little girl of a whore standing in a doorway beckoned to them. William saw her and smiled but said nothing to Alex.

'What a great place,' said Alex, moving his head in every direction, like an insect trying to get a sense of the whole by rapidly piecing together the visible fragments. 'What was that?' he said suddenly, searching to locate something that had swept rapidly across his narrow field of vision.

'What?' said William, also looking in all directions.

'Something went past me just then that looked and felt like a magnificent and sheer blue veil. I expected a fragrance of perfume to follow, but it didn't. Was it a woman or a curtain or something?'

'I don't know,' said William. 'I can't see anything around that looks like a blue veil.'

'Perhaps it was the wind,' said Alex, and they walked on.

They went up to Soho Square and sat down in the little park. It was a warm and pleasant afternoon. The sun broke through the sweeping patches of clouds and fell here, then there, then suddenly everywhere for a moment. Faces turned up towards it to absorb the warmth, newspapers collapsed for a moment in the hands of indifferent readers, and then stiffened again as the sun passed. They sat next to two old women, both of whom wore straw hats with artificial flowers, and ancient reading glasses. They were bundled in long skirts and sweaters and seemed to huddle together as they talked. Across the way a tall, unshaven youth was reading a book with near-sighted intensity. His thin legs were crossed and he rocked back and forth in a precise, cradle-like rhythm.

'Did you spend a lot of time here?' said Alex. 'I mean when you lived in London.'

'Yes,' said William, remembering those bleak days with Maggie. Sometimes after a murderous battle with her he would walk for miles, even in the dead of winter. Sometimes he would sit in Soho Square and wait and wait, as if something important was going to happen any minute, as if the solution would come. But it never came and the battles got worse, until at last they shrugged it all away and retreated into separate worlds. Big, beautiful, arrogant Maggie. She had the hands and the gestures of a saint and the will of a tiger. For a moment he saw those huge and fiery eyes again and that elegant, bony face.

'Does it remind you of Maggie?' said Alex. 'Does everything in this town remind you of your big broad?'

'Yes, everything. I didn't think it would.'

'I thought it was all over—finished.'

'You mean the marriage. Yes, the marriage was finished before it began. It was impossible. But there are other things.'

Alex was annoyed. He lit a cigarette and snapped his metal lighter closed with an angry gesture. 'Don't try to see her, Doc,' he said.

'Why not?' said William, still remembering one especially cold day when he sat there in Soho and allowed his tears to spill over, because he knew at last that though he loved this remarkable woman to whom he was married, he could no longer live with her, no longer tolerate her freedom, her generosity, her inability to commit herself to anyone or anything but herself. She belonged to no one and least of all to him. That was the way she had put it. She would accept no cage smaller than the entire universe, and even then would rattle at the bars and pound her bloody knuckles against the iron locks.

'Because she'll try to get you back and you won't be able to say no,' said Alex. 'And that will be the end of our pilgrimage.'

Alex had looked forward to their trip for a long time. He and William had talked about it for at least ten of the twenty years that they had known one another. 'Some day,' Alex would say, 'we'll go to Europe, just you and I. We'll take it by storm, a real pilgrimage. London, Paris, Rome, the islands, and finally Lourdes. We'll wind up in Lourdes, where we'll pick up a couple of miracles. I'll get my eyesight back, and——'

'And I'll be struck blind,' William would answer. It was a joke so often repeated between them that after a while William began to believe that it might be true, that he might, indeed, take this sentimental adventurer to Lourdes and there trade in his own sight, through some kind of divine economics, in order to have his friend's eyes restored. It was as though he secretly longed to do it, but so secretly that he could never even express the conscious wish. He would only laugh or scoff. 'Nothing would be more ironic. What a wonderful proof of God's playfulness and arbitrariness. What a great sense of theatre the old boy has.'

'It would serve you right,' said Alex on one occasion. 'It might even save you.'

'From what?' said William.

'From the mortal sin that enters through the eyeballs.'

'You mean a blind man can't be a lecher?'

And they were off again, accusing, bantering, arguing, another meandering segment of their endless twenty-year-old conversation. William sometimes wondered what it was that kept them talking, circling and circling as though there really was a centre, a point to arrive at, but slowly, cautiously, a point that one must sneak up on, disguised as a drunken, weeping, organ-playing Catholic mystic, or as a drunken Don Juan and serpent-tongued singer of poems. They talked in bars, in Alex's office, walking along the canal, in the car, at parties, sitting in the kitchen surrounded by children. They talked anywhere, with or without interruptions, with or without an audience. Sometimes, when other people were around, their talk became a public performance, almost a vaudeville routine, their wits sharpened by the applause implicit in the laughter and by the sudden sense of real competition between them. Was it possible, William wondered, that the talk was merely an end in itself? Was it possible, after all, that they were not reaching, as they imagined, for a truth, a revelation that lay always just around the next epigram or metaphor?

William admitted that he did not altogether understand, but Alex, who was more stubborn and prouder, insisted always that it was very simple, that they were two halves of a composite genius—or, better yet, that they were like two agents in a spy story, each carrying half of a hundred-dollar bill. Everything presumably would fall into place once the pieces were matched.

So they were on their way to Lourdes, though neither one of them understood why. And it was being en route to Lourdes that mattered as much as getting there. It was the pilgrimage that mattered, the journey. This much they knew instinctively, but because there was much that they did not know about the trip, about each other and themselves, they stumbled inevitably over the obvious questions. 'You don't really expect a miracle, do you?' said William.

'I don't know,' said Alex, looking uneasy. They had been in the Oaktree Bar in Seaville. Charlie Hawkins and Bill Kaup were playing shuffle-board. The sounds of sliding metal discs, subdued laughter, and ice tinkling in glasses intruded on their conversation. In another three days they would be on their way and Alex was alternately elated and depressed by the prospect. 'I'd rather not talk about it,' he said.

'I can understand the other part of it,' said William. 'Seeing Europe, I mean.' He leaned closer to Alex at the bar and put a hand on his shoulder. 'But damn it, don't expect too much—from Lourdes, I mean. Don't build it up in your mind as some romantic, lovely place. I've heard that it's full of souvenir shops and tourists.'

'So I've been told,' said Alex. 'But I've also been told a few other things about the place, about the strangeness of the atmosphere, the intensity and the beauty. But don't worry, Doc. I'm not altogether naïve.'

'You're not naïve at all,' said William. 'You're just a terrible idealist. I should add, however, that you're also a pretty greedy slob. You're convinced you can combine a two-week binge in the fleshpots of Europe with a pious journey to Lourdes.'

'It's the only way to do it, Doc,' he said with his clownish-wise grin. 'The way of the saints.'

The clouds above London parted again. The sunlight escaped and fell on Soho Square, drenching it for a moment in blinding light. The two old women next to them got up with grunts and sighs, folded their newspapers, put away their glasses, and shuffled off arm-in-arm.

The way of the saints echoed in William's mind. St. Maggie of Soho. 'We had a flat not far from here,' he said. 'Three small rooms, a fireplace, high ceilings.'

'Is she still living there?' said Alex.

'As far as I know, but I haven't heard from her in almost a year. After the divorce was final she stopped writing. Before that we kept up a curious, distant correspondence—a letter once or twice a month—newsy, chatty, witty, as though we were both trying to prove that the whole thing did not move us or destroy us. And then she stopped.'

'Perhaps she met somebody else,' said Alex.

'I don't think that that would have made any difference at all to Maggie. No, if she stopped writing it was for some other reason.'

'Maybe she has nothing more to say.'

'No, when Maggie has nothing to say, she talks quite freely. It's when she really has something on her mind that she is silent.'

Alex shifted nervously on the hard bench. He crossed his legs and lit another cigarette. 'Look, buddy,' he said, 'I didn't come all this way to get mixed up in your domestic chaos. Why didn't you warn me before we left?'

'There was nothing to warn you about. I told you it's done—finished. It's a dead issue.'

'Then why do you want to see her?'

'I don't know.' He hesitated. 'Why do you want to go to Lourdes?'

2

AT A QUARTER to eight William and his ward walked carefully out of the darkness of Wooley's pub into the dying grey light of the damp evening. Alex coughed and lit a cigarette. 'Lovely people, the English,' he said. 'So terribly civilized. Terribly, terribly, terribly,' he said, searching for the English pronunciation.

'We've got to pick up the girls at their flat on Manchester Street around eight o'clock,' said William. 'It's just another block or two; we can come back for the car.'

The traffic on Baker Street buzzed by, exhaling its poison into the already thick atmosphere. The shops were lit up. Neon signs pleaded pathetically or beckoned arrogantly. Hair Fashions by Arthur of Baker Street, Mardi Gras Boutique. 'There's a place over there called the Invisible Mending Company,' said William. 'What do you suppose that means?'

'Let's stop in,' said Alex, 'and ask them if they repair broken eyes.'

'Just around the corner now,' said William, wheeling his friend up the street. 'Do you suppose we're presentable enough for the young virgins?'

'We probably smell of booze.'

'Surely no one can object to that.' William straightened his tie and tucked his shirt more neatly into his trousers. He had to suck in his stomach to do it. And then, though it was uncomfortable, he tightened his belt.

'They probably think we're a pair of dirty old men from New York,' said Alex, 'with lots of American dollars to spend on goodies and girls.'

'Well,' said William, 'they're almost right—except for the money part, I mean.'

They stopped in front of a neat, three-story building with a little arched doorway. 'Charming,' said Alex.

'On the outside, anyway,' said William.

Lucy opened the door and ushered them surreptitiously into the dingy two-room flat. 'The landlady is a gossip,' she explained. William introduced Alex and they shook hands.

'Awfully good of you to accept my friend's rather crude invitation,' he said in his worst imitation British. Lucy laughed and blushed slightly. Her skin was cream-white, with a natural, healthy bloom. She had large black eyes and black hair that framed her face and fell to her shoulders. In such a setting her red painted lips looked shockingly sensual and lusty. She was a tall girl with a straight back and one of those deliciously large bosoms that the English often have. Those breasts that in youth ride excitingly high and then in early middle age begin to collapse into a general collection of fat and an awful stockiness that makes some English women of forty look like professional wrestlers.

'The Professor here is a bit forward,' said Alex,

'Oh, we don't mind,' said Lucy. 'I haven't met many Americans before. But do sit down and let me get you something. Jeanne is still dressing. She'll be out in a minute.'

The small living-room obviously doubled as a kitchen and dining-room. On a cluttered counter there was a gas-stove, and across from it a table with two chairs. The other end of the room was reserved for sitting, with its two stuffed chairs, a footstool and a fireplace. They sat down facing the fireplace, which no longer had an opening since it was fitted out with a stove, and Lucy brought them some whisky and an ashtray. 'This is all we have. I hope you don't mind. I hear that Americans like whisky.' She disappeared again and they sat there like two awkward strangers in the waiting-room of a dentist. They dared not say anything, because only a thin curtain separated this room from the bedroom. Alex's eyes gradually became adjusted to the dim light. He saw the Gauguin prints on the wall and the china dolls on the mantelpiece. William noticed that the bookshelf was overflowing with books and magazines and piles of letters. Everything was heaped so closely together in the room that he was afraid to move for fear of knocking something over. A floor lamp crowded him on one side and a very shaky end-table on the other.

Lucy came back with a glass of her own and sat down on the footstool. In a few moments the other girl appeared. The curtain was pulled aside and she stood there, a small fragile-looking creature with sad eyes, a pretty face and a very tiny waist. Her blonde hair was cut short and neatly curled. Lucy and Jeanne looked at one another and then there were introductions.

William grew more and more uneasy in the tiny room and after a few awkward pleasantries he said, 'It's time to eat. Find us a good place, Lucy. We put ourselves in your hands.' And then he looked automatically at her hands. They were large and delicate and white. Lovely hands he thought. Lovely hands!

They wound up at the Kashmiré Restaurant, laughing over the curious menu. The place was almost bare, except for the tables and chairs and a few potted plants. The waiter bowed a great deal and spoke very little.

'We've only been in London about six months,' said Lucy. 'And it's been rather difficult. I mean making friends and finding a flat and a good job and all that. London is such a large city that one gets lost in it.'

'You're not going to stay, then?' said Alex.

She shrugged her shoulders. 'I really don't know. My father would like me to come home to Scotland, naturally, but there's not much future at home. Here at least one meets a lot of people.'

'Like us, you mean,' said William.

'All kinds of people stay at the hotel. It's interesting. I do like people. Then there's the theatre and some concerts and I have a weekly course in world literature. But Jeanne doesn't care much for London. She's thinking of leaving.'

'Oh, please,' said Jeanne, 'let's not talk about all that.'

'Sorry! I only meant—'

'I don't mean to be such a bore,' she said apologetically. 'I really haven't been feeling well and I came along mainly as a favour to Lucy.' She looked from Alex to William and then down at her barely nibbled food.

'Well, whatever it is,' said Alex, 'forget it. Nothing can be that bad. Cheer up and enjoy the evening. After all, you're having dinner with two of the most fascinating men in the Western Hemisphere.'

She started to laugh, but tears came to her eyes instead. She tried to turn away, but then got up and without excusing herself walked out of the restaurant.

'I'm terribly sorry,' said Lucy. 'I'll see if she's all right. She's just had a very bad time with her boy friend.'

The girls were gone and William and Alex stared at one another. 'You can really pick 'em, Doc,' said Alex.

'How was I to know?'

'You ought to know that young girls like that are always suffering from something. If it isn't pimples, it's a broken heart. You should stick to grown-up women who know how to take care of themselves.'

'So what do we do now?'

'Eat our rotten curry, I suppose, and wait here for them. What else?'

'Too bad we can't get a drink in this place,' said William.

'Later,' said Alex. 'We'll find a bar.'

'That's not as easy as you think in this town.'

Lucy came back in about five minutes, shaking her head. 'Jeanne's gone home. I insisted on going with her, but she wouldn't have it. I feel badly about it.'

'Well let's finish up here and then take a ride over to your flat to see how she is,' suggested William.

'The poor girl,' said Alex. 'Is it something serious?'

'Yes, quite serious. You see, there's a man she met at her office. She's a secretary. They went off to Italy on a holiday this summer and now she's pregnant. Yesterday she discovered that he left London for good and gave no forwarding address. I'm worried about her. She comes from a strict family. Her father would literally kill her if he found out.'

Alex shook his head. 'We better find her,' he said.

They drove back to the flat on Manchester Street, but Jeanne was not there. 'Perhaps she went to see someone,' said Alex. 'Is there anyone that she is especially close to in London?'

'No,' said Lucy. 'She spent most of her time with that David character. Strange boy.'

'Could she be out for a walk somewhere?' said William. 'Everybody likes to walk when they're miserable. It's so dramatic, especially at night.'

'Yes, she was inclined to walk at night sometimes. She liked to walk over to the park and just sit there. A very odd girl, Jeanne. Always something of a brooder, you know.'

'She's not liable to do anything desperate, is she?' said Alex.

'I don't know,' said Lucy.

They got back in the car and drove up and down the various streets that she might have taken. A light rain began to fall and it was difficult to see clearly the people who passed. They went very slowly and pulled up once alongside someone who looked like Jeanne from a distance.

It was at least half an hour before they located her. By this time it was raining harder. She was sitting, wrapped in her raincoat, on a bench in the park, staring at the water. She said hello to them when they walked up to her, as though it were a perfectly ordinary chance meeting. Alex took Lucy aside and said quietly, 'Let me talk with her. I have a daughter almost the same age.'

'Yes,' said William, 'he's very good that way. Let him talk to her.'

'I'll walk her home,' he said. 'Why don't you and William go somewhere for a drink or a cup of coffee.'

Lucy agreed a bit reluctantly and she and William went off

in the Anglia. 'She will be all right with him, won't she?' said Lucy.

'Of course she will. Alex is the father of nine children and everybody's father confessor.'

'Nine children?'

'Yes. Remarkable, isn't it. Especially for a man who is going blind.'

'I think it's wonderful. I always wanted a very large family.'

'Why? Were you an only child?'

'No, I was one of seven—five boys and two girls.'

He saw her smile in the lights that flickered past. The rain stopped and he turned the wipers off.

'Isn't it odd,' she said dreamily.

'What's odd?'

'I mean that I should trust you both this way when we've only just met. But I do trust you. There is something very nice about your friend Alex, something very warm. About you too, though it doesn't show straight off.'

'Yes, some people meet and after a few hours feel as if they've known each other for years. I feel the same way about you.' Though there was some truth in what he said, he smiled a bit sadly to himself because the line was so old. He had used it half a dozen times before, and always it worked, and always it was partly true. He felt that way about certain women and they often felt that way about him.

At the Iron Gate they sat and drank brandy until closing time. 'I'm a writer,' he said. 'Though I've been other things—a professor of English no less, and an editor, a clerk, a husband.'

'You're married, then?'

'No, divorced.'

'Oh, I'm sorry.'

'I'm not. Why do people always say I'm sorry when they hear such things, as though someone has just died.'

'It is a kind of death, isn't it though?'

He looked at her as though he were seeing her for the first time. 'You're a smart girl, Lucy. So young and so wise!'

She blushed. 'I'm not wise at all. At twenty-one I should be a lot wiser.'

'What do you mean?' he said.

'I mean I've lived a very sheltered life until now, and there are many things I don't know. I feel absolutely stupid when I talk to some of my London girl friends. They are so terribly sophisticated about—about some things. I feel like a child.'

'I suppose you're talking about men?'

'Partly.'

After the pub closed down they went for a ride into the country. She told him about her father, who was a shop-keeper, and her mother, who came from a very good family in London and was disowned for marrying her father. And under the influence of the brandy she said quite freely that she had never been in love and had never been to bed with a man. 'Perhaps because I had such an odd childhood and a terrible experience when I was ten years old. We were living in London and we had a boarder, a Mr. Thurston. One night he tried to attack me. It was awful. He was an ugly man and I was so frightened.'

'Did he succeed?'

'Almost. In fact, I really don't know. The police took him away and we never talked about it again. But ever since then I've had this awful feeling that I've been spoiled by it and that I will never be quite normal—as a woman, I mean.'

He smiled. 'I don't see how that's possible. You're a very beautiful girl.' He stopped the car and turned off the lights. He had been watching the road for an appropriate place. 'Cigarette?' he said, leaning back in his seat. He offered her one and took one for himself. They sat quietly for a moment and watched the clearing sky. Everything was still. He could smell her beside him. He could hear her breathing and he could hear the delicate crackling of the cigarette as she puffed it into life and then tapped it on the ashtray. She wore an open sweater and her large bosom strained against her cotton blouse. He leaned towards her and kissed her—first on the cheek and then on the side of the neck and the ear. She did not move. She did not say anything. She just stared out the window as though nothing were happening. Then he found her mouth and pulled her towards him.

He felt her breasts, explored their shape and lifted them as though he were weighing them in his hand. He liked their firmness and heaviness. One by one he undid the buttons of her blouse until his hand could reach inside and feel the coolness of her flesh. She only resisted when he tried to unfasten her bra. 'No,' she said quietly, holding his hand away from her. 'You mustn't.' But he could tell she was excited.

'I'm sorry,' he said, 'I like the way you feel. I like to touch you.' And then Maggie's burning eyes flashed across his mind. That was her line—*I like to touch you.* With those greedy saintly hands of hers she touched everything—him, other men, round smooth stones at the beach, the clay she modelled with, everything.

He moved away from her and she looked at him in the darkness as though he were a boy with hurt feelings. She touched his arm. 'Please, William. You must know how I feel. I mean you're just passing through London and all this is just a lark for you.'

'Nothing is just a lark for me,' he said.'I take life quite seriously. What difference does it make that we only met? Something very nice has happened between us. We understand one another, and because we do I suddenly don't feel lonely any more.'

She came to him this time and kissed him passionately on the mouth and pressed herself against him. 'Let's get out and walk a bit,' she whispered. 'The rain has stopped.'

At Manchester Street Alex sat with Jeanne in the living-room. He had convinced her that a little whisky would warm her up after the walk in the rain. He had distracted her with a humorous account of his own life—his wife and children, his various businesses, his friends, his trouble with his eyes. After a while she began to smile again and he reached over and patted her on the head gently as though she were a small child. 'Perhaps you're doing your father an injustice by not trusting him. Believe me, Jeanne, his severeness with you comes out of love. It's his way of saying he cares.'

'Perhaps you're right,' she said. 'And besides, maybe David will write to me in a few days to say that everything is all right.'

Jeanne made some coffee and they talked some more. But it grew very late and after a while her eyes began to close with weariness, 'I'm sorry,' she said, 'I've just got to go to bed. Do you mind?'

'I would leave,' said Alex, 'but William is coming here with Lucy to pick me up. I don't know my way around at all. If you trust me to be a gentleman, feel free to go to bed and I'll sit up for them.'

'All right,' she said. She leaned over him, kissed him on the forehead and disappeared past the curtain into the bedroom. He could hear her getting undressed, and for a moment the thought excited him, but then he slipped into a grinning philosophical mood in which he saw himself as the sweetest and kindest of men. He stared into the fireplace as though it held a roaring beautiful fire and waited for his friend.

3

ALEX WAS STILL asleep at Woodbury Court when William left that morning to see George Hamilton, his publisher. When he woke up and staggered into the bathroom he found a note pasted on the mirror of the medicine cabinet with band-aids. 'Audience with his holiness George the ring-giver this morning. If all goes well I'll treat you to lunch. Otherwise have the river dragged. Agent 1066 and all that.' Alex removed the note and read it again in that painfully slow manner of his. His unshaven face eased into a sleepy affectionate smile and he folded the note and put it away in his suitcase. He was inclined to save such things and then, years later, produce them when in fits of sentimentality and nostalgia he needed them to sharpen his memory.

The city looked immense and beautiful and inviting in the clear air and sunshine. He had the whole morning to himself, he thought, and a thrill of excitement and fear went through him. Though he knew his limitations, he enjoyed doing things on his own, especially things that people could not believe he was capable of doing. He shaved and dressed quickly and went into the fresh morning to discover for himself the greatness of this ancient town.

He walked through the quiet neighbourhood in which they were staying, savouring in his own slow way all the sights and sounds. It was a different place, a very different place. Even the sidewalks felt different. The traffic moved up and down the wrong way. The cars and trucks were miniatures. He stopped to examine a milk wagon, a little trailer parked without its cab by the kerb, full of pint bottles. A tweedy woman walked by with a basket and a dog and he said, 'Good morning!' In his mind he tipped his hat and was Ronald Colman.

As he walked he thought of all the place-names he associated with London, names collected from novels or English films or conversations—Hyde Park, Piccadilly, Bloomsbury, Regent Street, Fleet Street, the British Museum, Trafalgar Square, Regent's Park. Like a small boy in a sweet shop he clutched his penny of a morning and tried to make a choice. Sherlock Holmes and Baker Street intruded, but no, he had already seen Baker Street and it was rather disappointing. There were St. Paul's and Westminster Abbey, but he could not imagine plunging into the shadows of a church on such a beautiful morning.

He came to a busy road and held his hand up for a taxi. 'Regent's Park,' he told the driver, who looked puzzled but drove on for a few minutes before asking him which part of the park he wanted. 'It doesn't make any difference,' said Alex, 'I'm only visiting.'

The driver let him out in front of the Zoological Gardens and Alex tipped him excessively. He kept a bunch of coins in his hand and touched them constantly, as though he were memorizing the denominations. At the main gate he offered his hoard of coins to the man at the ticket window. 'Help yourself,' he said, revealing with just those two words the fact that he was American, and, therefore, unable to read or write or count in English.

It was only mid-morning, but already the park was filled with parents and children, visitors from other parts of England with their curious accents, and tourists from overseas with their cameras and foggy, patient expressions. He was delighted by the colours, by the children, by the many foreign languages and the many varieties of English.

He followed the main path to a modern footbridge that crossed a canal and found himself staring at a group of camels. What is a camel? he said to himself. A horse made by a committee. And he laughed to himself. A little boy stared at his black eye-patch. 'Are you a pirate?' said the boy in his girlish voice.

'Of course I'm a pirate, son,' said Alex, poking playfully at the boy's curly blond hair.

'Well, if you're a pirate,' said the boy, 'where's your sword?'

'I left it aboard ship. We're anchored in the Thames.'

The boy half believed him and backed away a step or two. 'Well, my uncle Fred is a bobby and he'll have you hanged. They always hang pirates.'

Alex laughed. 'Don't you worry about it, lad.' He started to bend over to reassure the boy when suddenly he was gone. A mother's voice called 'Tommy!' and he slipped out of Alex's keyhole of light.

Further down the path he stopped to watch the crowd feeding the elephants, who were only separated from the spectators by a narrow moat. The lumbering, patient creatures reached across the moat with their trunks to suck up the edibles that were offered them. They rocked back and forth on the edge of the cliff of their concrete island and waited for peanuts and apples and bread. Little boys and girls screamed with delight as the damp and rubbery snouts inhaled the tiny offerings. Some children cried. They hid behind their coaxing parents and peeked out around skirts or trousers, wide-eyed and dubious.

Alex sat on a bench and watched the parade of visitors. Sometimes a young man went by with his arm around his girl and seemed unable to concentrate on any other animal but the one he clutched. Alex reminded himself that he was in another country, that he was in England, in London, at the zoo in Regent's Park, as if the idea was even more exciting than the experience itself. And then suddenly he grew lonely because he pictured the vast ocean that separated him from his noisy crowded home, his nine children, his wife, his friends, his army of relatives.

He had taken this trip partly to escape all that for a while, and now he was suddenly all soft and sentimental about it. It was only loneliness, he told himself. Or possibly he was unaccustomed to this much freedom. In the months before he had left he had become depressed. His family seemed to be falling apart. There had been trouble with the boys at school, real trouble. His oldest daughter was defying him daily to carry on a wild flirtation with an older boy, a man in fact. And he and his wife were no longer able to speak sensibly to one another. He still could not figure out what was happening to his world, to his dream of a kind of patriarchy, in which he reigned, benevolently, of course; in which he provided for everyone and taught them about goodness and truth and beauty. His children had turned on him. They called him a tyrant. And his own wife accused him of being a worthless drunk. What had he done wrong? Surely it was his privilege as a man to do things his own way, to exercise his authority, to rule his family. And it was also his privilege to condemn those things in his own society that he felt were harmful, those things that dulled the senses and corrupted the spirit.

Because he did not allow his children to play the American games of 'going steady' and 'raising hell' he was considered eccentric and harsh. And because he did not treat his wife as an equal, because he felt that her place was constantly at home, he was accused of being old-fashioned and European. But there was more to it than that. There was his failing eyesight; there was his own despair and restlessness. Yes, he drank a great deal and he was not very practical about money. And sometimes he reached for an idea or an experience and there was no one there to help him achieve it. In the midst of that great crowd of people that he had created and collected he was often lonely and dissatisfied. And still there was more to it than that. There was a darker streak in him that he never understood—a black and angry band of feeling that wound its way through his whole being. What was it? What was the secret cruelty or sin or pain or terror? What was it?

The roaring of lions woke him from his reverie. The crowd rushed past him in the direction of the sound in the hope, no doubt, of witnessing some thrilling exhibition of violence. Perhaps some child had crawled into the cage and was being clawed to death. He shook away the bloody image. Why had he done that? Why had such a thing even occurred to him? He walked back along the path the way he had come. Surely there was time for a drink, he thought, before he went back to the hotel. Or perhaps he would buy a bottle and bring it back with him.

4

AT ONE O'CLOCK in the morning at the Woodbury Court Hotel the only light that was still on was in room thirty-six, where Alex lay, propped up by pillows, on the uneven and sagging bed, and where William sat in the posture of a drunken and senile professor in a wooden armchair. In his slumped position he could feel the creasing of the fat around his middle and the rounding of his shoulders. What a feeling of heaviness old men must have, he thought, dragging around their thick old dying bodies, with no youthful surges of energy, no feeling of sheer physical power. He raised an arm and let it drop like so much dead flesh against the wood of the chair.

'I don't understand,' said Alex. 'How could he turn you down like that, the second most brilliant man in the Western world? You write like an angel.'

'When I write,' said William. 'He's tired of waiting. I haven't written a line in two years. No, almost three years. And old George Hamilton just doesn't dig sick oysters and pearls and all the fuss about art.'

'No more money,' said Alex.

'No more,' said William. 'At least until I produce a manuscript. I owe him a book.'

'Which book?'

'Any book. A novel. My next novel, the contract said. But I don't have a next novel. I may never have a next novel.'

'I hope you didn't tell him that.'

'Of course I told him. Why shouldn't I? I told him he'd have to gamble. But he said he wasn't a gambling man. Oh, he wasn't angry or anything. In fact, he was embarrassed. Very polite. Very sorry and all that. Even invited us to dinner at his home.'

Alex drank from the bottle. 'Well, anyway, it's a free meal.'

William heaved himself out of the chair and paced heavily across the room to the window. 'Yeah, a free meal,' he echoed. 'George said Maggie might be there. He was giving me fair warning.'

'You didn't by any chance try to get in touch with her, did you?' said Alex.

'No,' he said, turning slowly away from the window. 'No, I decided I wouldn't, or couldn't, or didn't want to after all. I don't know, I walked past the house three times, but I didn't go in.'

'Good,' said Alex. 'Stay away from her.'

'It's not easy,' said William. 'You don't know Maggie St. Claire. She's no ordinary woman.'

'All women are ordinary,' said Alex.

William laughed. 'Some day you'll meet her. Then you may understand.'

'Some day,' said Alex, 'but not this time. This is *my* trip—I mean *our* trip. Let's not louse it up. Let's not get bogged down. Remember what you said before we left. We need a few weeks of total freedom. Freedom to roam. Freedom from everyone and everything. No letters, no phones, no clawing women and children.'

William found his glass and emptied it. 'All right,' he said. 'All right. No women. No children. We'll have what Huck Finn calls an *adventure*.'

Alex relaxed against his pillow and smiled. 'Yeah,' he said

dreamily. 'We'll have this here adventure, and then we'll go home.'

'Sure,' said William. 'Then we'll go home. You can have your Paradise Island in the bay and I can be a teacher again.'

'You *are* a teacher,' said Alex.

'I am a teacher. I mean I was a teacher. I mean I shall have been a teacher. Should have been?'

'Shall have was. The future imperfect past tense.'

'We need more tenses. Break up this rigid sense of time. William Mariner's New Approach to Grammar. Future imperfect past tense, temporary present perfect, occasional present pluperfect past.'

Alex raised his heavy eyelid and smiled. He reached for the bottle of Scotch which stood on the table beside the bed and almost knocked it over. Then he had it by the neck and drank from it. It was half empty. The other bottle, which lay on the floor under William's chair, was altogether empty.

'Not to mention preverbs,' said Alex.

'What's a preverb?'

'You're the teacher; you tell me. There are adverbs; why not preverbs?'

'Oh, yes, I remember now, chapter six, section four. A preverb is something that happens before something else happens.'

'Like first you kiss her and then you screw her?'

'No Mr. Morgan. I'm afraid you flunk. First you screw her, then you kiss her.'

'Sorry, teach!'

'And why not projectives, adpositions, prenouns, and like that?'

'Is a mother a prenoun, Professor?'

'Right! Without which you would never have the baby noun.'

'A genius. What a genius we are, Doc. We need a new book. The True Grammar. None of this Mr. Jones has a square car stuff or John plays with Mary.'

'We'll make it required reading—the New Grammar, I mean —for everyone on Paradise Island.'

'Incorporated,' said Alex. 'Don't forget that it's a private company. None of this socialistic, Utopian, kibbutz, dream-world stuff. I have an option to buy. All I need now is about a hundred thousand dollars.'

'Not to mention another hundred thousand for improvements,' said William.

'Yeah,' said Alex, 'we better start lining up stockholders.'

'At a hundred bucks a share it's going to be a long line,' said William. 'That piece of sand out there is no more than three acres. Maybe you can sell off a few concessions. You know, the marina, the gas station, the restaurant——'

'No,' said Alex with drunken anger. 'No concessions. No compromises. We need the freedom. That's what we need. Freedom to make a world of our own.'

'On three acres?'

'I don't care how small it is; it's an island, a piece of sand totally surrounded by freedom. Paradise Island, Limited.'

'Oh, Brave New World,' said William, and then yawned. 'How can you start a new Utopia when you can't even get a liquor licence?'

'I'll think of something,' muttered Alex, 'when we get home.'

'Good,' said William. 'Build me a studio out there and I'll be your first legal resident.'

'What do you need with a studio if you can't write any more?'

'I need a place to take girls. Studios always impress them right out of their pants. Besides, it's not true that I can't write any more. I've got a thousand ideas for new books.'

'Oh!' Alex leaned back on the pillows and stared at the ceiling as though he were looking for something. 'Why don't you write a book about how you got fired from Fulton College because you wouldn't sleep with the dean's wife.'

'But I did sleep with the dean's wife.'

'Is that why you got fired?'

'Not entirely, though the dean was a little irked by the scandal. It was something much more trivial. This buxom little girl came in to see me one day about her mid-term paper and I grabbed her tit. I don't know why I did it. I was fed up with the place anyway and she was sitting there with this nice fuzzy sweater on, so I just put my hand on one of those nice round tits of hers and she got all hysterical.'

William stretched out across the bottom of the bed and put his hands behind his neck as a pillow. 'They were all very nice about it, though,' he said. 'They called it an impulse and they said they understood. I wonder what they meant by that.'

'Maybe they understood,' said Alex.

'Maybe,' said William, and then they were both quiet for a while.

'I guess it's about eight or nine o'clock on Long Island now,' said Alex. 'Some of the kids are watching television. Andy is fighting with Julie over who gets the leather hassock. Barbara is pouting on the couch at the other end of the room because her boy friend is working nights at Jones Beach. And Helen, poor Helen is probably ironing and trying to catch a glimpse of the television screen through the bobbing heads of her brood.'

'A touching scene,' said William sleepily.

'A madhouse,' said Alex, 'but I miss it.'

William got up and started to take his clothes off. 'You'll be back to all that soon enough. But first there's Paris and Rome and Mallorca and Lourdes. Just think of Lourdes when you get depressed. Think of the angel water and all those crutches hanging up over the grotto. Think of the miracle that might happen.'

'I can't think about it. I mean, I'm not supposed to think about it.'

'You mean you're afraid to think about it,' said William, pulling back the covers of the bed and forcing Alex to get up.

'Yes,' said Alex, 'that's what I mean. I'm afraid to think about it.'

5

MRS. EDITH SMILEY was a handsome, well-dressed lady of fifty-three who believed that the good life depended entirely on punctuality, cleanliness, good manners, and good books. She could never say exactly what she meant by 'good books', but she pronounced the word *literature* with such lusty fullness and shrill excitement that she always convinced all the ladies of the Wednesday-at-Four Literary Society that she had somehow achieved, through her reading habits, a rare and intense form of aesthetic orgasm, which they could only envy or long for in their dreamy, dull-housewifish way. Naturally, they always re-elected her as president and chairwoman of the Society.

Like many of her friends, Edith Smiley managed to raise her family of three without using up a fraction of that abundant energy with which so many English women are endowed, and without giving away more than half of her pitifully small supply of affection. At fifty-three, then, she was a kind of muscular, smiling anti-woman, who had had her last stumbling sexual encounter when she was forty-four and now welcomed the freedom that came with girdled middle-age. 'Now that the children are grown up at last,' she would say, 'I can turn my thoughts to those more intellectual pursuits which for so many years I have had to put aside.'

Edith Smiley played mother-hostess to William Mariner. She insisted that he arrive at least half an hour before the Wednesday-at-Four meeting so that they could have a little sherry and a chat. 'Only tea is served at the meeting,' she warned him over the phone.

Her enormous house was like a little museum or a Hollywood set for an English melodrama. William was led into a sitting-room by a plumpish maid, where he found his smiling hostess, her arm outstretched towards him as though she had been marooned on a desert island and help had come at last. 'Mr. Mariner,' she said, 'what a pleasure. I've heard so much about you,' she lied. Actually she knew next to nothing about him and had been persuaded to invite him finally by William's London agent, who insisted that Mariner was practically a household word in literary circles in America.

'It was awfully good of you to take time out of your busy schedule to speak to us today. All the members are looking forward to meeting you. But do sit down and have some sherry, or, if you prefer, something else.'

'Actually my schedule is not so busy,' said William, 'and I am eager to meet the members of your Society, which, I understand, has become a real force in the literary world.' After a long nap William was bright-eyed and ready to be civil. He smiled as he felt himself assuming his best academic pose. Professor Mariner, Ph.D. He liked to wave his title in front of himself at times, as a reminder that he had a respectable way of belonging to the world. It was especially nice to have one's name painted on an office door. He remembered his first teaching job, and the first time he had seen his name on a door. It was at Coleman College on the West Coast, a small co-ed school with very high standards. He taught there for two years before returning East to finish his doctorate. It was a sunny and pleasant time for him, though a bit dreamy and unreal. He had an interesting circle of friends, a book to write, and somebody to play tennis with. It seemed like such a long time ago. How young he was! How full of innocence and hope!

William accepted the sherry and complimented Mrs. Smiley on her lovely house. 'Are all the meetings held here?' he said.

'Oh, yes,' said Edith. 'You see I founded the Society some ten years ago. That is, Elizabeth Crestwood and I founded it. But she died four years ago and I have managed to keep it going since then. Fortunately I have this house, which has a lovely meeting-room, a kind of ballroom originally, I suppose.'

William cringed at the thought of addressing a large audience in a large room. He was always most comfortable with small groups. He liked relaxed discussions and seminars and was always very nervous when he had to deliver a formal lecture. Besides, on this occasion he had not prepared a lecture, though he had spent some time during the day drawing up a list of possible subjects. In a pub earlier he had narrowed down the possibilities to 'Hemingway's Puritanism' or something called 'Sex and Sexability in the American Novel'.

Mrs. Smiley talked a great deal and William listened patiently, only half-hearing what she said, but fixing his eyes on her face, her mouth, or nose, or painted left cheek, and nodding politely. 'You have no doubt heard of the annual awards we give to outstanding young writers.'

'Oh yes,' said William.

'This year we are adding the Crestwood Memorial Fellowship—in honour of Elizabeth, of course, who devoted so much of her time and energy to the Society.'

'Wonderful!' said William.

'Mr. Crestwood was most generous in helping us establish this award. A very remarkable man, terribly fond of writers and painters, a true patron.'

'How nice,' said William with growing impatience. Mrs. Smiley sipped her sherry with thin tight lips, and as she did so William could suddenly imagine himself strangling her. He shoved the image from his mind and gave his hostess an exaggerated, almost loving, smile. For a moment she seemed taken aback, but she went right on talking.

'Well, now, I suppose we should get down to business. Uh, have you decided on a subject for us? Oh, but of course you have. Since we have had no advance notice we are all enormously curious.'

In his mind William tossed a coin between his two possibilities and came out with Hemingway. What the hell's the difference, he thought. 'Hemingway,' he blurted out. 'I want to discuss something singularly American.'

'Of course, of course,' she said. 'We are so terribly curious over here about Americans, and especially about American writers. They are really quite unique, you know—not much like our English writers at all.'

'I want to talk about Hemingway's puritanism.'

'Oh, but how exciting! What a perfectly wonderful subject.'

He suddenly felt that it was the most ghastly subject in the world, and what's more a subject about which he had absolutely nothing to say. He had once enjoyed the man's works thoroughly, and now Hemingway seemed to be only a name, an entry in a syllabus. What the hell did he ever have in mind to say when he plucked this dumb subject out of the smoky air of the suffocating room at the Woodbury Court Hotel? He had a moment of panic in which he could not hear a word that Mrs. Smiley was saying. He saw her there opposite him, her mouth was moving, and her face was wrinkling into a smile, but he could not hear her. It was like a momentary deafness. He felt a throbbing in his neck and a tightening in his throat.

Then she was standing up in front of him, saying 'We ought to go in now Mr. Mariner. I think the meeting is about to begin.'

The next thing he knew he was sitting on a platform behind the girdled rear-end of Mrs. Smiley. She was leaning over a rostrum and addressing a colourful sea of hats and furs and printed silks. He caught words 'privilege', and 'American', and 'significant', and then his name. When the chairwoman turned to him with that outstretched hand again he recoiled, as though he had been watching a film of all this and suddenly one of the characters leapt from the screen into reality. He walked to the rostrum, still enveloped in his cocoon of panic and unreality, and started to speak. He could hear himself talking as though he, too, were another person. He almost listened with curiosity to what he was saying, or to what that strange lecturing voice of his was saying. Where was it all coming from, he wondered. There was a trembling in his knees and he wanted desperately to light a cigarette.

He heard the lecturer's voice say, 'Few people realize what a close connection there is in American literature between such writers as Mark Twain and Ernest Hemingway. They tend to think of Mark Twain as very American and Hemingway as very international, one of those artists who separated himself not only spiritually but physically from his mother country.'

He knew the voice was ad-libbing. He could not remember having said anything like that before. 'But Hemingway is as typically an American writer as Twain. He reflects the preoccupations and conflicts of his own country and his own generation. He was a romantic and a puritan, and a rebel against both romanticism and puritanism. He wanted to be liberated from that stifling American brand of sexuality and yet, like Twain, he could never bring himself to talk openly about sex in his books. Even in *The Sun Also Rises* all the sex is only referred to; it never takes place on stage. And, what's more, the problems that drive the characters to distraction and despair are peculiarly American problems—insecurity and guilt and violence. All the men in the novel would like to provoke all the women in the novel to murder them, and the women are too willing to oblige. The only recourse that Hemingway's men ever have, in the face of this grim view of sexuality and love, is suicide, alcohol, despair, or acts of violence and heroism.'

He paused for a moment, and when he spoke again it was with his own voice and he was startled to feel it coming out of his own mouth and to feel the ideas forming in his own head. 'I suppose I should be careful of what I say about women to such a charming group as this, but I assume that we are all sophisticated enough to realize that in literature there can be no restrictions placed on the kinds of ideas or feelings that are dealt with.'

A murmur of approval went through the audience, as if the ladies were saying, 'We mustn't allow ourselves to be petty about this. We are, after all, a literary society.'

'On the other hand, one is tempted to say that Hemingway doesn't really know much about women, that he is shy of them as so many American men are (and Englishmen for that matter).' A suppressed giggle forced him to hesitate for a moment. What the hell were they laughing at, he wondered. He stared at the ladies and began for the first time to distinguish individuals in the mass of faces and garments. His eyes settled on a toothless old bejewelled creature of ninety or so, whose lips kept disappearing into her squashed face, as though she were trying to eat them.

'And when we think of some of those wild generalizations he was inclined to make, we are almost sure that his point of view was distorted. He said, for instance, that all women today are lesbians. Surely, he must have meant something very special by that.' William could feel himself beginning to perspire. Was he losing his point? He had started out so well, so properly, like a real professor again, and now he was starting to say dumb things. 'All you ladies must know what a lesbian is. You've all lived long enough, and some of you must have gone to girls' schools. To say that all modern women are lesbians is very odd, indeed. I doubt, for instance, that more than ten per cent, or at the outside fifteen per cent of the women in this room are queer.'

There was suddenly a great twisting and turning and a grumble of disapproval. Heads leaned together, furpieces mated.

'Now, please, ladies,' said William, holding up his hands like a sheriff addressing a mob. 'Don't take any of this personally. In the name of literature and art, try to understand Hemingway's special use of the word, and try to see how it affected his treatment of characters, and try to see how all this is related to my initial point about romanticism and puritanism.' There, he sighed to himself, he was back on the track. A near disaster, a near derailment. Now stay there, he scolded, though he was sorely tempted. What fun it would be, what sport, to tear the old biddies apart! But no, one must not do it. One simply must not. So he hauled out his title again—William Mariner, Ph.D., Assistant Professor of English, Fulton College. But as he did so he remembered that he had just been fired for squeezing Miss Friedman's tit, and all the magic of the title-waving dissolved.

'What Hemingway really wanted to say was that there is meaning in the moment, in the immediate act, but not in the long run and not in any absolute and lasting way, and that hope for the absolute sits in our bellies like a piece of indigestible unripe fruit. We ought to wash it down and flush it out with lots of booze—get rid of the foolish romantic hope that springs eternal, and live solely in terms of a kind of existentialist appreciation of involvement and action that has no ultimate purpose.

'Actually,' he said, in a sudden British accent that surprised even him, 'the bloody fact of the matter is that every writer in the modern world finds himself in a dilemma. Anyone who writes is something of a mystic. He believes in the muse, or wants to believe in the muse. He wants to love her and love her and love her. But what if the bitch is a whore? What if she leads us up the garden path?'

He paused again. Something was becoming disconnected once again. What was the point of his lecture? Puritanism, puritanism, puritanism, he repeated to himself over and over again, and then aloud to his ladies. 'Puritanism, dears, is the problem. American history, Plymouth Rock, Hawthorne, the thorn in the side, Henry James, the ball-less wonder, Little Orphan Annie, Arf, Arf, and all the cuntless heroines of a thousand dirty-clean American movies. That's what Hemingway is all about. That's why he went to Paris and drank and that's why he shot himself. That's why he wrote *A Farewell to Arms* and *The Sun Also Rises*, and all the rest. Try to understand us. We are a poor brooding nation of prosperous, impotent insurance men. And you are all so articulate and civilized. Some day, perhaps, we will learn to behave ourselves properly.'

He sat down quickly and listened to the scattered, polite applause. A blushing and flustered Edith Smiley brought the meeting to a close without the usual discussion period, handed William an envelope with a cheque in it, and disappeared into the clucking crowd.

6

WILLIAM AND ALEX decided, at the last minute, to accept George Hamilton's invitation. William could not resist the possibility of meeting Maggie 'accidentally', and Alex could not resist the opportunity of meeting a whole new group of people, some of whom might even be important.

For both of them, however, the dinner party was something of a disappointment. Alex was seated between a pretty but uncommunicative lady named Mildred Kingsley and a disintegrating old newspaper columnist named Gladys Thornwood. Before dinner he chatted amiably but coldly with Horace Walton, a competent historian with more than a passing interest in literature.

Maggie St. Claire was conspicuously missing from the gathering. These were her friends, and through her William had come to know most of them. But he didn't trust them, and they, in turn, politely despised him. They considered him crude and insensitive, and they were convinced that Maggie was doing the right thing by staying away.

At the head of the table sat David Blumberg, whose new play was the occasion for George Hamilton's dinner party.

Alex was about to offer Mildred Kingsley a cigarette when a hand came down between them and a steaming broth appeared in front of him. For a moment he expected to hear the babbling of children, but he heard only the mumbling of polite adult conversation and the sound of silverware tapping gently against fragile china.

He waited until he saw Mildred lift her spoon to her mouth before he felt for the rim of his plate. And as he bent over the hot soup, he could hear her saying something to the man on her right. He felt suddenly self-conscious. He was sure everyone at the table was watching him to see whether or not he could manage. He straightened up slightly and felt a drop of hot, greasy liquid run off his lower lip and down his chin.

When he was finished, he automatically pushed his plate a few inches forward and rested his elbow on the edge of the table. At the far end he could see the gaunt and bearded Blumberg. If it were not for his receding hairline he might have looked like a presiding Christ. Several people were talking to him at once, and as he ate, he nodded patiently, or shook his head. Finally, he put his spoon down carefully in his empty plate, patted his mouth and beard with his napkin and said, 'The point of my play is that the Marquis de Sade is, in his own strange way, a hero and a revolutionary. He lived through the French revolution and took a part in it. He was in full agreement with the ideas it represented, and applied the sentiments of that upheaval to more personal matters. He is, in a way, a product of his age. His attack on traditional morality, religion, and social custom is not in itself remarkable, but his insistence on total freedom from these restricting philosophies and conventions is admirable, even though he committed what we think of as acts of cruelty. His violence is associated only with sex, which, after all, contains an unknown degree of violence and destruction. These elements in sex are traditionally condemned and suppressed, though they are often practised secretly anyway. Outside of his sexual preoccupations de Sade was not an unusually violent or cruel man. He was, perhaps, overly intellectual, but he was quite capable of living in what we call a *sane* fashion. In other words, he was not a madman.'

A huge and bleeding roast beef was set down on the table near William. Thin slices circled the wounded chunk of flesh. It was bound with roasted strings and decorated with greens. He imagined the Marquis de Sade seated cross-legged like a scholar or a doctor beside a bed on which a nude girl lay, her hands and feet tied to the posts. With a sharp blade de Sade drew thin red lines on her breasts and belly. The lines thickened and oozed blood. The girl screamed and struggled, but her terror was mixed with ecstasy. The Marquis smiled and sat back to study her, his eyes hot with excitement. He saw her arching back and straining thighs. With his sharp nails he clawed at her white soft buttocks.

Two slices of beef were dropped on William's plate and his mouth watered in anticipation. He helped himself to artichoke hearts and creamed potatoes.

Horace Walton looked intense and angry. He ignored his food and leaned forward to make his point. 'Look here,' he said to the unsmiling Christ at the head of the table, 'sanity is not merely a matter of common sense. A madman can often be precise and logical in the details of his behaviour and still have a purpose that is insane. A man might construct an ingenious bridge to cross a river, but if his reason for crossing the river is to commit a gratuitous act of violence on an innocent grazing sheep on the other side, then the fellow is insane.'

The word *gratuitous* stuck in William's mind as he sliced the meat on his plate. The warm gravy moved like lava against the white cliffs of potatoes. *Gratuitous*. Did it mean with no reason at all?

Alex sipped his wine and listened. He struggled to assemble his ideas, but his anger and outrage muddled his thoughts. Blumberg was his enemy; Blumberg was the anti-Christ, and he wanted to destroy him. He wanted to stand up and denounce him, but with what awful words?

'Freedom,' said Blumberg. 'Freedom even to believe that there is no meaning in life. Freedom to act as if there is no meaning, except the gratification of one's desires.'

'Freedom,' whispered Mildred Kingsley to Alex, but the rest of her sentence was inaudible.

'Yes,' he said. His hand brushed accidentally against her leg as he reached for his napkin. He felt her pull away.

'He's a frightening but exciting figure,' said Blumberg, holding up a goblet of water, as though he were toasting his hero.

The centrepiece of the table was a giant crystal bowl of fruit. Alex caught sight of it for the first time. The orchard freshness of it hypnotized him. *No one is free*, he thought. Total freedom is a madman's dream. And then he found himself saying it, barging into the conversation with his un-English accent. 'Freedom is a myth. To be human is to be bound. We're bound by our bodies, our desires, our families, our friends, the very food we eat. And by fear and love. To be human is to be tied to the world and to each other by a thousand wires of faith and passion.' He paused, his cheeks hot with embarrassment.

The table was silent. Everyone waited.

'The kind of freedom de Sade longed for,' he continued more calmly, 'was like death, a release from the responsibility of being human. No one ever fully achieves such freedom without destroying himself. It is the ultimate sin.'

William listened with secret delight and then looked at Blumberg to see his reaction. The tall, bony man poked at his salad. His dark face looked suddenly older. When Alex finished talking, he pointed a long finger at him, as though he were a patient but firm teacher. 'You're raising two different issues at once, and should sort them out in your own mind some day. One has to do with psychological detachment, and the other has to do with morality. A man can be evil without being insane; and he can be insane without being evil. But my point is that de Sade was neither evil nor insane. He absolved himself from judgement by rejecting the traditional moral order. He had no sense of guilt.'

'Everyone has a sense of guilt,' said Alex.

Several people spoke at once and Alex withdrew to his wine. He took a pear from the fruit bowl and held it in his hand. He felt its smoothness and its graceful shape, but he did not eat it.

'Let me answer for Alex,' said William, turning to Blumberg.

The two men stared at each other coldly. 'What you are implying is that there are no absolute standards for judging human behaviour, especially sexual behaviour; and that if a man enjoys himself sexually by sticking knives into young women or flogging them, or subjecting them to other perversions, he is only doing what comes naturally. Alex, on the other hand, is trying to say that there is a violation of nature in all this, and that it is, therefore, both neurotic and immoral.'

'de Sade admits that his acts are criminal.'

'Of course he does. Let me finish, if you don't mind,' said William, also in his lecturer's voice. Blumberg's thin face tightened. He flicked at the crumbs near his plate like a nervous, hungry bird. 'What Alex is trying to say is that the devil is real. Evil is a separate force in the world, inextricably entangled with good in the nature of things, but always definable.' Alex nodded in silent agreement. 'Judgement is imposed from the outside. No one can absolve himself—not even a maniac like de Sade. It is a mistake to assume that a man is a hero because he attacks authority. And it is a mistake to assume that all revolutions are good. Personally, I couldn't care less whether de Sade was insane or immoral. The important thing is that he is a bore as a thinker and he's a lousy writer. He contributes nothing to our understanding of ourselves. Because he got his kicks by cutting up little girls doesn't mean that he was either brave or wise. In fact, he was none of the things that we universally admire. He was a goddamn dirty old man, who should have been castrated when he was thirteen years old. And if you tried to make this double-talking queer old bastard into a hero then you've written a rotten play.'

'Perhaps you ought to see the play first, before you condemn it,' said Blumberg.

'No, thanks,' said William. 'I've got better things to do.'

Blumberg said something angrily, but William could no longer hear him. Too many conversations crossed their line of communication.

'Read your Milton,' someone said.

'And Dachau and Auschwitz . . .'

Alex smelled the coffee and brandy before it arrived and

leaned back as though he expected that mysterious hand to serve him any moment. Fragments of the splintered conversation reached him. The woman on his left turned to him for the first time all evening. 'I take it you're a good Catholic,' she said, as though she were accusing him of having bad breath.

'No,' said Alex, 'I'm not really very good at it.'

She smiled politely, though she was frowning, and pretended to be listening to someone across the table.

William sucked at a piece of food lodged between two of his back teeth. Where, he wondered, would Maggie be sitting if she were there. And what would she have said?

'Nature is not always right. Red in tooth and claw . . .'

'Discipline, restraint, reserve, guilt, compassion, consideration, sacrifice . . .'

'Freedom, honesty, expression, openness . . .'

'We must try to be ourselves. We must try to know ourselves.'

'And a man was nailed to the cross to help men do what they could not do for themselves . . .'

George Hamilton's composed face was jolted by a sudden burp.

After dinner William found Alex exercising his crude charm on the third Mrs. Walton and pulled him aside. 'I'm leaving,' he said. 'If you want to stay, take a taxi back to the hotel.'

'But, Doc, it's so early, and it's turned out to be a nice party after all,' said Alex.

'O.K., then. I'll see you back at Woodbury Court. I've got a couple of things to do.'

'All right, friend, but stay out of trouble.' Alex seemed to be talking to an invisible man over his left shoulder, because William had already found his way to the front door. He avoided any formal farewells and slipped into the damp night air, feeling a bit criminal. But the darkness was a comfort after the cold, blinding light of that dining-room, and he sighed as he walked quickly away.

After a few minutes he slowed his pace and became aware of the sound of his own footsteps on the hard pavement. It was not raining, but the air felt moist and heavy. There was a haze around the street-lamps and the sky was absolutely black. It was on a night like this that he had first met Maggie. They had left a party and wandered on Primrose Hill. By the time they got to the top of the hill he was not only breathless, but hopelessly in love with that big beautiful woman. Saint Maggie of Primrose, he called her. And later, in Italy, when they climbed another hill, it was less of a joke to call her *saint*. But that was in Assisi, where all things seem purer under that immense and friendly sky.

He paused at a corner, as if to decide which way to go. He looked back towards George's house, which he could no longer see, and then up the other streets. It was nice to have a choice, he thought.

7

MAGGIE ST. CLAIRE sat patiently in the dimly lighted lobby of the Woodbury Court Hotel. Lucy, who was working late that night, watched her with trembling curiosity. 'I really can't say when Mr. Mariner will be in,' she had told Maggie half an hour earlier. 'Perhaps you would like to leave a message.'

'I'll wait if you don't mind,' said Maggie, and sat down in a wing-back chair near the curtained bay window. She ignored the newspapers and magazines which were carefully arranged on the table beside her and stared at the faded rug or into the hazy darkness outside. In her brown suede jacket and green scarf she looked somewhat boyish. Her large features were more handsome than pretty. Her blonde hair was combed across her forehead and cut short before it reached her shoulders. Her eyes were very large and very broad, and their broadness was emphasized by her high cheek-bones and gently tapering face, giving her by nature an exotic and mysterious look. Her mouth, too, was wide and her lips soft and full with a perpetual hint of a smile and an almost imperceptible quiver. She moved silently, perfectly, with the natural grace and control of an animal—a predatory animal. Her eyes seemed to absorb everything in a sweeping glance, and she spoke very quietly.

Lucy sat behind the desk sorting out papers under an old lamp. Two or three times the phone rang and she made what seemed like complicated connections on the old switchboard. The wooden clock ticked agelessly on the wall over the desk, and then chimed once for half-past eleven. Lucy would go off duty at twelve and close down the desk for the night. She studied the tall American woman by the window and wondered what she was to William. Instinctively, however, she knew that the relationship was not trivial.

A few minutes before twelve William came in. He walked past Maggie without seeing her. 'Well, what a nice surprise,' he said as he noticed Lucy. 'What are you doing here?'

Lucy stood up. She was pale and speechless. She looked past William and saw Maggie get up and walk towards the desk with an odd smile on her face. 'Miss Foster's sick,' Lucy explained.

William leaned closer to Lucy over the desk and said, 'I hope you're spending the night.' Lucy moved away from him as Maggie approached.

'Still playing the mad artist for the co-eds?' said Maggie.

At the sound of her voice William's whole body contracted, as though he were trying to protect himself from an explosion. But when he turned to face her he seemed calm. 'Hello, Maggie,' he heard himself say. His voice was distant, detached, but his heart pounded and the surge of blood to his head made him dizzy.

'This young lady was good enough to let me wait in her lobby for you.'

Lucy blushed. 'I'm sorry Mr. Mariner. I was about to tell you—'

William introduced them and Maggie offered her hand. Lucy was flustered. She shook hands hastily and then said, 'It's closing time. I've got to shut the desk.' She turned away quickly and started gathering things together. William was afraid she might start crying. He took Maggie by the arm and led her to a couch in the lobby.

'Have you been messing around with that child?' said Maggie.

'Who? Me? Never!'

'What, never?' said Maggie.

'Well, hardly ever,' answered William, and they both laughed.

She touched his arm. 'How have you been?' she said warmly. 'It's been a long time.'

'Yes,' he said. 'Either too long or not long enough. I can't decide which. But you look good. Much the same, in fact. Even that jacket, that worn-out old thing.'

She leaned back and stared at him. 'Have you been working hard?'

'No,' he said. 'I haven't been working at all—except for teaching, that is.'

She hesitated. 'Then you've been drinking a lot.'

'Yes. Regularly and conscientiously. I suppose it shows.'

'Yes,' she said.

Lucy walked by and William stood up. 'Good night,' he said. 'Will you be in tomorrow?'

'No,' she said, without stopping. 'I've got the day off. Good night. Good night, Miss St. Claire.' The door closed behind her and William shrugged his shoulders.

'She's very young,' he said.

Maggie shook her head. 'And you're so old.'

'Almost forty,' he said.

Maggie was still seated and William looked suddenly restless and distracted. 'I've got something to drink upstairs, if you can trust an old lecher.'

'Sure,' she said, and they went up the squeaky carpeted steps.

In the room Maggie took off her jacket and made herself comfortable on the bed while William fixed the drinks. He handed her a glass and then offered her a cigarette. 'Well,' he said. 'What do we do now?'

'I don't know,' she said. 'It's as though no time at all has passed. I mean, wasn't it just yesterday, or the other day that we sat like this in our flat and smoked and drank and asked all the dumb questions?'

'Yes,' he said, 'it was just the other day. Nothing has happened since. Nothing at all. And if we were to ask those questions all over again, the answers would still be the same.'

She leaned on one elbow. Her black dress was sleeveless and pinched at the waist with a thin leather belt. William slouched in the stuffed chair and stretched out his legs. He watched her, studied her, as though he were trying to translate a dream into reality.

She looked around the small room. 'Where's your friend?' she said.

'How did you know I was here with a friend?'

'George called. George Hamilton. He wanted me to know that you were invited to his party. At the last minute I decided not to go. Not because I wanted to avoid you. Hardly. I just couldn't give George and his friends the satisfaction of watching us fumble in public.'

'I didn't have the impression we were fumbling.'

She laughed. 'Come off it, Bill. We're both as nervous as cats. When I heard you were in London, I didn't know what to do. I didn't know whether to call you or take the first plane out of the country.' She paused and stared into her drink. 'I don't suppose you wanted to see me.'

'Yes,' he said, 'I did want to see you, but I had just about decided not to.'

'Why not?'

'I don't know. Old wounds and all that, I suppose.'

'Surely you can think of a better cliché than that,' she said. 'You are, after all, a writer.'

'An ex-writer.'

'There's no such thing,' she said, sitting up suddenly as though she were about to scold him. 'Writers are born, not made. And they only stop being writers when they die.'

'Well, then maybe I'm dead,' he said. 'Maybe I'm dead and don't know it.'

'Oh Christ! Here we go again. What do you expect the world to do—weep for you?'

'I don't expect anything of the world, only of myself. I would like to be able to write another book—a good one.'

'If you want to do it badly enough, you'll do it.'

'I suppose eventually I will. Perhaps, as Alex says, when we get home.'

'Alex? Is it Alex you're travelling with?'

'Yes.'

'I feel as though I already know him.'

'If he can find his way back in the dark he'll be here soon.'

'Good. I want to meet this remarkable friend of yours.'

'You'll be disappointed.'

'We'll see.' Sitting on the edge of the bed she finished her drink and held out her glass for more. William got up slowly and reached for the bottle.

'Have you been working?' he said.

'Off and on. I did some designs and models for Peter Woodson. In fact, I've done quite a bit of work for him during the past two years.'

'And what else have you done for him?'

Maggie winced. 'Still asking dumb questions.'

'Just curious, dear girl,' he said. 'Just curious. I'd like to know how you've been living.'

She shrugged. 'I've been living much the same as always. I have to work. I have some friends. I live alone. I've been painting again.'

'And Peter Woodson?'

'He's a friend.'

'How good a friend?'

'Well, if you must know, he's asked me to marry him Does that answer your question?'

'Not quite, but it'll do.'

'What did you expect? Was I supposed to be faithful to you these past two years? I'm thirty-six years old and unmarried.'

'*Free*, you mean. Wasn't that what you always wanted? Wasn't that your eternal desire? Freedom. Independence.'

She got up and paced across the room. 'You haven't changed much after all, have you, Bill? Still as angry as ever. Still out to prove that all women are whores.'

He lit a cigarette nervously. 'Sorry,' he said. 'I keep forgetting that we're nothing to each other now.'

'Nothing?' She laughed ironically. 'Just because once we were married and once we were divorced; just because we submitted to a few legal technicalities—what does all that paperwork have to do with us? We are now to each other just what we always were to each other.'

'Do you mean you're still my wife or that you never were my wife?'

'I don't know what that means.'

'No, I'm sure you don't.'

For a moment they were silent. Then William crushed out his cigarette and looked away from her. 'Tell me, Maggie,' he said coldly, 'why did you come here? What do you want?'

She looked at him for a moment as though she were waiting for him to face her and then she said in that quiet, sad voice of hers, 'I don't want anything, Bill. But I was hoping that if we had some time together that we might want to stay together.'

He looked up slowly, feeling suddenly her anguish and awkwardness. She was too proud to talk that way. And he knew she would not say it again. He got up and went to her and took her long hand in his. 'I'm sorry, Maggie,' he said. 'I didn't mean to be angry.' He touched her hair and her shoulders. Her frown melted into a slow smile.

'You imagine you've been hurt,' she said. 'I never meant to hurt you.'

Then he turned away from her suddenly, as though he remembered something. 'It won't work, you know,' he said.

'Are you sure?'

'Yes, I'm sure. And I don't even know why, because I'm equally sure that we still love one another.'

'I'm tempted to argue with you, but I can't. You're probably right. In your own way you've often been right.'

William poured himself another drink. When he looked at her again he was smiling. 'Besides,' he said, 'I've got to take Alex to Lourdes. And Alex says that I'm not allowed to get involved with women because this is his trip.'

'Who's the ward and who's the warden on this little pilgrimage?'

'Well, it's kind of mutual. He's blind and I'm obnoxious.

But after Lourdes everything will be different. Alex will be a wise old man and I'll write a novel called *Moby Dick.*'

She laughed. 'I suppose he's trying to convert you.'

'Not at all. Actually he's trying to get me to destroy his faith and I keep refusing.'

She shook her head. 'That's too complicated for me. But if you can be serious for a minute tell me why you're taking this funny trip. I really don't understand. I mean, it's not like you to help old ladies across the street.'

'You mean I'm selfish?'

'Yes. Reasonably selfish. Certainly preoccupied with your own problems.'

'Alex calls it an *adventure*, and for him I suppose it is. After all, he's never been anywhere in his whole life. Perhaps I enjoy the innocent excitement with which he approaches things. Perhaps I even envy him.'

Her broad eyes glistened and she smiled gently and a bit sadly. 'What a strange man you are, Bill,' she said. 'So afraid to be kind.' She put her empty glass down on the night table beside an overflowing ashtray. 'It looks as though I may have intruded after all.' She got up and reached for her jacket.

He stopped her. 'No,' he said, 'you didn't intrude. At least not in the obvious way. What I wouldn't admit to Alex or to myself was that I made this trip partly to see you. I've missed you, damn it.' He held her face to face with him by her bare arms.

She allowed herself to be drawn closer to him. He put his arms around her and held her for a long moment. 'It's been lousy,' she whispered. 'I didn't stop writing to you; I just stopped mailing the letters.'

He kissed her on the forehead and the cheek and touched her hair. Then he stepped away again and looked at her. 'How would you like to join a drunken pilgrimage?' he said.

She smiled and shook her head. 'Alex wouldn't like that. Remember?'

'He'd love it. He doesn't know you.'

She thought for a moment as though she were trying to remember what she had to do. 'I'd have to finish up the job I'm working on—another three or four days.'

'In three or four days we'll be in Paris,' he said.
'I could meet you there.'
'All right. Thursday.'
'At the Deux Magots?' she said.
They remembered a time when they met once before at the same place. They were in Paris on a holiday shortly after their marriage. He had to sit there for two hours because she had stopped to see some friends and was very late.
'Sometime after nine in the evening,' she said. 'I'll wait if you're not there. It's my turn.'
William looked at his watch. 'It's almost one,' he said. 'I'm beginning to worry about that idiot. Perhaps I'd better call.'
'George's parties don't usually end until two,' she said.
'Alex is probably sound asleep under one of those phoney antique couches in George's living-room.'
He picked up the phone and started to dial, but he was interrupted by a distant thud. He put down the receiver and said, 'He's home, knocking over furniture in the lobby.'
They went down and found him lying on the rug beside a fallen chair and still-lighted lamp. William shook him awake and helped him up. Maggie picked up the lamp and chair.
'That you, Doc?' said Alex. 'I thought it was the wrong place. Somebody moved the staircase.'
'Drunk again,' said William, leading him to a couch.
'I am so!' protested Alex with a silly sleepy grin.
'Do you need some help?' said Maggie, and Alex looked up at the sound of her voice.
'Am I hearing things, Doc, or is there a woman here?'
'It's Maggie.'
Alex stood up suddenly but unsteadily. 'Maggie? You mean St. Claire? *That* Maggie?'
She reached for his hand to let him know where she was. 'I've heard all about you,' she said.
He clutched her hand gently. 'If you're as lovely as you sound, I'm going to steal you away from him. Let's turn on some lights so I can see.'
'No,' said William, 'let's go upstairs; the lobby is closed.'
They went up to their room and made more drinks.

'It was a good party, after all,' said Alex. 'It just takes a lot of booze to thaw out an Englishman.'

'I'm sure it was you and not the booze,' said Maggie.

'Actually,' said Alex in his newly acquired accent, 'I'm one of the most charming men I know. And I feel it's my duty to educate the English out of their primitive sense of shyness. A kind of counter-colonialism. I figure they need me.'

Maggie laughed. 'They sure need something—and it's not me.'

'You mean they're afraid of women?' said Alex.

'No,' said William. 'They're just afraid of Maggie.'

Alex squinted at her through his one uncovered eye. 'You know,' he said drowsily, 'you'd make a wonderful white goddess for one of those jungle flicks with lost cities and statues with giant emeralds for eyes.'

'I always wondered what I'd be good at. I've tried almost everything else.'

'You sure have,' said William.

Her smile disappeared, but she did not look angry.

'I'd like to try everything,' said Alex. 'Do everything. Be everything. So would you.'

'Would I?' said William. 'Maybe that's what we three have in common—greed. An enormous appetite. A kind of spiritual gluttony.'

Alex smiled. 'I owe you an apology, Doc. And you too, Maggie. I'm sorry I objected to you two seeing each other. I thought it would be another sloppy domestic scene and I didn't want to be caught in the middle.' He was beginning to fall asleep with his clownish grin still on his now sagging face.

'I'd better go,' Maggie said and got up. William helped her on with her jacket. She hesitated for a moment at the door. 'Did you mean it about Paris?' she said.

'Sure,' he said. 'Why not? Unless you've got something better to do.'

'No,' she said, 'I have nothing better to do.'

They looked at one another for a moment without saying anything, and then she nodded and turned away. He closed the door quietly behind her and heard her footsteps on the squeaking stairs.

8

'NO, IT WAS not like that at all.' Alex tried to listen, but the darkness thickened around him. Now and again his eyelids twitched, a muscle tightened, and a torn rag of light was waved before him. *My reality*, he thought, *is black. Light intrudes*. He closed his eyes again and after-images danced and exploded like miniature fireworks in his darkness. But then they too faded and he became conscious again of William's voice. 'It was almost the end, after less than a year, and we came here in desperation, thinking that the holiday or the beauty of Paris in May, or something would cut us loose from that deadly embrace—Paolo and Francesca, circling and circling.'

'Depraved May,' muttered Alex, and a picture of a dead tree in a desert of bleak rolling hills came to his mind. Was it a painting? It looked Japanese.

'When she heard that her father was dying she flew back to the States to show her pathetic, drunken mother how to be wise and brave. And made the poor widow feel that she had failed her husband in every one of a thousand fundamental ways. It was a chance that Maggie would not have missed—a chance to prove once more, and maybe for the last time, that only she, only Maggie knew what her father wanted. No other woman in the world could know him as she did. No wife or mother or sister or sweetheart could seduce him as she had seduced him all her life.'

A surf of blood lapped at the shores of his darkness. The Japanese tree spread out and drooped like a willow, and the hills moved like the parts of a huge beast bothered at these dark protrusions by flies and twitching to escape the annoyance.

Outside, the first ghost-like hint of morning touched the dark sky and brought with it a cool breeze. The quiet morning sounds rose like vapours from the damp Paris streets—the struggling engine of an old truck far away, the barking of a dog, the sweeping of a stiff broom over cobble-stones. William's eyes were closed and his head was heavy with wine. 'How good the wine is,' Alex kept saying all evening. 'How good the wine is.' And they walked and walked and remembered enough high-school French to buy cigarettes and gin and snails, and negotiated a tiny room in a narrow, tall, sagging old wooden hotel on the Rue Bonaparte that smelled of urine, tobacco, and clorox.

'She grew up on a pig farm. A pig farm in Pennsylvania. It was her secret and she lied about it to everyone, but only in that evasive way of hers. When someone probed, she put on her earth-mother smile, her big-eyed mysterious look. She preferred to think of herself as not having been born at all, as having sprung full-grown from the forehead of Zeus, or having boiled up out of the sea like a volcano to form the island of herself, the isolated, untouchable, unassailable rock that people called Maggie, but which she thought of as her nameless, exotic self—a private fire, protected by configurations of hardening stone.'

The dark landscape in Alex's semi-dream crumbled into an island. The blood-red sea washed into the caves and battered the cliffs of a rocky shore. An orange moon cast its light over plateaus of tropical vegetation—palm trees and grape-vines, ferns and moss and giant bell-like blossoms. On a broad and grassy terrace he could see his white two-story house. The olive trees danced in slow motion around it like a ballet group of ancient men and women. Their faces and limbs were grotesque. All wild lines and frantic scars. They smiled or grimaced or wept. Branches grew from their fingertips. Their legs twisted into the ground. They became a mad chorus and their cracking groaning song drowned out the sound of the sea and the sounds that came from his house. But then the house grew and he could see faces at all the windows. He named them all and counted as he named them to be sure they were all there—Helen, his wife; Barbara, his oldest girl and first-born; Alex junior, who was sixteen; Katharine, who was fourteen and almost too blonde to be his child; Julie, who was ten and more like the gypsy-Indian-pirate side of his family; Christopher, a handsome, poetic lad of twelve; Andrew, Mark, and William, three younger sons with a taste for mischief; and, finally, Jacqueline, the baby. There was always a baby in the house, always a new, innocent, crying creature, gasping for air, clinging to him and to Helen, as though every other person in the world meant death.

'So from the very beginning,' said William, opening his eyes to stare out into the thinning darkness, past the tall narrow shutters, past the iron railing of the balcony, towards a silhouetted army of chimneys, 'she pretended to be something she wasn't. She did not want to be a tall skinny girl with a broken tooth from a pig farm in Pennsylvania. She wanted to be the priestess of a cult, a white Watusi slave-girl, a female Gauguin dying of leprosy in Tahiti, a Garbo with raised eyebrows, slightly retired from the world, a siren, a sorceress, an artist, an avant-garde painter, a puppet-master in Buenos Aires, a free-lance photographer in San Francisco, a playwright in New York, a spiritual and bed companion of the near-great in London. She was embarrassed by the realities of her life, by the fact that she actually ate or slept or went to the bathroom. She had such a skilful way of minimizing her merely human activities that one could know her for months without ever becoming aware that she shared in the mundane and dreary aspects of living. She seemed to float there in front of one. She seemed, indeed, at times to be a saint—Saint Maggie of the pig farm!'

And then Alex's smiling family, his clan, his tribe, came out of the white house and wandered among the antique olive trees, and the children climbed into the arms of the trees, who received them and then held them and engulfed them. Pretty children in the arms of grey monsters. His heart pounded. The orange moon grew larger and larger, until it covered the whole sky. The jungle loomed on the plateau all around the olive grove. And William's voice spoke from the sea. That's William down there in the tossing sea, and William is wise, Alex thought, half caught in the half-dream. William was his wisest friend, his most honest and severest critic, his brother and guide. William laughed at him. William scolded and analysed and cursed. And what a good voice he had—the voice of a poet and a teacher. There was kindness in his voice and, yet, there was coldness. He both cared and did not care. The voice was in the wind now and it rose from the sea and swept through the slow-motion palms and sighed and smiled among the rocks and olive trees.

William was a voice, he thought, and he heard him reading lines from Dylan Thomas, and he heard him talking to his students and to friends in the late drunken sentimental hours, with the phonograph going and the empty beer bottles sticking out from under chairs in the room Alex called his office. There he and William had sobbed and laughed away all the cares of a twisted world. There they discovered, in those rambling idle talks, that neither of them was at the centre of the tragedy, that the stage belonged to what they called 'poor man, poor mankind'. Was it Hardy? Was it Conrad? Was it Yeats or Eliot or Thomas? William was always quoting, always sneaking in lines that were not his own. Poor Man, poor Mankind. And Edith Piaf moaned on the record-player, or Bessie Smith, or Ella, or Judy: Come Rain or Come Shine, Chicago, A Hymn to Love, Moonlight in Vermont, Somewhere Over the Rainbow, and that great, great classic, If You Don't Like My Peaches Why Do You Shake My Tree. And then he would be at the organ, bare-footed and dishevelled and high, dreaming of all the lives he might have lived, of the things he might have done—song and dance man, international spy, actor, writer, singer, poet, pirate, lover, adventurer.

And all his women were angelic and virgin, their blushing, flower-like faces half-hidden in the caressing strands of wind-blown hair. And they would serve him and love him and honour him. And when he was old his vast flock would gather around him and praise him and listen to his strong old words. And he would tell them the great things that only he knew. He would bless them one by one and they would kiss his hand or his robe and thank him and go away with tears of exultation and delight in their eyes, because he had given them so much, because he had touched them with a great kindness and they had felt his warmth and his great love. Yes, it was love. He loved them all. Their pain was his pain. Every sorrow in the world pierced him like a microscopic arrow, until his whole body felt as though it had been rolled in cactus and come away with a million invisible splinters. And then they all asked him why he found his life so difficult and painful. He smiled in his half-sleep. The probing doctor always asked, 'Where does it hurt?' He smiled again as he remembered the punch-line of his favourite joke—'It only hurts when I laugh.'

'Light falls and darkness breaks in *Romeo and Juliet* because day and night are reversed. They only live in darkness, which is their day, their safety. And all the terrors of night are, for them, the terrors of the daylight.' William's voice was a drowsy monotone. It did not matter any longer whether Alex heard him or not. He talked because he could not stop, because, he felt, if he stopped he would die. As long as he could put one word after another, as long as he could shape a thought, he knew he was neither dead nor mad. 'It was the best lecture I ever gave in my whole life, but she called it *romantic*, full of sloppy modern sentimentalism. And what's more she thought it was poorly organized, repetitious and facile. I agreed too easily, partly because I didn't really care whether or not it was good, and partly because I hate to defend the things that I do. What can I do if someone doesn't like what I say or write? What can I do if I cannot bridge the canyon between my private vision and theirs? And then she was sorry and tried to cheer me up. She played with the tassels on her shawl and tried to look girlish. We drank a lot of wine that night and made love until dawn, wrestling and playing among the twisted sheets and quilts in that freezing London flat.'

Sleep threatened. The landscape melted and shifted. Things began to fall apart. Rocks cracked. Trees bent and crashed to the ground. The sea spilled over. Alex was a boy, weeping in a dark room. He tried to call out but he had no voice. His throat was closed by a moment of terror. His child's heart pounded. He heard voices from another room, mingled women's voices. But in another moment they combined and deepened into a single male voice. It was William, still talking.

9

WILLIAM STOOD BEFORE the mirror in the narrow bathroom and lathered his face with shaving soap. He enjoyed shaving, especially first thing in the morning. It gave him a sense of newness and freshness. He used to get up sometimes at five or six, wash and shave and dress and throw open all the windows of the house to let the morning in. He would feel that all things were possible, that with a new handful of hours he could make something, that he might repair all the damage he had done during his lifetime, that he might take these hours as though they were clay and mould them into some infinitely graceful, infinitely exciting form. But somehow the day never turned out perfect. Something always went wrong, even if the work went well, even if he did not smoke too much or cough too much or feel sick by noon or three o'clock. His days never rounded into the perfection he longed for. He would have settled for just one, one perfect day. But it never came.

There was a white towel wrapped around his middle and a golden St. Christopher medal around his neck. He noticed the pendant nestled in the hair of his chest and felt its cold chain at the back of his neck. 'Where's your magic charm?' he said to Alex.

Alex sat on the edge of the big double bed with his face in his hands. He had on his shirt and socks and underwear, but seemed to have bogged down at that point in his effort to climb back to reality. He felt his chest and neck and then sat up as though he had heard a loud noise. 'It's gone!' he said, and stood up. 'My St. Christopher is gone.' He tore at the sheets and blankets of the bed and then fell on all fours to peer into the darkness under the bed. 'If we don't find it, the trip is off,' said Alex. 'We'll just have to take the next plane home. How the hell can I go to Lourdes without my St. Christopher?'

William draped the medal over the corner of the mirror and scratched at his face with his safety razor. 'You mean they won't let you in?' he said with a crooked mouth.

'My toothless old Irish mama gave me that St. Christopher as a special gift for this trip. She kissed it and prayed over it and asked me to wear it all the time. She'll be heartbroken if it's lost.' Alex sat down at the table by the open window and poured himself some coffee. He stared down blankly at the busy street. It was almost noon and the day was bathed in cool air and brilliant sunlight.

'Why don't you say a little prayer? Perhaps it will show up.' William unwound the towel from his waist and dried his face. He opened one of the shutters of the small window and ran the water in the tub.

'I haven't worn a medal of any kind since I got married,' said Alex. 'Helen gave me one and I wore it all during our honeymoon in Canada, and then I took it off one day at home and never found it again.'

'Why did you take it off?' said William, wrapping the towel around his middle again and coming to the table.

'It was one of those three thousand times in the past twenty years or so that I lost my faith, and I figured it just wasn't right to be wearing something like that.'

William stood by the table dangling the golden medal from his fingers not three feet from Alex's face, but Alex could not see it. Across the way a young woman watched them from between parted curtains. 'There's a girl over there,' said William, 'who thinks we're interesting.'

Alex peered around in his insect way until he located the window that William was referring to. 'Is she good-looking?'

'She's young—not bad.'

'Why don't you unwrap yourself,' said Alex, 'and see if she's interested in middle-aged circumcized Americans?'

William caught her eye and waved flirtatiously at her. The curtains snapped shut suddenly and the girl was gone. 'What did you do?' said Alex.

'I waved at her.'

'Your hand?'

'What else? I don't plan to be arrested in this crummy town.'

'I thought you liked Paris.'

He shrugged his shoulders. 'I have some old friends living here. That's what I like most about it. I also like driving in this crazy traffic.'

William sat down and carefully slipped the gold medal into Alex's coffee cup. After two more sips Alex felt or heard the object. He picked it out with his fingers and looked puzzled. 'How the hell . . .' Then his frown dissolved into a smile as he realized what had happened. 'You bastard! What kind of a trick is that?'

'I don't know what you're talking about. Maybe it's a miracle. Maybe it's a good sign.'

'You sacrilegious slob. Someday you're going to go too far and be struck by lightning.'

'Yeah,' said William, 'right in the balls.'

Alex shook his head. Then he looked up suddenly and frowned. 'I had a bunch of funny dreams last night. In one of them I was crawling around on all fours all over this gigantic woman. She must have covered half an acre lying down. Her skin was sort of tan and her tits were like hills.'

William leaned back in his chair and pretended to look over invisible glasses 'Tell me, ven did you start mit zese fantasies?'

'What does it mean, Doc? Don't be afraid to tell me; I can take it.'

'Vell, Herr Morgan, accordink to ze ortopedic Freudian

shkule you got vat is callt eine kleine castration complex. Zat fat nigger is a mudder figure, und you is eine teenie weenie knockwurst. Or maybe, on ze odder hand, you just like tall girls.'

Alex laughed. 'I think you're the one who likes tall girls, Doc.'

'Who, me? Not me. I like cute little effeminate boys with blond hair and little round asses. You know—cherubic and intelligent.'

'I suppose Lucy Gordon was a boy?' His tone was more serious.

'All right, all right, Jimminy Cricket, let's leave that one alone. Maybe I was wrong about her. I thought it would do her some good.'

'What you mean is you thought it would do *you* some good.'

'Well, for Christ's sake, friend, it's not the worst thing that can happen to a girl. Somebody's got to take her to bed sooner or later.'

Alex shook his head. 'I don't know how you can be so cold-blooded, Doc. It's the one vice I can't cultivate. Sometimes I wish I could. For twenty years I've been faithful to Helen. She's the only woman in my whole life I ever slept with. And I've vowed that I wouldn't die that way. What can I do? I fool around, and then when the time comes I can't do it. I just can't do it!'

'Well don't feel too badly about it, old thing; maybe you can have it fixed in Lourdes.'

Alex picked up a shoe and threw it in the direction of William's voice. 'Bastard!' But his good humour had returned and they both laughed.

It was noon and bells were ringing. 'The day is half gone already,' said William.

'Don't forget I want to see St. Germain,' said Alex, searching for his shoe.

'It's just around the corner,' said William. He stooped to locate the shoe and handed it to his friend.

10

ALEX CLIMBED INTO the chair at the barber shop and pointed to his head and to his face. '*Ma tête et ma visage*,' he said, remembering suddenly the ugly face of Miss Cavendish, his high-school French teacher. 'No, no,' she would have scolded. 'That is not the way to ask for a shave and a haircut. Study your vocabulary. Remember the idiomatic expressions.' But he could not remember anything except the simplest words—*hands*, *eyes*, *feet*, *face*. What was the word for *ears*? He always had trouble with that one. Something terribly unpronounceable. His mouth felt funny as he thought about certain words he might try out with the little bald-headed barber—like the puckering one feels when one thinks of lemons. The barber threw a sheet around him and stuffed a towel about his neck. He said something very rapidly in French which Alex did not understand. '*Parlez-vous Anglais*, *peut-être?*' he said.

The little man shook his head and looked embarrassed. '*Un peu.*'

'Oh well,' said Alex, and leaned back in the chair. The barber lathered his face and then sharpened his straight razor. Alex listened and in his mind he could see the sharp steel instrument.

His father had used a straight razor, which he kept in his bureau drawer. It had a handle of pearl and no one was ever allowed to touch it. In the bathroom of the old house in Seaville, where he lived as a child, there hung a razor strap. That rich brown sacred piece of leather was a vivid, living memory. He secretly touched it sometimes, and now he could recall in his very fingertips the slickness of one side and the roughness of the other.

There was a moment of silence and then he could feel the barber leaning towards him. His hands were small and cold and he smelled of hair tonic or cologne.

Around the corner William waited at the *Deux Magots*. He ordered a coffee and cognac and lit a cigarette. The smoke tasted bitter and somewhat medicinal in his scrubbed mouth. Paris was considerably warmer than London—almost hot, in fact. He had unpacked his light blue summer suit and wore it now with a white sports shirt open at the neck.

At the next table a good-looking young couple were speaking quietly in what he assumed was Swedish or Danish. They looked clean and healthy and eager for the world. Their guidebooks were heaped neatly on the table and a camera dangled from the man's shoulder. They were drinking coca-cola.

A pigeon circled, fluttered his wings, and descended a few feet from him. He watched it strut greedily, arrogantly, through the street. He wanted suddenly to be a little boy with a slingshot. He would have taken the ugly creature's head off with a rock. He hated pigeons with their tiny heads and beady red eyes; and he hated the ragged old women who devoted their lives and stale bread to keeping them alive.

Most of the tables of the café were already filled. He glanced about at the sipping and chattering crowd, as though he were looking for a familiar face. At one table sat an intense young Frenchman with black hair. He wore black horn-rimmed glasses and a black suit. He was sucking up the columns of his newspaper as though somewhere in that pulpy sheet he expected to find the key to the universe.

William could never understand avid newspaper readers. They made him uneasy. He could put up with headlines and sports news, but not much else. For years he had been bugged by dark-haired guys with glasses who read all the news and all the editorials and reviews and who talked about them glibly and smartly over coffee or drinks, as though they belonged to a private intellectual society that required as homework a cover-to-cover reading of *The New Yorker*, *The Saturday Review*, and the *New York Times*. Their agile references to Reston and Kerr and Chapman always made him feel that he had failed to do something terribly important. But his uneasiness was never enough to drive him into the arms of these prophets and interpreters of contemporary life and letters. However, once every three or four months he would have an impulse to reform, which would include giving up smoking and drinking, getting to bed before twelve and getting up before seven, writing at least five pages a day, eating sensibly, and reading all those standard publications everyone else read.

He would start out bravely, perhaps on a Sunday morning, with coffee and the book section of *The Times*. He would get through the feature review, a little dizzy from the lack of nicotine in his system, and then skip more and more quickly through the others. His attention would wander and he would find himself looking at ads instead of reviews. Then he would sit at his typewriter for an hour or so, trying to force five pages out of his now purified soul. By the end of such a day he would often find himself with a few ragged accomplishments and the awful sensation that his head was about to explode. The next day he would try again, but by three o'clock in the afternoon he would find himself pleasantly high on four martinis and half-way through his second pack of cigarettes.

He poured the cognac into his coffee and stirred it. Two American girls walked by, one, a blonde, in slacks and a sweater; the other, a brunette, in a simple sleeveless dress. He caught only a fragment of their conversation. 'We didn't do anything really,' said the blonde, 'except sit around and talk all night with this fantastic creature with a beard and . . .' Their voices faded and he watched them walk away. The girl in slacks had a small round rear-end that revealed its fleshy softness as she walked. He imagined himself placing his hands on her cheeks and squeezing. But then they were gone.

Across the way the old church looked comfortable and wise in the warm sunlight. People in colourful summer clothes walked in and out or stood around in two's and three's talking or laughing or pointing at something.

The cognac and coffee tasted good and the sun relaxed him. He was struck by the colours—the awnings, the cotton dresses, the shutters of buildings. Perhaps, he thought, he would stay in Paris, after all. How easy it would be just to sit there day after day. So many of his friends had done it, and perhaps they were right. He tried to imagine himself settling down into a room or an apartment, buying books, making shelves, wearing a beret, and growing a beard. In a moment he had transformed himself completely. He was even thinner. The bones of his face showed. His corduroy jacket was old and soft, with patches at the elbows. He could read French easily and he could talk to everyone. He would scribble notes at the café all day and talk all night with good friends. He would say wise things through his beard and people would listen and laugh. Then he would write it all down and his book would be applauded. *William Mariner, a well-known figure in Parisian expatriate and intellectual circles, has proven once again that he understands the dilemma of Western man. His new novel is a miracle of erudition and imagination. Never since Camus has a writer leapt at the truth with such swiftness and grace . . .*

'I'm a new man, Doc!' Alex was suddenly standing beside him rubbing his smooth face. 'How do I look?'

'Like the wrong end of the baby king of Jerusalem. Sit down, damn you; you just interrupted the most important moment of my life. I was about to award myself the Nobel Prize for literature. I had my acceptance speech all ready. I was going to say that Man's voice is puny and that it cannot be heard over the roaring of the angry sea; that Man will not only not prevail, he will not endure; that what we call the eternal problems of the human heart are really only the sex pangs and stomach rumblings of the moment . . . What have you got there in your dirty little hand? You look like a kid clutching candy.'

Alex sat down and opened his hand to show William his

collection of coins. 'I got a fist full of change, mostly one-franc pieces. I'm going to put some in every poor box in the church.'

'Well there's your old mother church over there. Help yourself.'

'Would you like to come?' said Alex.

'Only if you need me. Otherwise I'd better stay clear of the place.'

'I'm sure I can manage alone. I can't get into too much trouble in there, can I?'

William shrugged his shoulders and looked towards the old façade of St. Germain. 'Who knows! I don't trust churches myself. When I was a kid I was forced to go now and then and it always smelled of funerals. I mean the main business of a church, it seems to me, is to remind us that we are all going to die.'

'They also remind us that we have a reason for living,' said Alex. 'The Church is an earthly institution.'

'I suppose you're right. And there was nothing more earthly than that beautiful fat Pope everyone loved. I can just see him in the middle ages, winding up the road to Assisi on a tiny, staggering burro.'

More pigeons circled and landed. Someone from a near-by table tossed bread-crumbs into the street. The greedy birds strutted rapidly, competitively, towards the offerings.

'Are you going to wait here?' said Alex, standing up and jingling his coins.

'I may take a walk, but I'll be back soon.'

William watched his friend walk across the square to the church. In his business suit he looked somewhat out of place and drab, like a tired clerk in his lunch hour. His head moved continuously from side to side and up and down as he searched out the shape of the world. How sad, thought William. How terribly sad! And yet, did he really care about Alex? Did his disintegrating life mean something in terms of his own? William felt the distance growing between them. He used to say always that when people were out of sight he no longer thought of them. They somehow became unreal. The same was true of countries and cities and houses and objects. He had no feeling whatever of nostalgia or attachment to things. What he felt was what touched him at the moment—this sunshine in Paris, this coffee and cognac, these women who walked by in their full sweaters and rounded slacks. He felt a warmth in his groin and an urge to stretch the muscles in his thighs.

He paid the waiter, who stared dumbly at the coins William gave him, as though he were struggling to calculate his tip before turning on his automatic idiot smile of gratitude. With his hands in his trouser pockets he walked slowly in the direction of the street on which Edith Miller lived. It was Sunday and even if she had a job the chances were she wouldn't be working. He thought of calling first, but the temptation to surprise her was too great.

He turned the corner into a side street with cobblestones and narrow pavements. The old houses that rose on each side of the street, with their balconies and shutters and chimneys, seemed to lean towards each other, cutting out all but a strip of blue sky and a slant of sunlight. The neighbourhood reminded him of the Village in New York, where he had lived at one point for more than five years. After his first two years of teaching, at Coleman College in California, he had come back to Columbia to work on his doctorate. During that time he lived in the Village and taught occasional courses at The New School and New York University.

They were the years in which he wrote *The Full Circle*, in which he finished his doctorate, in which he made love to fifteen or twenty different women and was seriously involved with none, with the exception, perhaps, of Edith Miller whom he saw regularly for all of those five years, and with whom he lived in an apartment on Thompson Street for almost two years. And even after he decided that he wanted a place of his own he spent a part of each day with her. He helped her find a place on King Street, which, after two or three weeks, she converted from three bare rooms into a comfortable place that reflected the warmth and intelligence of her own being.

Edith left her mark on anything she touched. She was good with her hands and sensitive to form and colour. She enjoyed shopping for old pieces of furniture and flowers. She made rugs and lampshades and curtains. Probably what she needed all along, he thought now, was a lot of kids and a big house to fuss with. She came from a Jewish family in the Bronx that smelled always of herring and sour cream and her father's cigars. It was a big family and a happy one, but somehow she could not create a similar family for herself. She could not hold on to the traditions. She was educated out of a way of life that she secretly longed for and was rammed into another way of life in which she could never quite find a place. After college she taught school for a year, switched to publishing, where she could only be an underpaid editorial assistant, tried rather half-heartedly to pursue a singing career with a guitar and a repertoire of folksongs, and then settled into a kind of drifting or waiting, until, finally, she married a painter named Jeff O'Connor and moved with him to Paris, where, after a year, he ran off with a French girl and then discovered that he was dying of cancer.

It was Edith who nursed him in his final months, selflessly, with apparently no feelings about the past. It was she who, efficiently and patiently and lovingly, did all that might be done for this strange, wild man to whom she had once attached herself as a wife. The old urges, the old traditions came back to her. She knew instinctively what was right. And she knew what was right for William, too. She had wanted to marry him, but each time the subject came up he fled from it into levity or drunken indifference. Though he did not love her, perhaps he should have married her. He could have trusted her always. He could have depended on her. His house would have been warm. The sting of doubt and the pinch of lust might never have haunted such a house.

He wondered now why he hadn't taken her more seriously, why he always wanted to reduce her to a naked, cringing animal. He would take her to bed often and she was very good and very sweet, but he would go away always feeling inside of him a tight sense of dissatisfaction, as though something stayed locked in his belly that he or she or they could not release. He knew he could not be faithful to her or to any woman. But there was still something else—something worse. He didn't know how to put it. Perhaps he was afraid of himself. Yes, that was it. He was afraid of something in him that was both a part of him and yet separate from him. But he could find no name for it. If only he could name it, he could know it.

Alex lingered outside the church, his fist curled around the now hot and moist coins, a smile of anticipation on his smooth-shaven, boyish face. He lingered in the sunshine, among the tourists, hearing in his mind a vast organ and imagining cathedrals with vibrating columns and walls and windows that rose heavenward, that arched over him like miracles, like God's own work. He trembled with excitement and felt his heart pounding in his chest. It had been almost two months since he had been inside of a church and even longer since he had made his confession. He had gone through one of those bad times when he turned on God and all things benevolent, when he could not believe that his own tragedy was absorbed by some greater harmony and beauty, when he could not believe that anyone really cared whether he laughed or cried or loved or died. But now he was going back. The trip to Europe, the pilgrimage, the talks with William, the longing for his wife and children—all these things brought him back. He needed to believe in the goodness he felt. He needed his wise and mysterious God and all the familiar agonies and comforts of that gentle suffering soul on the cross. He needed the smiling Virgin Mother and the rhythmic chanting of the Mass. Fragments of prayers ran through his head. *Pray for us sinners now and at the hour of our death. Pray for us now . . .*

He touched the hard stone of the outside wall of the church and waited, as though for permission to enter. He should take time to prepare himself, he thought. Preparation is everything. Drain the mind of its fear and excitement. Learn to give one's self. The coins grew heavy in his hand. Was this his price of admission, he wondered. After his retreat and anger, was this his way of coming back. He shook the thought away and closed his eyes for a moment. He could feel the warmth of the sun on his cheek. 'Let me come to you,' he said, as though he were speaking in familiar tones to a familiar friend. 'Let me walk through these doors into your house. I need the comfort of your fire and the nourishment of your love. Forgive me for these months of bitterness. Help me to put it aside.'

And then he opened his eyes and saw the wooden doors that opened into the cave-like darkness. He straightened his tie, rubbed his face once more, and then plunged into the cool dark interior of God's house. A whimpering rush of air surrounded him and invisible bodies brushed against him. He felt as though he had not entered an enclosure but that he had left one. The sunlit world outside had dimensions and limits; this dark world seemed to stretch out and up infinitely. Everything was reversed. It was like leaving a well-lighted house and plunging into the vastness of the dark starless, moonless night. He could see absolutely nothing. But his feet kept moving, as though his initial momentum carried him forward. There were quiet voices all around him and footsteps. He heard the sound of his own shoes on the stone floor. And then miles and miles away, as though in another city or another country, there was the sound of organ music. He hesitated and reached out a hand but could feel nothing. Perhaps he was crossing in front of the altar, he thought, and started to kneel and make the sign of the cross. But his face brushed against some coarse material and a man's voice whispered, '*Pardon!*' He stood up quickly and felt the pistol shot of rage and humiliation explode in his chest. *Damn, damn, damn!* he screamed to himself and charged forward three or four more steps until he felt the crushing, immovable, stone against his forehead. He reeled back in the midst of a rude splash of coins and covered his eyes with both hands. The tears rushed from every part of his body and waited to be released, but he held them back and turned to search for the light of the entrance. It was a milky blur at the end of a tunnel and he rushed for it quietly and swiftly as voices and footsteps pursued him.

When William returned to the café he found Alex sitting thin-lipped and erect at a table on which there was a bottle of cognac and two glasses. 'She wasn't in,' said William, collapsing into a chair and reaching for the bottle. 'Did you light a candle for me in there?'

Alex smiled. 'Sure, Doc, I lit a candle for you. I lit candles for everyone.'

'And your money is all gone?'

'Yeah, it's all gone.' He poured himself another drink. 'And now I'm performing a holy communion on myself.'

'Ho, not so fast, fella; we promised to show up at Larry Grossman's at five. And I'll be damned if I'm going to carry you home again tonight.'

'Did you carry me home last night, Doc?'

'After midnight your feet never touched the ground.'

Alex laughed. 'Yeah,' he said. 'I get that way sometimes. Next time it happens I'm going to try walking on water. Maybe that's how He did it.'

'You're in great form, buddy. What the hell happened in there?'

'Nothing. Nothing at all. Say does this Hemingway friend of yours by any chance run with the bulls at Pamplona?'

'Why?'

'I don't know. I've always heard about it and I'd like to meet somebody who actually did it.'

'You mean you would like to do it yourself.'

'Yeah, that's what I mean.' He stared blankly towards the church on the opposite side and then poured another drink.

11

LARRY GROSSMAN LIVED in an apartment off the Boulevard Raspail with his wife and two small sons. It was an expensive four-room apartment in an old street in exactly the part of Paris that Larry preferred. It was close to the Select and the Dome and the Falstaff and the Deux Magots and the American Bar. His principal reason for living in Paris at all was that he tended to go mad after dinner. In America, he said, no one knows what to do in the evening—or, rather, *he* never knew what to do. Everyone eats at about six or seven o'clock, and dinner is one of those swift, efficient affairs, because, being Americans, they cannot stand even the pleasure of lingering over a meal. And by eight o'clock he would have the screaming willies because he didn't like to read and he didn't enjoy television and he hated his wife and he needed a drink. (The wife he hated was his first one: Lydia was his third. The one he really loved was the second, a girl with an exquisite mouth and long legs, who ran off with a Negro graduate student from N.Y.U.) So he decided on Paris, because in the evening he could escape from the dreary confines of his apartment, and from the fussing of his small children, and from the depressing sight of his loyal young wife, and wander from café to café in search of friends and conversations and a purely animal sense of freedom.

Larry was forty years old, bearded, stocky, and hairy. He was blessed and cursed with such an abundance of energy and such a lack of insight that he was almost always restless. Because he could not stop to think about what he did, he did a great deal. He served in the war, and was, in fact, a hero; he finished college under the G.I. Bill; he started a little magazine; he married three women, by whom he had four children; he taught school; worked for a newspaper; travelled in Africa and the Middle East and India; he wrote free-lance articles about everything; he wrote and published a novel; he fought with the underground in Israel, where he castrated an Arab and watched his best friend tortured to death; he smuggled cigarettes out of Tangiers by boat; he lived in a Kibbutz; and, finally, and perhaps most important of all, he ran with the bulls at Pamplona. Sometimes, when his beard was dripping with wine and his teeth were purple and his eyes were wild, he would shake his head tensely, as though he were quivering with excitement, and say, 'I just love it. I love life. I love wine. I love people. I love me. I love my balls and my feet and my hands.' And his wife Lydia, if she were there, would smile a patient Jewish smile and wait for him to vomit, which he invariably did after too much wine.

Larry Grossman knew everyone in Paris. That is to say, he knew all the Americans who had come to live more or less permanently. But he shunned the English and, even without the help of wine, said quite freely that he hated them. 'I just hate the bastards,' he would say. 'I hate them. They're all queer.' For a writer he was singularly inarticulate, relying for communication on grunts and exclamations, table-pounding, and a collection of wild and spastic gestures that could mean almost anything. At times he was frightening, at other times merely ludicrous. Most people, however, liked him.

It was almost eight o'clock before William and Alex found the right house. Large wooden doors opened into a courtyard, where half-brown potted plants lay dying in the shadows, and baby carriages mingled with the garbage cans and rusting collection of pipes that some plumber must have misplaced fifteen years earlier. At the ground level an inquisitive old woman leaned out of her curtained window to look at the foreigners, who babbled in English and walked cautiously, arm-in-arm, like lost boys invading the ruins of an old schoolhouse. She sucked at her gums, batted her tiny eyes, and waited for them to ask directions. 'Grossman!' said William, with what he imagined was the French pronunciation.

She cupped her hand to her ear and he repeated the name several times. '*Dix-huit, dix-huit,*' she said, imitating his fumbling approach to the language and pointing to a pair of glass doors that led to a dark staircase. Alex, who had finally zeroed in on the old lady amidst her flapping curtains and flowerpots, smiled and thanked her gallantly. His bitterness had been converted by the cognac into a reckless light-heartedness, and in his mind he spoke French fluently, with the juicy lips and raised eyebrows of a Charles Boyer.

They went up the narrow passageway with its rough plaster walls marked by stains like eternally seeping brown water, its worn stone steps and heavy wooden banister, and its single dangling light-bulb. 'Where the hell are we?' said Alex, climbing one more step than there actually was to reach the first landing and arresting his awkward motion with a semblance of dignity if not grace. There were five doors on each landing and William read off the faded numbers—'eight, nine, ten. Christ, we've got two more flights to go.'

By the time they reached the next landing Alex was beginning to make out the shadowy shapes of things. He held on less firmly to his friend and began to chuckle quietly to himself. 'I can't help thinking about that car of ours. How the hell could we lose something that big?'

'I just forgot where we left it. I know it was a side street not far from Harry's Bar, but I think somebody must have sealed it off this afternoon. It's like one of those dreams in which you are just trying to cross over a little bridge or walk across a field and the shape of things keeps changing and you can't seem to get there.'

'Yeah,' said Alex. 'Maybe you just can't get there from here.'

They found apartment number eighteen and knocked. When no one answered, William tried the antique electric buzzer. From the pool of sounds on the other side of the door a set of footsteps emerged, grew louder and more distinct. The door was jerked open and a band of yellow light yawned suddenly at them, against which was silhouetted the growling gorilla shape of Larry Grossman. 'Ha, at last, you crummy bastards. Lost or drunk? Don't tell me, I can guess. Come in, come in.'

Alex shuffled a few steps into the room and then held back, blinded again by the change of light to which he was always slow to adjust. Larry had grabbed William's hand and hauled him into a hairy embrace. 'You look terrible, you slob, but it's great to see you. I was afraid you wouldn't make it at all.'

William threw a playful football block at him and their combined four hundred pounds of flesh thumped together. 'The bull of the forward wall.' Their handshake became suddenly more formal. 'You're looking good, Larry. The place must agree with you.'

'Oh, yeah, yeah, I like it. I'm going to talk you into staying. It's just the place for you.' Over William's shoulder he saw Alex smiling politely and patiently.

'Oh,' said William, 'this is a buddy of mine, one of my oldest friends in the States, Alex Morgan, the pirate of Seaville.'

Alex held out his hand and Larry found it. He was surprisingly gentle, as though he imagined that Alex's bones must surely be brittle just because he wore a patch over one blind eye.

'So this is your pirate friend, the guy with the patch. Good to meet you at last, Alex. Bill told me all about you. The guy with nine kids and an organ, or is it nine organs and a kid?' He laughed heartily at his own joke and took Alex by the arm to lead him into the room where a dozen people stood or sat, talking and posing.

Alex hesitated. 'I need a minute to get used to the light.'

'He's a little near-sighted,' said William. 'He can't see past his eyeballs.'

'That's rough,' said Grossman. He shook his head. 'That's

real hard. I mean the eyes. I don't know what I would do if—you know. How bad is it, anyhow? I mean can you see to get around or read?'

'Oh, yeah,' said Alex, 'I manage more or less. I'm only legally blind. They give me an extra exemption on my tax form. I haven't paid any taxes in years.'

'With nine kids I guess you don't,' said Grossman, feeling his way clumsily into the courtyard of Alex's congenial nature.

As his two friends chatted in the foyer William glanced into the living-room to see who was there. A pretty young blonde caught his eye for a moment. She was talking with a small skeleton of a man with enormous eyes and wild black hair. But just beyond them, with her more kindly version of the Mona Lisa smile, was Edith Miller. In the soft light of the big room she looked younger and more beautiful than he remembered her. She leaned against the wall and seemed to be a painting come to life with her white skin, her very black hair and her deep burgundy turtle-neck sweater. She held up a glass towards him but did not move. His stomach tightened and his heart seemed to rise as fragments of memories doused him, like the fine spray from a crashing wave. He could not have believed beforehand that he would be so glad to see her.

He had never even really felt that he missed her. She was settled in his past like a hard, dead fact, lined up on the shelf of his mind, along with scores of other people whom he no longer saw or wrote to, like statues, frozen into a state of suspended animation at precisely that moment when he last spoke to them, waved goodbye at the airport to them, or loved them. He had no sense of their reality after that living moment, and refused to imagine them eating and sleeping and thinking and loving in a world that did not include him. He had what Alex once called 'the egocentricity of a cat'. But now life was breathed once more into the statue and it was as if no time at all had passed since their last meeting. He would cross the room and talk to her just as he had talked to Maggie, as if nothing had happened and nothing were different. And, indeed, for this very reason, nothing would be different between them.

Alex watched his friend disappear into the fuzz of colour and light. He saw it all as a technicolor film out of focus. 'Nice place you've got here,' he said a bit nervously to Larry.

'I like it. It's got everything I need, except maybe a quiet place to work. You know how kids are. God, do *you* know. *I* should complain.'

Alex followed Larry into the living-room, where someone lifted his hand gently and wrapped it around a glass. He recognized William's touch. 'Thanks, buddy,' he said, but William was gone again. He found himself in front of an empty chair. He eased himself into it and sipped his cognac. It was warm and sharp in his mouth and then in his chest and stomach. His sight grew clearer and he studied the faces around the room and the room itself.

'What did you do to your forehead?' said Larry, who had come back. Alex could hear him breathing before he could actually see him. He touched the small dry cut and smiled.

'I think I was struck by lightning,' he said. Larry's bearded face spread into a smile of stained teeth. Someone interrupted and took Larry away, and once again Alex was alone. Plunging this way into a crowd of new people both excited and depressed him. He collected himself and sipped again at his cognac. They all looked quite different from the people he was accustomed to. They were animated and colourful and talkative—almost exhibitionists. He sensed an intensity in the atmosphere which made him curious and uneasy. For a terrifying moment he was sure that he would have nothing to say to them, that his mouth would open and no words or thoughts would form.

What, after all, did he have in common with them: They were probably painters and writers and scholars, and he was an ex-labourer turned real estate broker and contractor. In the local tavern in Seaville he was sure of his ground. Bill Carney would buy him a drink and tell him dirty jokes about Italians and Jews; Charlie would complain about the wiring job in his house; Tom Burns would kid him and tell him that he heard his wife was pregnant again. He would lean on the heavy wooden bar. People would sit beside him or come up behind him and put their hand on his shoulder or grab him by the arm.

He would know always who it was and how to talk to him. He'd ask about Fred Schumann, who was in the hospital, and somebody would know, or he would ask Willie, the bartender, to drop a quarter in the jukebox and play the theme song from *Tunes of Glory* or something from *Gigi* like 'Thank Heaven for Little Girls.' He sipped again at his cognac and heard in his mind the voice of Maurice Chevalier.

'Alex, this is Edith Miller,' said William, who was standing in front of him with his arm around a pretty brunette.

Alex stood up and shook her hand. 'A pleasure,' he said.

She smiled warmly at him and he felt as though he had been embraced. He liked her immediately. He expanded. 'I'm a professional father,' he said, when she asked him what he did.

Her laugh was soft and her voice reached out like a friendly hand to touch him on the ears and cheek and mouth.

It was a buffet dinner and Edith served Alex as though she were tending a child. William watched, amused at first, but then also annoyed. She brought Alex a plate of food and moved his hand towards his fork and knife. She placed his glass of wine where he would not spill it, and showed him where the ashtray was. 'I suppose your wife does all this for you at home,' she said.

'It's easier at home,' he said, his face glowing now with food and drink and attention. 'She's wonderful with the kids and the house, but I never get to talk to her. Perhaps I should take a second wife—as a companion, I mean. Just to talk to and go out with. Helen is always too tired, or else she is just not interested. She's never read a book in her life.'

'Well, you can't have everything, Alex. After all, you married her because she was a simple domestic girl.'

'Yes, very simple and very domestic. The prettiest girl in high school. The first time I saw her was in a school play. I fell madly in love with her and asked everybody who she was. It took me a week to run into her in the hallway between periods. I had cooked up this elaborate plan for introducing myself, but when I finally stopped her and she smiled and said, "Hello, Alex," the whole plan dissolved. She knew who I was. She knew my brother and my sister. I blurted out something stupid about the play and she laughed at me and rushed off to class.'

'And how long did it finally take you to get her to say yes?' said Edith.

'About two years. I was the school clown and I had a hard time convincing her that I was also serious about life. We were both nineteen when we got married.'

'Just children,' she said, somewhat wistfully.

'Yeah, but we grew up early in Seaville. I didn't go to college. I found a job with the lighting company working on high-tension wires. Besides, I wasn't a very good bachelor. I wanted to be married. I wanted a house full of kids.'

'Well, your dream certainly came true, didn't it?' said Edith.

'With a vengeance.'

'And now you want a harem.'

'Not exactly a harem; just an intelligent woman to talk to.'

'Just to talk to?'

'Yes, I think that would be enough.'

'Well, maybe you're right. Maybe it's the best solution. Women are expected to be too many things today—childbearers, housekeepers, mistresses, friends, psychiatrists. And what's more they *want* to be all these things. Finally they discover that by trying to be all of them they are none of them.' She looked sad, as though she were thinking of someone specific. Alex felt her sadness and it tempered his own momentary joy. He noticed now that her face was not quite so youthful and perfect as he first imagined. There were slight lines about her eyes and mouth, and the beginnings of lines across her forehead that soon would become permanent. She sat close to him and when she reached in front of him to pick up his plate or move his glass he would see some grey in the soft blackness of her hair. He had a sudden impulse to comfort her.

William, too, felt Edith's sadness. He touched her shoulder and then quickly withdrew his hand. She looked up at him and smiled and he caught in that smile not only affection, but resignation, as though her vice was that she could not help but serve, as though she had learned a thousand years ago that we must all go on trying to be what we most want to be though a mysterious fate has already made it clear that we will not be allowed that privilege, that the truth will be bent by suffering, that we will be arbitrarily tormented and even destroyed, and that there is no bargain to be made, no possible compromise or deception that will make any difference. Like Job, she seemed in that moment haunted equally by the sense of injustice and the feeling that surely she had done something wrong, something offensive. She served and expected to be punished for serving; she loved, and expected to be destroyed for loving.

What a good woman, thought William. And all their days together in New York exploded in his mind, a moment of piercing reality. She would have served him. She would have loved him.

'Why don't you come back to Seaville with me?' said Alex, 'and be my other wife?'

'Sure. I'd love to, but how would you explain me to Helen?'

'Oh, she won't mind. You can be a governess or something for the children, Or, better yet, you can be *my* governess.'

'What have you been doing?' said William.

'I'm a secretary in an American firm.' She spoke as though the fact that she was forced to talk about herself was distasteful.

'And your music?'

She shook her head without explaining further. 'I'm taking lessons in Chinese. A fascinating language. You must take it up sometime.'

'Some day,' said William.

'There are ideas that one can express in Chinese that cannot be expressed in any other language. For instance—do you have a pencil?'

Alex handed her a ball-point pen from his inside pocket. She took a paper napkin and drew an elaborate Chinese character. 'Do you know what this means?'

William shook his head.

'It is the Chinese character for the fog that develops between a man and a woman who love each other but do not understand each other. It took Henry James a whole novel to convey the same idea.'

Alex picked up the piece of paper and studied her meticulous drawing. It looked like a small cottage perched on slanting stilts, with animals or children running about through the uprights. 'Amazing,' he said. 'How intricate and subtle. But do you think that people like us can ever really learn to understand them?'

She hesitated as though she were weighing the question and then said, 'No, I don't suppose we ever can.'

The party grew smaller but louder. Alex wandered, sniffing here and there like a curious cat. But William sat alone with Edith. They drank a great deal of wine and commented from the side-lines on Larry Grossman's cast of characters.

Larry finally intruded. He draped his heavy arm around William and said, 'How's the writing going, old buddy?'

'Not bad,' he lied. 'How about you? Have you got a new book yet?'

'Oh, man, that's a real drag. I don't know, I just can't get hold of it. I wrote about eight drafts of the first chapter and I'm still not satisfied with it. Meantime, I'm running out of dough. The advance is gone. My other money is gone. Even the money you loaned me is used up. No, I haven't forgotten that, Bill. I'd give it back to you right now if I had it.'

'Never mind the money. What's the matter with the book? It's the book that counts.' He could feel the perspiration forming on his forehead and in the palms of his hands. 'Life's never as important as art. To write another book, a better book, that's the thing.' He emptied his glass.

'I sent my editor a few pages last month and he wrote back that it's not enough to tell anything yet. He said my style is too thin, too distilled. What the hell does that mean?'

'It means you don't use enough adjectives.'

'Too bad! I'm not going to use adjectives. A book is a picture of action. What people do and say—that's all. It worked all right for *The Siege of Karem*. Anyhow, you thought so, and I have more respect for you than that little old grammar-school teacher who calls himself my editor.'

The bottle tipped in someone's hand between Larry and William and suddenly both of their glasses were filled with dark wine. William glanced at Alex across the room. The shadows on his smiling face made him look ancient and bony. William saw the deathhead blossom there and then fade again. He heard Larry's voice but was no longer listening to what he was saying. After a while Larry wandered away. William went across the room and put his hand on Alex's shoulder.

'Is that you, Doc?' said Alex. He took William by the arm and drew him closer. 'Listen,' he said, 'why don't you and I and Edith go somewhere else. I've had enough of this.'

'Sure,' said William, looking around the room for Edith.

Without saying good night to anyone the three of them went out of the door, tiptoed down the narrow staircase like conspirators, and then burst into laughter when they reached the dark pavement and the cool night breeze swept gently over them.

Alex inhaled deeply. 'Let's go somewhere quiet,' he said. 'Just the three of us.'

'Let's go to my place,' said Edith.

They walked arm-in-arm through the silent, empty streets. Alex hummed quietly to himself and felt the warmth of Edith's arm.

12

IN THE SOFT light and calm of Edith's apartment they sipped black coffee and brandy. The phonograph played *Plaisir d'Amour*. The sensual, wistful voice of a woman sang first in French and then in English, 'The joys of love last but a moment; the pain of love lasts all life long.'

The music combined with Alex's weariness and all the brandy he had been drinking to melt his insides and bring tears to his eyes. 'How sad it is,' he said, trying to smile away the tears. 'How terribly sad everything is.' He remembered the long kisses he gave his wife when she was a young girl. He remembered her soft blonde hair and her hands on his rough face. 'We always imagine we have hold of something permanent and perfect; but it always slips away.'

'Nothing is ever the same,' said William.

'No,' said Edith, 'nothing is ever the same.' And they looked at each other as though they longed to be deeply, romantically, in love. But even this longing and this understanding bound them together for the moment and William put his arm around her and moved closer.

'I thought I might go to Greece to live for a while. They say it is very beautiful, but I never seem to do anything about it. The days pass. I work. There are little things to do. There are friends.'

'And your music?' he said.

'My music? How flattering you are. I wrote two little songs in the past two years—very little songs. Very simple. Sometime I will sing them for you.'

'Sing them for us,' said Alex.

'Yes,' said William, 'why don't you.'

Without saying anything she got up and went into the next room. William and Alex sat quietly, looking at one another and at the paintings and flowers and shelves of books. Were they Jeff's paintings, William wondered. The music stopped and all that came now from the phonograph was the circling whispering of the needle in an empty groove.

'How quiet it is,' said Alex, leaning forward over the coffee table in his blue-cushioned bamboo chair. He raised his glass and then paused, as though he was distracted by a nagging idea.

The painting that William stared at was a large canvas with an exploding entanglement of pyramids and triangles. Crystal formations, he thought, remembering the time in high school when he first looked through a microscope.

The force that kept Alex suspended gave way and his raised arm moved again. He emptied half the small glass and said to William, without looking at him, 'What are you going to do with her?'

'She's not mine to do anything with,' said William.

'She would be if you married her.'

Edith came back with flowers in her hair and a guitar. She sat in the shadows, away from the glare of the lamp and away from them. They waited. She played a few notes and then a few more. The melody emerged. She sang her gentle, dreamy song.

The red rose falls on the white snow.
The snow falls where no birds go.
The old sun smiles away
Memories of a summer day.

Alex listened to the slow, whispered, mournful song. And

he remembered how one morning, one cold winter morning, he walked out to the canal and sat in the freezing morning air, amidst heaps of snow, to watch the sun rise. The salt water was still. Swollen ghosts of boats under canvas lined the shore. And the air was brittle and clear. Dog-tracks in the snow of his back-yard betrayed the wanderings of some lonely creature. It was a Sunday morning, after a drunken party at McGuire's. His head throbbed with nicotine and liquor and the foggy memory of some woman whose breasts he was feeling in the kitchen, and to whom he was telling gallant lies about her beauty—her eyes, her hair, her mouth. He was carried home and put to bed about one a.m. And then at five or six he could no longer sleep because he was suffocated by dreams.

He put on his clothes in the silent house and tiptoed out into the white world. The cold was painful but good against his hot flesh. The air filled his lungs and sent chills across his shoulders and down his back. The light came across the water and the sky softened to grey-blue. With the light came such a feeling of despair that he wanted to pray, but at first he did not know what to say. He just knelt in the snow and waited, feeling the dampness numb his legs. Then he said, 'Are you taking away my sight because I've abused it? Have I abused it? I have tried to see the simple beauty of things. I love your world. Please don't lock me in this cold, dark place. Please, please, please.' The tears that ran down his cheeks were cold and salty when they reached his lips. He was embarrassed, though he was alone, and his pride burned in his throat. His humiliation made him angry and self-conscious. He made a hasty sign of the cross, stood up, and trudged back through the snow to his warm house.

The snow falls where no birds go.

William, too, remembered the snow. He remembered a day years earlier when he walked through the white field that was Washington Square Park on his way to have lunch at Edith's place. He saw a Negro girl sitting alone on one of the uncleared benches. She wore an old coat with a fur collar and red woollen stockings. She was tall and thin and the dark brown of her elegant face was such a contrast to the white snow that

William could not pass her without finding an excuse to stop and look at her. He lit a cigarette, blowing the combination of smoke and steam into the grey dampness. Then he stood in front of the girl and said, 'You must be cold; have a cigarette.' She accepted without a word. Later, in his apartment, he discovered that her name was Clara Williams, that she was from Cincinnati, and that the job she was promised by mail had been given to someone else. 'Because I'm black,' she said. 'I ain't so dumb. They didn't know I was black.' They drank wine and he studied her young face and body. He had never been to bed with a Negress before and the prospect excited him.

He cooked bacon and eggs and toast and served her at the small wooden table in his kitchen. She accepted everything without apologies or thanks, as though she fully expected everything that he gave her. After some more wine and cigarettes in his combination living-room and study, he sat with her on the couch and touched her face and shoulders and breasts. Still she said nothing. Still she accepted whatever he did. When he took her by her hand and led her into the bedroom, she came, carrying her wine in one hand and saying drowsily, 'I never slept with no white boy.' But she allowed him to undress her and put her down on the bed.

As he made love to her he stared down at the whiteness of his skin against the darkness of hers. He was fascinated—not by her, but by the act in which he was involved, and he wanted to feel that act deeply and sharply. He wanted to see it; to remember it, as though he was already sure that it would never happen again. And it never did. She got dressed afterwards and went out again into the winter evening. She did not even say goodbye.

After her two little songs Edith continued to play, humming familiar melodies. Alex's compliment was somewhat delayed, as though he did not know where her music left off and the old songs began. 'Lovely, Edith. Really lovely.'

After a while Alex fell asleep in his chair and William said, 'He's a weary pilgrim with a long way yet to go.'

'I like him very much,' said Edith.

Alex's breathing was heavy and even, threatening at any

moment to break into a snore. 'I'd better take him home,' said William.

She held his arm. 'No, let him sleep. In fact, why don't both of you spend the night. There's plenty of room.'

William considered for a moment and then said, 'All right.'

'I'll see if I can make him comfortable where he is,' she said, and went into the bedroom for a blanket and a pillow.

William lit a cigarette and leaned back. He felt the silence in the room, but then it was shattered by the memory of something Maggie once said to him a long time ago. 'You must decide what you want—whatever it is, however bizarre or mad. The fear of one's private madness often makes one truly insane. And to deny life and involvement with reality is the worst form of insanity.' He would listen to these lectures of hers in the darkness—her stern but patient voice winding in a slow, serpentine fashion around slippery ideas—and wonder whether she was talking to him or to herself. When he accused her of this confusion, she would get angry and say that his way of seeing things was too intellectual, that there was a fatal separation between his head and his heart. And, finally, he would agree, because he knew there was some truth in what she said. He would agree and say, jokingly, 'All right, Saint Maggie, build me a bridge.' And she would turn towards him and playfully pretend to strangle him. Then they would hold each other in the night, and without another word, make love until they fell asleep, their arms and legs tangled comfortably about one another.

And now it was Edith, forcing him to decide, to choose, offering him the animal comfort of a warm house, a good wife and children (he was sure she wanted and needed children). He could picture himself in a house in the suburbs with Edith. The waxen figures of his unimaginable children—one boy and one girl—were waving goodbye eternally as they set off for school with their neatly combed hair and their schoolbags. His aproned wife, like a mannequin, or the starched lady in a *Better Homes and Gardens* ad, smiled over her Hotpoint stove or sparkled by her giant Westinghouse refrigerator. And he, complete with tie and hat and attaché case, eased his Ford out of the garage and headed for the seven fifty-five on the Long Island Railroad or The New Haven or The Jersey Central. He would read his *Times* and smoke one cigarette and never think an evil thought.

But perhaps he was being unfair. Certainly it would not have to be that way, children or no children. She had more sense, more originality and imagination. She would know instinctively what to do for him. They could buy a piece of land, design their own house. He might even have a study of his own, separate from the house—a place of his own where he could work or sleep or brood. It would mean getting a job, some kind of a job. He had been an editor; he could do that again. Eventually he could teach. There would be summer vacations and week-ends for writing. His studio in the woods mushroomed into reality. It had a fireplace and walls of books. Sheepskin rugs warmed the floor and the large desk was heaped high with manuscripts, magazines, and letters.

Yes, he thought, it was quite possible. And all he had to surrender for it was his drifting, foggy, drunken quest. His secret strength—the thing that kept him sane—had always been the feeling that he was moving towards some great revelation, that he was lending himself to some force that moved him in a right direction, even if he swept past the simple comforts of life, the temptations, even if he turned away from people, even if he neglected himself and his work. He always knew that something was falling into place. But now, lately, he was not so sure. He was almost forty and the promise of roundness and harmony, love and wisdom, was fading instead of growing. Things were falling apart. Could he have been so wrong all these years? Was there, after all, no place to go? No revelation? No sense of wholeness within?

He looked out of the window towards the black sky and imagined a malevolent god smiling down at him out of the darkness with cruel satisfaction.

A wave of dreams washed over Alex in his bamboo chair, a rag bag of images, fragrances, and conversations. His father's long hands were knotted with arthritis. He rubbed them in slow motion over the wood-burning kitchen stove and complained that he left his gloves at the shop where he worked as a cabinet-maker. His mother moved through the small kitchen like a swollen cow. His daughter, Barbara, stripped to the waist, combed her hair in front of the bathroom mirror. Her hair was very long, reaching down past her hips. 'Hurry up, Katie,' she said, 'the children are waiting.' Helen was asleep beside him with a fever. She was pregnant and tried to turn over but couldn't. He felt her pain through his back and stomach.

Out on the dock his cousin Ralph was running up the sails on a three-masted schooner. He called to Alex to come before the sun gave out. The wind blew them out to sea and the boat glided like a toy boat on a pond, too fast in proportion to its size. Ralph laughed and laughed like an excited schoolboy. He was all in white, with a sweater and a tie and white tennis shoes. His dark hair tossed in the wind. The boat leaned and the water washed over it. Ralph's pleading voice came from the rough waters, but Alex could not see him. He rushed up and down the deck, holding on to a tangle of lines. 'Where are you?' he called. 'Where are you? Ralph! Ralph!' Ralph's voice called again, but it was weak and distant: 'Tell Mama to light the candles in St. Jude.' And then the sea was calm and the boat glided gently through the tropical night.

Alex tried to turn in his chair and the chair slipped away from under him. In his dream world he was parachuting through miles of sunny space, free-falling, gliding, sailing on the air, like sky-divers in films he had seen. Then the hard ground greeted his stiff and aching body and he woke up, puzzled and lost, in the darkness of the strange room.

Edith and William helped him to the couch and covered him with a blanket. He mumbled for a moment and shook his head, but then soon was asleep again.

'Poor man,' she said. 'He wants so much to enjoy everything.'

'He does enjoy everything, especially his own suffering.'

'He does play Jesus Christ sometimes, doesn't he?'

'Yeah, a comic Christ. And yet he takes it all very seriously.'

'Does he really mean it, about Lourdes?'

'I think he's more serious about it than he admits.'

'Then perhaps something will happen after all.'

In the bedroom they turned out the lights and opened the window. 'You always liked to look out at the night,' she said quietly. They lay down side by side under a single sheet.

'Yes,' he said. 'I like the feeling of being inside looking out at all that endless space.'

'Your escape hatch,' she said. He could not see her smile.

'That's right,' he said. 'Among the cold, indifferent stars. If heaven meant floating up there for ever like a star, I wouldn't mind too much, so long as I could look down and see the earth. I would settle for seeing it, for watching it turn, looking in on the lives of the living. It would be better than death absolute.'

'Death absolute,' she repeated. 'What an ugly term.'

He put his arm around her shoulders and drew her against him. Her warmth distracted him and aroused him. He faced her and pressed himself against her belly. 'It's good to see you again, Bill,' she whispered.

He felt her hair and her back and the roundness of her hips. Her mouth searched for his and he pulled her on top of him. He liked the lightness of her body on his own sturdy form. She leaned her head against his shoulder and he could see past her out the open window. It was a warm clear night but a cold shiver went through him. He turned away from the stars and eased Edith gently down to her pillow. He made love to her slowly, carefully, enjoying every touch, every kiss. When they parted again and she once more lay curled against his shoulder, under his protective arm, she whispered, 'I love you.'

He wanted to say those words to her, but they did not come. He said nothing as he stared once more out the window, and soon he could feel that she was asleep. He removed his arm without disturbing her and closed his weary eyes.

13

THURSDAY MORNING ARRIVED and still William had not told anyone that Maggie was coming to Paris. But Alex could tell that William was preoccupied and it was safe to assume that it had something to do with Maggie. 'It's simple,' he said. 'Men fall in love with women like Maggie, but they marry women like Edith.'

'I suppose you call that *folksy wisdom*,' said William.

'I don't care what you call it,' said Alex, 'it's true.'

'To hell with the truth,' said William.

They sat at a café in the clear air of the sparkling new day drinking coffee and smoking. The noisy morning traffic clotted the boulevard. Tourists wandered, bathing themselves in the carnival colours and cool sunlight that filtered through the leaves of a thousand pavement trees.

William shook his head. 'I guess I'll never understand women,' he said, and leaned back to watch the people pass. 'Or maybe I don't want to.'

'Then why don't you stop trying,' said Alex. 'Why don't you leave them alone?'

'I can't,' said William. 'They bother me. They're so nice and soft and warm. I think I'm hooked on them. You know, like an alcoholic.'

'Well you can't have them all, old buddy, even if you worked at it day and night.'

'Yeah,' said William. 'Isn't it a pity! I tried to work it out mathematically once and it's discouraging. I figured if you went to bed with five different women every day of your mature life that after forty years (assuming you weren't dead in a week) you would have made love to only 73,000 of them.'

'Is that all?' said Alex sarcastically.

'Well, it's not much when you figure there must be at least a couple of hundred million eligible broads in the world.'

'It's downright depressing, Doc. What are you going to do?'

'I don't know.'

'I guess you'll have to console yourself with those miserable 73,000.'

William laughed and caught the waiter by the arm as he went by. 'Two cognacs and two black coffees,' he said.

Alex smiled. 'And I've been eating cornflakes for breakfast all these years.'

William took out a pencil and a piece of paper. 'All right,' he said, 'let's get down to business. Today I'm going to make a list.'

'What for?'

'Because we never get anything done that we set out to do and time is running out. Today we're going to make a list.' He started to write. 'American Express. Right?'

'Right,' said Alex. 'Put down postcards, shoelaces, Notre Dame.'

William scribbled these things on the slip of paper. 'And I have to call Larry and Edith and a guy named Stanley Ripple.'

'Who?'

'He teaches at an American school here—at an airforce base, I think. I want to find out what the chances are of picking up some work.'

'You mean you want to stay here?' said Alex.

'I have to settle somewhere, and my prospects are getting

blacker by the hour. If I go back to the rat-race in New York, even assuming I can find a job, I'll drink myself to death and never write another line. If I go back to teaching it means waiting until next year for something to turn up. And, besides, I hate teaching. I don't have a rich patron. I don't even have a working wife. I've thought of manual labour, but who's going to hire a guy with a Ph.D. to dig holes in the ground? On top of everything else I'm fed up with America, with New York, the whole academic world, Madison Avenue, Mainstreet U.S.A., television, deodorized American girls, supermarkets, big fat fast cars, credit cards, bills, the New York *Times*, phony intellectual parties, high fidelity, the whole bit. I've had it.'

'Oh, come off it, Doc,' said Alex. 'You know damn well it doesn't matter where you live. America is no worse than any other country. It's got its advantages too. It's got space and variety and energy.'

'No, Alex,' he said, 'it isn't so. I used to think it didn't matter where I lived or what I did for a living. But now I know it does matter, and America bothers me. For one thing there's never any place to sit down either in the city or in the country, except for an occasional park full of kids and pigeons. No cafés, no plazas with fountains where you can just hang around. Only the Latin countries here know how important it is to do nothing.'

'Americans are afraid to do nothing,' said Alex. 'But, on the other hand, they get a lot done.'

'That's fine if you believe in progress. I don't happen to believe in it. I don't want to be cleaner and travel faster. I want to be dirty and move very slowly. That makes me, automatically, un-American.'

Alex poured his cognac into his coffee and stirred the mixture. 'I can't argue with you, Doc,' he said. 'I've been complaining about the same things for years, but it's my country. I mean it's home and I figure I've got to find a way to live there.' He paused. 'That's why I have to get that island.'

'Another bait station in the bay?'

'No. A private colony. A little world. I don't care what you call it.'

'Paradise Island, Incorporated,' mumbled William.

'We could do it, Doc. Together we could do it.' He leaned over the table towards William. 'It's a solid piece of land. All it needs is bulkheads and plenty of dock space. We can get fifteen or twenty lots out of those three acres.'

'Yeah, and wind up with Levittown-in-the-Bay.'

'All right, then, we'll build a hotel or something.'

'What you need is a plan, a principle. Either you want to make money or you want to create a Utopia. You can't do both. There's no money in dream-worlds.'

'It's not a dream-world; it's real.'

'Sure, it's real. All your schemes are real.'

Alex dropped his cigarette on the ground and stepped where he thought it might be, but missed. 'All right, Doc, forget it. I'll find somebody else.'

'Oh, for Christ sake, stop looking so wounded,' said William.

'I'm not wounded, just disappointed.'

William shifted uneasily in his seat and crossed his legs. 'I'm sorry, Alex. I didn't mean to sound discouraging, but, damn it, it's not an easy thing to do.'

'Of course it's not easy. I never said it was easy.'

'Well, let me think about it. Right now we've got a thousand things to do.'

'Where's your list?' said Alex. 'Put down Chartres and Versailles. I always wanted to see them.'

'It'll take a whole day.'

'All right put it down for tomorrow. And put down the Louvre, the Eiffel Tower, Sacre Cœur, the Bois de Boulogne, Montmartre, and half a dozen cafés.'

By noon they had not yet found the American Express office and were puzzling out the geography of Paris over a couple of beers in another café.

By three o'clock they were finished with lunch and set out again. 'Why can't we find anything?' said Alex. His tie was undone and he was squinting drunkenly in the afternoon sun.

'I guess we don't try hard enough,' said William.

At another café they talked to a man who looked like Maurice

Chevalier and who turned out to be a farmer on a holiday in the big city.

Late that afternoon they were propositioned in a side street and laughed so hard that the women were scared away. The incident naturally called for a drink. They picked up a couple of American college girls, bought them each a rum and coke and then, after a futile attempt at conversation, sent them off on their touristy rounds.

At six o'clock somebody tried to assassinate De Gaulle, and by seven the streets were full of honking police vans and gendarmes armed with sub-machine guns. The round-up of suspects continued on into the night.

'Something's going on,' said Alex. 'I can tell.' He leaned against the open window of the car, half-dozing. 'Remind me to call home. Got to see if everything is all right.'

They were lost again. William turned into a narrow street and pulled over to look at the map. Two gendarmes came up to the car and drew their guns. They pointed to Alex, who now was sound asleep. Draped over the window, with his dark hair and eye-patch, he looked like a dead Algerian. 'I don't understand,' said William. 'We're Americans.' He pointed to Alex and made a drinking motion. The gendarmes apologized and went away.

It was after nine and Maggie was waiting. By the time they arrived at the Deux Magots it was after ten and Alex was awake again.

'Where are we, Doc?' said Alex.

'At the Deux Magots. St. Germain. Remember? I promised to meet Maggie here tonight.'

Alex looked up suddenly as though he had been doused with cold water. 'Maggie? Here?'

'I guess I didn't tell you. She's coming along with us.'

Alex shook his head as though he couldn't believe what he was hearing. 'You mean all the way to Lourdes?'

'Sure. Why not?'

'Because I won't have it—that's why not. This was supposed to be a private trip. Just you and me—remember?'

'Well I already told her she could come.'

'That's great. Very considerate. Did it ever occur to you to ask me beforehand?'

'Sure it occurred to me, but I decided not to because you were bound to say *no*. This way you have no choice.'

'That's what you think, Professor.' Alex fumbled with the door of the car. 'You go about your business, you horny bastard, and I'll find my own way to wherever I want to go.' He opened the door and stepped out into the darkness. He could only see the lights of the café and he groped his way towards them.

'Come on back here, you idiot,' shouted William. He leapt out of the car and ran after him.

'Go to hell,' said Alex.

William held him by the arm, but before he could say anything further Maggie appeared. 'Who's leading who?' she said cheerfully.

Alex yanked his arm away from William, but did not walk away.

'He's sore at me,' said William.

'Forget it,' said Alex.

'He's sore because——'

'I said forget it,' insisted Alex more loudly. 'Let's have a drink.'

They found a table and sat down. For a moment they were all awkwardly silent. Then Maggie said, 'I bet he didn't tell you I was coming.'

Alex broke into a smile. 'Boy, have you got his number, lady.' He put his hand out. 'Where are you? I'd like to shake hands with the only other person in the world who understands this bastard.'

She put her hand in his and almost immediately he softened. 'I'm sorry, Doc,' he said. 'But all you had to do was tell me.'

'All right,' said William. 'I owe you an apology. But you can be pretty obnoxious about certain things—and stubborn. You would have said *no*.'

'As a matter of fact I don't think I would have. Not after we met in London anyway. But that's not the point.'

'The real point,' intruded Maggie, 'is that right now we're all here and we've got to decide what to do. If you two want to go on alone, that's fine with me. I've got plenty of friends to visit here in Paris for a couple of days.'

'Don't be stupid,' said Alex. 'You're coming with us.'

'I won't be offended,' she said. 'I told William to begin with that it seemed to be a for-men-only party.'

'Well you don't count,' said Alex. 'Not that you're not a woman, but you're not an ordinary broad. You're one of us. I could tell the minute we met.'

'That's me,' she said. 'Just one of the boys.'

They had dinner at a restaurant off St. Michel that William and Maggie had been to before. 'It hasn't changed,' she said. 'I even recognize the waiter.'

'I don't recognize anything,' said William. 'These places all look alike to me.'

'That's what I like about him,' said Maggie to Alex; 'he's so sentimental.'

'He's about as sentimental as an amoeba, except when he's loaded, of course. Then he gets all emotional and starts talking like real people.'

Maggie laughed and put her hand on Alex's shoulder. 'There, there, old thing, don't overdo it, just because he treated you like a little boy.'

'That's the way he treats everyone. He thinks we're all kids.'

'Well maybe we are,' she said. 'Sometimes I still feel as if I'm about eight years old. Haven't you ever felt that way? I mean, as though your own childhood is still alive inside of you somewhere?' She pressed her long fingers against her chest. She was wearing a white cotton blouse and a black skirt and did, indeed, look like an overgrown schoolgirl.

'When you two get through picking me apart,' said William, 'just sweep the pieces under the table, will you.'

'How long has this little war being going on?' she said. 'And isn't it time we declared a truce?'

'I'm willing,' said William, 'if Napoleon here will put down his bayonet.'

'Well, damn it, Doc, somebody's got to tell you. You just can't treat people that way.'

'What way?' said William, genuinely confused.

'As if they weren't people,' shouted Alex.

Maggie the peacemaker leaned back in her chair. Her broad smile collapsed into an expression of resigned sadness. How often she had tried to tell him the same thing; and how often she had failed. Perhaps now it would mean something, coming from him, from Alex, from his closest and possibly his only friend.

But William resisted. He leaned forward and said, 'Look, Alex, you have your way of surviving and I have mine. When you're feeling bad, you want the whole world to love you; when I'm feeling bad, I just want to be left the hell alone. I've got this private little cave into which I crawl, complete with weapons, great books, and erotic nightmares. It's not always fun, but it's safe. It's a way of saying that I can take care of things myself.'

'The original loner,' muttered Alex.

'All right, I'm a loner. And you're a non-loner.'

'And Maggie?' said Alex. 'Since you're handing out labels, what's she?'

He looked at her for a moment, at the few loose strands of hair that fell across her shining eyes, at the dampness of her lips. 'She's an untouchable,' he said. 'The sacred, sainted whore of Lourdes, the other Bernadette.'

Alex frowned, and a magnificently contained fire spread through Maggie's entire body. Inside she winced, but outside she smiled and nodded. 'The grandest, most complicated compliment I've received all week,' she said.

And then it was Alex's turn to play peacemaker, a job at which he was infinitely more successful than Maggie. 'As soon as we mop up the blood,' he said, 'I'm going to offer a series of toasts to every great French writer from whoever the hell wrote the *Song of Roland* to Albert Camus.'

For the moment it was possible to talk of other things.

When they returned to the hotel they arranged for a room for Maggie. William was amused by the studied expression of indifference on the young clerk's face. What would the young man think, he wondered, if he tried to explain that Maggie was his wife.

Alex went to sleep right away, but William lay awake smoking and reviewing over and over again the events of the day. He was troubled by the argument with Alex, and he was afraid that before the trip was over it would happen again. The antagonism between them seemed suddenly to be as real as the affection, and he didn't understand it.

After a while he got up, put on his pants, and went to Maggie's room. He found her awake, sitting by the window in a blue silk robe. He knew that she had nothing on under it.

'I'm sorry about the scene this evening,' he said, 'but Alex has some peculiar ideas.'

'You should have told him,' she said. The tall windows were open and the cool night air blew against them as they sat in the darkness.

'You don't understand,' he said. 'Alex has a thing about power and authority. He wants to be obeyed. He thinks it's a kind of castration if his wife and kids have minds of their own. Why do you think he has such a big family?'

'I thought he liked children,' she said.

'He does. But what he likes more is being a father. No, not just a father, an overlord, a king, a tribal chieftain.'

Maggie thought of her own father, of his silent arbitrary manner about the farm. And of his feeble, feverish last days. 'Perhaps he's right,' she said. 'Perhaps that's the way it ought to be.'

'Maybe,' said William. 'I don't know.'

They stood by the window for a long time without saying anything. William stood beside her but didn't touch her. Finally, she looked at him and said, 'I suppose we should have had a child.' Then he put his hand on her shoulder and felt her back and neck.

'Let's not talk about it,' he said. He took her arm and led her to the bed. They lay down under the light blanket and the sheet as though it were an ordinary day in their married life and without saying another word made love quietly, and held each other as they slept.

14

THINGS ARE ALWAYS different in Italy, thought William, remembering another summer, a time when he and Maggie had been together before. Sharp edges grow blunt. Faces soften in the caressing sun. The days lengthen out lazily and one has a sense of roundness.

They had come to Assisi from the east in the early part of the day so that the sun caught the heaped-up, hilltop town of Saint Francis, and drew it, mirage-like, away from the clinging earth, the rich surrounding valleys, towards an embracing sky so blue and delicate that William's angry heart softened and he stopped the car along the road to let this first distant view filter down through his whole body, hoping that Maggie, too, would see it as he did.

He leaned against the fender of the car as she wandered down the road with her camera. It was the only picture she took on the whole trip. He watched her walk away from him slowly, her feet almost naked in simple monkish sandals, her blonde hair held together gypsy-fashion by a knotted bandana. Over her dress she wore that old brown suede jacket that tied around the middle and emphasized her thin waist. She stood for a while, staring at the miracle of form and light that is Assisi, at the monastery walls that rise like cliffs, at the humble, huddling houses below. How graceful she looked at that moment. How simple. How lonely. He watched her while she adjusted the camera, looked through the viewer, adjusted something again, moved a few steps off the road into a field of stubble, and took the picture.

She walked back towards him with such a look of satisfaction that he might have imagined, had he any faith, that she had undergone a spiritual conversion just by taking that picture. 'Isn't it lovely?' she said, her face a gentle, rosy smile, after days of cold, business-like politeness. 'I know what the expression *breath-taking* means now. That quiet excitement inside does take your breath away.'

They drove a long time towards that shining town, and in their windings sometimes lost sight of it. 'Perhaps there is no such place,' he said when once the town was hidden from their view behind a hill. 'Perhaps we only imagined it.'

She laughed. 'Romantic yearnings.'

But then it appeared again, closer and larger and more real than ever. When they climbed the hill into the main piazza of the town the reality depressed them momentarily. They were blinded not by the golden halo of light that singled out that holy place, but by giant aluminium tourist buses. Gas-pumps and parking attendants, souvenir shops and cafés conspired to tear apart that distant vision. 'It can't be the same place,' said Maggie. 'Damn them! Why do they have to do this? Why don't they insist that all these cars and buses be left down below, so that anyone who really wants to come up here can walk up the hill?'

'Carrying crosses?'

'Yes, why not?'

They were unable to find a room in the main part of the town and were forced to search up higher towards the monastery, where certain private homes rented out spare bedrooms to visitors. After dinner, with the sun settling like the swollen fiery king of the world, they walked up narrow streets, searching out a route to the top. They felt the roundness of the earth in this sphere of sky, at first aflame with the dying sun, then eased into darkness and flooded with stars. They lingered along the road, looking now and again towards the silhouetted fortress-like monastery that they never seemed to reach.

'It's like being inside of the sky,' she said, standing straight and still on a flat rock by the side of the narrowing road. The lights of the town below them became dim imitations of the brilliant stars that shone not only over them but all around them. He sat down quietly beside the road and watched her and smoked, blowing the whitish-blue clouds into the cool air of that still and silent night.

They did not speak much, but held hands as they walked and told each other with every movement, every slow step and turn of the head, that they were glad to be there and that they were happy to be together. After the clawing arguments, the patronizing explanations and the cruelty, there was no other way to say what they meant.

Then they stood together at the highest point they dared to reach. They studied the stars, searching for familiar constellations. 'Do you know,' he said, 'that the light from some of those distant stars takes over a million years to reach us, and that some of those stars that we are now looking at no longer exist, because sometime during that million years they have died or exploded?'

'You mean they're no longer there though I see them?'

'Even now,' he said, 'close as we are, my voice must travel that short distance from me to you, and you do not hear it exactly at the moment that I speak.'

'Does that mean that people can never be entirely together?'

'I don't know what it means,' he said, 'but the immensity of all that makes me see all this much more clearly.'

'The microcosm and—what's the other?'

'Macrocosm.'

'That's right. I never knew which was which.'

He put his hand around her waist and drew her closer to him. He looked at her face near his in the darkness and saw that only a last strand of stubborn pride kept her from weeping. He kissed her on the cheek and allowed his lips to linger there until he felt her relax and lean towards him. Then they kissed, their warm, familiar lips touching gently, their mouths parted and moving slowly, instinctively, almost musically, in wordless conversation. They held each other for a long time under the immense, curving sky. They felt themselves growing towards it, as though they were themselves a church on a mountain top, reaching into the mystery of the fire and darkness. They were afloat in the night, their eyes closed. Then he heard himself whisper to her, 'Marry me here—secretly, privately, under this heaven, for all of time in this whole black universe.' And she listened and held him and he felt her face nodding against his cheek. He did not know whether the tears were hers or his but he welcomed the blessing, the mutual acceptance of a private ritual that he could never forget, though the time would come when he would scoff at it or laugh or curse, when he would say, 'We held hands like high-school kids and imagined ourselves the first and last lovers in the whole world.'

William roused himself from the bed and stretched his weary body before the open window, as though once again he was reaching for some still glittering but extinguished star whose light was only now arriving from a remote graveyard in the universe, like a ghost come to taunt him into action.

It was not quite dawn. Maggie was still asleep. William glanced at her as she lay quietly under the white sheet, her naked form clearly outlined, her long legs bent slightly, her arms embracing the pillow.

In the pre-dawn silence the streets of Rome, like empty hallways, echoed every incidental sound. An invisible horse-drawn wagon plodded by over the cobble-stones. Ageless, thought William. The ageless rhythm of a patient beast. Old men in beards swaying in their bent chairs, waiting for the sun to set or rise, waiting for a sign from the more patient mountains and the infinitely patient sea. How swift time is, he thought, and how slow. Hours creep. Years slide away. Nature pulses on like the beating of a giant heart. Would it make any difference, he wondered, whether we lived for a thousand years or just these few. Would it really, finally, make any difference?

Maggie stirred in her sleep, as though in response to his question. Did she feel it too? The pressure of time? Was time also running out for her? Certainly it was for him, and certainly for Alex. There are things that must be done before one is forty or never at all, he thought, but then he could not name those things.

The darkness grew thinner and melted into morning. How long, he wondered, had he been sitting by the window. One hour? Two? Three? It was impossible to tell.

When he looked again Maggie was awake, lying on her back and staring at him with her wondering eyes. 'Good morning, sugar,' she said in her sleepy seductive voice. 'Always up early.'

He sat down at the foot of the bed. 'The best part of the day,' he said.

She stretched and ran her hands through her hair as she lay there. 'I used to wake up to the sound of your typewriter in the next room. And I used to listen to it the way some people listen to birds, hoping to discover a pattern or rhythm.'

'And did you?' he said. He had a large towel wrapped around his waist and rubbed gently at his naked chest as though he were searching for his own heartbeat.

'I imagined I could tell when it was going right,' she said, 'not because you were typing very quickly, but because it came in bursts.'

'Like a machine-gun,' he smiled.

'Yes. I could hear the anger being ground into language in your machine. I could hear the rhythm of a single long sentence, the rising and falling, the alliteration, the force, and finally the end, the pause. I could almost tell what it was you were saying. You were like a fighter, circling your enemy.'

'Sometimes I think I'm afraid to fight' he said.

'It depends on the fight.'

William smiled as he remembered a night in Seaville when he and Alex sat in the Shady Lounge celebrating the birth of Alex's ninth child. 'I'm going to buy you nine martinis,' he had said to his friend. And then did, indeed, buy him nine martinis, while he himself drank nine bloody marys. By midnight they were sagging over the bar reciting poetry and singing hymns. Two wild young men came in looking as though they had spent three days on the beach or at sea, and tried to join them. But Alex said, 'This is a private party, Buster. Take off.'

'You talk that way, mister,' said the big young man, 'and somebody's going to poke your other eye out.' The smaller man stood by William, swaying, red-eyed and angry.

William said, 'There's plenty of room down the other end of the bar.'

'I like it here,' he said.

Alex put his hand on William's arm. 'You know what I'm going to do, Doc,' he said. 'I'm going to finish this drink and then throw these two creeps into the bay.'

The big man clenched his fists and stepped back. 'All right big-mouth, whenever you're ready.'

Alex took a slow sip at his drink and then turned to get off his stool. William reached surreptitiously for a handful of coins piled before him on the bar. They felt heavy and firm in his hand. He waited until he was sure the other man was not going to back off and then shouted, 'You lay one finger on him and I'll kill you.' The man rushed at him and was met by a fierce blow in the face that dropped him like so much dead meat. But the smaller man was also on William, wrestling more than hitting. And soon the bigger one recovered and the brawl was on. William staggered around warding off blows and was backed through the plate-glass window. The crash halted the fight and someone yelled, 'Get the police.'

'We can't afford that,' said the big man, pulling at his friend's torn shirt. 'Let's get the hell out of here.'

Alex still sat at the bar. His face was drawn and pale. William's arm was covered with blood. 'You all right, buddy?' said the bartender.

'Sure,' said William. 'Don't worry about the window. We'll take care of it.'

For about fifteen minutes Alex and William sat quietly at the bar. Finally, Alex said, 'I'm sorry, Doc. It was my fault. If I could have seen him, I would have hit him.'

William put his arm around his friend's shoulders. 'It's all right. I didn't mind. I just wish you could have seen the look on that slob's face when I hit him.'

William was pleased. He enjoyed the fight, much in the same way that he used to enjoy playing football.

'But about other things you're a coward,' said Maggie.

He stood up and stared at her. 'You mean, I'm afraid of you?'

'That's not what I meant, though maybe you are.'

'I don't think so,' he said. He undid the towel and put on his pants. He had a sudden desire to walk through the quiet, empty streets of the city. And he did not want to hear what Maggie was about to say.

'No, I'm talking about your work.'

He winced. 'It's a nice morning. I think I'll go for a walk.'

She sat up suddenly and held the sheet to her breast. 'Wait,' she said. 'Just give me a minute to say what I mean. Don't always run away.'

'I know what you're going to say.'

'No, you don't. You think you can't write because you have nothing to say. The fact is that you're just plain scared to say anything true about yourself. You're afraid of yourself. You think of yourself as some kind of physical and spiritual monster. You won't let go. You're full of fury and you hug it and cuddle it——'

'Oh, for Christ sake knock it off,' he shouted. 'You sound like a goddamn amateur psychologist.'

'Look,' he said, 'I'm not angry and I'm not scared. I don't write any more because I found out I'm a fraud, a phoney. I once saw myself from a distance as a successful writer. It was only the success I wanted, the applause and the money. The work itself didn't matter.'

'That's a lie, Bill,' she said.

'What difference would it make if I never wrote another lousy word? Tell me, what difference would it make to anyone? The wheels would go on spinning, the world would turn, Alex would get drunk, you would go on chasing adventure and romance. In another hundred years no one will remember that any of us ever existed. Time will swallow everything. That's why I don't write. It doesn't mean anything. It never did.'

'I suppose Shakespeare never meant anything. I suppose the Greeks were forgotten.'

William hesitated and then said quietly, 'Time will get them all eventually. No wisdom is absolute.'

'You say it, but you don't believe it. I've seen you weep over a line of poetry or a passage in a book—and I've seen you hide the tears.' She leaned back against the pillow. 'No. You're like a man wrestling with his faith. You don't want to believe that God exists, and yet you find it hard to deny that he does. Tell me, would it be so awful if there really was a God?'

He looked away. 'I never seriously considered the possibility.'

'And yet you fight against it all the time. Why?'

Once more he raised his voice. 'Because I don't trust my own faith. Because I don't trust God or art or love or people or anything. That's why! And because I keep feeling that maybe—just maybe, my secret instinct is the right one.'

'Your secret instinct?'

'Yes. I can't purge myself of the feeling that something miraculous, something wonderful will happen if only I can put one word after another in some special way, if only I can knock down one more wall, tear aside one more curtain, if only I can say something so utterly and eternally true that it would ring like a bell with a perfect tone in the very eyes and marrow of whoever read it.'

And even as he said these words his voice rang in the room like a bell and disturbed the silence that followed. Tears rushed to Maggie's eyes but she would not let them fall.

After a while he turned away from the window and said, 'Maybe I hate you for knowing me so well. Maybe that's why it will never work for us.'

'It might, if you trusted me,' she said.

'Between people like us, I no longer know what that word means. And damn it, if you give me that nineteenth-century nonsense about being faithful in your fashion, I swear I'll tear this hotel apart room by room!'

He stood trembling by the bed with clenched fists. She stared at him but did not cower. Then he shook his head as if to drive away the fury and unclenched his fists. The next words he spoke were in a voice so calm and matter-of-fact that Maggie could not believe it was the same person standing there beside him. 'I'm going to take Alex to see a few things today. I assume you can find something to do.'

'Yes,' she said, trying to smile. 'I brought a sketch pad along.'

He went to the door, turned to say something but then decided not to and went out.

15

THE GHOSTLY CROWD roared in the immense arena. In his mind Alex remade the skeleton of massive, crumbling stones that was the Colosseum. He lined the walls with pink and white marble quarried in remote regions of the empire, he rebuilt staircases and seats, filled the archways with statues of emperors and heroes, and heard once more the rattling of chains in the underground cells and dungeons, and the roaring of frightened, hungry beasts, jammed in the damp labyrinthine passageways that led to the dazzling circle of death.

Alexander Publius Septimus Marius Claudius Morganus. No! Io, Ego, Morganus. One name only. Like Plato. Like Spartacus. Morganus, the immortal gladiator. Morganus, the scarred, battered, unbeaten, proud warrior, favourite of the crowd and special favourite of Helena, wife of Claudius. Was it she, then, who condemned the beautiful Marguerita to death, the Christian slave-girl who could not speak. The crumpled message from Marguerita lay on the ground by his feet. 'Today it is God's will that I die in the arena.' He leaned forward on his wooden stool, his bearded face in his huge iron hands.

Julius, his slave, stood by him, holding out a piece of glittering armour, a breastplate, especially moulded for his broad chest. 'She is a jealous woman,' whispered Julius. The other fighters in the large windowless room strapped on their armour and tested their weapons. Grim-faced and silent, they prepared themselves. Though they were all friends, they treated one another as strangers now. Their eyes were blank, not with hatred, but with necessary inhumanness. To feel one ounce of pity or sentiment was fatal.

'When will she die?' said Morganus.

'At the very end,' said Julius. 'Forty Christian women will be sent naked into the arena, and forty black panthers will vie for the meat. Severus feels the simple black-and-white colour scheme will please the emperor.'

Morganus heaved a great sigh of weariness and despair. 'And who am I to fight?'

Julius looked away as though he were reluctant to answer. 'Who?' roared Morganus. He stood up and shook the scrawny creature by his dirty rags.

'The rumour is that her highness is angry at you because of the Christian slave-girl. She has brought back Nemo, the giant of Galaeta.'

The other men in the room heard the name and froze in their various postures. A silent terror and tension filled the room. Then the preparations began again, more slowly and more quietly than before.

Morganus let the frightened slave fall to the ground. He smiled and adjusted the black patch over his eye. 'It is about time that this black giant and I met face to face.'

'They say he is as swift as a tiger and as strong as a bull. Swords have been broken on his bare flesh without drawing blood,' said Julius.

'Send a message to the empress,' said Morganus, smiling with bravado, 'and tell her that when I have Nemo down I will trade his life for Marguerita's.'

A warm breeze played in the dark cavities of the haunted old arena. They walked slowly around the corridor, pausing in each archway or passageway to view once more, from a shifting angle, the open place where, almost two thousand years earlier real blood gushed from real flesh, where bones cracked and men panted and twitched to murder more quickly whatever enemy was sent against them. A short dark man went by behind them, dangling strips of postcards. Somewhere William could hear a heavy hammer pounding against stone.

He squinted at the broken rows of seats until they blurred into the crowds of faces. The sound that he heard, the sound that tightened his stomach and sent currents of fear and joy through his chest, was the sound he remembered from his last football game, the game that earned him his trophy, the Curtiss Memorial Award. He played as though he was possessed, as though his life depended on that game, and yet, even as he did it, he knew it wasn't so, that the game did not matter, that he did not even want the trophy. But what he wanted at the moment was to take the ball and run through everyone. He wanted to break them, to kill them. He had been hit very hard during the game, but refused to be taken out. After each play he got up painfully and walked in a daze back to the huddle.

It was in those last few minutes, with the score tied, that he remembered the crowd. They screamed hysterically for the last ten minutes. He saw faces, thousands of faces, as though in a dream. Blood dried on his cheek. Two fingers of his left hand were crushed and taped together. His ribs and hips were bruised. He heard his own breathing and felt his own sweat inside his uniform on his back and belly and groin. Even the voices of his own team were distant and unreal. They thumped him on the backside; they growled and crouched. And, facing them, an army of fleshy enemies, also crouched and growled. They had been driven back deep into their own territory by the heavier team.

The signal was given and the two lines of men collided, fell, rolled, spread out, bellowing and grunting. His man went past him for a moment and heads turned up to watch the short pass into the end zone. The ball was just over his head, floating there like a shimmering mysterious piece of ripe fruit in some purgatorial garden. He was off the ground at the right moment, going up and up for ever, until the hard leather banged against his broken fingers and he was hurled once more to the real ground by the pain.

But the ball was his. He felt it pressed against his body. His heart pounded and his mouth was dry. He was an animal now, a wounded animal and they thundered down on him. But the treasure was his and he would kill them before he would surrender it. He headed back up field, avoiding three tacklers at the very start. One he caught in the chin as the man fell. Another he bumped off balance with his shoulder. When he looked up again he saw open space in front of him and charged. He felt himself, not running, but galloping, his legs heavy but still strong. As he headed for the sidelines two more men closed in on him, swift and lean and fresh. They would force him out in a second. A wave of anger ran through him and he turned into them, instead of away from them. They hesitated for a moment and he ran right through them, his legs flying wildly, his free arm a menacing weapon. He caught the look of fear on one man's face as he butted his way past him, and he was secretly pleased.

That was what he finally wanted from this stupid war. He wanted a personal victory, a sheer physical triumph, over them and over himself. He wanted to fly, to gallop, to be invincible. He stood in the end zone for a moment as his team charged towards him to raise him up on their shoulders and as the crowd praised him with their hoarse exhausted voices. He imagined himself at a the moment dripping with blood and sweat. He was satisfied.

'Why did they do it?' said Alex, leaning on a wooden railing that barred them from the arena. Across the way he could see the large cross dedicated to the martyrs who died there.

'Cruelty,' said William, leaning back against a stone wall and lighting a cigarette. 'They were amused by cruelty. We all are, in a way.'

'But not by injustice,' said Alex, his mouth tight with grimness. 'I can't imagine what they were thinking as they sat there.' He stared up at the first row of seats.

William, too, stared at the places where the spectators sat. 'They did not consider life sacred.' He shrugged his shoulders.

'They're all dead now—all of them, slaves and emperors alike. It's so stupid. It's even stupid to mourn for them.' He put his hand on Alex's shoulder. 'They were all out there once, breathing and thinking, eating and fighting—real people. They imagined that they knew what they were doing, but they were all mad—even the martyrs. There was no point to it at all. Ludicrous. Absolutely ludicrous. In another two thousand years two other tired guys like you and I will stand beside other ruins and say the same thing about us. Madison Avenue will be a stony ruin. The subway system will puzzle curious visitors from other planets. Everyone will ask the old questions all over again—why did they live this way? Why did they kill each other? No one will really be able to recover the stench of bleeding bodies, the moments of panic, the rumbling in the guts, the excitement, the fits of passion and love, the poetry, the moment of joy as one stands on a cliff and looks out over miles of ocean on a clear and windy day. History murders us all.'

'History,' mumbled Alex, and they walked on along the corridor.

'There's no meaning in it,' said William. 'No lesson to be learned from it. There is only the living moment—for you and me and everyone. There is no conclusion to be drawn.'

'Except the one you are now drawing,' said Alex.

William laughed quietly. 'The Jesuit mind at work.'

Alex retreated into his fantasy and confronted the black giant of Galaeta. 'We who are about to die . . .' he heard himself say. Then, 'Pray for us sinners now and at the hour of our death . . .' His stomach turned at the thought of driving his sword into human flesh. His arm grew weak. The two warriors stared at each other and understood what was going on. Morganus threw his sword aside and undid his armour. A whisper of awe went through the crowd. He stretched out his arms like Christ and shouted at the emperor, 'All men are my brothers.' The emperor looked puzzled for a moment and then started to laugh. Helena leaned towards him and said something that made him raise his eyebrows joyfully. He ordered the Christian slave-girl into the arena. 'Kill her,' he shouted to Nemo. 'Kill her or die!'

The black man hovered over the naked body of Marguerita with raised spear, eyeing Morganus like an animal. And there the tableau froze in Alex's mind for all of time. The girl cried out for ever. The black man was poised for murder. And he, twitching to kill, but preferring to die, held his ground and waited. In that hopeless circle they were suddenly all united —victim, killer, defender. They were bound more by love than hate, more by necessity than anger. The vision melted into a serpentine statue in which all three were entangled, rising heavenward in an agony of wrestling flesh.

'I want to write a book about the Tullian Prisons, where Peter and Paul were held for a hundred days before they were crucified. I can see them now in that dungeon, talking endlessly to the hundreds of prisoners that were thrown in from the hole above. I can smell the stench of their filth and see the slime on the rough stone walls.' William could see that Alex was only half listening. He paused.

'I'm sorry,' said Alex. 'I was thinking of something else.'

'Plutarch called it "The Abyss". There Peter and Paul converted forty-seven prisoners and two guards before they were killed. Can you imagine the arguments, the violence, the muddle of languages.'

'It was there, wasn't it,' said Alex, 'that Peter struck the rock to produce water?'

'Yes. A famous miracle.'

'And why do you suddenly want to do a novel on a Catholic subject?'

'I don't consider it a Catholic subject,' said William. 'It's the drama that interests me, the situation. I want to pit St. Peter against a bunch of hard-hearted, moth-eaten, fatalistic prisoners.'

'You think the legend's not true?'

'It doesn't matter whether it's true or not.'

'Of course it matters.'

'How can you be a good Catholic and worry about the historical truth?' said William. They were out of the Colosseum now and walking in the fierce sun back towards the Forum.

'I think it's important that miracles be recorded.'

'And do you believe in miracles?'

Alex stopped to light a cigarette. He inhaled deeply and blew the smoke away towards the street. 'I don't know,' he said. 'Yes, I suppose I do. I accept the fact that they exist. I do not believe, as you do, that history is meaningless. I see in it a coherent chronicle.'

'The great drama of mankind struggling to recover his lost perfection,' said William sarcastically.

Alex refused to answer. An unexpected coldness separated them as they walked. Both of them were disturbed by it. After a while Alex allowed himself to break into a smile. 'Let's buy a drink for the dead gladiators.'

'A good idea,' said William, taking his friend once more by the arm to lead him.

16

MAGGIE'S PENCIL, LIKE a weapon, hovered over the unfinished sketch. Her steady hand practised lines in the air just inches above the paper, where a few bold lines already began to reveal not the arch or the ruined wall of a once magnificent Palatine mansion but the passage of time, the squandered energy and wealth, the wasted genius, the lost hope, the dreamy sensuality and the mad optimism that one associates with these ruins.

Where must the next line go, she wondered. Where will her hand, like a separate being, descend? How will it move? And with what force? She leaned against a railing in the fierce sun, allowing the heat to dazzle her, to unfocus her eyes and dampen her face. The whiteness of her untanned skin was heightened here on this ancient hill under the huge expanse of pale blue sky. Behind her and below the hill stretched the Circus Maximus; before her the crumbling brick walls of the fallen house.

Whose house was it, she wondered. What emperor, what senator or consul, now less than dust, once planned those arches, once watched with pride as the bricks heaped up through the hot summer and became his house, his monument, his exhibition of power and wealth?

Her pencil swooped down suddenly and shot a line into the distance, towards some imaginary horizon. What was it? A path? A street? A highway? Space was suddenly created. A second line completed the illusion and an avenue stretched into the mere paper separating two collections of ruined walls.

Maggie never finished a sketch because she never changed a line. She would keep going as long as each line was exactly what she wanted, but once she faltered, once her hand did not commit what her mind or heart ordered, she stopped, turned the page, and began again.

In the heat of the Roman afternoon she was almost alone on the Palatine. No voices intruded, no tourists. The ghosts of all those ancient men and women were free to wander in what was left of this most fashionable part of the old city. And Maggie wandered with them, imagining herself in a white gown, strolling in a formal garden or lounging on a couch. She was a famous courtesan, Clodia herself, perhaps, entertaining with her wit and wealth all the handsome and talented men of Rome. Statesmen and poets courted her. Women envied her and hated her not only because of her beauty and grace, but because of her aloofness, because of her sense of freedom. She was above the law and beyond all tradition and custom. Nothing could bind her; nothing could intrude on her quest.

Maggie allowed her hand to draw. It suggested a window, a garden, a fountain. A broad flight of stairs led somewhere. Was there a terrace beyond the garden? The ruins in the sketch were no longer merely ruins. She was reconstructing them but not entirely. The picture that slowly emerged was like a double exposure, collapsing two thousand years of history. Real men and women gathered under the vines and palms, laughed in the stone rooms, made love, felt cool wine in their hot throats, and talked endlessly about each other and themselves. She could hear them. She could almost make out their sentences. They were gossiping and planning; they were posing, complaining, seducing, weeping. The babble of voices grew louder before it suddenly stopped and by a trick of the eyes one saw instead of the perfect old arch merely the ruin of an arch, and heard instead of living voices only the whispering ghostly silence.

A cold shiver went through Maggie as though all those deaths impinged directly on her, as though she had herself been all those people once and had died when they died.

She paused for a long time and studied her sketch. It was still right, still what she wanted, and yet it seemed unfinished. What was missing? Where could she put a line now that would complete the vision? Her hand moved over the sheet of paper like a hunting hawk. But there was no where to land, no clear place at all. Had she, at last, finished something? Was it the picture she wanted? She shook her head, her stomach tightening with the tension. No, no, no, she muttered, it's not right, not finished. It's never finished. One always adds a line, one always goes on. Her hand twitched. The pencil was damp between her fingers. A kind of panic seized her and she stabbed at the picture. A dark, impulsive line broke an arch and cracked all perspective. The sketch was ruined. She closed her eyes for a moment to hold back the tears and then opened them again. Without looking at what she had either created or destroyed, she turned the page and faced the clean white emptiness with an enormous sense of relief.

But she did not begin to draw again. She wandered from the railing and found a place along a narrow path where she could sit under a tree. In the shade the grass was thick and very green. She leaned against the tree and smoked a cigarette. For the moment she lost the sense of being in a dead city. She looked out on gardens and lawns, decorated with statues and columns. People began to appear again as the afternoon heat subsided. Maggie watched a young man in a yellow sports shirt who ambled towards her and then sat under another tree just across the path from her. He watched her, waiting, perhaps, for the slightest hint of interest on her part.

But Maggie turned away and looked back towards the houses she had tried to sketch. She took up the pad again and rolled her pencil nervously between her fingers. Why, she wondered, could she never finish anything? Was William right after all? He called her a perfectionist, but a destructive perfectionist.

She heard his voice, his stronger, angrier, younger voice. 'Your standards are impossibly high. And you unconsciously set them high in order to fail, and in order to watch others fail. You are not interested in success; you are only interested in punishing yourself. But what your secret sin is, I do not know. What is it, Maggie? What is the secret sin, the transgression for which you know you must be beaten? Haven't you escaped all moral judgement? Haven't you found a private innocence? Haven't you asserted your own goodness and generosity? Haven't you justified every act you ever committed? No one I know has been so right so often.'

She shook her head as though she were still arguing with him. 'You don't understand,' she had said at the time. 'I believe in a kind of perfection; I believe in truth and beauty and goodness and love.'

His laughter snapped in the night like a whip. 'Your fantasies of saintly purity are only a reaction to your secret sense of immorality. You don't like yourself. You want to wade through corruption but come out clean and pure. You're for ever purging yourself of guilt and weakness. You keep trying to be a saint because you're afraid to be an ordinary woman. Tell me, is it really so awful to be a woman?'

He was attacking her. He was always attacking her. All she ever wanted to do was to express herself honestly; to find out what she really was; to find out what it meant to be alive. She did not abandon herself to sensual pleasures. The people with whom she made love were all people for whom she cared, if only because they needed her. She enjoyed being needed, and yet she hated it. When Michael poured out his heart to her and wept, she not only scolded him for his weakness, she also comforted him. And she made love with him because it brought them closer to each other, and because there is a comfort in that closeness, even though she could say, even to him, even while they lay in bed, that she did not love him, at least not in the way he hoped or imagined she might. And the same was true of others, many others. How, then, could William condemn her? How could he ask her to condemn herself? She was not wrong. She was not dishonest. She never misled anyone, never lied or deceived. And still he beat her and beat her with an old morality which he himself defied and mocked with his own behaviour.

No, she thought angrily, he was not right. There was no secret sin, only his own fury and self-pity. He wanted her to be a sweet and innocent virgin, a peasant girl conjured up in his feverish brain. It was he who was really the perfectionist, the dreamer. It was he who destroyed himself with an idealism that he must constantly violate. She only gave herself to life. She only lived, devouring experience, pleasure and pain. She only searched for meaning, for goodness. She searched in human feelings, and in art, not only her own but the art that others created. She stalked the truth in galleries and museums, in books, in the theatre. And she pursued it in her own writing and painting, even though she never finished a major piece of work. It was not finishing that mattered, she always insisted, it was starting and being immersed in an artistic effort, whatever the medium.

She was not ashamed of her life, though William kept implying she should be; she was proud of it. She did the things she wanted to do. She followed wherever her instincts led. She protected her freedom. Why did he want her to fall on her knees like a weeping schoolgirl and plead for forgiveness? She was damned if she would ask anyone to forgive her for anything—and least of all him. What presumption, what arrogance to think that he even had the right or privilege of doling out forgiveness. She had not tried to judge *him*. She had not offered *him* forgiveness. But he did not understand this. He called it indifference or amorality.

Maggie knew better. She knew that her whole life was a restless journey, that she was quite possibly going nowhere, that life itself might have no meaning. And at the same time she knew that she had a stubborn, child-like faith in life, that she loved it and embraced it. She enjoyed people. She enjoyed nature. She liked to use her hands. Making love was in itself a beautiful act, part of the miracle of being alive. Why couldn't William see that? Why couldn't he understand?

Her reverie was suddenly interrupted by a soft masculine

voice. The young man in the yellow shirt was standing over her, smiling and saying something in Italian. His hair was very black and he was quite handsome.

'I'm sorry,' she said, 'I don't speak very much Italian.'

'You are American?' he said with a heavy accent.

'Yes.'

'Do you mind if I sit?' he said.

She moved a bit, as if to make room for him. She was accustomed to such flirtations in Rome and did not usually mind. In fact, they amused her, especially when the men were young and somewhat embarrassed.

'Your English is very good,' she said.

'Oh, no,' he said shyly. 'It is bad. Very bad. I cannot remember the words. You have to forgive.'

She smiled at the word *forgive* and said, 'It must be late; I have to go.'

'No, please,' he said, holding her by the arm. 'I saw you making a picture. You looked to be so lonely.'

'No,' she said, 'I'm not lonely. I came here to sketch the ruins.'

'Ah, the ruins,' he said. 'You like them? And the Forum?'

'Very much.'

'You must let me show you sometime. I know well the ruins. You must let me buy for you some cold drink and I will tell you about them.'

They got up and walked along the path.

'Yes?' he said. 'You will come?'

'Yes,' she said. Her voice was flat and sad, almost exhausted. He was not quite as tall as she and he took her arm as they walked.

17

THE FAT SHIMMERING, orange sun squatted on distant rooftops. The air remained warm and windless in the heaped and sprawling city of monuments and ruins and dismal new apartment houses. The dome of St. Peter's caught the last rays of light, but in the narrow, stifling streets and alleyways the shadows thickened and occasional electric lights went on. The invisible river was a humid presence. In the air one could feel the nearness of mud and slow-moving water. William thought of mosquitoes breeding in steaming grassy pools, and, then, for some reason, of leopards, sleek, stalking, suspicious leopards, translated, after a moment, into decorative skins.

'Everything is made of stone,' said Alex. They turned into a dark street full of children and old women.

'Not everything,' said William, dragging Alex along by the arm. They stepped off the narrow pavement to get around a clot of women in black. A motor-bike buzzed past them.

'What a noisy neighbourhood,' said Alex.

'Italians are noisy people. Short, degenerate, and noisy. But they enjoy life. They even enjoy their misery.'

They stopped in a small square while William tried to remember which of three streets was the right one.

'I still don't know why you've got to see this guy Mario so urgently. Couldn't it wait?'

'No,' said William. 'I just had a brilliant idea back there at the café.'

'What now?'

'I'm going to live in Rome and write books about Catholic saints.'

'Sure you are, Doc, and I'm going to be the pizza peddler next door,' said Alex.

'Mario's the key to the whole plan.'

'Why? Does he know all the saints in town?'

'No, he's an intellectual con-man. He starts little magazines, makes documentary films, and sleeps with a lot of important men and women.'

'You mean he's queer?'

'He's not queer; he's Italian.'

William's voice turned to a half whisper as they entered an old building. He led Alex down a dark hallway to a rear apartment.

'I smell fish,' said Alex. 'Somebody is cooking.' The air in the hallway was suffocating.

William knocked gently. In a moment a man came to the door, opened it half-way and studied them with a worn, confused look. It was Mario's father, a handsome man of sixty with a thin black moustache and greying hair. 'I'm looking for Mario Rossano,' said William. 'I'm a friend of his from New York. We were at the university together. Do you remember me?'

The man in the doorway looked again and then broke into a smile. 'Come in, come in,' he said. 'Sure I remember you now. Mr. Marino; Beel.'

'We can't stay,' said William. 'I just wanted to see Mario. It's been such a long time.'

'Marguerita,' he called. 'Come and see who is here.' And then in a subdued voice he half-apologized to William. 'Perhaps she will not remember you. She is very shy.'

Mario's sister came into the small room through a curtained doorway. She was a beautiful unadorned woman of twenty-five with long black hair and large sad eyes. She smiled and nodded towards William, who stood up. Alex also stood up and said, 'Pleased to meet you,' but he could not see her.

'She cannot speak,' said Mr. Rossano.

'That's all right,' said Alex. 'I can't see. We should get along fine.'

'It is too bad about your eyes. I am so sorry.'

'It's all right. In a minute I will adjust to the light in here.'

'I'm afraid the light is not very good.'

'How have you been, Marguerita?' said William. She nodded again. In her simple cotton dress she looked full and ripe. The dress buttoned down the front and where it passed over her large breasts, it was drawn tight and almost parted.

'Bring some coffee,' ordered her father, and she disappeared quietly through the curtains.

William always thought of Mario Rossano as the handsomest young man in the world. His hair was very black and loosely curled. His face was lean and smooth. When he smiled, his soft mouth opened slightly to reveal his perfect white teeth, and his large eyes shone with genuine amusement and affection. He had one of those slight but perfectly proportioned bodies, with square shoulders tapering to a thin waist. But William also thought of him as a victim of his own beauty and joyful confusion. He had come to the States on a fellowship to do graduate work in comparative literature. From the very beginning, however, he did nothing but talk and pose and fall in love. He would say frequently to William that he was afraid of becoming like his father, a gigolo. 'But if I go to work, what can I do? I can be a waiter, maybe. Can you imagine me serving spaghetti to junior executives and smart young secretaries on Madison Avenue? I can't do it. I won't do it.'

His mother was American and died while he was in graduate school. He flew back home and William did not see him until he and Maggie stopped in Rome after their trip to Paris. 'He's like a beautiful boy out of a Botticelli painting,' Maggie said at the time. 'What a gorgeous face.'

'I hope you don't mind my asking,' said Alex to Mr. Rossano, 'but what kind of work do you do?'

The older man smiled uneasily and stirred his coffee. 'A little cognac perhaps?' he said, passing the bottle towards Alex.

Marguerita, who stood now behind her father, as though for protection, took the bottle from his hand and poured some cognac into Alex's coffee. 'Thank you.' He squinted at her. 'You have a lovely daughter,' he said to Mr. Rossano.

'Yes, she is quite beautiful.' He looked proudly at her. 'Little Marguerita. Not so little any more. She looks like her mother.'

William's fantasy world was populated by half a dozen beautiful women whom he had only met briefly. One of these women was Marguerita. At certain odd moments he would parade out one of these beauties and arrange a special and exciting form of seduction in his mind. In many ways the fantasy was better than reality, since he could vary the circumstances as he pleased each time. All was new and untried—a promise of some ultimate and satisfying pleasure. In his mind he had seen Marguerita nude. He had broken into her bedroom at night while she slept only with a sheet. He had raped her violently in the middle of the afternoon, knowing that she could not cry out. And he had melted her with kindness and brotherly affection. Now they stared at each other over her father's head as Alex and the old man talked.

'What did you say you did?' said Alex.

'Educational tours,' said Mr. Rossano. 'I do a lot of work with visiting teachers.'

William suppressed a smile. He remembered Mario's description of his father as an ageing professional escort, a man with charm and a few statistics, who could thrill the visiting schoolmarm from Iowa or Pennsylvania for a fee, or for free meals and a little *affection*.

'How interesting,' said Alex. 'You should arrange a tour for me. This is my first trip to Europe. I'd hate to miss anything really important.'

'I would have to find out first what was important to you. Some people, you know, go for churches, some want the ruins, some the art or architecture. The business men like the night-clubs and the modern hotels. Are you a business man in New York?'

'It's difficult to explain. I do a bit of everything—contracting, real estate, insurance. I'm a broker.'

Mr. Rossano frowned and looked at William. 'An agent,' William explained. 'For other people.'

He accepted the explanation politely, as though he really understood and nodded to indicate that he was impressed with Alex's importance. 'And you like our city?'

'Yes,' said Alex. 'It gives me such a sense of history.'

'Ah, yes, history. The story of Rome is the story of the world. The centre of pagan civilization and the centre of Christianity.'

William could imagine him using his old conversational tricks, his obliging air, his automatic affected enthusiasm. And then he could imagine him trimming his moustache and shaving in the dreary bathroom of that small musty apartment. He could see him coughing in the morning, sipping his coffee, lighting a cigarette. He could see him strolling about town in his best clothes, eternally searching, like an old shark, for his routine diet of naïve fish. How weary of it all he must get. How similar his victims must be. How many times, William wondered, did Mario's father use the same line, the same words. How many times did he hold a Midwestern schoolteacher by the hand and say, 'Rome will remind you that you are a passionate and beautiful woman.' *And when Miss Pimpel felt his thick but gentle hand on her gartered thigh she tried to remember whether or not she had used her deodorant that morning.*

Could he also have been indifferent in bed? Could he, after a while, have developed a counterfeit passion that fooled even him? A theatrical approximation of the panting romantic helplessness by which Latin lovers are supposed to be possessed. Perhaps it went even further. Perhaps his whole life was only an act, so often repeated by now that it was more than mere habit to pose and to lie. William remembered how Mario used to talk about Italian men. He knew suddenly what Mario meant when he said that all Italian men were chronic liars; that they had no sense of reality and no respect for it. 'Life for them is an elaborate fantasy, a dream of manliness, love, and pleasure. More than romantic. The truth is unimportant. Only puritans and madmen search for the truth.' And then he thought of Maggie's grinding motto—'Know thyself.' The truth at any cost! And there was Marguerita, silently serving her father, without questioning his way of life. Surely she did not care about Maggie's God of Truth. He looked from one to the other, from father to daughter, and wondered if possibly, living alone this way, they had ever slept together. The thought excited him and annoyed him. He pushed it away.

William suddenly felt too large for the room. He wanted to leap up and run for the door. 'What's Mario doing now?' he said impatiently. 'Is he working?'

'Yes, he has a very good position with Count Bolognesi.'

'Count Bolognesi!' said Alex, imagining ballrooms of uniformed heroes and perfumed ladies.

'What sort of work?' said William.

'He's a kind of secretary. A very important position. He lives in the Count's household at the Villa Merdeluna. He has his own car and a huge wardrobe. Very elegant. Very successful.'

William took down the address and stood up to go. Marguerita was standing very close to him and did not move away until he brushed gently against her. He smiled at her and her eyes smiled back.

When they were outside again William led Alex to the nearest café. 'What are we doing now?' said Alex.

'Waiting,' said William.

'For what?'

William shrugged. 'Just waiting.'

18

WILLIAM RAISED HIS glass unsteadily towards Alex and Marguerita. 'To Romulus and Remus,' he said.

Marguerita sipped at her champagne and smiled. The waiter came with another bottle and took away the empty one. They sat amidst potted plants under red and yellow lights in a sidewalk restaurant. A large man in a white suit with three chins and rimless glasses looked over at them from a near-by table. His permanent look of disgust did not change. Two elderly American women at another table smiled politely. The waiter was a small man with too much hair for his thin pale face. He bowed automatically every time he delivered something to their table.

'Who did we forget?' said William, his low, bony forehead wrinkled into a frown. The air was still in the hot humid night and perspiration shone on his temples and cheeks. He was flushed with wine and excitement. It had been building all day, through the Forum and the Colosseum. His blue eyes were intense and playful.

'How about Cicero?' said Alex.

'Oh, Jesus Christ! How could we have forgotten poor Cicero. That much maligned, that much underrated, that colossal bore. Nailed his head to the Rostrum they did. Nailed his bloody head to the Rostrum just because he couldn't make up his mind to join up with the bad guys. Only the bad guys were the good guys—Julius and his boys. Isn't that right, Marguerita? I bet they taught you all that in school the way we learn about Lincoln throwing logs across the Potomac and how somebody bought Alaska for a buck and a half or something.'

'Did you go to school, Marguerita?' said Alex.

She nodded, amused by both of them. Her long black hair was parted in the middle and fell down past her shoulders.

'Beware of Marguerita,' said William, leaning towards Alex. 'She's an Italian witch, a siren, like the Mona Lisa and Lucrezia Borgia. She does magic in the night under full moons with bat wings and pasta and little boys' testicles.'

Marguerita sat poised and beautiful in her cotton dress.

'Will your father be angry if he finds out?' said Alex.

Marguerita nodded.

'But you're a grown woman of about twenty-five,' said Alex.

Marguerita shook her head and held up four fingers.

'All right, twenty-four. Sorry.'

'She'll be home long before him,' said William. 'He's out tracking down schoolteachers.'

'I thought he was a nice guy. I liked him.'

'Of course he's a nice guy. He has to be in his business.'

Marguerita looked suddenly sad. She stared into her glass as though she were not listening. 'Now she's having one of her Anna Magnani moods,' said William. 'Look at those sad eyes, that Latin passion.'

'If she could talk she would curse you, you bastard,' said Alex. Then he turned to Marguerita and put his hand on her bare arm. 'Would you like me to say something dirty to him? He deserves it.'

Her tragic expression dissolved. She got up half-way in her seat and kissed Alex on the forehead and then turned and stuck her tongue out at William.

'I don't understand,' said William. 'Why does everyone love you so much and hate me so much? I'm more intelligent than you. I'm kind and generous and articulate, but all the women think you're such a sweet lovable guy and I'm no good. Why?'

'Because you're no good, Doc,' he said, finishing his champagne and shoving the empty glass toward William.

'Oh! I thought there was a logical explanation.' William filled all the glasses again. 'Now, let's see, where were we? Cicero. We got him. Caesar? Three times already. Marius, Sulla, Nero, Claudius, Augustus, Spartacus. Catullus? No, we haven't drunk to the saddest poet of all times, Catullus. Dead at thirty from a broken heart and a cough. Done in by that bitch Clodia. Shall I recite *Odi et Amo*?'

'Don't bother,' said Alex. 'Let's just drink to him.'

'How about that bit in another poem about Clodia's Spanish lover who washed his teeth in the urine of homosexual Spanish rabbits? Do you want to hear that? I only know Horace Gregory's translation.'

'I don't trust translations.'

'All right, then, I'll do it in Latin.'

'Don't you dare; it's the language of the Church.'

'Why don't you ever let me recite? I love to recite. When I was a teacher I always used to astound my students by memorizing a poem before I came to class and then reciting it as though I knew it all my life and it had just come up casually in the discussion. What a ploy for a teacher.'

'He was a great teacher,' said Alex to Marguerita. 'He never believed it or cared much, but he was great. They still talk about him at Fulton College.'

William grew meditative for a moment, as though he was recalling those years at Fulton. His head was supported in his hand and his eyelids were half closed. 'I never believed a word I said. I lied to them. But sometimes—sometimes I said something worth-while. It didn't matter whether I believed it or not. Yes, he's right, I was brilliant. But I lacked what every good teacher needs. I didn't care a damn whether or not the students learned anything. I only cared that my own performance was good. They could have rotted in abysmal ignorance after they left my class for all I cared. They could have gone off into their father's corporation never to be heard of again, stuttering, ill-informed, narrow-minded, and it was no skin off my ass. When they were gone they were gone—just names in a roll book, just pieces of paper to be graded. And how I hated grading those papers. How I hated finding out things about them. Some of them got personal in their themes and I didn't want to know what their personal tragedies were. And once a kid died, a good-looking boy in my class just dropped dead. I hated him for doing that. I had to talk to his mother, who came a week later to see me and to say something stupid about how she was hoping he could finish school. He had a fatal disease and they knew he would not live long. But I didn't know. How was I to know?'

'You really should call him "Doctor",' said Alex. 'He has a Ph.D. He deserves a lot of respect.'

'Yeah, take off your clothes and respect me,' said William.

'Don't mind him,' said Alex. 'He gets this way every once in a while. I think the full moon has something to do with it.'

She shrugged her shoulders and pointed to the sky. William looked up but he could see nothing but the heavy darkness of the night. Then he stood up and said, 'It's time to go. To hell with Rome—I mean ancient Rome. It's all so dead.' He raised his glass toward the Forum, or what he imagined was the Forum, and said, 'To all the orators and statesmen and heroes, and to all the ladies who were faithful and true, *adieu*, *adieu*! We who are about to salute you, die.' He drank his champagne and banged his glass down. 'Have we eaten already?'

'Yes,' said Alex.

'What did I have?'

'Saltimboca.'

'But I wanted oysters.'

'There were no oysters.'

'Don't be ridiculous. We'll go somewhere else and get oysters.'

Before they left he ordered two unopened bottles of champagne. They wandered through the streets arm-in-arm with Marguerita in the middle. 'If you don't find me some oysters to go with my champagne I will recite Pericles' Funeral Oration,' he said. 'After which, I warn you, I will run through the Greek alphabet, portions of *Ulysses*, beginning with "Leopold Bloom ate with relish . . ." and a flock of poems by Emily Dickinson, including that one about the fly that buzzed when she died.'

'We're going back to the hotel,' said Alex. 'And she's going home.'

'Oh no,' said William, putting his arm around her waist. 'She comes with us or else I'm not going.'

'Haven't you forgotten something, Doc?'

'What have I forgotten? Cicero, Caesar, Pompey——'

'Maggie.'

'Was she a Roman emperor? Oh! Miss St. Claire. My ex-wife,' he explained to Marguerita.

'I don't think she'd appreciate your sense of humour,' said Alex.

'I have no sense of humour,' said William, making a comically grim face. 'I'm dead serious. Anyhow Maggie is not my wife, except in some Catholic sense.'

'Well you happen to be completely surrounded by Catholics.'

'Good Lord!' he said. 'Will I have to fight my way out?'

Alex shrugged and they walked on. 'It's your funeral, Doc.'

'You don't know Maggie,' said William. 'Nobody knows Maggie.' He could hear himself breathing heavily and he could not focus his eyes easily, but words swam gracefully through his head. He imagined he could say anything he wanted to. 'Perhaps I should write when I'm drunk,' he said. 'I think I can say whatever I please. Only trouble is I don't have anything to say. Isn't that sad. When I was eighteen years old I thought I had so much to say and needed only the right words. Now, twenty years later, I think I can say anything, but I have nothing to say. To hell with it. I'll be a hermit. I'll take vows of silence and poverty. I already have the poverty; all I need is the silence. Silence is all. No, ripeness is all. That's why I quit teaching.'

'Here we are,' said Alex.

William tore himself away from them and stood with mock

outrage on the pavement in front of the hotel. 'We forgot to toast Leonardo! How could we have forgotten that poor old madman?'

'We were drinking to dead Romans,' said Alex.

'Well at least he's dead. And a great wild man he was. Didn't he invent tanks, or something, and catapults and airplanes? Crazy old bastard. Didn't even know how to mix paint. Ah, but the *Mona Lisa*, now there's something. If he never did anything else . . .'

He unwrapped one of his bottles and popped the cork. The bottle oozed white foam that dripped down over his hand. He drank and passed it to Alex.

'I'll wait until we get upstairs. Now straighten up and look civilized or we'll all get tossed out.'

'Civilized? Who's not civilized? You're looking at the most civilized man in the Western world. William Mariner, Ph.D. I used to go to faculty teas and balance cookies on my knee; that's how civilized I am. Nobody knew that I was feeling up the dean's wife in the crowded corridor. That was *our* secret. The poor old girl had such hot pants she was about to go up in smoke.'

The neon light over the narrow entrance-way spelled out *Albergo da Vinci*. They went into the carpeted musty hallway and tiptoed past the empty desk. 'Number twenty-three,' whispered Alex, and Marguerita took the key off the board. They led William up the staircase to the first floor and then into the hot little room. They dropped him on the bed and locked the door.

William propped himself up against both pillows of the double bed and looked around the room. Alex took off his jacket and sat down beside a small table, on which he placed the open bottle of champagne. William still cradled the other bottle in one arm as though it were a football and he were about to repeat the broken-field heroics that eighteen years earlier made him famous.

The room had a high ceiling and a tall, shuttered window at one end. The light fixture that dangled from the ceiling by a long twisting wire was made of dusty pink glass and gave a curious tint to everything in the room. There was a lamp beside the bed with a small wax shade, on which were painted cartoon-like faded replicas of the *Mona Lisa* William switched on the lamp and studied the shade. 'Hey, fellas,' he said, 'did you know there were forty little *Mona Lisas*. on this lamp-shade? That's great. That's what I call bringing art into the home. We should do more of that in the States. Maybe we can get up a company of some kind—we'll call it BringArtHome incorporated. We'll put Eiffel Towers on toilet paper. No! No! Too phallic. We'll use *Le Penseur*. His posture is very suggestive. Very good for constipated art lovers. And we'll decorate coffee cups and spoons and forks. Every knob in the house will be carved into a replica of something—Moses on the knob of the hi-fi set; David on the handle of the ice-box; and a lot of little Berninis on the beds. You know, *Apollo and Daphne* and the *Rape of Proserpine*.'

Alex found two glasses in the bathroom and poured champagne into them on the little table. 'We'll have to share the glasses,' he said.

Marguerita walked cautiously about the room, like a cat in new surroundings. William watched her. She glanced at a framed picture of the Vatican that had been clipped from a magazine, and then at a mirror that hung over a miniature washbasin. She brushed a few stray hairs from her forehead and removed the wilting flower. He could see the softness of her full round hips through the cotton dress. Her legs were bare and smoothly shaven. 'Don't be afraid, my dear,' said William, twirling his imaginary moustache. 'There's nobody in here but us lechers.'

Alex laughed and handed Marguerita a water-glass full of champagne. She took it and sat down in a wooden armchair that was covered with carved lions. 'That chair,' said William, 'is a perfect example of what we need in America—lots of carved wood and marble and ceramics. Down with paper plates and Swedish modern. Right, Alex?'

'Right, Professor! You're always so right. Who was it who wanted to do that? One of your Utopian dreamers. He wanted everything to be made by hand so that it would have the stench of the artist about it.'

'William Morris. Good old William Morris. He wanted to turn the world into a garden, a series of charming medieval villages, where all those English ladies could satisfy their need for arts and crafts.'

'He was a socialist, wasn't he?' said Alex.

'He was an idiot,' said William. 'He didn't know anything at all about people. People don't want to live in a garden world. Their garden was lost a long time ago, as you ought to know. And it was a great garden because there was a snake in it. Without the snake it's no good.'

'And with the snake it's no good,' said Alex. 'So where are you?'

'Right here,' said William, 'in the Leonardo da Vinci Hotel under a pink light, drinking second-rate champagne. That's where we are. Contemplating the earthly beauty of this woman, wondering whether or not to make love to her and how. Wondering whether she is Eve or the Madonna or the fish-peddler's daughter.'

He undid the buttons of his shirt and rubbed the sweating hair of his chest with his hand.

'Do you understand?' said Alex to Marguerita.

She smiled and nodded, and then put her hand over her mouth to suppress a fit of laughter. Alex studied her face, puzzled completely by her beauty and openness and apparent innocence. He lifted his eye-patch, rubbed his eye, and flipped the patch down again. 'I can finally see her,' he said to William. 'What a Renaissance creature.'

Marguerita pouted to show her displeasure. 'She's insulted,' said William. 'She thinks you consider her too fat.'

'Oh, no, not at all. That's not what I meant.' He came to her with the bottle and refilled her glass. 'I mean you are much woman. Understand?'

She pretended to consider the apology, indicating her deliberations with her eyes and mouth and the tilt of her head. Finally, she beckoned to Alex to lean forward and raised her puckered lips to him. He kissed her and they were friends again.

'It's amazing what she can do without saying a word,' said William.

'It was always my contention that women should not be allowed to speak,' said Alex. 'Think of what a difference it would have made if Eve couldn't talk.'

'Yeah,' said William, 'Adam would still be playing with himself in the garden. In immortal innocence, of course.'

William looked at Marguerita with an affected leer. 'Bring me some holy water, oh lady of the lost word!'

She brought her glass to him and sat down beside him on the bed. He drank it all with one slow tilt of his head and felt a few drops run down his chin and onto his chest. 'Some day I'd like to take a bath in this stuff,' he said, putting the glass down under the *Mona Lisa* lamp-shade. 'Come closer,' he said to Marguerita. She moved closer and he put his hand around her waist.

'Watch out, Marguerita, he's got a sultan complex,' said Alex.

'Yeah, I dream of harems of fruity women.' He pulled her against him and kissed her on the mouth. She did not resist or seem surprised. William held her away from him and looked at her for a moment and then began to laugh.

'If you two are going to bed, then I'm going out for a walk,' said Alex, slipping on his shoes and standing up. 'Ever since my eyes went bad I've been a lousy *voyeur*. Besides, it makes me nervous.'

'You don't have to leave. Marguerita belongs to both of us. Don't you,' he said to her.

She nodded pleasantly towards Alex to reassure him.

'If you were smart, Doc, you'd send her home to her old man right now.'

'She doesn't want to go home to her old man. She wants to stay out and play with us.' He kissed her again and cupped his hand over her large breast. He heard the door open and close and knew that Alex was gone. He pulled Marguerita down on the bed beside him and, leaning on one elbow, stared down at her. She picked at the buttons on the front of her dress and he helped her with them. She stood up and allowed her dress to fall to the floor. William turned off the overhead light and undressed. In the dim light of the little lamp he could see her take off her bra. She was statuesque and very white. He tore back the covers of the bed and drew her down onto the cool sheet.

There he made love to her with drunken abandon and she followed his every desire with limp obedience. He ran his tongue over her whole body and rubbed his face in her abundant bosom. He squeezed her thighs until she winced, and pressed himself heavily against her and into her.

He never said a word to her. And when he was satisfied he moved away from her and lit a cigarette. She lay very still beside him, her eyes closed as though she were asleep. He was puzzled by her composure and the hint of a smile on her face. And then he heard a voice, a cold, distant voice speaking perfect English. 'Was that good?' He stared at the woman beside him as though she had suddenly risen from the dead.

He sat up and shook his head. 'I don't understand.'

She got out of bed and started to dress. 'There's nothing to understand.'

'But you can speak.'

'Yes. Is that so remarkable?'

'Then why——'

'Because men prefer it that way. They are not interested in what women say. They do not want to think of us as people, but they want us to listen. I never pretend to be deaf.'

William laughed. 'Then you've done this before.'

She shrugged her shoulders. 'My silence is appreciated.'

'You mean you expect to be paid?'

'Do you think I am here out of passion? I don't even know you. I have my own life and I live it in my own way.' She stood before him fully dressed like a smiling shop clerk waiting for the transaction to be completed.

William was too shocked and too angry to say anything further. He reached down and found his trousers lying in a heap near the bed. He took out his wallet and tossed it at her. It landed with a flat thud at her feet. She picked it up, took a large note and tossed the wallet back on the bed. In another moment she was gone and William was left staring blankly at the door. After a few minutes his anger gave way to bitter amusement. So the madonna is a whore, after all, he thought. Like the Muse. And he muttered aloud in the empty room, 'One must love her and love her and love her.'

When Alex left William he went directly to Maggie's room, determined to keep her there as long as possible. He found the staircase and went up one more flight. He remembered the room number but he could not see well enough to find the right door. He waited for a while in the comparative darkness of the hallway and then used his cigarette-lighter to read the large numerals on each door.

He knocked gently and in a moment he could hear Maggie come to the door. She opened it cautiously and said, 'Come in, Alex.'

'What are you afraid of?' he said.

'I thought it was someone else,' she said.

'Who?'

'Oh, just someone I met earlier.'

She led him to a seat by the window and then lay down on the bed. 'In this town I bet you meet a lot of people. I mean these Italians really go for tall blondes.'

'They're pretty bold. At least in Rome. It's not the same in the country. The men in the smaller towns and villages are very polite. Here they make a game of seducing tourists.'

'Did they bother you today?' He crossed his legs and tried to look relaxed, but he was obviously nervous and too obviously trying to make conversation.

'A young guy followed me around half the day. He wanted to show me the ruins. Actually, he was very nice. He even paid for the drinks.'

'I guess his investment didn't pay off,' said Alex.

'I guess not, unless all he wanted was company on a hot afternoon. But it's not likely. When I left him I think he followed me for a while.'

'You should have told him your husband was waiting for you.'

'It wasn't really necessary.' She paused. 'A strange boy. Very strange. Full of clumsy bravado and quite intelligent.'

'Maybe you should have been nicer to him,' said Alex, betraying a trace of bitterness.

Maggie said nothing. She lit a cigarette and came to the window where he was sitting. 'Where's William?' she said.

'I don't know,' said Alex. 'He went out for a while. He didn't say where.'

'That's odd, isn't it?'

'Not especially. Not for him.'

'No, nothing's odd for him. He was always going out, always restless.'

'Maybe he's got some friends to look up. He knows people in this town, doesn't he?'

'Oh, for Christ sake, Alex,' she said, 'stop being so loyal. You know where he is and so do I.'

'What do you mean?' said Alex.

'I mean I saw you all come into the hotel. I was standing right here by the window.'

'Oh,' he said and then lit a cigarette. 'I'm sorry.'

'What for?'

'I don't know. The whole situation has me confused. I think you're both crazy. And I don't like lying—for anybody. Why don't you two just make up and get it over with?'

'Ask him.'

'I have, but I don't understand his answer. I don't think he knows what he's doing any more. I don't think he knows what he feels. The other day he wanted to settle in Paris. Now he wants to settle in Rome. He's so unhooked from the world and himself that he's beginning to rattle around. Somebody's got to get hold of him. I've tried but he won't listen to me any more. You're the only one who can do it.'

'Me? I can't do anything for him.' She hesitated. 'I offered him whatever I have to offer.'

'Did you tell him you want to try again?'

'Yes. But he says it won't work.'

'Do you think it would work?'

She thought for a moment. 'No,' she said.

Alex smiled and then stood up. 'Let's get the hell out of here,' he said. 'Let's go out somewhere and get drunk.'

19

AT NINETY COUNT RUDOLFI BOLOGNESI could no longer ride a horse. Because of the arthritic stiffness in his back he spent much of his time setting in straight-backed chairs reading or playing chess or thinking about the sculptured perfection of his long life. He was neat and poised in every way, his moustache and hair delicately trimmed, his mouth somewhat pinched, as if to indicate that he never spoke an uncensored word, and his clothing so carefully fitted and selected that it seemed to be a part of his anatomy, a vital replacement, immortal in its own way, for that insubstantial and ageing piece of flesh he knew secretly to be his real body.

Even at ninety the Count continued to chisel away gently at that magnificent form that was his life, refining certain curves and smoothing over certain rough places by grinding down the truth in what he proudly called his 'infallible memory'. Incidents that might have been distasteful half a century earlier were now fitted into the aesthetic whole and explained away as necessary for that special Renaissance perfection of body, mind, and spirit towards which he always aimed. His philosophy was a very small thing, a piece of fruit that he could hold in his manicured hands and admire for its external perfection—a piece of fruit into which he never dared to bite for fear of a disappointing unripeness or a hidden worm.

In his time the Count had done everything any man in search of the good life could hope to do, and he had done it well. His first great accomplishment, of course, was to be born into a rich and noble family. He also had the foresight to be the first-born, which guaranteed him titles and properties extensive enough to support him in his lifelong journey towards Platonic perfection.

As a young man he was studious, literary, athletic, and amorous. Between seductions and horse shows he wrote poetry and earned degrees in law. He adored women with an intense intellectual interest, but for horses he had simply a passion. In the first great war he served as an artillery officer of substantial rank, but by this time he was already past forty. Before he rushed to the service of his country he had already dabbled in politics, published two books of verse, collected scores of trophies for his riding, and married the beautiful Lucrezia Canzoni, on whom he fathered three children before the war, all of whom died, and three children after the war, all of whom, unfortunately, lived.

His many affairs with household servants, shopgirls, young opera singers, and other men's wives, were long ago packed into a handsome parcel, wrapped in blue ribbon, attached to a large stone, and dropped into the deep river of his 'infallible memory'. They meant nothing to him in purely human or sentimental terms, though several of the illegitimate consequences of these 'non-involvements' still dragged out their dreary lives in the back-streets of Rome or Milan.

His political career was temporarily hampered by the rise of Mussolini, but not before he served briefly as ambassador to an insignificant, but picturesque little nation in southern Europe, where he could satisfy a life-long urge to paint and gamble. It did not take him long to learn how to speak the language of the new leader, though his interest in politics was already beginning to wane. The grimness and crudeness of post-war politics drove him to more pleasant and safer pursuits. He developed an interest in ancient Roman plumbing and Etruscan painting.

Though his family fortune declined steadily through wars and fits of spending, he still managed to keep the Villa Merdeluna and several other large estates, and some large balances in Swiss banks. The giant sewers through which much of his money seeped away were his three children, motherless now for almost thirty years, and lost in the exploding vagaries of a modern world, to which the Count himself could not pay much attention. Theodora was the oldest, hardly a child at forty-five, though she seemed to strive eternally for that simple state of innocence which is governed only by fits of temper, erotic play, and a general unawareness of other people. The two boys, Aldo and Angelo, were only this or that side of forty. They were light, like hollowed-out egg-shells, and bobbed around on little waves of unreality. Aldo pretended to be interested in architecture and Angelo played the harpsichord. Most of their time was spent in devising ingenious schemes for satisfying their bizarre sexual whims. The Countess Theodora, as her friends called her, was more than helpful and often constructively, in this quest for what their loving father might have called 'the Platonically perfect idea of an orgasm'.

It was eleven o'clock in the morning when William, Alex, and Maggie drove through the giant unguarded Baroque gates of the Villa Merdeluna. The stone wall around the villa was twelve feet high and covered with ivy and moss. 'Whenever I see a wall like that,' said Alex, 'I think of the poor slobs who built it, hauling and lifting and chipping. I think of a particular day, a hot afternoon, maybe, and I imagine that I'm one of the men. Do you suppose they cursed at the old Count or his great-grandfather or whoever built it?'

'Who knows? Maybe they enjoyed lifting stones all day,' said Maggie.

The old house with its closed shutters and its encrustation of balconies looked asleep or dead. It rose from the neglected, jungle-like greenery, a structure suggesting a combination post-office and monastery that might have been abandoned by over-ambitious missionaries who left it to the strangling verdure of the steaming forest after deciding not to create a great city around it after all.

They drove towards it on a dirt road that ended in a circular driveway paved with cobble-stones. 'It looks haunted,' said Alex.

'It probably is,' said William. 'It would make a great setting for an Italian version of a Tennessee Williams play.'

They parked the car and stepped out into the warm sunlight and silence. The land behind the house sloped away into an olive-grove, but the gardens closer to the house were crowded with expanding shrubs, proliferating flowers, and trees half devoured by parasitical vines.

They stood there before the huge, carved front doors like waifs about to abandon themselves on the steps of the church. The doors were fifteen feet high and looked as though they had not been opened for a hundred years.

William lifted the heavy iron knocker and let it fall once. It sounded like a hammer dropping on an anvil.

'Jesus Christ,' said Alex.

They stepped back from the door and waited. To the left of the house William saw a smaller gate that led to a formal garden, in the centre of which was a fish pond. Alex lit a cigarette and shifted nervously from foot to foot. 'There's nobody home, Doc,' he said. 'Let's go.'

William reached for the knocker again, but he was interrupted by the squeaking voice of an old woman. She shuffled towards them in a mass of skirts and shawls, apparently having dropped from one of the dying trees. She was beckoning for them to come around the other side of the house, but her toothless Italian reached them only as a curious cackle. They looked at one another and then followed the old lady down a narrow path that led to a side entrance, a weatherbeaten door made for medieval dwarfs. She led them through a dark kitchen, where Alex stumbled into a rack of pots and pans, down a corridor so narrow that they had to walk single file, and then into a cathedral of a living-room or *entrada* with marble floors and a monster of a crystal chandelier that threatened at any moment to fall from its single chain and crush them into powdered flesh.

The old woman went mumbling past William and up the

broad staircase. As she went by, an ancient remnant of something that once was human, he could see her brown scalp through her few remaining hairs.

Suddenly a bolt of sunlight struck the floor in front of them as someone flung open the shutters on the landing.

'What happened?' said Alex, blinking his eyes.

Before he could answer, William saw a young man gliding down the curving staircase, his arms gracefully outstretched as though he were about to part the waters of the Red Sea. 'Ah,' said the young man. 'At last you are here. Ah, how good to see you, William. I knew it must be you. And Maggie. Beautiful Maggie.' He descended on them like a Renaissance painting come to life in full technicolor. His red silk robe and white scarf made his black hair seem all the blacker, and matched the redness and whiteness of his lips and face. William retreated half a step from his embrace, as though Mario were Death come to claim him at last. But Mario's cold hands caught him by the shoulders and neck and he kissed William on the cheek. Then he took Maggie's hand and also kissed it. Alex smiled patiently, like an embarrassed tourist watching the bizarre sexual rituals of a primitive tribe.

Mario stepped back to look at his friend. 'My father telephoned me last night to tell me that you were in Rome. I would have tried to reach you but he didn't know where you were staying. I was afraid that you would not bother to come all the way out here.'

'We rented a car,' said William.

Mario's eyes moved quickly as he talked, as though he was searching for the old friend hidden somewhere inside the man who stood in front of him. He and Alex shook hands without an introduction.

'I'm sorry,' said William. 'I feel as though you two already know each other.'

'I'm sure we know about each other,' said Alex.

Mario forced his gaunt face into a polite smile. 'Yes,' he said blankly, and then turned his attention again to William 'You've changed since I last saw you.'

'Have I?'

'Yes, but I don't know exactly how, except there.' He poked playfully at William's belly. 'You'll never win any more trophies with that.'

'There are all kinds of trophies,' said William.

Mario laughed and invited them out to the terrace for coffee. 'Everyone in this house sleeps late,' he said.

The terrace was enclosed by an elaborate balustrade and partly shaded by an arbour of grape-vines. 'What a beautiful view,' said Maggie.

'Yes,' said Mario, 'it's a fertile valley. This part here, from the house to that road out there, belongs to the Count. His grandfather used to own the whole thing.'

'These must be rough times for the nobility,' said Alex.

'The taxes are ridiculous. We have to keep selling the land.'

William noticed Mario's curious use of *we*. It reminded him of all those dapper young friends of his in New York who worked for giant corporations and also said *we*, as though they had been ingested into some enormous invisible personality and could no longer refer to themselves as individuals.

Mario was thinner, more remote, and more effeminate than when William last saw him. In those two years he had aged ten. The leanness that once made him beautiful now made him ugly. The boy in him was suffocating, not under the burden of manhood, but the harder burden of some grotesque substitute for manhood that time was imposing on him.

'Well, Mr. Rossano,' said William, with his mock professorial tone. 'How do you explain all this? The last time I saw you you were thinking of writing a novel about the human condition like any other normal healthy neurotic intellectual, and now you're living in baronial splendour in this palace.'

Mario blushed slightly and shrugged his shoulders. 'I hardly know where to begin. Life is full of marvellous and awful surprises. I met the Contessa Theodora at Domenico's Bar one night. But that's a long story in itself. She was in the process of destroying the place with a chair (she's quite moody), and I tried to disarm her. Some hours later we found ourselves here, and the next morning she offered me the position of secretary to her father. That is the barest outline of what happened. Another time I will try to fill in the details. Theodora will be down soon and you can meet her for yourself. Perhaps her brothers will also come down. They are probably watching us this very minute from their bedroom windows.'

William glanced up at the rows of closed shutters and then out across the fertile valley. The land was a patch-quilt of green and brown and yellow. 'And what's happened to your work?' he said.

Mario frowned. 'My work? What do you mean?'

'Your academic work. The movie script. The novel. The magazine you started.'

'Oh, my juvenilia,' said Mario, dismissing them all with a wave of his hand. 'Everybody wants to write a novel or start a magazine. Some people outgrow the desire; others don't.' He adjusted his white silk scarf and pointed his profile towards the sky as though he were posing for a picture or daring the world to contradict him. 'I can't take art seriously any more; or scholarship. I don't want to be a bearded, itchy old professor, and I don't want to be a successful novelist. I just want to live.'

'Ideas don't interest you any longer?'

'Oh, yes. Ideas are fine. I love ideas. I spend a great deal of time in bed, just wallowing in ideas. I have a painted ceiling in my room. You know, like a chapel. I just lie there and think about Michelangelo and da Vinci and Marcel Proust. I think about my father and dialectical materialism. I even think about the church and all the saints. Charming people. Have you ever read the lives?'

'But you do nothing?'

'I do a great deal. I read to the Countess. The other night I finished *To the Lighthouse*. What a marvellous book. And, you know, when Lily Briscoe puts that last line on her canvas, when she stands on the shore and has her vision, Theodora actually cried. She was a little drunk, of course, but nevertheless she cried. How many people do you know who have cried over Virginia Woolf?'

Maggie smiled as though she were remembering something.

'You, for one,' said William.

Mario looked puzzled and shook his head. 'I don't remember. I don't remember anything.' He got up abruptly and said, 'Come, I'll show you the place. It's full of history and second-rate statues. And the fish-pond is full of cannibal fish from South America.'

They stalked through the overgrown gardens while Mario recited genealogies and architectural facts, and then went quickly through the house, except for the bedrooms on the third floor.

When they came back to the terrace, the Countess greeted them. She was wearing skin-tight silver pants and a black cashmere sweater. Her hair was platinum blonde. Her make-up was so carefully applied that from a distance she might have been taken for a shopgirl on an extravagant vacation in Miami Beach. She was one of those very thin women who always look about forty, whether they are sixteen or sixty. She greeted them with cat-like caution and ordered more coffee.

'We've met somewhere before,' she said to Maggie.

'Yes.'

'At Portofino?'

'No, Athens. You said you were going to Beirut and Cairo and Jerusalem.'

'I remember now. At the home of Felix Topolous. There was a masquerade party and you were Diana the Huntress.'

'What a memory!'

'But how could I forget? Your costume was the talk of the evening. So daring.' She laughed. 'How I hated you for having such courage.'

'I was trying to be authentic,' said Maggie.

'It must have been quite a costume,' said Alex.

'It was,' said William coldly, remembering a friend's description of the sheer tunic that covered only one breast and the golden sandals that strapped around her ankles.

'You were beautiful that night,' said Theodora. 'So perfect for the role you played. No one should have objected.'

'And did you ever get to Jerusalem?' said Maggie.

'No,' said the Countess, 'we went to Crete instead, and

Sicily, Sardinia, Corsica, and Mallorca. We were looking for islands.'

William watched her, fascinated by the variety of moods that swept by behind the twitching curtain that was her face. Her eyes darted from person to person, then suddenly across the distant fields, then back to the terrace and to another face. He had the feeling that she was disintegrating before his very eyes, that at any moment she would start to fly to pieces. Her hair would fall out, her voice would crack, her eyes would go wild, and she would crumble into a heap of bones and pearls right there on the stone floor of the terrace. Her madness made him uneasy, especially because it didn't show itself openly, but only lurked there just below the surface.

'I want some day to buy an island,' she said. 'A small island where I can live for the rest of my life in exactly the way I choose. I will invite all my closest friends. We will make our own world. We will be wise and free and happy there.'

William looked at Alex and smiled, but he knew that Alex did not see him. He thought of his friend's Utopia, his Paradise Island, and he assumed that Alex too was at that moment also thinking about it. Would he mention it, he wondered. Would he associate his dream with the dream of this mad countess?

Alex remained silent. His face was tight and hard.

'There is an island off the coast of Africa,' said Mario. 'We are thinking of it. It is beautiful. Just right for what we want.'

'How wonderful,' said Maggie. 'What sort of society did you have in mind?'

'Not a democracy, I hope,' said William.

She laughed. 'Oh no, nothing like that. No government at all, as a matter of fact.'

'Just people,' said Mario. 'Just people, living.'

They all waited, but he did not go on.

'Living?' said Maggie.

'Yes,' said Theodora. 'Just doing what they please, exploring their talents, meditating, exercising—whatever suits them at the moment.'

'Anarchy?' said William. 'Suppose one of your friends has an urge to kill?'

'Then I think he should kill,' she said.

'But whom?'

She smiled enigmatically and shrugged her shoulders. 'Which friend are you talking about?'

'It won't work without laws of some kind,' said Maggie.

'No, no,' said Mario, his tone now a parroting of Theodora's, 'laws are impossible. Laws would ruin everything. We have to take chances.'

William sighed and tried to shake away his uneasy feeling. 'Everybody wants an island,' he said. 'Everybody is looking for Utopia. What's wrong with the world as it is? Aren't you satisfied?'

'Are you?' said Theodora, and William felt that her question was annoyingly personal.

'Ah, but I don't have all this.' He waved his hand at the house and the surrounding countryside.

'Do you think it makes any difference how large one's house is?' she said.

'I don't know,' he said. 'Perhaps it does.'

'No,' she said. 'No, it makes no difference at all.' Then she stood up suddenly. 'You'll excuse me, I have a few things to attend to. Please feel at home and plan to spend the night.'

Before they could refuse or accept she was gone, striding with glittering poise along the terrace and then through the giant French doors.

After lunch William insisted on seeing Theodora's collection of automobiles. She was delighted. She drove cars as some women ride horses, with that arrogant posture and erectness that seems to suggest not only a triumph over the beast but also a revenge against men. Theodora also rode horses, but she preferred the greater driving force and destructive possibilities of a Ferrari or a Jaguar.

By the time they walked down to the garage William was absolutely sure that the Countess was mad, but he no longer thought of her as a ludicrous middle-aged lady trying, in some childish way, to cling to her youth. She was intelligent, witty, and utterly insane. It was a high and expensive form of madness. She was convinced that she had psychic powers, and that she was literally two people, one of whom lived inside of her and was immortal. After her death, she explained at lunch, her outer body would fall away and her other body would emerge, eternally young and beautiful. She would, in short, give birth to herself. 'Are you sure you're not talking about your soul?' said Alex.

'I have no soul,' she said angrily. 'I have been many bodies, moving through many worlds.'

Perhaps, thought William, she had had a drunken conversation with a Hindu mystic and only half listened to what he was saying. Or perhaps she was even more subtle and facetious than he imagined and was assuming the pose for her own amusement. 'Conventional ways of knowing the truth,' she said, 'are not good enough. Science leads nowhere. Logic is a joke. The geometrical imagination is a prison. Art is a subjective distortion. We need something else; some direct route.'

Drugs he wanted to say, but instead he nodded politely and said, 'The way of the mystic.'

She looked at him suspiciously with her heavily painted, oriental eyes. The pupils seemed to shrink under the drooping blue lids. 'I hope, Mr. Mariner,' she said, 'that you are not laughing at me.'

'Not at all, not at all,' he said hastily. 'I'm something of a mystic myself. I've read Evelyn Underhill and counted the steps of St. John of the Cross with T. S. Eliot.'

She looked confused by his references and said, 'I'm afraid we are not yet talking about the same things.'

As she walked in front of him down the narrow path that led to the garage he studied her lean body. Her legs were long and her small round hips moved invitingly. Her silver pants glistened in the sun. The wine he had drunk with lunch warmed him inside and he wonder how approachable this woman might be.

Theodora had a Mercedes convertible, a Bentley, and three sports cars—an Alfa Romeo, a Jaguar XK140, and a red Ferrari. 'I find driving very exciting,' she said. 'If I were a man I would have raced.'

'I've wanted to try it myself,' said William, examining the dashboard of the Ferrari. 'What a beautiful piece of work.' He toyed with the steering-wheel and felt the black leather of the bucket seats.

'Come, I'll take you for a ride,' she said. She climbed in behind the wheel and he got in beside her. They drove through the big gate and down the road. 'Such a lovely animal.' The low, heavy car surged forward. 'So responsive. It will do almost anything I want it to do.'

He held on to the door and pressed his foot against an imaginary brake. He felt the force of the car against his body, but said nothing. He remembered the little MG he had in California, and the sense of freedom it gave him to drive it aimlessly and sometimes dangerously along the coast highway. He liked the sound of a powerful engine and speed awoke in him some smiling devil. But he preferred to be at the wheel. He had always hated being driven around by someone else, especially a woman. Whenever Maggie had insisted on driving he allowed her to, but he remained silently furious with her throughout the trip.

'Take it easy,' he said, as they squealed around a tight curve.

Theodora laughed and went faster. 'Are you afraid, a big man like you?'

'No, but unlike you I don't have any bodies to spare. This old corpse is the only one I've got and I'd like to be wearing it when we arrive. Where are we heading for?'

'Anywhere you like. I have friends in Formia. We could stop for a drink. Or we could go into the mountains—Perugia maybe. Or even Naples. Anywhere. It doesn't matter to me. I enjoy you. You are a very peculiar man.'

The air rushed past them noisily and they had to raise their voices to be heard. Occasional cars came at them from the other direction and veered to the side of the road to let the big Ferrari by.

'Any good old-fashioned bar or café will do. I think I need a drink.'

She laughed again, but took her foot off the gas and shifted down. In a few moments they were idling along at a sensible speed. They were going downhill and in the distance William could see a hazy line of blue. 'Is that the sea?'

'Yes,' she said. 'When we come around this hill you will see it better.' She went on a little further and then pulled into a rocky dirt road that seemed to be nothing more than a terraced piece of land on a hillside full of olive trees. She stopped the car and said, 'From up here you can see it all. My father owns this land. We have a little house here, but we seldom use it.'

They got out and walked further along the road. William felt the cooler breeze from the sea. For a moment they were silent and the whole world seemed to lie before them in death-like noiseless splendour.

He looked at her as she looked away. The lines on her face seemed relaxed and there was a lucidity and softness about her for a moment that made her look not only sane, but a little sad and innocent. In another moment, however, she turned to him abruptly, the wildness building again in her eyes, and said, 'Do you want to make love?'

'I don't know,' said William, unable to hide his surprise. 'I suppose so. I mean, I usually do.'

'Then come with me,' she said, leading him by the hand to a patch of new grass under an ancient olive tree.

They sat down beside one another and smoked a cigarette without saying anything. Finally, she threw away the red-tipped butt and said, 'Well? What are you waiting for?'

He laughed and leaned back on one elbow. 'I guess I've changed my mind. I mean, usually a woman waits to be seduced.'

'Nonsense,' she said. 'I've seduced many men. They prefer to be relieved of that awful awkwardness of approaching a woman. Kissing her and feeling her until with her body she says *yes*.'

'Well, frankly,' he said, 'I don't feel seduced, just propositioned.'

'All right, then,' she said, 'give me your hand.' He let her take his hand, which she pressed woodenly to her breast. 'Do you like that?'

He nodded and tried to pull her towards him, but she held tightly to his hand. She lifted her sweater and allowed him to touch the bare skin of her belly. Her flesh was cold, but very soft. 'Have you made love to many women?' she said.

'Not as many as I would have liked to,' he said.

'Tell me how you made love to them.'

'What difference does it make?'

'No, I want to know all the things you did. Were you gentle? Did you beat them?'

A chill of anger and excitement went through him. He tried to pull away his hand, but she held on to it. He tried to get up and she pulled him down again. 'Don't you dare leave,' she said. 'I won't allow you to insult me this way.'

'I'm sorry,' he said. 'Let's go somewhere for a drink. I don't want to make love. I don't enjoy this kind of thing. You may find this insulting, but frankly I like to choose the time and place—and the woman.'

She released her grip and stood up. 'I'm sorry,' she said. 'I'm so used to giving orders. I keep forgetting that you are an American and that Americans don't like to take orders.' Her mouth was trembling and her eyelids fluttered nervously.

He offered her another cigarette and they walked back to the car.

When William went up to his room at the Villa Merdeluna it was late in the afternoon. He had passed once again the garden with the fishpond, where he saw Aldo feeding the fish. He had heard the splashing of water and the mumbling of a single voice. As he climbed the wide stairs to his room he imagined Aldo with a maniac grin tossing new-born babies to the cannibal fish, and he remembered a story about a restaurant-owner in North Africa who was arrested for serving human flesh to his customers—a stew of wandering street boys whom he captured in the night.

He opened the door and was startled by the silhouetted figure of Alex, who sat, his face in his hands, in front of the open window. In the distance, slanting sunlight deepened the colours of the checkered fields, but the room, by contrast, was almost dark. Alex did not turn around to see who it was, as though he already knew by the sound alone and would not let himself be roused from his stubborn meditation.

William went to him and put his hand on his shoulder. 'What's the matter, Mr. Grim? Intimations of mortality?'

Without turning around Alex said, 'Let's go home, Doc. I've had enough.'

William pulled up a chair. 'Homesick already?'

'I've been homesick since we left. It's worse than that. I'm disgusted with Europe. I don't like Europeans. And I especially don't like these people. I want to go back to Seaville, to the raging stupidity of my middle-class Brave New World. I miss my kids. I want to go back and watch them ground up into more selfish and materialistic versions of myself. All these years I've been kidding myself. I'm not a poet or a pirate; I'm an ordinary American father and business man, puritanical, ill-informed, restless, and greedy, just like the next guy. I don't trust intellectuals and I don't really like them. I'm only envious of them the way all good red-blooded Americans are envious of everything they don't have.'

'Hey,' said William, 'slow down a minute and tell me what started all this. What happened?'

'Nothing. I suddenly realized that these people were laughing at me. I'm the naïve little American savage in a loin cloth, full of primitive superstitions and fears, and they are the safari of sophisticated hunters trying to trade me candy-wrappers and broken mirrors for my hand-made philosophy. I made the mistake of being serious and honest with them and they made me feel like a fool. Your friend Mario is the worst one of the lot. So precious and affected! He's full of information and ideas, but they rattle around inside of him like the broken filaments of a light bulb.'

William took off his jacket and undid his tie. He lay down on the oversized bed and looked at Alex. 'So you want to go home, then?' he said.

'To tell you the truth, Doc, I don't even remember now why we came. Sure I wanted to go to Lourdes, but I don't think that was my main reason. I probably just wanted to get to Europe before my eyes gave out. I'm just a tourist at heart. All my life I've heard about people taking a trip to Europe and it seemed to me such a luxury, such an absolutely elegant thing to do. I used to see myself aboard a huge ship with white pants and a sports coat with one of those coat-of-arms on the pocket. I'd be standing at the bar holding a Scotch and soda and talking to Lauren Bacall. In the evening there would be music and a magnificent dinner served by perfect French waiters. You know, the whole bit—and without an acid stomach or headaches or a foul-tasting mouth in the morning; without this constant and horrible discovery that people are real and that life goes on more or less the same all over the world. Everybody is loused up. Everybody struggles to survive in their own way. Maybe I got it all from the movies. Maybe I'm immature or something. I keep expecting my dreams to come true. That's the miracle that I really want out of life, not a good pair of eyes, though I wouldn't mind that either.' He paused and rubbed the fist of one hand into the palm of the other. 'What I can't seem to get rid of is this eternal optimism of mine. After each disappointment, I get up off the ground and start all over again. Tomorrow will be better! Next year we'll all be rich! I'll feel young again and strong. My children will be beautiful and intelligent. I will take my sweet wife on holidays and cruises and we will relive our honeymoon days over and over again. The years and years of dirty diapers and wailing children, the arguments and illnesses, the broken plumbing, the debts, will all fade into unreality. I keep working and working as if all this can be true, but every now and then I know that it cannot be true, that life is always made up of heartburn and unbalanced check books and insomnia.'

'You know it, but you don't believe it,' said William.

'No, I don't believe it. I don't want to believe it. I long for perfection. I would like to feel it just once, in just one thing, one action, one object. A kiss or a conversation, or—or something I made with my own hands. I would like to go away totally satisfied, without feeling, as I always do, that it fell just short of what I hoped for or expected.'

'It's deadly to expect too much of the world,' said William.

'It's an old cliché that perfection is impossible, at least in *this* life.'

'I know,' said Alex.

'And about the next life I don't know very much.'

'Neither do I. I probably know less about it than you.'

William got up and poured two cognacs. 'That makes us even,' he said, 'because I know less about this one than you do.'

'Only because you refuse to live it, Doc.'

'Ouch,' said William.

'No,' said Alex, 'I think your way is better. If you never expect anything you can never be disappointed.'

'What makes you think I never expect anything?'

'Do you?'

'Sometimes I think I expect too much. I expect people to accept me as I am. I am willing to be loved without being able to return that love.'

'Perhaps it's better never to love,' said Alex.

'No,' said William. 'It's not better, It's not even possible. I mean, one *can't* live without it. I've spent half my life in a crazy vacillation, trying to escape it and plunging headlong at it like a madman. I keep imagining that I will tear it from the heart of the very next woman that I meet, that I will force her to abandon herself with such completeness and such devotion that I will never want to look at another woman again. But it's a lie and I know it. Yet I go on doing it. And I go on envying you, because you're so much more gentle with people and with life.'

'I'm not gentle, Doc, just scared. I don't want to be hurt and I don't want to hurt anyone. That's why I get angry with you sometimes. You hurt people, Doc. You hurt them real bad sometimes.'

William did not say anything. His long chronicle of affairs and seductions erupted in his mind like a cloud of suffocating black smoke. Faces emerged, arms and hands. He heard fragments of conversation, protestations of love, and he felt the softness of naked bodies. 'I don't want it,' he said. 'I just don't want it. I want to strip away all decent good things. I want to cut all ties, end all business, finish with the rotten lie. I want to be able to live as though nothing really mattered, but I can't.'

'Keep trying, Doc. You may make it yet,' said Alex.

'I'm sorry,' said William, 'I'm sorry if the way I live offends you.'

'It does offend me, Doc; and yet I'm forced time and time again to forgive you. I don't know why.'

William tried to laugh. 'Playing Christ again?'

Alex shook his head. 'You haven't found a way yet to turn me against you, Doc, but I'm afraid one of these days you will. And that will be a very terrible day for both of us.'

William shrugged and turned away.

20

'THE CHAPEL,' said the old Count, 'was built by my grandfather in memory of his young wife, who died in childbirth, a mere girl of nineteen. The stones were brought from a ruined church in Padua.'

Maggie listened with a combination of affected and genuine fascination. She marvelled at the clear strong voice that came from the dried flesh and bone that was his face. William watched her from the other end of the table, where he was frequently attacked into conversation by Mario and Theodora.

'I play the electric organ,' said Alex to Aldo, lifting his wine glass. 'But I've always been interested in harpsichords. Some day perhaps I'll buy one.'

'After dinner I will show you my collection,' said Aldo. His round face beamed. 'But I am not a performer. I've studied the instrument for years, but,' he threw up his hands in a gesture of hopelessness, 'I have no sense of music. It's the construction that interests me.'

'Mr. William is a mystic,' said Theodora to Mario, but with her eyes on William. 'He believes in the journey of the human spirit.'

Mario smiled. 'Mr. William, my dear, is an atheist.'

'No,' said William, 'I'm not an atheist. I'm just afraid to believe in anything.'

'Everybody is afraid of something,' said Angelo.

Theodora had undergone a complete transformation since her ride with William. She appeared at the dinner-table in a sedate linen suit with a simple string of pearls and a hair-do that might have been worn by an attractive lady doctor. She talked calmly.

'Fear, I think, is overrated,' she said. 'This is the mistake the psychologists make. They imagine that we are all frightened. Guilt, punishment, birth-trauma, survival. If we are afraid at all, it is in another sense entirely. It is not pain or death that frightens us; it is something much more important.'

'The loss of identity, I suppose,' said William.

'No,' she said. 'Not quite. The death of the god in us.'

William frowned and looked at Mario as if for a further explanation. 'I don't know what you mean.'

'She means that there are two kinds of death,' said Mario.

'Exactly,' she said. 'Physical death is unimportant and may not even be a reality. But we are holy creatures, capable of all kinds of miracles, and we can lose that power, which is another kind of death. To remain strong in our special strength we must exercise it constantly. We must see the invisible and know the unknowable. We must not be seduced into being mere animals. I, for instance have developed my psychic powers to the point where I can know what everyone in this room is thinking.'

'How terrible,' said William.

'No, not at all. Shall I give you a demonstration?'

'By all means,' said William. 'But pick on someone else.'

She turned to Alex. Everyone at the table fell silent. Alex's smile was almost a sneer. 'Your friend, for instance, is collecting his contempt for me and trying to frame, in his own mind, an abusive phrase with which to attack me. He thinks I am insane and evil. And yet he hesitates because he is not quite sure.'

'My daughter is a remarkable woman,' said the Count quietly to Maggie. She nodded in polite agreement.

After dinner more guests arrived. Theodora introduced William to a stocky young man who was accompanied by a terrified woman with a purple birthmark on her neck. She cowered behind the man as they were introduced. 'Professor Mariner,' said Theodora, 'I want you to meet Carlos Bugati, one of our most dangerous columnists; and Viola, his charming wife.' She ignored Maggie.

'This is Maggie St. Claire,' said William to the new couple.

By midnight there were a dozen people in the large sitting-room—a man with a turban, two young women in slacks who William assumed were lesbians, a beady-eyed man named Franco wearing evening clothes, a young French couple, an Italian actor named Guido with long hair and muscles, who was accompanied by two adoring females, and three men in sports clothes, who looked as though they might have just come alongside in their yacht.

Alex burrowed through the party, sampling and probing, supported by a confidence that came from anger, curiosity, and alcohol. He collected information as though he were preparing for an inquisition, wrenching from pretty women, by charm and flirtation, black secrets about their pasts and innocent dreams about their futures. He courted one of the two Brigitte Bardot girls who accompanied the Herculean Guido. Her English was very bad, but she managed to tell him that she was twenty-one, that she had been in love eight times in her life, that she had played a bit part in Guido's last movie, and that she hoped some day to have six children. He could not remember that she said anything about getting married.

The man in the turban, he discovered, was not oriental after all, but a former schoolteacher from Sicily, who was promoting himself as an expert on Zen Buddhism. He refused the drink that Alex offered him and suggested, almost in the same breath, that he might cure his ailing eyes within three months, if Alex would place himself, heart, soul, and money, in his hands entirely for that brief period. 'And where would we conduct these spiritual exercises?' said Alex.

'In a warm and soothing climate—the Riviera, perhaps,' said the wise man.

'I'm afraid I can't make it this year, Mac,' said Alex, 'I've got to go to the West Indies on business and then rush back to Zurich for a pre-frontal lobotomy.'

By the time Alex searched out Theodora he was quite drunk. 'Countess, baby,' he said, taking her by the arm, 'I've been looking for you all evening. But, you know, I can't see too well. I wanted to thank you on behalf of my buddy and myself for a great time. And you know what? You were absolutely right about what you said at the table.'

Theodora tried to pull away from him, but he held on to her. 'I'm sorry,' she said. 'I imagine I owe you an apology, but I felt your anger and contempt.'

'I don't doubt it. You don't have to be psychic to see such things. But what you probably didn't notice was my pity and compassion. I'm also a very compassionate man.' He swayed towards her as though he was going to kiss her. She held him back with an outstretched arm.

'No,' she said, 'I didn't feel your pity and compassion, and I wish you would let go of me. I don't like you.' The composure that she had managed to muster for the evening threatened to explode into hysteria.

'All right,' he said, releasing her arm, 'but let me finish what I came to tell you. At the table you said I was searching for a phrase with which to attack you. Well I found one—quite an ordinary one. You're an indecent woman, an insult to God's vision of the world. I could forgive you for being crazy, but lady, you're just plain *dirty*.'

In a blur of pearls and white linen she slipped out of his field of vision, like something on a microscope slide. He imagined that everyone was looking at him, though, in fact, they weren't. The humming of their voices made him dizzy. He felt his way towards an open door and went out into the warm darkness of the garden.

William and Maggie were also outside. They were sitting on the ground with two bottles of champagne and two glasses between them. They enjoyed their invisibility as they looked towards the blazing lights of the villa, which now had its immense front doors flung wide open.

'I still don't understand,' said William, filling both glasses again. As he sat there, his knees bent and his legs spread apart, he could feel the layer of fat around his middle.

He leaned back and rested, Roman-fashion, on his left elbow. Maggie, on the other hand, could quite comfortably hug her knees and rest her chin on them, a huddled posture that William remembered all too sharply. It was one of several positions she assumed when she had something serious to explain. She had sat that way once at the foot of their bed to explain to him why she had been unfaithful, why she had gone back to see an old lover of hers in London only two months after they were married. She showered on herself a purifying rain of theories and excuses. Marriage was not easy for her. An old habit of independence. An assertion of the will. Old loyalties. Nobody can own anybody entirely. Such things could not harm their own relationship. All avenues of experience must be explored. And so on into the shivering, polluted night, until, weary even with his own anger and disappointment, he forgave her. It was not until much later that he realized that he never really did forgive her for anything, not even the things that had happened before their marriage, which she recited to him, all too willingly, like a mischievous young girl savouring her sins in the confessional and at that very moment committing even subtler, more profound sins.

He had discovered that his disappointment was not real because he had never held any illusions about her. From the beginning he had called her an amoral animal. He knew that she could never surrender herself to him like a peasant bride, that she was too large and evasive a woman ever to be contained in that fashion. But still he was hurt, or imagined he was; still, when it was convenient, he invoked all the old-fashioned codes and rules and lashed her with them until her pride broke or doubled itself into a cold defensive arrogance.

'I don't understand why you wanted to come with us,' he said.

'That's what I've been trying to explain to you,' she said, shaking her head and holding out the palm of her long slender hand to him, as though she were begging for a penny's worth of understanding. 'The moment I saw you in London I knew that something important was happening. I have never seen you so precariously close to either total despair or real joy. It has something to do with Alex and this whole trip. I think it means more to you than it does to him.'

'You mean I'm about to fall into the arms of the Mother Church?'

'No,' she said. 'I don't think that's very likely. But you're in a very strange state of mind—a dangerous state of mind, like a man with a raging fever. It will either break or it will kill you.'

He raised his eyebrows. 'How dramatic! Are you sure you're not making all this up? Are you sure it isn't you who has the fever?'

She hesitated. 'I'm not sure of anything at this point, Bill.'

He tore up a few blades of grass and tossed them into the air. 'I'm sorry,' he said. 'I didn't mean to make fun of you. You're too close to being right, and I suppose I don't want to talk about it.'

'Why not?'

'Because I don't know what to say. I've thought about things for the past two years. I've watched myself slip deeper and deeper into the quicksand without knowing why; without knowing how to climb out. Oh, I offer myself theoretical explanations. I'm so full of self-analysis I could vomit. Self-destruction, I call it at times. The urge to fail. I sometimes think I want to be a bum, a real vagabond, with no ties, no commitments, no hopes or dreams. Perhaps that's what I'm secretly striving for. Perhaps that's all I deserve.'

'Ah, now you've touched it; now you've left a clue.'

'What do you mean?'

'That's all you *deserve*,' she said. 'It is *you*, after all, who harbours the secret sin, and therefore deserve nothing. And now I can ask you as you once asked me—what is it? With what awful stick do you beat yourself?'

There was a long silence. William played nervously with the grass. 'I don't know,' he said. 'I don't understand. I only wanted to live a quiet, simple life. I only wanted to write my books and love a woman and walk in the country or by the sea. For so many years everything seemed so simple. I mean, what I wanted seemed so simple. But it never came. I never let it happen.'

'Why?' she said, like an insistent school teacher. 'Why?'

'I don't know,' he said more loudly. 'How can I tell you what I myself don't know?'

'And did you hope to discover these things on this trip?'

'I don't know what I hoped to discover,' he said. 'I have always envied Alex for his sheer humanity, his real connection with the world. Perhaps I hoped to learn something from him. Perhaps he is my only friend.'

'The only one you can accept you mean.'

'Yes, because he makes it easy. Because he accepts me. Because nothing I ever do alienates him. We are like brothers who never question the bond between them. What connects us is as fundamental as that; and yet we are not brothers, so the connection is complicated—mysterious.'

'It's a kind of love,' she said.

'Yes. A kind of love.' His voice trailed off into a whisper. 'And I would like to be God for just one minute in Lourdes so that I could perform just one miracle.'

'And you would give that miracle to him?'

'Yes, I would. I would let him see again, and I would be satisfied. It is the thing he needs most right now, and it is the one thing that nobody can give him.'

'He needs more than his eyesight,' she said.

'Of course he does,' said William, 'but that's all I'm talking about.'

'And you?' she said. 'What do you need?'

He smiled. 'Me? Perhaps what I need is just that—to be God for one minute, to enjoy unlimited power and wisdom, if only for a split second, to escape for one moment from this creeping, rotting animal that I call myself.'

'There are ways of doing that without being God,' she said.

'No. It's not the same. Even being in love is not the same. Even art is not the same.'

'Yes,' she said, 'love is the same. It's the only way by which we can escape being merely human. It is God's way of allowing us to share in his wisdom and being.'

He looked up through the black branches of the trees to the scattered stars in the darkness, and he remembered that night in Assisi with such a combination of pain and fury that all he could do was laugh. 'The gospel according to Saint Maggie.'

She shook her head. 'You're an old black-hearted heathen.'

'Would you prefer me as a romantic, sentimental slob?'

'You *are* a romantic, sentimental slob,' she said. 'Do you remember the drunken night you threatened to read aloud all the sonnets of Shakespeare?'

'What about Shakespeare?' said another voice from the darkness.

Maggie stood up suddenly and dropped her glass of champagne. A figure staggered towards them, silhouetted against the light of the house. 'No, I am not Prince Hamlet, nor was meant to be . . .' mumbled the intruder.

'Alex!' said William, annoyed but relieved. 'What the hell are you doing wandering around in the dark?'

'I've been walking around in the dark for years, haven't you heard?' He bumped into a tree and said, 'I beg your pardon.' Then he held on to it. 'This is the ghost of Alexander Morgan speaking. Where are you? You have to keep talking so that I know where you are.'

William came over to him and took him by the arm. 'Is that you, Doc?' said Alex. 'I thought I heard you lecturing in the wilderness.' He spoke with a drunken smile and leaned heavily against William. 'And there's a woman here, somewhere. I can tell.' He sniffed the air. 'Fee, fi, fo, fum!' Maggie laughed. 'Ah, I knew it. Maggie Saint Pig-Farm Claire.' She came over and took his other arm. He burped elaborately.

'Are you going to be sick?' said William.

'Not *going to be*, Doc; *shall have should been*! Don't you remember our new grammar book?'

'Come on, we'll walk it off,' said William. He and Maggie supported him as they stepped aimlessly about the dark lawn.

'I didn't mean to interrupt, folks,' said Alex. 'But I heard these voices, see, and then somebody said Shakespeare. It was like a drop of rain in the desert. Shakespeare. Willy Shakespeare, the genius of Stratford. Why didn't we get up there to see the place?'

'Another time,' said William.

'Damn it, there won't be another time. You know that. You should have forced me to go. Why didn't you force me?'

'How long have you been wandering around?' said Maggie.

'Oh, about forty years or so,' he said. 'Forty years, forty, forty years. That's a quotation from something, isn't it Doc? I remember you reading that to me once. Ahab, wasn't it? *Moby Dick*?'

'Yes,' said William. 'I remember that night. You forced me to read to you until three in the morning.'

'Forced you? I couldn't stop you.' He turned to Maggie. 'He's a real ham, you know. But, of course, you know. He should have been an actor or something. In a way I guess teachers are actors, and what a great teacher he was! He taught me everything I know about literature. He told me what books to read; he told me about Faulkner and Hemingway and Virginia Woolf. He would get drunk and sentimental and read to me. Huxley, and Orwell. Remember that story about shooting an elephant, old buddy? And Dylan Thomas, "There was a saviour", and "Death Shall Have No Dominion", and "In My Craft and Sullen Art", and then the last part of *A Farewell to Arms*, with Catharine saying "it's a dirty joke" and he trying to kiss her after she was dead—dead like a statue and it was no good. Remember? We cried that night. We laughed and cried. And Billy Budd, who ascended when they hanged him, "and in ascending took the full rose of the dawn". I'll never forget that line, Doc. Never. Such a beautiful line. It makes me dizzy even to think about it. "Certain uncatalogued creatures of the deep." Was that the line? How did it go? "Natural depravity." From Plato, wasn't it? "Natural depravity." A depravity according to nature. Certain madmen . . .'

A woman's high-pitched scream shattered the night and trailed away into a moan that was followed in a moment by another scream and the general roar of mixed voices, some calling, some simply crying out. The three of them stood frozen in the woods looking towards the house. Dark figures rushed about, doors opened and slammed, a startled dog barked. The diminutive, puppet-like figures moved towards the garden to the left of the house and were swallowed up by darkness. But there the hysteria was loudest.

Alex clutched William's arm and trembled. 'What is it? What's happened?'

'I'll find out,' said William, releasing himself. 'Stay here with Maggie.' He glanced around at her and saw that her face was ghost-pale. But she took Alex's arm and said, 'Yes, we'll wait here.'

William ran off towards the crowd in the garden. He could see them gathered around the fish-pond. Some were turned away. Others were throwing things into the water and shouting. One man took off his coat and flung it into the pond in a vain attempt to frighten away the man-eating fish. Another man stood there holding his head and screaming, 'Oh, no, no, no!' The man in the turban walked aimlessly away from the scene as though he had been dazed by a blow.

William pushed past several people and came to the edge of the water. And then he staggered back. The water was a small ocean of choppy, splashing waves, from the centre of which a black ooze spread like an expanding cloud. Shreds of white linen twitched like torn sails in the tiny hurricane.

He turned away quickly and covered his eyes. He shook his head but could not drive out the sight. As he walked back towards the lawn he passed Mario sitting on a marble bench surrounded by neo-classical nudes. They stared at one another. Mario's face was drawn and empty. 'She threw herself in,' he said. 'We were just standing there talking and she walked over to the edge and started to laugh to herself. Then she spread her arms out and fell forward.

William walked away without saying a word and went back to Maggie and Alex. He told them what had happened and they all stood there for a moment unable to speak. Then Alex moaned, 'Oh my God, my God!' and started to weep.

'Let's get out of here,' said William, 'before the police come.'

He and Maggie helped Alex to the car. The three of them huddled together in the narrow front seat and William started the engine. They drove away in silence along the dark road. After a while Alex fell into an uneasy sleep and Maggie pulled him towards her and rested his head on her shoulder.

21

'SO THIS IS the city of palms?' said Alex, as he sat uncomfortably in the imitation eighteenth-century dining-room of the Hermitage Club. In his white coat and black tie he looked like a weary international playboy trying to recover from the excesses of a Riviera holiday.

'I don't know,' said William. He sat with one elbow resting on the table and contemplated a silver candlestick. In his newly pressed suit and clean shirt he felt resentfully civilized. It was Maggie's idea, her plan to restore in all of them a sense of order.

Maggie sparkled in dark silk and pearls. 'Yes,' she said, 'it's the city of palms.'

'But it's not Palm Sunday by any chance, is it?' said Alex. The tall, handsome captain, immaculate in ancient tails and black tie, eyed them with a combination of suspicion and servile protectiveness. He was, after all, not only the guardian of their pleasure, but the defender of the candle-lit, upholstered atmosphere of Palma's most expensive restaurant.

'No,' said Maggie, 'it's not Palm Sunday and there will be no crucifixions here.'

'No crucifixions,' said Alex with mock outrage. 'No crucifixions!' He sipped quickly at his martini. 'Then why did you bring me here? I thought you were going to buy me a burro and whip me with palms.'

'Sorry, old boy,' said William, 'but you don't qualify. You're not a Jew.'

'O, come on now, Doc, let's not get technical,' said Alex.

'It's not only that,' said Maggie. 'You don't even have a beard. Besides, your mother wasn't a virgin.'

'How do you know?' said Alex. 'You never met my mother. She's a big, fat drunken Irishwoman who hates men. Isn't that good enough? I mean, that practically makes her a virgin, doesn't it?'

'It's not the same,' said William. 'She has to be pure of heart.'

'Mary may be pure, but Joseph are you sure?' mumbled Alex, his grin spreading into a smile.

'Besides,' said William, 'you have the whole damn thing wrong. A crucifixion is not a punishment, and all you want is some appropriate punishment to fit your imaginary crime.'

Alex shook his head. 'No, no, Professor. That's not the way it goes at all. You may be a good teacher, but you're a lousy Catholic. That lynching was a punishment. The flesh was pierced, the pain was real. And when that guy hauled that cross up the hill he was you and me and Maggie and anyone who ever winced at a bruise or sickened at the sight of blood. He was a man, a stinking Jew with a beard who could lose his faith like you or me or Job at the first plague of boils. When they nailed him to the cross he cried out with his man's voice, 'Oh, my God, why hast thou forsaken me?' The ultimate punishment was death, and he died like a man, which is to say that he died like an animal, full of fear and trembling and real ugly human pain and disappointment. Because, God damn it, none of us believe it will ever happen!' He raised his voice, and the handsome emperor of the dining-room cast a cold glance in his direction.

They were all silent for a moment. Alex explored his silverware with slightly quivering fingers. Maggie studied the baroque chandelier in the centre of the room, under which stood a round table heaped with fruits and cheeses and other delicacies.

Smoked salmon and caviar, thought William. Serpentine brass vines sprouted into tiny shaded lamps on the maroon walls.

'I told her she was a dirty woman,' said Alex.

'She didn't need you to tell her,' said Maggie. 'She lived with the truth about herself for a long time—too long.'

'Alex is sad because he doesn't believe in suicide,' said William. 'Personally, I couldn't care less, but nobody likes to be so close to such things.'

'Reality is always harder,' said Maggie.

'Oh, reality, reality! I'm sick of the word,' said William. 'When the hell are you going to stop talking about reality? You sound like some damned sophomore from Sarah Lawrence.'

They fell into an awkward, heavy silence again. It had been a mistake, thought William, to allow her to come along. She couldn't possibly understand Alex. Now she would only try to cheer him up. He turned on her suddenly and said, 'Tell us about your adventures in Mallorca, Maggie. Didn't you once live here with a puppet-master named Juan Rieras?'

Maggie blushed and Alex looked up with curiosity. Her recovery was swift and smooth. With her eyes fixed on William she leaned back in her chair and smiled. 'Poor Juan. What a marvellous man. You would have liked him, Alex. He inherited an old puppet theatre from his father and he asked me to help him reopen it.'

'Yeah,' said William, 'so they climbed into bed to talk it over.'

She went on, ignoring him. 'He was touring Europe as a street magician and juggler. I met him in Greece. He was a real artist with his hands.'

'I bet he was,' said William.

'Oh, hell,' said Maggie. 'You just can't leave things alone. You know the story as well as I do; why don't you tell it?'

'No, no,' said Alex. 'Let me tell it. I bet I know it better than either of you.'

The evening settled over them. They drank a great deal of wine and the Countess faded into a bad dream.

'Why have we come here?' said Alex.

'To see an old man named Gregory Winters in a village called Caladea,' said William.

'A horny old bastard who writes mediocre love poetry,' said Maggie. 'William likes him.'

'I never said I liked him. I said he was a good poet. And what's more, at his age he's still knocking off sixteen-year-old virgins, which is pretty impressive.'

'I don't believe it. He's got a beard down to his belly and he never takes a bath.'

William shrugged. 'There's no accounting for taste, is there. Some women like clean-shaven young boys and others like dirty old men.'

'I wish somebody would footnote this conversation for me,' said Alex. 'It's much too subtle.'

'Don't worry about it,' said Maggie. 'It will all get clearer soon.'

The *sirocco* swept across the island, the hot wind from Africa. They had come out of the air-conditioned unreality of the Hermitage Club into the gusty furnace of the oppressive night. William could not breathe. His chest was like lead and his temples throbbed. He took Maggie's arm to steady himself, and she seemed to know without his telling her what was wrong.

At the hotel where they had adjoining rooms they threw open all the windows, but there was no way to escape the heavy air. It was inside and outside and all around them. Alex complained drunkenly, and then grew very drowsy. They put him to bed in the large double room and sat for a while on the small terrace of the other room, the one intended for Maggie.

'It will last for at least three days,' she said. 'It's always about the same—three days.' She lit a cigarette and stared out towards the harbour. The water was dark and calm. A wide semicircle of lights marked the hotel-infested shore.

They sat in bamboo chairs that were separated by a small

round table. William undid his tie and also lit a cigarette. 'Is this the famous wind that drives everyone mad?' he said.

'Yes. And I think it's true.'

'I've never felt so strange in all my life.'

'Some people are more sensitive to it than others,' she said.

'On the way to the hotel I was sure I was going to fall down.'

'I could feel you leaning on my arm. Maybe you had too much to drink?'

'No. No, this is quite different. Suffocation and derangement! I couldn't breathe, and I thought my brain was disintegrating. I mean, I had the peculiar feeling that it wasn't going to function any more, that I was going to ask it to do something or think something, and then nothing would happen, or else something totally unexpected would happen. I can't describe it.'

'Madness,' she said with a quiet laugh. 'It's exactly how I always imagined it!'

'No,' he said. 'There's a rotten hot wind blowing. The air pressure has probably gone up or down drastically, whatever it does at times like these, and done something to my sinus, that lowly cavity, which, in turn, has given me an oppressive headache.'

A gust of wind swirled with a rushing sound through the branches of the trees below them in the courtyard. A shutter banged on the next terrace. William slouched in his chair but said nothing. The wind died down for a moment, but then began again, stronger than before.

William got up and went inside. He turned on the lamp over the bed and sprawled out. Maggie followed him and sat down at the foot of the bed. 'So here we are,' he said. 'You and me and the blind pirate.' He smiled and shook his head. 'And in my sirocco-nutty mind I keep thinking I should strangle you, or that I might without being able to help myself.' The perspiration glistened on his forehead and he pressed the palms of his hands together near his mouth as though he were about to pray.

'Perhaps you will before the night is over.'

His eyes narrowed as he stared at her. She came in and out of focus like a colour-slide being adjusted in a projector. The green of her dress blurred, and with it the clear outline of her long graceful body as she stretched herself along the foot of the bed, leaning on one elbow to face him. Her string of pearls faded into a streak of white, and for a moment he saw again the composed face of the Countess as she appeared for dinner. The pearls! She also wore them. The same pearls. He was walking in Regent Street on a rare and beautiful sunlit day in the autumn. It was Maggie's birthday, a little more than three months after their marriage. He searched the town for books and records, antiques and jewellery with no idea in the world of what to get her. How impossible it always was to buy things for her! Each idea was washed away with another double Scotch, until, with flushed face and mind, he thought of pearls. He reeled home late to a spoiled surprise dinner and wrestled Maggie out of her sad patience and anger with bear hugs and flying fragments of lectures on the beautiful agony of the sick oyster and the symbolic power of the pearl in myth and legend and life itself.

'Do you remember where you got those pearls?' he said.

She nodded. 'And I also remember what we almost had for dinner that night.'

'Don't tell me; let me guess.' He looked towards the ceiling, his brow wrinkled, like a slow-witted student searching for one of those obvious dates in history. 'Spare-ribs, sweet and sour, mashed potatoes, artichokes, a simple, unassuming red wine, and a heaping bowl of fruit.'

She laughed. 'Yes. It could have been that.'

'You were thirty-three years old and I called you Lady Christ.'

'You always made nasty little religious jokes about me—or are they anti-religious jokes? Or just anti-Maggie jokes?'

'You inspired them with that silence and pride and tall dignity of yours. You were always so tolerant and patient. You never condemned me for anything, never threw a rolling-pin. I was the fitful, dirty, wandering child, and you were the saintly fountain of all forgiveness, saying always "I understand. I understand. We are all what we must be." You spread out those long arms of comforting kindness and all I wanted to do was to drive nails through those generous hands of yours.'

'Would you have preferred a nagging, bitchy little wife with suburban ambitions and a profound distrust of men? Someone who would make you sign in and out of your own house as though it were a girls' dormitory?'

'No. I preferred you, but you drove me nuts with that aloof, all-forgiving benevolence of yours, as though you were constantly reminding me that big Maggie St. Claire encompasses all foibles and peccadilloes and understands even the most complex evils of the human heart. When I played around with that pink little girl at Stanley's party, you said absolutely nothing, though you knew damned well what happened.'

'It wasn't important.' Maggie turned on to her stomach across the bed and tapped ashes on the floor. 'No more important than what happened in Rome with Marguerita.'

The muscles of his face tightened. 'You knew about that?' He was damp and his breathing was laboured. He leaned forward towards her and swayed back and forth like a cobra. 'Did Alex tell you?' She raised herself up again on one elbow, but otherwise was very still. The two of them suggested at that moment the snake and the charmer, though she might also have been the transfixed bird.

'No,' she said. 'I saw you from the window.'

'I don't believe you,' he said.

She looked away from him and said nothing. The distant sound of traffic along the harbour road and music from another room intruded on their silence. At last, William leaned back for a moment and then got out of bed and started to undo the buttons of his shirt.

'I'll take a shower,' he said quietly. 'This heat is too much.' He went into the bathroom and closed the door half-way. She heard him undressing and then she heard the water running. It reminded her of that hazy army of days they called their marriage, five hundred days and nights, coffee in the morning, at first around ten or eleven, and then afterwards, when William decided that it was time to work hard again, at seven or eight; the sound of his typewriter, or the long silences between sudden outbursts; the smell of tobacco in the small flat, the heaped-up ashtrays; the tiny wardrobe where their unpressed clothes intermingled; and the long evenings in bed. Talking. Fighting. Making love. The long nights. The wakeful nights. She would stare out the window in the darkness of their small bedroom at three or four in the morning, listening to the sleeping animal beside her and wondering what she was doing there and how she could bear to spend the rest of her life with this angry, restless, uneasy man. On warm days she could smell the stale perspiration in the wrinkled, stained bed. She would get up quietly and smoke a cigarette by the window, allowing the cool night air to explore her naked body.

Visions of green rolling hills filled her mind, and white beaches and curling crashing seas under giant skies and searing sunlight. She filled her lungs with the cool air and stretched her arms out as if to embrace the world itself. She thought often of leaving suddenly, in the middle of the night, without so much as a note—of taking a train or a boat to almost any city or country, if only to be moving, to be getting away from the shadowy prison of that flat in London and the deadly, clawing embrace of this strange man who now called her his wife and demanded excesses of affection and admiration that she could never deliver.

And now, once more, she found herself alone with him in a small room, subjected again to him without knowing that that was what she intended to do. Once more she stood by a window and looked out longingly across the waters of the *bahia*. But this was another country, one of those exotic places after which, in those cold London days, she lusted. Now she was here, and still lusting, still longing.

She dropped her cigarette on the terrace floor and stepped on it slowly, feeling the slight heat penetrate the thin sole of her black shoe. She went into the next room and looked at the sprawling figure of Alex on the big double bed. He lay there in his underwear on top of the covers, breathing as though he were about to strangle. With a corner of the bedclothes she wiped his sweating face, lifting his eye-patch gently and then replacing it. He stirred but did not wake.

She went back into the dim light of the other room and stared once again out the window. A moon was rising over the silhouette of the cathedral. It was past midnight and the city was growing quiet. The wind was a hot breath from a leering, universal mouth. And now she could feel it, wrapping itself about her, pressing against her breasts and belly. Her body sagged with heaviness and a chill of murky excitement went through her.

William looked up towards the cold shower. The water rained on his face and ran in rivulets down his chest and shoulders. His spine was a river bed and his groin a delta. The heat was driven away and he recalled an old boyish impulse to run into the driving rain along the beach near Seaville. His hair would flatten over his head and stream down into his eyes. His shirt would cling to his warm wet skin. He would run and leap and shout on the empty stretch of sand until the cool breeze would reach him and he would feel the chills run through him as his shirt flapped against his stomach and back. Then he would run all the way home and strip down in the bathroom while his mother pleaded with him from the other side of the locked door to dry his hair and put on an undershirt.

He turned off the shower and pulled back the plastic curtain. As he did so he saw Maggie leaning in the doorway, smoking a cigarette. 'Hel-lo,' she said in that singing playful tone that always meant she was embarrassed or amused.

He picked up a towel and snapped it at her playfully. 'Get out of here you whore.' She backed up, laughing, and fell onto the bed. He followed her and threw himself on her like a wrestler about to pin his opponent. She punched ineffectually at his thick arms and shoulders. He threatened her with a growl and pretended to bite at her jugular vein.

'Vampire! Brute!' She tried to raise her knee towards his stomach, but he shifted his weight and flattened her against the bed. 'All right, all right!' she said. 'I give up. The triumph of brute force over beauty and brains.'

His growl became a laugh and instead of biting her neck he kissed it. She held his head against her chest and he could hear the rapid beat of her heart. A full minute went by and neither one spoke or moved. Then he pulled himself away from her slowly and, without looking at her again, went back into the bathroom and started to put on his clothes.

22

'THERE MUST BE an easier way of getting there,' said William. He shifted down as the road grew steeper and snaked its way along the terraced slopes of mountains that over the years were crumbling into ravines and cliffs, against which, hundreds of feet below, the immense, dazzling, hazy blue sea pounded like the gentlest but strongest of blue-eyed giants.

'Yes,' said Maggie. 'There is a more direct route, but it's not as beautiful, not as dramatic as this one.'

They were following the west coast of the island and heading north through Andraitx and Bañalbufar, climbing steadily higher into the spectacular mountains that guarded the peasant simplicity and remoteness of Caladea, the village where Gregory Winters chose to live.

Alex was lost in the colours and forms that showered him through a thousand keyhole glimpses. Sometimes he saw the blue of the sea, stretching out towards an indistinct horizon, and his breath quickened. He thought of his own town, the canal that came right up to his back-yard, the bay that he had sailed on and fished in all his life, the bay, never quite so blue as this water, in which his cousin drowned because he, Alex, could not see to save him. And then the car went around another sharp turn and the sea was replaced in Alex's field of vision by whizzing splashes of vegetation, some very close to the road, some further away. He imagined olive trees and palm trees, and he saw green patches laid against the sides of more distant mountains like ragged pieces of carpeting or small patches of moss. As the car slowed for another sharp curve a giant cactus plant came into focus, but just for a split second, and then a forest of pines. He could smell the freshness of the air. And everywhere, as they drove, he saw, punctuating his curious glimpses of sea and greenery, endless walls, blurred structures, slashes, columns, fields and mountains of stone. The island seemed to him a mass of crumbling rocks.

'Some of those trees are three thousand years old,' said Maggie. 'Just as ancient and grey as they look, old men subsisting on next to nothing, sucking a little dampness from the rocks. Incredible creatures.'

William watched the olive trees as he drove. Each one was different. Each one had found its own shape, adapting to the elements over hundreds and hundreds of years, to the wind and soil, the pruning, the violence of storms. They bent, turned, twisted, split, sprouted new limbs, fell and rose again—brave, immortal, wise old trees, driven by some ancient, mysterious impulse to go on living and bearing fruit, and revealing, as the lines in an old man's face reveal, every trial and tragedy, every tortured moment, every pleasure and instant of joy.

Now we are alone, thought Alex, sensing more than seeing the simple and grand juxtaposition of mountains, fields, and sea. He wanted the car to stop. He wanted to get out and sit quietly somewhere and listen to the church-like stillness of the place. But he said nothing.

They came to a village and stopped at a local store for some food and wine. The hot wind was still blowing steadily from the south and the sun baked the stone houses of the village. At a café they sat quietly and had a drink while flies buzzed dreamily about the sticky table-top. And then they were out on their way again, the busy, ambitious engine of the little Fiat intruding once again on the unreal silence of that post-card world.

At a place called Son Marroig, a crumbling grand estate built by the Archduke, they got out of the car at Maggie's insistence, and, carrying the two-litre jug of wine, the bread and cheese and smoked ham, started down a long, winding, rocky path towards a desolate precipitous peninsula called La Foradada, a thin ridge of trees and stone that reached out into the sea and culminated in a bare, hard, arrogant cliff, into which nature had bored an almost perfectly symmetrical hole, the huge eye in a thick, crude needle of land. Once the Archduke maintained a house out there for one of his mistresses, but now the house had fallen into ruin, and the road that lead there had also given way to wind and rain, so that it was, in most places, no more than a bed of rocks from which the packed soil had sifted away.

Maggie led the way. In her tennis shoes and tapering black slacks she was a tall, graceful creature. She leaped from stone to stone, the wine-jug in its straw covering swinging at her side. 'Come on,' she sang out from fifty yards ahead of them.

William and Alex had given up their suits for sports shirts and slacks. 'Take it easy, Doc,' said Alex as William urged him on. 'It's a sheer drop along here.' William carried Maggie's canvas sack, which contained the rest of their picnic.

'Look up for a minute at the weird formations in these cliffs,' said William. They paused and Alex inspected the cave-like openings, the damp, dripping, almost metallic surfaces of the eroded mountainside which they were descending. 'See the dragon's teeth and the huge broken wing of a bird.'

Alex nodded. He felt the sea pounding below them among the boulders and in the shadowy coves. There was comfort and terror in the sound.

'The path seems pretty good from here on,' said William. 'Just hold on and we'll catch up with our girl guide.'

'She can really fly over these rocks,' said Alex.

'Being so close to nature drives her slightly wild. She's like Rima the bird-girl come home to her native forest to gossip and giggle with the birds and listen to the ancient wisdom of the wind.'

'Me Tarzan; you Jane,' said Alex with a grin.

'I sometimes think she really does have an in with Nature,' said William. 'At Castiglioncello she swam and drifted among those rocks for hours and hours and then basked out there like a mermaid. When she finally came in she always looked a little different. She had a smile on her face that made you feel that she was harbouring some wonderful or terrible secret, but a secret that was half-hidden even from her and would fade altogether the moment she had her feet firmly planted on the shore.'

Alex nodded. 'A strange and wonderful woman.'

'Be careful,' said William. 'Her charms are fatal.'

When they reached the ruins of the old house Maggie was waiting for them, her face flushed and her hair wild. 'From out there,' she said, pointing to the cliff at the point, 'you can see the whole coast, and the mountains on the shore behind us, and a whole semicircle of sea.' She waved her long arms around and then went skipping off toward the stone steps that led to the terrace of the crumbling house.

To William the house looked like a pretty young girl who had been beaten up and raped and then left there, perched on those rocks, bruised and dirty and unprotected.

On the terrace Maggie took out the bread and cheese and broke off pieces for them. They passed the wine bottle and drank in turns. The walk had made them hungry and the food and wine were good. But the air was still warm and thick and soon they were all drowsy. They went to the base of the peninsula, where the land broadened into a steep, beautiful, rocky forest. Pine needles softened the ground and the trees provided a protective shade. There they rested, smoking cigarettes and sipping occasionally from the wine jug.

'Pirates roamed these waters once,' said William.

'Maybe we should give it a try,' said Alex. 'All three of us.'

'I don't have an eye-patch,' said Maggie.

'And I'm afraid of deep water,' said William.

'A fine crew,' said Alex. 'All any of us can do is talk.'

They laughed and stumbled their way up the rocky path. When they reached the top, sweating and winded, they paused to look back towards the rocks and the sea. 'Do you think we'll ever come this way again?' said Alex. Maggie and William looked at each other, but neither answered him. The warm wind curled around them and whispered through the olive trees.

23

GREGORY WINTERS COMMITTED his first formal act of cold-blooded rebellion in 1905, when, at the age of ten, he took his mother's ·poodle, diamond-studded collar and all, to the rooftop of the fashionable apartment building on Park Avenue in which they lived and threw the squealing, over-fed, over-petted creature into the sun-blessed street below. Prior to that time his brooding had been more passive, more Hamlet-like. He would refuse to eat. He would hide in his room and draw pictures in which he hanged his entire family, his fat father (a judge), his skinny mother (a psychotic social-climber), and his pimple-faced teen-age sister (destined years later to become a short-haired feminist).

Before he was sixteen he was, quite justly, disowned by his Victorian daddy, who not only feared for the boy's immortal soul but for his own skin. Little Gregory was by then six feet tall and quite capable of murder. The break was swift and final. There never was again communication of any kind between Gregory and his family. He went to sea, painted in Paris, escaped the war by pleading homosexuality, and then disappeared behind a beard into the wilds of Brooklyn, where he lived in erotic obscurity with a series of mistresses and two wives. In 1928 he moved to Greenwich Village, drank himself into a liver condition, started a little magazine called *Orfeo*, and acquired a degree of notoriety for a dirty novel called *The Nymphomaniac*. Poems leaked from him like premature ejaculations, and his work was called *experimental*. He wrote about love, about how it doesn't exist or does exist, about how much it hurts and about how it doesn't matter. He attacked his middle-class American society. He preached, at various times, anarchy, socialism, monarchy, free love, ritualistic masturbation, cannibalism, Zen Buddhism, hedonism, racial integration, and existentialism. But, finally, he decided that philosophy was a bore and that one should be guided always by instincts and visions. He read Plotinus and T. S. Eliot, E. E. Cummings and Robert Graves. He flirted with Christianity and was much taken with the lives of the saints. Meanwhile he was growing older and his teeth went bad. He divorced his second wife because she refused to sleep with a friend of his, and took up with two young lesbians named Georgia and Virginia, who called him Daddy Winters and encouraged him to start a bacchanalian cult of his own, built around his mystical leanings and his sexual perversions. He wrote a little book called, *Passion, Pity, Penis-Envy, and Paradise*, in which he stated that God is the great Penis in the Sky, and that one should celebrate him and try to achieve a union with him through a humble abandonment to all the natural impulses. He was arrested for conducting orgies in New York and was forced to flee to Europe in order to continue his work as priest and prophet. After brief adventures in half a dozen countries, he settled in Mallorca, in the ancient seaside village of Caladea. There he bought the ruins of an old fisherman's house built into one of the many caves that puncture the eroding cliffs along the sea.

For ten years he reigned in his primitive little kingdom by the sea, a combination painter and poet, Poseidon and Satan. In the winter he was a lonely old man who swam in the nude in the icy waters and paced through the village like a ghost of himself. The villagers dismissed him as *loco*, but the literary world, enchanted by his eccentricities, began to read his books.

In the summer he attracted a small colony of beatniks and drifters who sat at his feet, listened to his gibberish and delighted in his antics, as though he were, indeed, leading them to the promised land of full identity, free sex, and marijuana. His two lesbian daughter-figures had long ago been replaced by a middle-aged English woman who looked deceptively like a retired nurse or librarian, but was actually the alcoholic former wife of a member of parliament. The embarrassed Conservative bribed her with monthly cheques to stay out of the country. She took good care of Gregory, especially of his public relations.

The summer crowd came mostly from the Village in New York and equivalent areas in London and Paris. Occasionally some guilty-looking Germans showed up and tried very hard, but with no success, to learn how to surrender themselves to a life of sheer lazy pleasure. The permanent foreign residents and the natives of the place both resented the summer people and the old rotten melon who attracted them like flies. And hence the community was, like all communities, divided.

Into Caladea, then, came Alex and William and Maggie, a bit dreamy and excited; a bit pre-occupied. They sat at the café. An ageless waiter with a round, indifferent face glided across the shaded terrace with a tray of drinks. The ice tinkled in the glasses as he set them down. The afternoon sun roasted the mountain village. The long siesta was over and people began to stir. A burro cart went by slowly on the road, an old man bent over in the seat as though he were trying to escape the heat. The sound of the wheels on the paving was the ancient sound of wood on stone—dull, rumbling, full of patience and history.

At the next table a small group collected and gradually expanded to eight or ten. The men were all bearded. The women were all bored. They mumbled or sighed and looked away from one another towards the mountains or the houses of the village or the road. They sounded as though they wanted to converse but didn't know how. At another table two men played chess. They were young, and almost certainly American. One of them drank orange soda and nibbled at packaged cakes.

The crumbs dribbled down his beard. He moved his pieces on the board very quickly, and each time he moved his opponent twitched as though he were taken completely by surprise.

'I was only here once,' said Maggie, 'and that was a long time ago. It's a beautiful place.'

'Where's the beach?' said Alex.

'About a mile down the mountains,' she said.

William drifted. He imagined himself living in this village. With a beret and a beard he walked through the hills and along the cliffs. His bleached blue shirt hung loosely on his hard, brown shoulders. His face was lined and lean. Perhaps he would be a fisherman, setting out each morning before dawn and returning at noon with his catch. He would be alone on the gentle sea all day. He would abstain from everything and learn to enjoy the soothing, hypnotic mysteries of Nature.

'It was an awful winter in London,' he heard Maggie say. 'Very cold and damp.'

'Were you working?' said Alex.

'Not regularly. Some theatre work, mostly costumes.'

'What happened to the play?' said William. 'Your play.'

Maggie shrugged. 'I did another draft, but it's still not right. I'm afraid I made some of the characters too realistic. The original notion was to keep them looking like marionettes.'

'It all takes place on a merry-go-round,' William explained to Alex. 'With circus characters.'

Alex nodded.

'Surrealistic is not quite the word to describe it.'

'No,' said Maggie. 'I only wanted a device that would make the people involved more universal—and,' she hesitated, 'and more ghastly. In the sense that a clown is ghastly. With his painted face he suggests always a mask of joy over a real face that is not quite so happy, and often tragically sad. The concept is medieval.'

'The mask?' said Alex, interested and leaning forward on the café table.

'Yes, and the dualism,' said Maggie. 'The body and the soul, appearance and reality, heaven and hell, good and evil—are all medieval concepts.'

'And magic?' said William.

'Magic?' She looked at him curiously, as though she suspected that he might be mocking her. But he seemed quite serious.

'Yes, magic.'

'You mean magic in the mask?'

'No, I mean a world view based on magic and miracles.' He seemed reluctant to explain further.

'I think what he means,' said Alex, 'is that there is a common denominator in all the things that you have been talking about.'

'I'm sure there is,' she said, and noticed that several heads were turned in their direction. The people at the next table began to talk and fragments of their conversation were audible. Their mumbled statements were punctuated by tired laughter.

'Palma is the most *booring* city in the world.' The accent was French and the young man's voice was melodious and charming. 'Not a fucking thing to do all day, except sit at the Formentor Bar and watch the fucking tourists go by.'

'Paul is hitch-hiking from Paris with this wench he found there named Tina . . .'

A skinny blonde in skin-tight pants and a loose polo shirt sat reading with her knees bent up and her feet on the edge of her chair. 'What are you reading, Barbara,' said the shaggy young man next to her.

'None of your goddamned business.'

'Gee, I wish I knew how to read!'

'Try comic books.'

'And San Antonio is full of fat whores. Fifty pesetas for a piece of ass. Much easier than . . .'

'Kierkegaard! Jesus Christ!'

'She's been reading the same book for two years.'

'He says there's no more pot in Palma.'

'Yeah, but when Paul comes . . .'

'Tonight?'

'Yeah, tonight. His birthday. Don't you remember? At the *cala*. Like last year. In the caves, with fires and all that. We were down there this morning already collecting wood. Peter wanted us to carry the fucking piano down there.'

'Shee-it!' The girl giggled.

'And all those phoney cave drawings he's been doing. He even *looks* like a caveman.'

'Who?'

'What?'

'The sickness unto death?'

'Lend me a hundred p's.'

'I'm waiting for a check. The fucking *correos* must come by mule. Oh, man . . .'

Alex ordered another gin and tonic. He brightened suddenly, as though a happy thought passed through his mind.

Maggie lit a cigarette. 'We ought to be thinking about finding a pension or hotel for the night. I think there's one right up the hill behind this café.'

Alex leaned forward and half whispered, 'Hey, are you guys sure we're in Spain? I haven't heard any Spanish since we arrived. All I hear right now is English.'

Maggie and William decided to walk up the hill to the pension Mirador to inquire about a room. Alex insisted on waiting at the café. 'I promise not to move from this table,' he said with a devilish smile.

'By the time we get back he won't be able to move at all,' said William, as they made their way up the dirt road.

The higher they went the more they could see of the village. The houses were made of stone, brown mortar, and clay roof tiles; they seemed to grow out of the very earth itself, ascending the hill haphazardly towards the church at the top. Every inch of earth on the terraced hillside was cultivated. The stones were softened with ivy and morning-glories; there were lemon trees and orange trees, palms and almonds. 'It looks a little like Assisi,' said Maggie. William stared at the hillside and then towards the higher mountains that rose above the town, but said nothing.

At the pension a thin, middle-aged woman with a gold tooth explained to them in a combination of languages what accommodations were available. She stood there in the *entrada* smiling and frowning all at once and wiping her hands on her dirty apron. Maggie negotiated in a broken Spanish that impressed

William. They selected two rooms and dismissed the landlady by handing her their passports. Maggie closed the door behind them and stretched out on the double bed.

He watched her. She sat up dreamily and took off her blouse. 'It's very warm,' she said.

William lay down beside her. He pressed his mouth against her bare shoulder, and then reached behind her back and undid her bra. He saw the smooth white curves and the brown nipples close to his face. He reached towards her with his tongue like a slow-motion serpent, hesitated, and then barely touched the tip of her erect nipple. She shivered slightly and sank back onto the pillow. 'Devil!' she whispered.

He took off the rest of her clothes and then his own. Side by side, their legs and arms touching, they waited, as though neither one wanted to begin, as though this moment just before they flung themselves down into the sea was the real climax, the moment of greatest tension and most delicious anticipation. Maggie stared away from him out the window towards a white-blue sky and mountain peaks, but her hand moved towards him as though it were acting uncontrollably or with a will of its own. She touched his hip and his thigh. The warm air pressed him to the bed. He imagined he heard the throbbing of the sea. Then Maggie turned towards him and he felt the weight of her body against his. He pressed the palms of his hands against her small, round buttocks and drew her closer still. The drums inside them grew louder and they could not speak. Their bodies were fiercely entangled, as though they were both lovers and wrestling enemies. He wanted to sink his teeth into her soft breasts. He wanted to squeeze her thighs until she screamed. Their mouths were joined hungrily, almost desperately. They turned as one graceful, monstrous body and were completely joined as he pressed himself full-length against her.

Time dissolved. They floated. They drifted, luxuriating in the hardness and softness of their bodies. Unstrung words tumbled over them and fell away like loose pearls, and their nakedness became profound. They unfolded like all life evolving and discovered secrets in the marrow of their bones and the chambers o ftheir hearts. Reality wavered; everything lost its shape—language, flesh, faces, furniture, mountains, sky, and even all memories of places and people and concrete objects.

Together, through their very flesh, they threatened to tear away from their flesh-bound world. But something held and they were snapped like the end of a whip and exploded back into time. Awareness descended like ice, and they lay once more side-by-side in stunned silence.

24

'HAVE WE DIED already and gone to hell?' said Alex.

'No,' said William, 'it's only the middle of the Journey. I am Virgil and this is Beatrice, whom you loved at the age of nine. We have come to show you all. We will show you all. The hot flames flicker in this underworld. See the shadow-shapes of damned souls. See them squirming in their agony.'

'I only see shadows,' said Alex. 'Fire and shadows.'

'Plato's cave. The shadows cast on these walls are your reality. Some day one of us will escape and see the world as it really is. He will come back to this cave and tell everyone what he saw and they will say he is mad.'

Stalactites hung from the high ceiling of the yawning cave like swords or dragons' teeth. Torches rammed into crevices and pockets illuminated the giant room. The slimy rock glistened like serpent's skin. Cathedrals and grottoes, organs of the body, eyes, hands, breasts, mountain villages, craters of the moon, and an endless hint of ghastly faces. A huge fire in the centre of the place hypnotized the satyrs and maenads, who sat in a circle or lounged on balcony-like ledges. The smoke was sucked up into the high, vaulting darkness above.

'There's an opening up there,' said Maggie, her face tinted yellow-red in the firelight.

'What's going to happen?' said Alex. 'Who's voice is that?'

The old man droned:

The pomegranate springs from my spilt blood.
Twice-born I rise again,
Horns curving through serpents,
The shifting shapes of animals
Stalking through vineyards
To strike fear and wonder
In the dazzled minds
Of evil kings and innocent maids.

'It's the old bastard himself, Gregory Winters. He's reading from small white squares of paper and his hand is shaking.'

'Why is he trembling?' said Maggie. 'He looks so old.'

On rocks heaped like a throne overlooking the fire sat the withered poet, his thin face and bulging eyes almost lost in the encroaching hair and beard.

'I haven't seen him for ten years,' said William. They found a shelf of rock and squeezed together on it, comfortably lost in the shadows.

Music came from above the throne—two guitars and a penny whistle. Gregory Winters paused, leaned forward as though he were searching for someone in the recesses of the cave, scratched at the bare shoulder that his sheepskin did not cover, and then began again:

Madness whirls me
In wandering conquest.
Rivers of blood burst from the rocks,
Wine laps the shores
Wherever my wild foot comes down.
From Egypt to India
The murdered goats scream.
Ammon is saved
And Lycurgus cuts apart his own son.
The vine-bridge spans the Euphrates
And the east is ours.

Then Thrace, Boetia, and Thebes,
And still no end to rage and lust,
No peace until the weary, joyless world
Succumbs,
And I am placed among the holy twelve,
Secure in heaven
With my father Zeus.

'What the hell is he talking about?' said Alex, wiping the perspiration from his face and forehead with the back of his hand.

'I think he's lost his mind,' whispered William. 'He thinks he's Dionysus.'

'It's only a poem,' said Maggie. 'And not bad either. Powerful. Intense. Not even obscure.'

'Not to you, maybe,' said Alex, 'but I don't know what he's talking about. Except the wine lapping the shore. Does that mean Dionysus? Is that what he's referring to? The wine god? Or is that Bacchus?'

'Hence, the bacchanal,' said William.

'Which reminds me,' said Alex. 'Is there a bar in this hole?'

They looked around. 'There's a waterfall of wine,' said Maggie. 'Oooo! And pretty by torchlight. Look at that.' A huge barrel was perched high on some rocks and allowed to seep out its contents slowly over steps of stone. The rivulets ran splashing down into a large wooden basin at the bottom, which was periodically emptied into the barrel again, but en route the wine was caught in cups and glasses by the members of the curious gathering. Gregory Winters was served a silver goblet on a silver tray. He raised it in a toast, which the noisy crowd echoed. 'To the forces of darkness,' he bellowed, and his followers chanted in unison, 'To the forces of darkness.' 'To the unshackled Bull!' he growled, and they answered again in chorus. 'To the nymphs of the Hyades! To Persephone and Hermes! To freedom and joy and the fruit of the vine!'

Shouts and applause followed the toasting ritual and William was reminded of a football rally he once took part in. Beat Navy! Beat Army! Beat Notre Dame! Whichever it was. Tear them to pieces. Drown them in blood. The blood of the goat. The blood of the lamb. Victory is ours. And he, too, stamped his feet and pounded his fist on the wooden railing. He wanted blood. He wanted to destroy the helmeted, faceless enemy. And because they were the enemy they were evil. But because he was their destroyer he, too, was evil. God is on nobody's side. He protects no one, neither victim nor murderer. He cares for no one. He sits in airy silence watching with indifference the stupidity of heroism or cowardice, love and hate. To him it means nothing. He is not even amused.

'I want a cold beer,' said Alex. 'I wish we were in Seaville, where the refrigerator is full of beer. On a hot night like this we could sit out on the canal and wait for a cool breeze from across the bay. We could see the lights of the house and know that all was well, that the children had all been put to bed, that Helen was inside picking up toys or folding clothes.'

'I'll get you some wine,' said Maggie.

'No, I'll go,' said William, but before he could move Maggie was gone, into the restless, shifting circle of bearded young men and unpainted girls. He watched her go, watched her pick her way through the hot pack of lean young bodies. They greeted her. They touched her. She held someone's naked arm. He was tall and stripped to the waist. He wore a Western moustache and sideburns that made him look like a prospector or a cowboy. Tight-fitting blue jeans emphasized the flatness of his sweating belly and his lean hips.

At the waterfall some girls in bikinis giggled as the wine splashed against the rocks and landed in purple-red beads on their white skin. They leapt away with empty cups, their breasts bouncing and limbs flying. But then they returned daringly, stubbornly, to try again. One girl stood there boldly, the wine running into her cup, and splashing from the rocks onto her chest and belly. She stood there, her eyes half closed, long after her cup was filled and rubbed the dampness into her hot skin.

Maggie approached cautiously, her clinging white jersey as yet unmarked. Excitement showed in her lighted face and open-mouthed smile. She wants to take her clothes off and dive in, thought William. She wants to feel the wine running through her golden hair and over her body. He remembered how he teased her in bed once, as she lay there naked. He held the wine-glass high over her belly and threatened to pour it out. She laughed and dared him and he tipped the glass further until a thin stream trickled down, made ribs across her flesh, stained the sheets, collected in her navel. And then with his hands he smeared the wine over her breasts and she arched her back with pleasure. He was laughing too, and drunk already. He rubbed his face against her and licked up the combination of wine and sweat, lingering at her navel as though it were a trough, and pressing his mouth over her nipples.

Maggie approached and retreated several times, until the cowboy came to her, took the cup from her hand and plunged into the waterfall. He handed it back to her with a broad, muscular grin. She asked for another and he repeated the exhibition. He followed her with his eyes as she walked away, and then rejoined the circle, which was tightening again for another ritual. Gregory Winters was standing over them with his arms spread out and his eyes fixed on the darkness above.

'Can you see him?' said William.

'Yes,' said Alex. 'When he stands there I can see him. He looks as though he wants to fly, but I don't think he'll ever get off the ground.'

'He wants to look like Christ.'

'Everybody wants to look like Christ,' said Alex.

'The urge to suffer.'

Alex shook his head. 'The urge to live.'

'To be embraced by Big Daddy God?'

'No, to be nailed into immortality. It's worth it, don't you think? What, after all, did Christ have to lose? He knew he belonged to heaven.'

'That's more than we can ever know.'

Alex watched the old man. 'He can't be both Christ and Dionysus.'

'Why not?'

'It's like a mixed metaphor, Doc. You know that.'

'History is full of mixed metaphors. Christianity is full of pagan rituals and symbols. Cannibalism, blood, and all that.'

This is the blood and the body of Jesus Christ Our Lord, thought Alex. The Sunday morning service in Seaville sprang into his mind, his children dressed in starched clothes, the girls in white shoes with miniature purses and flowered hats. Easter. Dinner at his brother's house. Uncles and aunts, mothers and fathers, gravy on the new dresses. He knelt at the altar and took the wafer from the priest. The body of Christ. Cannibal! And the wine which the priest held. The wine that poured now in this waterfall of blood. This is the blood of Christ. Candles and incense and Helen McGuire at the organ. A choir of voices from above—*Ave! Ave Maria!*

Maggie returned, holding out two brown crockery cups overflowing with wine. 'We'll have to share,' she said. 'I couldn't carry three. That waterfall is great fun. Somebody had a stroke of genius.' She looked at her shirt. 'Damn,' she said. 'It's all stained. I thought I was careful.'

'You had help,' said William.

A hush fell over the room. People took seats. Burning eyes peered from the darkness of the niches and shelves. Hunted animals! 'I think they're going to kill a goat,' said Maggie, her voice descending gradually into a whisper as the silence thickened in the cave.

'Where? Where?' said Alex.

'They're dragging him in now,' said William.

Three executioners in beards and brief black bathing-suits pulled at a rope to which was tied a terrified white goat, a ram with beautiful curving horns. They hauled him into the centre of firelight and the circle fell back further as he thrashed and kicked. More ropes were tied to him and he was pulled in three different directions so that he was unable to move. Murmurs went through the crowd.

They're not really going to do it, thought Alex, and then poked William, who was also fascinated. 'Are they really going to kill it?' he said.

'It looks that way,' said William.

'Why not?' said Maggie. 'Might as well do it right. Old Gregory may be a slob, but he has a good sense of theatre.'

Two young women and an older man moved into the shadow

of the ledge on which they were sitting and leaned against the rocks. One of them lit a cigarette and inhaled deeply. Then it was passed to one of the girls. She did the same and stifled a cough. Once more it was passed and then a pair of pretty eyes looked around and up and saw the three figures on the ledge. The girl smiled and handed the cigarette up to William. He took it and smelled it. 'What is it?' said Maggie. He handed it back to the girl, who shrugged her shoulders and took another drag.

'What do you think it is?'

'Oh,' she said. 'Why don't you give it a try?'

'No thanks! Why don't you?'

'I'd like to some time, just for the hell of it.'

'Well, there's plenty of it around here, I'm sure.'

'What's going on?' said Alex.

'They're all smoking pot,' said Maggie. 'Have you ever tried it?'

'You mean marijuana? No. I prefer brandy.'

She nudged him. 'Go ahead, Alex, be brave. The next time it comes around . . .'

He laughed. 'What do you think, Doc? Aren't you curious?'

'No. But you do what you please. I'm not your warden.'

'You are so! I can't do anything without your permission.'

'All right! You have my permission. Do you want me to write you out a note?'

'He's angry,' Maggie whispered to Alex, leaning close to him on the narrow slab of rock. William heard her but said nothing. He stared at the circle of faces and the struggling goat.

He folded his arms across his chest and clenched his fists. He hated them all for their youthful holiday spirit and their brutality, but still he wanted to see them kill this poor animal. If they hesitated now or called it off he would have been disappointed. He wanted them to prove that they were bloodthirsty little bastards, so that he could go on hating them, knowing that he was right all along, that even as a teacher he was right.

The group that sat and sprawled around this fire could have been a group of his students. He had gone with them once on a week-end excursion that they called the Spring Festival. It was at Coleman College when he was very young, still mistaken at times for a student himself. There were bonfires on the beach and songs. The camp was pitched among the dunes. But as the night wore on and the drinking grew more serious, the polite sons and daughters of middle-class bankers and plumbers dipped into savagery, revealed their contempt for all conventions and authority. They swam nude. They fought. They made love even within sight of the fires. The faculty consulted in desperation, and the next morning a solemn dean condemned them all in ministerial tones and announced that this would be the last of the Spring Festivals. With dazed indifference the weary students listened, remembering with secret delight the revels of the wild night. And even he laughed at the pompous and frightened dean, his sympathies in those days more with the students than with authority.

And he, too, had been an offender—half against himself, because he had lain in cosy darkness with two co-eds and talked about Dostoevsky and existentialism while his hands wandered, accidentally, to their naked thighs and breasts. They conspired with him and went on talking, knowing that he could admit nothing, that he was trapped in his official position, but enjoying nevertheless, his youthful good looks and strength, enjoying it, in fact, even more, because he was their teacher, one of the wise men, one of the father figures who beat them into responsibility and maturity. One girl lay on her belly, her cheek resting on his thigh. With innocent nonchalance she drew one arm up over his leg and leaned it against the swelling bulge in his bathing suit. Even in the darkness he could see her small round buttocks flexing now and again with excitement. He let his hand wander to her legs and then fall between them. He felt the soft curve of her cheek and the edge of her bathing-suit, but he could not allow himself to go any further. Whatever they did as they lay there had to be subtle and surreptitious. The American way! Everyone had to pretend to be ignorant of what was going on. Everyone had to go on talking. 'You remember I mentioned the similarity between Faulkner and Dostoevsky.' And the other girl pressed her large, half-naked breast against his arm as she reached across him for her pack of cigarettes.

When he thought about it afterwards he grew more and more furious with them and with himself—not because of his lust, but because of his willingness to take part in the lying and hypocrisy. They had seduced him not into sexual revels, but into a kind of anti-sexuality, a situation in which they were all perfectly safe. Nothing could be worse. Nothing could be more puritanical. Dirty little bitches. Eternal virgins, growing up to fill their frame houses with the stench of their cleanliness and efficiency, pretending to their desperate husbands that they are too tired or sick to perform the ritual of sex, and beating their children into stainless-steel images of themselves. It was the game they really wanted. The bonfire on the beach. The flirtation. Even an occasional abandonment in the dark, but only to achieve the necessary status of non-virgin. In broad sunlight, stricken with conscience and fear, they retreated to their sorority houses and coca-cola dives to scribble dutiful letters to daddy and mom.

And here, too, they played a game. It was a dance, a ritual, and therefore all right. They were sucked into nakedness, raped by their own suppressed excitement and desire—and not only for sex, but for blood, and maybe more for the blood than the sex. They rocked back and forth and began to clap rhythmically as the goat was prepared for the slaughter.

A girl in an over-sized and tattered blue shirt stood up beside Alex. 'Oooo!' she said, 'the man with one eye!'

'It used to be in the middle of my forehead, but I had it moved,' said Alex laughing.

'You mean a Cyclops,' she giggled.

'What a clever little girl,' said William sarcastically. 'I bet your mother's proud of you.'

'Who's your square friend?' she said to Alex, leaning against his leg.

'Be careful what you say about him. He's the ghost of a very famous gynaecologist from Boston.'

Maggie laughed and after a moment of reluctance William too laughed and raised his cup in a toast to Alex. 'Two points for you, Tiresias.'

'Hey, that's a great name,' said the girl. 'Is that your name?

Tiresias? I remember that from some course I took once.'

'No, that's only my nickname,' said Alex. 'My real name is Irving Schwartz. I'm a crucifix salesman.'

'And what's *your* name?' said Maggie, friendly but a bit patronizing.

'Marcia. My real name, believe it or not.' Someone tapped her on the shoulder and she turned. A tall blond boy handed her a cigarette.

'For the lonesome threesome from Daddy-O,' he said.

She held the cigarette out to Alex, who took it and looked at the twisted tip. He took out his lighter and lit the end. It flared up and the girl pushed his hand towards his mouth. 'Don't waste it, man!' He took a puff and inhaled. Then he coughed and shook his head.

'What a stink,' said Maggie. 'Don't get sick.'

Suddenly the clapping stopped and a single drum sounded. The girl disappeared and all eyes were fixed on Gregory Winters. In the silence even the goat stood still, his eyes shifting from face to face, his head lowered.

After a moment of dizziness Alex brightened. His heart fluttered once or twice and his head cleared. He chuckled to himself and took another drag.

'We are ready for the offering,' said the old man in his deep but raspy voice. He held up a large knife and slashed at the air. 'He is the lecherous destroyer of our vines. We offer his life as a gift to the gods. Their holy fire will consume his lust and strength. His blood will be turned to wine and we will drink it to absorb his wild spirit.' He stepped down off his platform cautiously, his skinny old man's legs protruding a bit ludicrously from his sheepskin skirt.

'A bad costuming job,' said Maggie.

'He should have consulted you,' said William.

'I would have dressed him in a simple white robe and put real snakes in his hair.'

The goat and the old man eyed one another for a tense moment. The ropes were drawn tighter. Gregory circled around and approached the animal from the rear. The guitar players came out into the open and joined the drummer. Together they played a slow funereal rhythm. A girl with black hair and a white abbreviated poncho held a large brown bowl a few feet from the goat's head. 'She'll catch the blood when he cuts its throat,' said Maggie.

Alex smiled. 'That'll teach him to crush our vines, our tender vines.'

'Tender grapes,' said Maggie.

'Roast him and eat him,' said Alex, taking a final puff on the cigarette. 'Shove a stake up his ass and throw him on the fire.'

'Is he drunk already?' said William.

'It's the pot. He smoked the whole thing,' said Maggie. 'Do him good. He can boast about it to his friends back in Seaville. That's what he really wants.'

'How do you know what he really wants?'

'He's a simple man, Bill. Simple and lovable. He's afraid he's missing a lot in life.'

'He hasn't missed anything,' muttered William. 'He's greedy. Just like you. Can't pass up any opportunity. Can't say *no*.'

'Except to women.'

'He would if he could, but nothing happens.'

'Conscience?'

'I don't know. Fear, maybe. Impotence. Guilt. Who knows.'

'What a pity.'

'But he's fine with his wife and has lots of kids.'

'I don't understand either.'

'He's just chronically faithful. The fool!'

Maggie looked at the smiling pirate. His face was relaxed though he squinted slightly to see as much as possible of the performance that was taking place in the centre of the cave.

Like Romans, thought Alex, straightening his back and imaging himself at the Colosseum in Rome once again. He sat like a magistrate in his choice box, surrounded by senators and beautiful women. His heart was steel. Let them die. Let them all die. Animals! Slaves! He tipped his head back and emptied his wine cup.

Gregory mounted the animal and, with his bare forearm, yanked up his head to expose his throat. The girl in the blue shirt came back and stood next to Alex again. She turned away from the scene. 'I can't stand the sight of blood,' she said. 'I wish he would get it over with.'

The goat struggled as Gregory raised the knife with ritual slowness. The girl in the white tunic came closer with her bowl. But just as the knife started to descend the terrified animal bucked and Gregory lost his balance. The ropes slackened. The goat kicked. Gregory dropped the knife and landed on his backside, his face an apoplectic fiery red. 'Hold the bastard,' he roared, struggling to his feet.

Maggie covered her mouth with both hands to keep from laughing. 'I haven't seen anything so funny since the Keystone Cops. Too bad. He was doing so well.'

Alex's expression did not change. He was Roman and stoical. It did not matter which animal was killed. William felt a moment of pity and embarrassment for the old man, of the sort that one feels sometimes at the theatre when an actor trips or drops something unexpectedly.

Three strong young men rushed to Gregory's assistance. They held the raging animal and wrestled him to the ground. The ropes were fixed again and once more the old man approached with his weapon. This time he did not wait. One mishap was enough. With vengeful fury he tore back the goat's head and slashed his throat. The blood spurted out towards the girl with the bowl, splashing over her white tunic. Sighs of relief and shouts of approval greeted the execution.

At the sight of the blood Maggie winced, but not because she was unaccustomed to such things. Her head was suddenly filled with the squeals of dying pigs, and she remembered that one day in particular when they sent for Stoney the butcher to kill a giant hog which they had been fattening up all season. Stoney came out in his station wagon, which was full of the tools of his trade. And Maggie came out to watch—not only the pig-killing but Stoney's son Jason, a strapping lad of sixteen who had come along to help.

She was fifteen at the time and beginning to blossom. Her father no longer kissed her and touched her the way he did when she was younger. Her tall thin boy's body was rounding into curves and bulges, and inside she felt very strange, at times dreamy and poetic, and at other times vicious and mean. She snapped at her father for nothing at all. But he, a handsome, lean man in his early forties, seemed to understand and said nothing. He almost seemed to be avoiding her and she was furious at him. Meanwhile her mother lay 'sick' in the house, which meant, she discovered a few years later, that she was drunk. The pig was very big and very tough. He took a long time to die and squirted oceans of blood through the slit in his throat. 'Bleed him good,' she remembered her father saying. It took five men to hold the creature still for his disgraceful exit from the world. There was a nip in the autumn air and steaming breath puffed from their mouths and from the pig's snout. The wrestling and screeching stirred something in her. Her heart galloped and her breath grew short. The men grunted over the kicking animal, pushing it, hugging it. When it was over, Jason backed away, his hands and arms covered with blood. She came to him and said, 'Do you want to wash up? Come, there's another pump around the side of the barn.' Jason followed her, innocent, shy, a handsome, lumbering farm boy. She took him through the barn and there threw her arms around him and kissed him hard on the mouth, until his surprise passed and his arms, blood and all, went around her in a clumsy embrace. Then they stood apart, both stunned, both stained with the pig's blood. They stared in silence for a moment and heard the babble of voices outside. 'Can you come here tonight?' she said. 'I mean right here to the barn about ten?' He nodded dumbly and she turned and fled through the back door and into the house to wash herself and her clothes in the locked bathroom. That night Jason met her and there in that barn, in the straw of the loft, she allowed him to make love to her, abandoning at fifteen her least prized possession.

Gregory Winters held aloft the bowl of goat's blood. 'Let this be our wine tonight,' he shouted, and handed the bowl to a young man in white calypso pants who carried it to the wine barrel and emptied it.

'I just went on the wagon for the night,' said William.

'Maybe it's good,' said Maggie.

Alex handed his empty cup to the girl in the blue shirt.

'Marcia, my dear, fetch me a drop of that stinking brew.'

The circle broke and a crowd gathered around the waterfall. Eager arms reached in to fill cups and glasses. Sometimes a head turned up to catch the cascading wine and blood. The goat was opened and cleaned and spitted over the fire.

'A good show,' said Maggie. 'Let's go backstage and shake the old man's hand. He's come a long way since he left the Village.'

They found him surrounded by half a dozen of his disciples, including a beautiful mulatto, rather conservatively dressed in a skirt and blouse. She looked like an aspiring young journalist from a Negro college in the South, trying to prove to the world that she could be just as passionless, efficient, and articulate as any blonde American beauty. But when she turned suddenly to look at the intruders her long dangling earrings glittered and her eyes flashed a combination of anger and desire.

Gregory pushed his way through the adoring circle and gave William an enthusiastic greeting. 'I saw you out there,' he said. 'I didn't think you would come.'

'I promised myself that this year I would make it,' said William. 'I think you've met Maggie sometime or other.'

He searched his memory. 'A long time ago, I think. Either in New York or Paris.'

'And this is Alexander Morgan, a very old friend.'

'I don't know whether I should shake hands with him or not,' said Alex. 'It might be grounds for instant excommunication.'

They laughed. 'He's a Catholic,' William explained.

'So am I,' said Gregory. 'Most of the time. I'm only a part-time pagan god.'

Alex felt Marcia standing next to him. He put his arm around her and said, 'Gee, Mr. Dionysus, I hope you don't mind if I borrow this little handmaiden for the evening. She's great.'

'Be my guest.'

William leaned towards the old man. 'Listen, Gregory, what have you got to drink around here?'

Gregory took him by the arm and said, 'Come into the house. We'll have a look at the private stock. I personally can't stand wine. And the idea of drinking blood makes my liver quiver.'

Alex had been dragged off again by his little nymph and Maggie was staring after him. 'I think I'd better keep an eye on your ward. He's beginning to stumble. Besides, you two probably want to talk.' She patted him on the arm and turned quickly away.

'Bitch!' muttered William as Gregory led him through a dark tunnel to an ancient wooden door.

'An ingenious arrangement. I think the place was once used by smugglers. You'd never guess there were all those caves behind the house. The tunnel is man-made.'

In the old fisherman's shack they sat opposite one another at a crude olive-wood table. Gregory brought out a bottle of Scotch and a kerosene lamp. 'It's the only thing I can drink these days.' His wasted old body still glistened with perspiration and his grey hair and beard hung damp and limp about his face and head. The room in which they sat was surprisingly ordinary with its white plaster walls, its stone floor and stone fireplace. A few modest abstracts decorated the walls, but they were not at all intrusive.

'I like those,' said William. 'Anyone I know?'

'Ralph Woodson. A very talented boy. American. He went mad a couple of years ago and threw himself into the sea. I think his work is just being discovered.'

Through a half-open door William could see into Gregory's study, a crowded little room full of books and an enormous desk. 'Talk about discoveries, did you know that Gregory Winters is now famous in the States?'

'So I hear. Almost what you might call posthumous fame.' He smiled and revealed a row of crooked yellow teeth. 'It should have happened thirty years ago.'

'Maybe you're a late bloomer,' said William.

'Late bloomer, shit! I had to come here and raise hell before anyone paid attention to my work.'

'As I remember, you weren't exactly a model citizen in New York.'

They drank the Scotch straight. Gregory coughed and

laughed and then drank again. A huge grey cat ambled into the room—from where, William could not tell. Perhaps he had come out of the wall.

'An Abyssinian,' said Gregory. They both stared at the animal as it posed in the middle of the floor. 'The last one on the island as far as I know.' Then he looked away and let his fist drop wearily, heavily on the table. 'The fact is that Americans don't know anything about literature, especially poetry. The mild resurgence of interest in the last ten years or so hasn't been in the poetry so much as in the poets—you know, Ginsberg and that crowd. It's the bearded, bleeding rebel that fascinates the middle-class son-of-a-bitch who has to catch his train every morning and sit behind a desk, or the school teacher, who has to stare at blank-eyed teen-agers all day.'

'And the college professor,' added William, 'whose life is just as dull.'

'In his fantasy-life the typical American is a sadistic detective surrounded by nymphomaniac blondes whom he alternately beats up and screws. His car is a big, glorified phallic symbol, a weapon—to make up no doubt for the concern he feels over his subtle castration, and not only by the little woman in the kitchen with her brand new combination electric can-opener and castrating gadget, but by the whole society that conspires to scare the shit out of every red-blooded male who thinks that he can still be a cowboy, that he can still exhibit some daring and individuality. If an American man is not scared, he is in a sense subversive. He has to go to the dentist once a year, surround himself with insurance, build a fence around his stinking little suburban house, send his wife for a cancer check-up, investigate the school system to make sure he's getting his tax-money's worth, bring his car in for a thousand-mile check-up, take vitamins, quit smoking and keep himself on a low-fat diet. That kind of goddamn Germanic discipline is enough to depress anyone. No wonder they go around committing suicide and murder all over the place. I don't blame them. But it's also why they like to talk about crazy bastards like me. Last year a guy from *Life* magazine came out to take some pictures and interview me. He didn't really want to know anything about my work or my serious ideas; all he wanted was the bizarre, far-out stuff—you know, this sheepskin bit, swimming off the rocks, the beatniks. So I gave it to him and a few months later my books were selling like dirty novels.'

William helped himself to more Scotch and leaned back in his chair. 'So you don't mean it after all? I mean, all this Dionysus jazz?'

Gregory frowned and scratched at his ragged head of hair. 'Sure I mean it. I think the Greek myths tell us more truth about the world than nuclear physics and Catholicism combined—if you could ever combine two such things.'

'It's been done, I hear,' said William.

Gregory rolled his bulging eyes towards heaven. 'O the genius and diplomacy of the Mother Church. Leave it to them Jesuits to find a way.'

'What I meant to say was, I don't understand whether you're doing this sort of thing to build yourself up as a legendary figure or because you really believe in it. I'm sorry, Gregory, I'm beginning to sound like some journalist who's been assigned to interview you on the occasion of your nine-hundredth birthday.'

'Listen, Bill, today I turned seventy, and I might as well be nine hundred. Old age is lousy. I hate it. But let me answer the question. I've had to answer it for myself anyway. No, I don't take it all literally. This Dionysus jazz is all drama, like the theatre. But even if the details are not literal, the sentiments or emotions can be real. I do believe in the life-force, though I'll be damned if I understand it. I don't believe in the conventional ways of conducting society. I gave up a long time ago trying to be sane in the usual sense. I found out when I was quite young that I was a crazy mixed-up guy. I figured I could do only one of two things—try to get with it, which would have meant a life-time of psychoanalysis and ulcers; or try to find a way of life that suited my peculiarities, which has meant a life-time of friction, rebellion, and pretty queer behaviour. No, I don't mean queer in that sense, though I wouldn't draw the line anywhere. If a guy is queer I think he should screw boys and not see his psychiatrist. That's what I mean. Either you suit the world to yourself or you try to bend yourself to suit the world. And many a poor bastard has broken himself that way because people just aren't that flexible or changeable. We are what we are!'

'Yeah,' said William. 'But people grow up. They mature. They think differently after a while.'

'Oh, sure! That's not what I'm talking about. Besides, they only grow up within their potential. They can't change basically. A rosebud can only open up into a rose; it can never become a tulip.'

William let the idea sink in while Gregory shifted nervously in his seat and turned his glass in its own wet circle on the table. 'I don't know why you're trying to pin me down, Bill. It's that goddamned metaphysical turn of mind of yours. Even in New York, I remember, you played young Socrates, always testing out other people's ideas—as if you were trying them on for size. Damn it, don't you have any of your own?'

'Suspended judgement,' said William. 'I'm waiting for the wisdom that comes with old age.'

Gregory squinted at him. 'Ah, now there's the mean streak in you—the healthy part. You're making fun of me. Good! Why not!'

William lit a cigarette and inhaled deeply, as though he were giving himself time to think. The Scotch relaxed him and lightened his head. Metaphors began to accumulate in his throat and chest. 'Now you're getting suspicious,' he said. 'Now I have to tell you why I'm so interested in all this. The fact is that I see a vague similarity between your life and mine, though one might not imagine it offhand. Naturally, then, I'd like to know what the hell you think you're doing.'

'I don't understand,' said Gregory. 'I'm doing now what I've always done, and the only thing I can do—I'm living.'

'I know, I know,' said William. 'That's a good stock answer, but be more specific. Does that mean you believe in nothing? Does it mean you're stymied? Does it mean you're in it for kicks?'

Suspicion and anger descended on his old face. He sipped at his drink and studied William's impassive expression. Was there a hint of a smile in the young man's face. Was he playing a game? Or was he dead serious? 'You're pushing me to the wall, Bill.'

'I mean to do just that.'

'It's not fair.'

'Why not?'

The old man got up and paced across the room. He toyed with a candlestick on the mantelpiece. 'Because I'm twice as old as you and I'm going to die soon. It's harder for me to say honest things.'

'I thought the older you got the more you could afford to be honest.'

'With other people, yes, but not with yourself.' He turned around slowly and stared at William as though he might suddenly leap on him. 'All right,' he said, 'I'll tell you what I really think. Caladea is a quiet place. In the winter it's remote. No one comes here. I spend a lot of time alone, except for Elizabeth. I find it lonely. I keep telling myself I should go to Paris for the winter, like the old days, but, frankly I don't have the energy for it, and, what's more, I don't believe in it any more.' He paused and chewed at his protruding lower lip. 'What I am trying to say is that I don't think my life means anything. It's taken me seventy years of knocking around to discover this abysmal truth. On the other hand, I think life *is* something, which is why I have never thrown it away. But it can *be* something without meaning anything. It's a bundle of guts wallowing in blood and nightmares. It's aching bones and warm jugs of wine. It's a hard-on at the beach and a big pair of white tits. It's love and hate, lust and anger, comedy and tragedy, all rolled into a fiery ball heading nowhere. That's the real message of Dionysus if you read it closely. Logic has nothing to do with understanding. And, what's worse, understanding has nothing to do with life. And what's still worse, life has nothing to do with anything else except itself. It's self-contained. No umbilical cord connects us with God. The universe is a glorious display of fireworks, but that's all. It means nothing.'

'So what does one do?' said William.

Gregory exploded into laughter. 'You dumb bastard. You're as bad as the typical American businessman. You want a pragmatic solution. What does one do? What's the plan? How do you beat the system? Oh, shit, Bill, get off it! There's no way to beat the system, because there ain't no system. You let go, that's what you do. Just let go, without being afraid of making a bad deal with life or yourself. No deals, boy. There are no deals.' He stepped slowly closer, his eyes wild with fury and excitement. 'You begin by living and end by dying. If you don't let go you never begin. If you never begin you might as well be dead. You have to throw yourself into the water, even though it's cold and you're bound to get your brains knocked out on the rocks. Jump in and raise a little hell. Stop figuring and figuring as though it were a horse-race that you think you can handicap.'

'But one has to make choices,' said William. He grew quiet and uncomfortable. He felt young and boyish in the face of this inevitably paternal howling.

'It doesn't matter what the choices are. It only matters that you choose swiftly and often. I never hesitated in my life. And I've never felt any remorse for anything I've done. Fuck if you want to. Write if you want to. Break rocks for all I care. Drink, paint, travel, fight, grow flowers, have kids, build houses or bridges. I've done my share of most of these things—but not to get to heaven; just to keep from dying. And here in this beautiful place I can play god and emperor. It's great sport in the summer-time. I amuse the kids and they amuse me. I tell them not to be afraid of life, and they jump around with their naked little asses hanging out. They're fascinated by life, by sex and a little violence. They come from London and New York, where their middle-aged daddies are all hanging themselves in the attic and their mothers are all secretly laying for the butcher boy. It's their holiday, but it's also mine—even if I can't get it up much any more.'

William poured them both another drink.

In the cave Maggie danced. The bare-chested cowboy sweated near by, clapping his hands and grinding his hips. She had tasted the wine-blood and the air was filled with smoke. Over the hot coals the dead goat roasted into black scabs and oozing juice. Usurping musicians cluttered the vacant throne. A wild boy with a blond beard pounded the back of his guitar. The whistler wailed and the drum signalled across the Mediterranean to black brothers crouching in the steaming jungle.

The circle had re-formed around the dancers, who performed alone, seized by the endless improvised rhythm. Three or four at a time they squirmed, twisted, jerked, and rolled, as though they were trying to shake loose from their bodies or from the circle or the world. They urged Maggie on. She felt the drum in her stomach. Her long legs parted. Her white jersey clung to her sweating body. The cowboy grinned, his eyelids drooping. 'All the way, baby,' he panted. 'All the way. Yeah. Yeah. Move it around. Move it around.'

And Maggie's hips churned and swayed. Her arms snaked over her head and around her own body. She wanted to tear the clothes off her hot body. She wanted to plunge into cool water. She turned and turned, and the fiery walls spun before her eyes. The cave tilted. The burnt and ghastly goat swept past her. She was twirling uncontrollably, falling towards the fire, then towards the wet body of the cowboy. 'Ah, baby. Ahhh.' And then his arms were around her, holding her on her feet. She felt his broad back, and his firm arms. 'One more time. One more time.'

She held her head. 'No. No, I can't.' Laughing and gasping, she left the circle, her arm still around the young man.

Others took her place. The crowd now chanted to a girl named Lola. They all knew her. The circle tightened and the rhythm grew faster. 'Roll it around, baby. Thump, Thump. Put it here, baby. Push hard. Push hard.' The buxom girl in the bikini grew wilder. Her breasts bounced under the narrow bra. Her round hips rolled and sucked in an imaginary phallus. The crowd rocked with dreamy eyes and wet lips.

The cowboy handed Maggie a drink and they crouched on a rock. She could hear nothing but the thumping of the instruments, which multiplied in the cave; and she could see nothing but the blur of heads, twitching and rocking, and the possessed, almost naked body of the black-haired girl. She danced around the goat, holding her breasts out to the fire, luring the dead creature with her seductive thighs, as though she expected any moment the spirit of Dionysus himself to leap out of the corpse and ravage her. A Negro joined her, lean and hard and shiny. He danced behind her, imitating her, like a shadow. He pumped his hips at her white buttocks and the circle yelled, 'Yeah, yeah!' His white teeth sparkled. His eyes laughed. They saw the joke, the black man's joke. His secret. He crouched. He leapt. A drama in pantomime of attack, of rape.

And she danced on, waiting, hoping, growing more and more excited at the threat. She knew the drama too. And all was still contained in the theatre. Reality did not intrude. The tension mounted and was perfect. Don't let it break, the circle thought. Hold it, baby. Hold it right there, but push it, man, push it! The drummer screamed and pounded harder. The Negro picked up the signal and with a graceful sweeping motion he tore the bra from the girl's body.

She whirled away from him, her arms outspread, and fell to her knees. Her back arched. Her eyes were closed. She trembled and shook. Her shoulders moved more and more quickly back and forth as she rose again. The motion rocked her breasts, bounced them from side to side. They slapped against each other and against her body. She was up again and still dancing, but then her pace slowed as though she were sinking into a dream. She squirmed. She quivered. The drum slowed. The Negro crouched over her, waiting, as though she were a dying animal. The crowd grew more quiet. Would he do it? Would he do it? The cowboy leaned forward, his hand pressing against Maggie's thigh.

The girl sank slowly to the ground, as though she were fainting in slow motion. The Negro stood over her, between her legs. Everything depended on the balance now. One false word, one hesitation in the rhythm of the drum and it was all destroyed. The beat continued. All the other instruments had stopped. He undid the simple knot of his loincloth and pulled away the rest of her bikini. The rhythm of the drum now grew firmer and louder.

The girl's head rolled back and turned from side to side. Her legs opened and her hips reached towards the black figure. For a moment the Negro was frozen into stillness like a predatory cat, his muscles tensed, his erection curving upward like a sword. Then he fell forward onto her body and with four or five quick strokes, like a fierce animal, he emptied himself into her struggling white flesh. The circle roared and clapped and jumped to its feet. The music picked up again and the two performers were separated and absorbed into the crowd.

'What happened' said Maggie, also standing, raising herself higher to search for the girl and her Negro lover.

'It's over,' said the cowboy. 'He did it. I didn't think he would.'

Maggie was flushed with excitement and anger. Why did they stop? Why did they smother it? It could have gone on and on. She had danced too. She could have danced again. But she had hesitated. She had not taken off her clothes, and no satyr ravaged her. Why hadn't she done it when she had the chance, sweating out there in the fiery circle. But now it was too late. The tension had broken and reality threatened.

'Crazy Sam,' said the cowboy. 'He got his in the arm tonight.'

Maggie looked at the hard face of her self-appointed escort. He was not as young as he looked earlier. Lines were forming around his eyes and mouth and his hands were not boyish. 'What's your name?' she said, swaying slightly in front of him.

'Albert Schweitzer,' he said.

'No, seriously.'

'What's the difference. I don't care what yours is.'

'I want to know. Your real name. Please.'

'Jim. Jim O'Hara.'

She was dizzy. She wiped her eyes with the back of her hand and held on to his bare shoulder.

'Come on,' he said. 'We'll get some air. We'll swim out to the boat.'

'The boat?'

'Yeah. My boat. I live on it out there in the *cala*.' He took her by the hand firmly and led her away from the fiery darkness of the cave into a gentler, cooler darkness. The surf grumbled lazily among the rocks.

Alex descended.

Marcia dragged him along by one arm, the torch she held, flickering dangerously near her shiny black hair. A frail blonde named Diana, also dressed in a bikini and a ragged man's shirt, tugged at his other arm. The stony path divided and they staggered into opposite directions. 'This way,' giggled Marcia.

'No, this way,' insisted Diana in a singing argumentative voice.

Alex felt their warm little hands on his bare forearms and wrists. He wobbled drunkenly and smiled into the darkness. The light of the torch swept past his field of vision erratically. 'To the sea. To the sea, my little nymphs, my mermaids. I long for the swelling breast of the sea.'

'The sea comes up through the bottom of the cave. It makes a pool down here. And it's around here past these awful gates and dragons' teeth and things. Don't you remember, you idiot.'

Diana stopped pulling. She looked around at the pockets and coves and shafts, at the jungle of forms, the nightmares of animals and ruined cities, and then shrugged her narrow shoulders. 'All right, Marcia,' she said, 'but if we get lost it's your fault.'

Diana punctuated her little speech with a hiccup and they were off again, half slipping, half stumbling, lower and lower into the bowels of the cliff. I have wings, thought Alex. I have wings and I will fly up through this rocky night like a giant bird. 'Are we flying, now?' he said.

'Man, are you flying,' said Marcia. 'And me too. Me too. My head is like clouds.'

'We can swim down there,' said Diana. 'It's warm. I remember how warm it was. Remember?'

'Yeah. And Daddy-O here will swim too, won't you, Daddy?'

'Like sharks, my little lovelies. Like sharks!'

'Hey, look at that one, Marcia,' said Diana, pointing to a stalagmite that grew from the floor of the cave. 'Looks like you-know-what, like Sam's big old pecker.'

'Brrr!' said Marcia. 'Did you see him. Gives me chills all over. That long hot thing.'

'And Lola eating it up.'

'Oh, rude little girls,' scolded Alex, like a benevolent and senile grandfather. 'Dirty rude little girls. Mustn't talk that way. No sex for dirty little girls. No candy. No dessert. Daddy will spank you. Daddy will take down the old razor strap and beat your little ass until it glows like a neon sign.' He saw the razor strap hanging in the bathroom at the old house. His father's hands were swollen. Arthritis. Pumping gas all day at Marty's station in the middle of winter. Poor old bastard. All he ever wanted was lots of coffee and a place to sit like a dog in front of the fire. Never said much. Nodded. Grunted. Farted sometimes. And his big fat Irish wife bellowing in the kitchen, cursing and scolding and drinking. He never did anything, she said. He never had fun. To bed always at nine o'clock. And up at six. One New Year's Eve he fell asleep in his chair while the party of noisy relatives whirled around him, and she reeled into the room, flushed with wine and started beating him on the head with a cushion from the sofa.

'I have mastered the art of walking on water,' said Alex to the staggering, laughing nymphs. 'A matter of mind over water. Sheer desire. If you want something badly enough . . .' Rough walls rubbed against him. Rocks fell away from under his feet. He was St. Peter in the dungeon waiting for his execution. Wormy prisoners lay about the dark room in hot misery, moaning and praying. He made signs of the cross over them. He struck water from the rock. 'I have worked a few little miracles in my time,' he said. 'Before you girls were born. Before my own girls . . .'

'I hear the water,' said Marcia. 'Wait. Be quiet. Listen.'

They listened. The pulse of the sea throbbed in the cave.

'But that was in another country,' said William, his head heavy with the oppressive air of the African night.

'And a long time ago,' said Gregory Winters, his nose a mass of bursting capillaries.

'Maybe you're right, though. Maybe I should have done it.'

'I think you should have done it. I think you should have been a professional football player. Not for the money, just for the pleasure. I used to follow the game in those days. I remember your ugly face all over the sports page. Crew cut, swivel hips, ovaltine smile.'

'Yeah,' said William. 'I was real healthy in those days. I could have made it, too. I even had offers. An easy life. Nothing to think about except the next game and the next contract. No stupid intellectual problems, no metaphysics, no nothing, except your own muscles and the enemy. Just have to remember all the damn plays. Some guy—who was it?—wanted to put little radio receiving sets in the helmets, so the coach could call the plays from the sidelines. He'd make us into robots. Next they'd shove a couple of electrodes or something up the poor guy's rear end and turn him completely into a machine. I should have done it. Nice train rides, or these days airplanes—jets. Good hotels. Mountains of food, steaks, vitamins, milk. Movies of the games, over and over, so you could see what went wrong or right. Narcissus leaning over the pool. Don't fall in. There goes big Bill Mariner off tackle. Keep your head a little lower. Bring up your knees. Crowds roaring all the time, and more coverage in the papers than if you were three senators.'

'Don't belittle it,' said Gregory. 'It's a kind of heroism. Better than art. Every little shit-head with a pimple on his ass and an unhappy childhood wants to be an artist. What's the big deal about art? Think of all the bad painters you know who could have been great dentists, or all the lousy sculptors who could have been brilliant plumbers. If I was smart I would have been a preacher when I was younger, instead of picking my nose in the Village. I could have been a great evangelist. Plenty of money. Plenty of women. Women love preachers.'

'Because they're all prostitutes at heart. Sadie Thompsons. They love to get the innocent bastard by the short hairs, and prove that he's human, that he's a man, and therefore seducible. Women hate men that they can't get to sexually, because for them there's no other way. Intellectually, men always prefer other men. Who the hell wants to talk to some pretty broad about Aristotle or Longinus. They're not really interested, and usually they don't know what the hell it all means anyway. All they really want is your hand between their legs.'

'Conversation is a sexual experience for women,' said Gregory. He shared the last inch of Scotch with William and they raised their glasses in a toast.

'To the many-cunted she-devil of the haunted world,' said William.

Gregory's hairy mouth stretched into a smile of broken yellow teeth.

On the rocky beach Jim O'Hara took off his skin-tight blue jeans and stood naked in the hazy heavy moonlight. 'Come on,' he said. 'It's only fifty or a hundred yards out.' The mountains rose behind them, a semicircle of giant walls, blocking out the hot southern wind. But the air was like molten lead. It pressed the surface of the water flat and diffused the yellow light of the moon. Maggie stood there, looking out over the vast surface of gently curving water. *Mare nostrum*, she thought. The same sea that touches Greece and Italy. How they feared it in the ancient days. Terrified sailors, thinking about home, about olive groves and wives and rolling solid hills. We swam in it at Castiglioncello. We basked in the sun among those rocks and listened to its long sad and happy tale, a million years of history. 'The sea is an old man,' she said, almost to herself.

Jim waded into the water up to his knees. 'Come on,' he called. 'It's warm and clear.'

Maggie pulled her jersey over her head and then undid her bra. Near the farm there was a lake, where, on nights like this, she swam nude and alone, dreaming of Greece and Spain, of Crete and Rhodes and Sardinia. What a lovely sound that was —*Sardinia*. It sang in her girl's mind with the voices of mermaids. Distant shores beckoned—places she had never seen and could hardly imagine, except in that dreamy way. The hypnotizing sun caressed the graceful palms. Schooners moored in coves and bays waited sleepily for her and her tall lover. They were her castles and cathedrals—those ships with their masts rising to heaven, piercing the blue sky or the dark night. And the pigs grunted in the distant pens, shoving their ugly noses into the mud and garbage of that horrible reality. And the lights burnt deep into the night in that musty house where her mother and father quarrelled and wept themselves into old age and despair.

She unhooked her slacks and stepped out of them. For a moment she hesitated, feeling her flat belly and pubic hair through the silk underpants that heightened rather than covered her nudeness. She took them off finally and walked into the water towards the silhouetted cowboy.

'It's deep, real deep,' said Diana. 'Nobody has ever touched the bottom.'

'Daddy Winters says it comes out in Hades a million feet down,' said Marcia.

'It's only the sea coming up,' said Alex.

'No, it's not the sea. It's something else.'

'It's a huge big giant hole in the ground.'

'Hold the torch still. Let me see,' said Alex. They stood on a flat rock, a ledge that hung out over the water. Marcia held the torch as high as she could. Its light shone on the surface of the black water. 'But I can hear the sea,' he said.

'It must be coming through the walls,' said Diana. 'We're far down.'

'Below the sea?' He said.

'Sure,' said Marcia. 'Under the bloody sea.'

The murky air turned to water in his mind. Underwater jungles tangled upward, lifted by the water. An upside down world. Hanging gardens. And myriads of golden fish. Striped, silver, black, big-eyed fish with silken fins, and sliding enormous silent monsters of the deep—prowling. How quick they are. How silent!

'Uncatalogued monsters of the deep,' he muttered.

'Let's throw him in and see if the fishes eat him,' said Diana.

'Yes, throw me in. Throw me in; I want to feel the black water. I want to swim.' He started to step off the ledge. His head was burning. His heart was pounding. The little hands that touched him all over were like the hands of his children.

'Wait! Wait! Take off your clothes.' And Marcia stuck the torch into a crevice and started to undo his shoes.

'Off with the rags. Strip to the bare flesh,' he said. 'And plunge in. Let's all go. Whoops, into the big black hole, into the water. Whoops, into Hades, down, down, down, into the old shark's mouth. Girls and all. Balls and all.'

They took off his shirt and pants. 'All of it,' said Marcia, and down came his underpants, tripping him. He fell onto the smooth flat rock, naked, bruised on the hip. They laughed, falling on him as they tried to help him up, their faces flushed, their legs unsteady. 'Big old fish,' said Marcia, her hand brushing his groin. He felt the weight of their tumbling little bodies.

'Come with me, little daughters, little nymphs of my darkness. I can't go alone into the big hole.' And he held onto them, an arm around each, as they laughed and struggled. 'Together we'll go down, all the way to the bottom and out the other end where the fires and shadows are, the roasting heathens.' A breast filled his hand and he squeezed it hard.

'Oh,' cried Diana. 'You mean old man. I'll show you.' And she reached between his legs for revenge. She tugged playfully and felt him growing stiff in her hand. She lingered and the wrestling grew less fierce.

'I'm going in too,' said Marcia, taking off her shirt and bikini. 'My head is so warm. I can hardly breathe.'

Alex lay stretched out on his back on the flat rock. Marcia stood astride his limp body and tried to drag him up by his wrists. 'Come on,' she said. 'Into the water old Daddy fish. Down into Hades with you, you dirty old man.'

Diana took off her clothes and came to Marcia's aid. She lifted a leg and held it like the end of a log. 'Ugh. What a beast. We'll never lift him. Let's roll him in. He'll sink like a rock.' She let his leg fall and it slapped against the damp rock. She crumpled, exhausted, between his legs. She panted and leaned forward. He could feel her breath on his groin. Marcia, too, gave up and kneeled over his chest, rubbing her hair against his.

'How strong you are, old man,' she said.

His hands held her thighs, and moved over the curves of her buttocks. 'I used to be a fisherman. A thousand years ago in another land I fished for whales alone in a small boat. I burned my hands on ropes and caught nothing. But the sun burnt my skin and my muscles turned to stone.' He pulled her towards him and her breasts touched his face. Diana held him with both hands between his legs and put her mouth on him. He felt her quiver, and he felt her tongue moving quickly. His whole body trembled with excitement. 'Oh, babies of the dark night. Sweet children. Little white hands and ruby mouths.' He kissed the flesh of Marcia's breasts and licked at her bead-like nipples.

'How hard he is,' sighed Diana, climbing on him now behind Marcia. Her frail body settled on him and he could feel her little hand guiding him into her as her hips came down. Then she leaned against Marcia as she moved up and down, round and round. Her arms went around Marcia's waist and her hand searched the hair between her legs.

The dark world swam around and away. Sharp rocks pierced his head but he floated in seas of clouds and rolled in billows of airy flesh. Blood pounded in his neck. His breath stopped for an eternal moment. His jaws tightened. His teeth sank into the girl's breast, his hips heaved up. They pressed against him and sighed with satisfaction as he surrendered himself to the chaos in his whirling brain and the monster in his guts.

They felt him collapse beneath them, but they clutched him still and kissed him—but gently, like a dead father.

The new bottle glistened on the bare table beside the hot lamp. The two men leaned towards one another, face to face, sweating and swaying, while the Abyssinian cat watched with ancient patience and wisdom, as though he were judging a metaphysical tennis match. 'Thirty love,' he meowed as Gregory aced his metaphor down the middle. 'The Muse is a whore but I love her.'

'I hate her,' said William. 'Remember Flaubert? He said just love her and love her and love her. But it was easy for him. She never left him, never stuck her hatpin up his ass.'

Gregory waved a wooden finger. 'But she did, she did. Tortured him. Deceived him.'

'But he loved her.'

'Yes. As a true lover must—whore or no whore.'

'And can't I hate her, then, as a true hater must?'

'No, no, no, no. Can't. You can't. Say it a thousand times and you can't. Wanting to hate is not the same. Just like wanting to love. Not the same at all. You want to hate her but you can't. I can't. We kick her and abuse her. Revenge. That's what it is. Revenge because each line we write doesn't produce instant immortality. That's what every writer, every poet wants. That's what every lover wants. Instant and final immortality, Nirvana, Beulah land, Utopia, music of the spheres, paradise.'

'She hates us,' said William. 'The Muse hates us. God hates us. She won't let me write any more, like a lovely lady who won't let you kiss her, who spits in your face and sneers at you. She puckers out her wine-wet lips but says *don't kiss me*, and bares her breasts to you and says *don't touch me*. I've had a million ideas, but they're all still-born, all abortions. I wanted once to write an enormous novel. *War and Peace* or *Moby Dick*. I wanted a huge stage so that I could say something universal. I was tired of all these little homosexual English novels about sad young men. I was tired of picking on my own scabs. No more autobiography, I told myself. No social realism and protest. No little issues—sex, love, anger, and rebellion. No. I wanted to get beyond all that to something that mattered for all of time. Shakespeare didn't write about his unhappy childhood, did he?'

'But Aeschylus wrote about Oedipus.'

'Fault,' meowed the Abyssinian.

'Not fair, not fair,' said William. 'That was myth. Much more important than merely a tale of psychological disaster. And *Hamlet* is more. Ahab is more. And Raskolnikov.'

'Yes,' said Gregory, 'myths are important. I write myths. I create myths. I say I am Dionysus come down from Olympus to spread madness and truth in the heaving hearts and guts of the squirming young boys and girls.'

'Corrupter of youth,' said William, nailing down his point with an elaborate burp.

'Impossible. Youth is itself a corruption, an unsettled whirling of forces. Children are beasts. They would eat us if we didn't scold them for it or eat them first. Blind animal urge. Amoral life force. Ramming its way through darkness, going nowhere.'

The cat yawned and stretched out on the straw mat in front of the empty fireplace, like an old and inarticulate professor who harboured the truth but could not convey it to his sticky-minded students.

'Exactly,' said William. 'Which is why it doesn't matter what I write. I even thought of articles. Why not? Recipes for the *Ladies Home Journal*, travel guides for tired accountants, how-to-do-it pieces for the man who can't do it.' He laughed at his own joke. 'And what sport. The more absurd the better. A brief dental history of all the presidents.'

Gregory gurgled and coughed and laughed, whisky running down his tattered grey beard. He pounded his applause on the table. The cat jumped and stared.

'Grow Your Own Marijuana. Get More Out of Death. Deliver Your Own Baby. Knit-picking in Kenya. Mama I Want to be a Mau-Mau.'

Gregory cleared his throat and spat on the floor. They roared and coughed as William filled their glasses. The cat squinted with wise indifference and contemplated sleep.

Eyelids half-drawn I breathe with the breathing sea. It holds me, enfolds me, the silken, liquid breast of the world. Mother of us all. Giver of life. Maggie swam through the gently swelling, sadly sighing water, her body naked and weightless, moving with sure and perfect rhythm. Her white arms lifted, arched slowly, dipped, one after the other, into the salty coolness of the sea, and she glided, floated, rocked in the darkness towards the dim lights of the ghostly boat. The fever that spun her around subsided. The pounding of drums faded behind her and was replaced now by the sound of barely disturbed water that splashed about her intruding form. She swam as though she were trying to persuade the sea that she was one of its creatures, as though she were assuring it that she was not an enemy, not a warrior from the land come to fight it and conquer it. Let me be part of you, she thought. Absorb me. I have been outside of nature too long. Too long in the unfriendly world.

The water caressed her face, lingered near her mouth, whispered in her ears. What was it saying? Soft and strong it whispered but she could not understand. She had heard it before. An old man taking a little girl in his arms to protect her from the dark night, to tell her that all was well, that all would be well. Was that the message from the sea? No more strife. No more hunger. No more fever. Only the soothing, motherly-fatherly half-whispered song. Come to me. I will hold you, enfold you, protect you from the demons of the night, the crawling beasts of the forest, the hawks of the air. No rough rocks will bruise you. No fires will touch you. She turned and floated on her back. She could see the vast dark sky overhead, the stars, the haze-enlarged moon, the silhouetted peaks. What was it he tried to say at Assisi? They were inside the sky. It was all around them, pressing them together. Who spoke? What was the secret? Or was it only a dream of words—only the wind and the silence?

'Over here! Over here!' a voice called across the water. She turned towards the voice and found that she was swimming past the boat. 'Towards the light,' said the shadow standing on the deck.

She did not answer. She hesitated, looking from the boat to the darkness beyond and then back towards the shore, where the entrance to the cave was an eye of light, and where, further to the left, a dimmer patch of yellow marked the old man's house. 'Come on,' shouted Jim. But still she waited, longing to swim out into the darkness until she could swim no more, yet anchored by some invisible chain to the shore.

She drifted closer to the boat. 'Are you all right?' said the silhouette.

Finally she answered. 'I'm all right.' Her voice was reassuring and calm, not even breathless. 'The water is lovely.'

'Come aboard,' he said. 'We'll open a bottle and celebrate.'

'What are we celebrating?' she said, with forced amusement.

'What's the difference? We'll find something. The ladder is here. Right where I'm standing. See it?'

The boat grew larger. Its side rose above her, rocking gently. She caught the heavy rope ladder and pulled herself up, feeling the sudden weight of her body, and becoming conscious again of its nakedness. She peered over the rail, 'Have you got something for me to put on?' she said.

'An old shirt maybe. That's about all.'

'Okay,' she said, and he disappeared into the cabin below deck. She came all the way up and sat against the low railing.

He came back along the narrow, slanting deck. 'Here,' he said, tossing the shirt at her. 'But I don't know why you bother. There's nobody here but us ghosts.' He held out his arm with a gesture of triumph. 'Look!' He was clutching a bottle of champagne. 'French,' he said. 'None of that cheap Spanish soda-pop.'

She smiled weakly and walked away from him, buttoning the only two remaining buttons of the tattered garment. She stared up at the twin masts and felt the solid roundness of the boom. The teak deck was warm and smooth under her feet. 'A beautiful boat,' she said.

He followed her, still holding the unopened champagne. 'You like it?'

'It's the sort of boat you see in movies about the South Seas.'

'It's only a forty-footer. But fifty years old. Built before the first war.'

She turned to face him. 'All right,' she said, 'we'll drink to the boat. What's her name?'

'Thalia.'

'Thalia?'

'Something from Greek mythology. A Muse, I think, but I don't know what a Muse is. I could never keep all that straight. You know, Furies and Muses and nymphs and all those gods and demi-gods. The old man explained it to me once, but I couldn't follow it. I think Apollo made it with her once. Maybe that's her claim to fame.'

'I don't know, but it's a lovely name for a boat.'

Leaning against the cabin, Jim popped the cork of the champagne. It flew out into the darkness, but they could not hear it land. The wine bubbled up and oozed over his hands. 'Ahh!' he said. 'The sexiest drink in the world. Let's have it from the bottle.' He tipped back his head and drank, still holding the bottle with both hands. Then he passed it to Maggie, who also drank. He took the bottle from her and set it down on the deck behind him. He stood close to her and put his hand on her shoulder and rubbed the back of her neck. She stood up to move away but he pulled her towards him and kissed her. Their naked bodies touched where the shirt parted.

'No,' she said, without resisting. 'I've got to go back. I shouldn't have come in the first place, but I thought the swim would be good.'

He didn't answer. She felt his warm breath near her ear and the softness of his moustache. His hands caressed her back and then reached past the shirt to her buttocks and thighs. She looked past him through the rigging of the boat towards the shore. It was too late, she thought—too late to say no, too late to turn back. He rubbed himself against her and she felt him throbbing, pleading. Yes, she thought, she would comfort him, this stranger, this boy or man, whatever he was. And she allowed him to undo the shirt and slip it from her shoulders.

He made love to her on the deck, silently, distantly. She felt the muscles of his back and shoulders and stared into the curving universe of stars. She held him, steadied him, comforted him, her long maternal fingers telling him that it was all right, that it was over now and that he needn't be ashamed or angry or obliged or anything.

Later they sat and smoked and drank the rest of the champagne. He told her about himself and the boat, how he had worked for seven years to buy it, how he starved himself in a rooming house in New York, cursing his extravagant friends, surviving on bread and soup and milk. 'I did it all myself,' he said. 'I had a plan a long time ago and nothing would stop me. I wasn't going to be trapped in any goddamned factory or office the rest of my life. I wanted a boat and my freedom. I put everything into stocks, except what I spent on this boat. I worked two jobs for a while, three hundred bucks a week.' He laughed angrily. 'I figured there was a way, after all, to beat the system, to get the hell out. I saw my old man rot away as a drunken salesman, and I said to myself, even when I was a kid, that it wouldn't happen to me.'

'And now that you've got it,' said Maggie, 'are you satisfied?'

'You're damn right, I'm satisfied. I go where I want to, stop when I please. I'm not rich, mind you, but I've got enough to keep me going indefinitely—couple of hundred a month. In Spain that's not bad. I live on the boat. I even save a little now and then. And the girls are easy when you have a boat. I took it up to France last spring and had a ball. And then I spent the winter in the Canary Islands. No sweat. No work.'

She winced and turned away. 'The good life,' she said somewhat sarcastically, and his line echoed in her head: *the girls are easy*.

He was puzzled by her sudden coldness. 'What is it?' he said. 'A pinch of conscience? I thought we understood one another.'

'Not conscience,' she said, standing up in front of him and looking down on him, 'just pity, dear boy. Pity!'

'I don't understand.'

'Never mind. Be careful or I'll deliver you one of Mother St. Claire's famous sermons. But I've got to go back.' She took off his shirt again and climbed onto the railing.

'Hey, wait a minute. Wait.' He leapt towards her, but before he could reach her she dived into the water. He stood there, clinging to the ropes and watched her swim gracefully, silently away.

'I don't want to go back,' moaned Alex. 'I don't want to go anywhere. I want to die. Why didn't you push me into the water like you promised, rotten little brats, ungrateful daughters.' He held his clothes in a bundle under his arm as the giggling girls tugged at his sweating stumbling body.

'He's so drunk he doesn't know what happened,' said Marcia.

Diana now carried the torch. 'We should have thrown him in the water to sober him up.'

'He would have drowned.'

'So what?'

The dying torchlight flickered in the grotesque windings of the cave. Stone eyes peered at them, monstrous mouths with broken teeth yawned. Walls rippled and folded like the hide of prehistoric beasts.

'Watch where you step,' said Marcia. 'The place is full of holes and canyons and things. We'll all be swallowed up.'

Alex resisted and his damp arms slipped away from their clawing young hands. He fell backwards against some rocks and landed in a sitting position. 'Come on, you fool,' said Diana, 'before the light goes out.'

'No, no, no,' he said, half crying. 'I don't want to go anywhere.' They reached for him again. 'Wait,' he pleaded. 'Wait. I'll tell you what you can do. Please, sweet children, O lovely nymphs of my old age. Listen. Just lead me to the precipice. That's all I ask. Stand me at the edge of a cliff and let me throw myself in.'

The girls looked at one another and shook their heads. Then Marcia leaned towards Diana and whispered something in her ear that made them both laugh. 'All right, Daddy-O,' she said 'Come on. This way to the precipice. Be careful now. There's a wonderful ledge over here. It goes way down, down, down, right into the black old mouth of Hades. Oh, see how dark and deep it is.'

'Hurry,' he said. 'Show me. Put my feet where I can feel the edge.'

Diana covered her mouth with one hand and her cheeks billowed with suppressed laughter. 'Right here, right here,' said Marcia, guiding his foot by the ankle. 'That's it. One foot here, and the other one here.'

'Is this it?' he said. 'Are you sure this is it? A deep canyon? A black hole?'

'Yes,' she said. 'We'll go away now and leave you. And don't forget to say your prayers before you jump.'

'All right,' he sobbed, like a scolded boy. 'All right.' He

clutched his clothes and trembled on the brink. With his toes he could feel the edge. He reached out one foot and felt nothing. The girls backed away as though they were going.

'Goodbye,' they said. 'Goodbye old Daddy-O.' They crouched behind a large boulder to watch.

'Am I alone now?' he said. 'Am I all alone?' He waited, as though for an answer. 'Is this the final darkness, the final agony?' He waited again. 'Then Oh God forgive me for what I have done and for what I am about to do. If I offend you it is only because you have offended me. You have torn me and dirtied me and spat in my face. You have made me an animal for your own sport. You have made me a fool.' The tears streamed down his cheeks and mingled with his sweat. 'I hate you, but forgive me, forgive me for hating you, and let me hurl myself into this darkness as you have already hurled me into that other darkness by plucking out my eyes.' He squeezed his bundle of clothes against his chest as though they were alive and he were embracing them, and then with a spastic, awkward motion he leapt from the ledge of rock into the blackness.

The devilish girls howled with amusement as he landed on his rump just three feet down from where he started. He sat there stunned, still hugging his clothes, and heard his nymphs charging away through the tunnel, their high-pitched voices hysterical with mockery.

'Don't leave me, boy,' said Gregory Winters. He and William struggled drunkenly in the doorway that led from the house to the cave. The old man's legs sagged. William's vision blurred. 'We were just coming to it. We were moving in on it—the final truth, the ultimate word. Another hour, half an hour, and we would have had it by the throat. Come on, boy, one more drink. One more.'

'There's no more,' said William. 'All the fucking juice is gone.' He squinted to focus his eyes on the empty bottle that lay on its side on the table. 'And we didn't solve anything. Only more talk. Talk, talk, talk. That's all we ever do. Wagging serpent tongues. The devil in the word, out to kill us all.'

'Unless we kill it first. The coupling serpents. Bad omen. Bash them both. Not only the she-snake. Remember your mythology, boy. Bash them both with the same quick sword. Otherwise blindness. Blindness and despair.'

'Let go of my arm, old man,' said William. 'Tiresias is out there walking into the dragon's teeth and walls of this rotten darkness. He needs me.'

'I need you too. I need you here. Now. If you leave me I'll level a curse on you and all your sons for a thousand years. I am old. I have powers. Serpents and bulls.'

'There's burning flesh out there, you old fool. It's time for the feast. The sacrifice is over. The goat is dead. Let go of my arm.'

Gregory held him, but his hold grew weaker. His face wrinkled and quivered. Tears were wrenched from his dry bones. At last he let go and staggered back to a chair. 'We were almost there,' he said to the Abyssinian cat. 'We were almost there.'

William swayed in the doorway, unaware of his freedom, almost seduced by pity. 'Go to sleep, old man,' he said, hanging on to the swinging door. 'Go to sleep and forget.'

Gregory and the cat stared at one another compassionately. The empty bottle rolled across the table and then smashed on the stone floor. 'Duty calls, and love,' said William, as though he were about to mount a horse. 'Farewell!' He turned away from the dimly lighted room and stumbled into the darkness of the tunnel. He tripped on the rough ground and fell. The world spun around him. Slowly he lifted himself to his feet and went on.

He staggered past the still-roasting goat, through the sea of snuggling, sliding, whispering, dancing youths, to another opening in the cave. He stood on a rock and surveyed the steaming cavity for Maggie and Alex, but saw them nowhere. 'He's down in the cave, drunk as a priest,' said a girl's voice, but when he turned to find the girl he saw no one. His stomach churned. His chest tightened. If he didn't get some air he knew he would be sick.

He made his way outside and climbed down to the seaweed-encrusted beach. There he sat down and let his head fall between his knees. A terrible lethargy threatened him. He wanted to let himself fall forward into unconsciousness. He wanted to sleep. But his guts rebelled and his mouth watered with nausea. His whole body contracted as he heaved up everything in his stomach. When the seizure was over, he picked himself up shakily and went down to the edge of the water. He splashed water on his face and head and took several deep breaths. The world settled somewhat into place. He saw the sea and then looked back to see the cave and the mountains beyond. His breath came more evenly. His eyes began to focus more clearly.

'The hermit-crab,' said a female voice out of the darkness.

He looked up and saw Maggie standing no more than six feet from him, fully dressed, but with her wet hair dripping over her forehead and down her neck. He held his head and rubbed his eyes. 'Go away,' he said. 'You look drowned.'

'I am drowned,' she said, and sat down beside him. 'I've been swimming.'

'Why didn't you keep going? It's only a hundred miles to Barcelona or somewhere out there. Maybe you could have made it to the Acropolis.'

'I was tempted.'

'I bet you were.'

They sat silently for a moment, listening to the gentle surf. Finally William looked at her as though he were trying to remember something. 'Where's Alex?' he said.

'I don't know. I thought he was with you.'

'He was with you when I left.'

'No, he was with that little girl—what's her name?'

'The black-haired one.' He stood up uncertainly. 'You should never have left him. You don't know him.'

'What can happen to him?' she said, also standing.

'Almost anything if he's drunk enough.'

Without another word they climbed back up the rocks to the cave.

Alex got up, bruised and blind, tangled in the clothes he still tried to carry. Coins and keys dropped from his trouser pockets, clinked and echoed in the dark and shapeless chamber. The house keys, he thought. I've lost the house keys. All my pretty babies are there, my boys, my sweet girls. Strength and comfort for an old man. He went down on all fours like an animal and searched with his trembling hands. He found a large coin, which he recognized with his fingers as English. He threw it into the darkness and heard it rattle among the rocks. Rotten, dirty money. Filthy money. Ruining everybody, ruining everything.

He searched again and his hand touched a small square of metal, slick and familiar. His cigarette lighter. His heart leapt and he sat up clutching it in both hands. O Blessed Mother of God! A little light. He worked it with his thumb—once, twice—and the third time it caught. A dull point of light attacked the darkness and grew brighter slowly as his eye adjusted to it. He could see the flame and then his hand and fingers, but nothing else. *Light a candle for me*, someone had said. Who was it? William? His mother? *A candle for St. Jude?* There was a retreat house and a seminary where he and his brother used to go for one long week-end every year. The room was monkish and bare. The meals were simple. He read and rested and prayed. There was a small window from which he stared into the magnificent garden with its medieval paths and squares of flowers, roses, azaleas, rhododendra. And the fruit trees in blossom in the spring. He went in May. Depraved May. Where had he heard that? And he tried very hard to do and say the right things, to find his way to God. Purity, pride, humility. What was it that he was missing? Father Jerome had tried to tell him. They sat on a white stone bench in the garden and talked. The talk was quiet at first and friendly. But soon it boiled into an argument, and Father Jerome, an old, mild Irish priest with the weathered face of a seaman, smiled as if to say, *now do you see what I mean?* And for a moment he saw, but his anger threatened his understanding.

The light flickered in his hand. He held it high over his head and tried to see around him, but all he could see was his own nakedness, his white forty-year-old body, still somewhat youthful, but not entirely. He saw his knees in front of him as he sat there, and then his thighs, his groin, and his belly. A wave of repulsion swam through him. *Flesh*, he thought. His mouth and tongue uncontrollably formed the word and he muttered it slowly, 'Flesh.' He heard his own voice. How strange it sounded down there under the sea in the darkness. Once more he said the word, but out loud, so that it echoed against the rough walls. The sound died away into absolute silence. The light was beginning to fade. Let it go, he thought. Let it go! He closed the lid and put the lighter away in his trouser pocket. He balanced himself against some overhanging rocks and put on his pants and shirt. But where were his shoes? He felt around again but couldn't find them.

Barefooted and alone, then, he began his journey, feeling his way along walls, reaching out to feel the ground in front of him. But was he going up or down? He could not tell. The walls fell away into grottoes and coves. He cut his feet on sharp stones. There were no corners, no simple forms that would give him a clue to the shape of the place. Was it big or small? Where did it turn? He stopped at a ledge and tried to find more ground in front of him, but there was none. He stepped out tentatively with first one foot and then the other, but there was nothing. Then he lay down flat on his stomach and reached down with his hands. Still nothing. He took a loose stone and dropped it into the void. He heard nothing for a long time and then a distant sound of water. He collapsed inside with fear and anger and felt the tears rushing to his eyes. 'O merciful Jesus, don't let this happen to me. Dear God, kill me if you must, but don't beat me and beat me with my own pride and stubborn hope. Let me give up, at least. Let me just lie here and die without thinking about anything.' He buried his head in his folded arms and silence whirled about him.

William carried the torch and led the way. Maggie followed him through the winding, twisting shafts. 'What a pair of little bitches,' he said. 'If they weren't so potted I'd kick their asses in for them. A warped idea of fun.'

'Blame your friend Gregory,' said Maggie.

'No. I blame them. Not the old man or the devil or anyone else.'

'And Alex?'

'He's just irresponsible.'

'Is that a virtue?'

He turned on her suddenly and she almost walked into the flame of the torch. 'What the hell do you know about virtue, you dirty whore!'

She stepped back away from him, frightened by his fury and the satanic redness of his face in the close light of the fire. He stared at her for a moment and then turned away to continue the search. Again she followed.

The path subdivided several times and then disappeared, leaving them to inch their way along ledges or climb down underground waterfalls. 'Would it do any good to shout?' she said.

'Try it and see.'

She cleared her throat and called, 'Alex.' And then louder. 'Alex.' They waited for a moment but heard nothing. 'At least we're still going down,' she said.

He did not answer.

Alex started to doze but awoke with a start. He imagined he heard a babble of voices. They were laughing and weeping. 'Who is it?' he shouted, his heart pounding in his chest, his face quivering. The voices came first from one direction and then from another. 'I'm here. Can't you see me? Can't you hear me?' The voices faded and then grew louder again, but this time they came from the depths of the canyon he could not cross. He felt for the ledge again and looked over into the darkness. 'Hey, you bastards,' he called. 'I'm up here. I can't move.' He waited. His own voice echoed in the cave.

'Pray for us now,' said a whispering deep voice.

'Mary, Mary, sweet contrary,' sang a little girl.

'I went round and round and down to the bottom of the sea.' It was a familiar voice. 'The one-eyed idiot staggered on the deck, blind and drunk.'

'Who are you?' said Alex.

And then a voice came from behind him out of the rocks. 'Be careful, you dirty old man.' He spun around and waved his arms in front of him, banging his hands against stone. 'I'll make you leap into that hole.'

Alex shook his head to drive out the voices. They were unreal. He knew they were unreal, but still he heard them. He heard them like wind rushing past his ears.

'Shall I chop off your hands? Can you see the bloody stumps? Next year you'll be rich. The kids will love you. The girls will kiss your rough, unshaven face. Your wife will play with you under the warm sheets and feed you. Mama will wrap you in her bosom, smother you with her pillows. The little pirate from Seaville. Humpty Dumpty humped her. And the old man cut it off with a cleaver. Ding dong bell, ding, dong, bell, ding, dong, bell . . .' The voice died into distant laughter.

They reached a hopeless impasse and doubled back. 'We'll have to find the path again and try to stay with it,' said William. 'There is a way down to that pool.'

'We should have brought them with us,' said Maggie, brushing strands of wet hair from her forehead.

'They were in no condition.'

The shaft narrowed and they went through the narrow opening sideways. On the other side there was another huge chamber, hung with ancient stalactites, cathedral-like in its Gothic immensity. 'My God,' said Maggie. 'I've never seen anything like this.'

'We didn't come this way,' said William, 'but we seem to be going up hill.'

'Perhaps Alex has found his way back alone.'

'Sure. Guided by flights of angels, no doubt.'

His anger turned in her chest and stomach. And she accepted it. Someone had seen her go off with Jim O'Hara and mentioned it. William only looked at her at the time, but said nothing. She knew he would either wait until some other time or simply turn away from her entirely. She remembered her feeble tricky explanations in the past, and even her benevolent lies. How stupid it all was. How utterly stupid. A little girl dreaming of schooners and castles and exotic islands. His crouching form moved in front of her. She wanted to reach out and touch him. She wanted to tell him how sorry she was—for this, for everything. For him, for Alex, for her mother and father, and Edith, and for all the men she had lived with and slept with, and the one who had died in an automobile crash, drunk with a mad dream of love for her. But she said nothing. She only followed after him as he searched this and that avenue for some sign of a path.

At last he stopped and studied the ground. 'There,' he said, holding the torch over a rock on which there was a blue streak of paint. 'A marker.' He went on for a few more yards and found another. 'It turns here and goes down. Come on.'

They walked more quickly and soon were on a definite path.

When Alex heard them shout he stiffened again with panic. They were coming back again, those ghostly voices. 'Go away,' he growled. 'Go away and leave me alone. I haven't done anything.'

They followed his voice. 'Hello!' Maggie called. 'We're here.'

'Can you see the light?' shouted William.

Alex sucked at his bleeding fingers and tried to blot out the voices. Lie still, he thought, pressing against the rock. Lie still. Perhaps they would pass by without seeing him. He lay down and curled into a shivering ball, his arms pulled in to his chest, his knees bent up towards his belly. 'Shh!' he whispered to himself. 'Lie still in the darkness and be good.'

William and Maggie stopped and listened. 'Why doesn't he answer?' she said. 'It was Alex. I'm sure it was him.'

'It was. I don't understand.'

They listened again and then heard a quiet sobbing off to their right. They came to the ravine and looked down. 'Jesus Christ!' said William. A natural stone bridge brought them to the other side and there they found Alex. He sat up in confusion and tried to fight them off. Maggie took the torch from William, who picked up his friend bodily and hugged him firmly in his arms until the ghosts and shadows were driven from his mind. 'It's all right, old buddy. It's all right now.' Alex clung to him and stifled his tears. His trembling subsided.

'We'll be out of here before you know it,' said Maggie, taking him by one arm, while William held him by the other.

They made their way back along the path, all three of them stumbling a bit. Finally Alex hesitated and held them back. He shook his head and said, 'Hey, Doc, are you sure you're real?'

They all laughed weakly and went on.

25

ON A COLD morning in February Bernadette Soubirous started out with her sister Antoinette and a young friend named Jeanne Abadie towards the forest to collect wood for her mother. She was a dark-haired girl of fourteen with large eyes and a serious, intelligent expression, a combination of curiosity, and fear. She had already felt the stirrings of young womanhood in her and watched, with dreamy suspicion, the changes in her body. Her father was a miller in Lourdes, a solid, handsome peasant of fifty. He too noticed that she was growing up. In the dull light of their small house he watched her move about the kitchen with her long skirts and her apron. His wife, Louisa, had been only a few years older than this girl when he married her.

Bernadette and the other two children crossed the River Gave on the Old Bridge and headed for the woods. But they met a washerwoman who told them that there was plenty of wood to be had on the Ile du Chalet, only a short distance from the bridge. The island in the Gave was a piece of land barely separated from the shore by a canal.

They were collecting branches when Bernadette looked

across the canal towards a large rock formation called Massabielle, in which there was a grotto. It was a lonely, somewhat forbidding place that she and the others had never explored. She suggested that they follow the canal a little further in order to have a better look. They found the grotto, and above it saw a small oval cave at the entrance of which grew a wild rose bush. Eager to explore further, Antoinette and Jeanne took off their shoes and waded across the canal. Bernadette hesitated. She had been bothered by attacks of asthma, and her mother insisted that she wear stockings in the cold weather. In a moment the other two children were gone and she found herself alone. She was puzzled by the strangeness of the place and a little frightened. The Angelus sounded in the village of Lourdes, but in this valley she could not hear it. She decided to remove her stockings and follow the others, but before she could get them off she heard the whirling of a great wind, as though there was a storm. She looked about but saw nothing. The other bank of the canal was calm. Massabielle loomed in rocky silence.

She removed her stockings quickly and started to step into the water, but once more she heard the strange wind. When she looked up she saw the beautiful face of a young woman in the small cave above the grotto. She was smiling with tenderness and grace and her hands were slightly extended as though she were inviting Bernadette to approach more closely. But Bernadette was frightened. She rubbed her eyes and trembled, but she could not run away. The vision grew clearer. The young woman was dressed in a white tunic and a white veil, and a mysterious light surrounded her. Bernadette tried to make the sign of the cross but could not raise her hand to her forehead. She dropped her rosary and fell to her knees. After a moment she recovered her rosary and tried once more to cross herself, this time successfully. The lady in white smiled down at her as though to encourage her, and Bernadette began to pray. The lady followed her on the beads of her own rosary but did not move her lips or utter a sound.

When the other children returned, in about fifteen minutes, they found Bernadette barefooted and on her knees. Her eyes were rolled back in her head and her face was as white as death.

This was the first vision. There would be seventeen others, and the world would come to Lourdes to pray and hope.

Here was a place where the invisible became visible. Here was a place, a solid piece of rock, that one could look at as though it were indeed a physical link with the other world, a bridge, a tower (not the Tower of Babel), that reached to heaven, not because presumptuous men attempted an invasion of God's sacred fortress, but because, out of pity and compassion for man's smallness and weakness, out of a profound understanding of man's Euclidean simplicity of mind, his inability to know and his tendency to doubt, and as a divine demonstration of tenderness and humility, God chose to provide a comforting sign, a miracle—not the ultimate miracle of salvation through grace—that would slay, like a holy arrow, the beast of logic and common sense.

After such a miracle one could believe that all things are possible. Therefore, one must believe in the miracle. Secretly, openly, somehow, one must believe in it. One must. He is driven into the mouth of it. He is devoured. Without it nothing follows. Without it man is nothing—a hopeless, twitching creature with rotting teeth and nowhere to go but, stumbling and coughing, into total annihilation. Between him and that grim fate there kneels a fourteen-year-old girl at Lourdes, a round-faced, big-eyed, asthmatic daughter of a French peasant, who would have, without the fame of his little girl, chewed and sweated away his ordinary life in total obscurity.

She knelt, barefooted and ecstatic, before the grotto in the rock called Massabielle and talked with the pretty lady in white, who, after some modesty or shyness, admitted that she was the virgin mother of Christ. Who would really want to doubt her? Who would really want to call her a liar? So much depends on the miracle, the sign. And yet, and yet—just fourteen years old, a mere girl, and asthmatic, which we all know means—what does it mean? But the innocence of children! The innocence. The innocence. The plea rings in one's heart. And the guilt, the brutality, the playfulness of them—of children. Are they, after all, creatures of the devil? Wouldn't that be just as good, just as strong a link with another world? No. It's not the same. Not the same at all. It's the innocence that matters, the pity and compassion and purity and simplicity. One can only trust innocence. No truth can ever be built on evil. So there is no other way, no other choice but to believe her, and to believe in the miracle, if only to avoid the yawning, indifferent darkness. And if the miracle is true (Oh, if only it were true), the gentle mother of us all would lay her soft hand on us, press her loving lips against our feverish cheeks and whisper her sweet song to us in the bleak night: 'All will be well, child. All will be well.'

William stared through the rain-streaked window into the narrow winding street below. Shops and houses huddled together. Umbrellas passed, as though on feet of their own, black turtles jostling each other in the crowded town. Bent women in bandanas shuffled by close to the ancient, uneven walls. Yellow and red signs squeaked in the wet breeze. And, in spite of the rain and the heavy grey clouds, or possibly because of it, the voices of singing pilgrims drifted up from the valley, spread through the narrow streets and hung in the thick air. *Laudate, laudate, laudate Maria.*

'The place is haunted,' said William, his hands rammed into his pockets as he stood before the window. Raindrops collected on the upper frame of the window, waited, ripened, shook themselves free and raced down the window pane, sliding, diminishing, sometimes disappearing before they reached the bottom of the frame.

Alex was stretched out on the bed, his legs crossed and his hands folded on his chest as though he were a corpse. He stared towards the ceiling of the small room, studying the streaks and stains in the plaster. 'We won't be able to do anything today,' he said. 'It's too late.'

'It's only five o'clock,' said Maggie, who was slouched in a straight-backed chair with her feet up on the edge of the bed. In her snug green slacks and her white turtle-neck sweater she looked comparatively spring-like in the midst of the dreary, heavy furniture that cluttered the room. Her raincoat was draped over the back of another chair. It was a tan, military-looking garment, that seemed now to serve as a rather unconvincing scarecrow.

'It's too late,' said Alex again. 'Besides, we can't go out in this miserable rain.'

'Why not?' said Maggie.

'Yeah,' said William, turning suddenly away from the window. 'Maybe it's full of magic like that angel water that comes out of the grotto. Baptism straight from heaven. You never know.' He lit a cigarette and paced back and forth in the confined space between the bed and the window.

Alex glared at him. 'Your humour's a little sick today, Doc.'

'*I'm* a little sick today,' he said. 'This place gives me the creeps. There are more souvenir shops here per square inch than in Coney Island.'

'What did you expect,' said Maggie, 'formal gardens, pink clouds, a virgin in every niche and grotto?'

'I didn't expect anything,' he said, turning back to the window.

Alex sat up in bed. 'I think I'll go down and hunt up a liquor store.'

'Oh no,' said Maggie, pointing a scolding finger at him. 'Not this time. You came all this way for a reason. Don't forget what it is.'

'Hey, Doc, what is she talking about? What is the funny lady trying to say?'

'She's trying to say that you're a jerk.' He tapped ashes on the floor.

'Oh,' said Alex, 'why didn't you say so in the first place. I never said I wasn't. But what's that got to do with anything?'

'Forget it,' she said. 'You're impossible. You're both impossible.'

'All right, all right,' said Alex, forcing a smile. 'I'm sorry. I'm a little disappointed, I guess. I mean it took us so long to get here and now it's raining and everybody's so depressed.'

'The place reeks with tourists,' said William, still staring into the street.

'Not tourists,' said Alex. 'Pilgrims. Pilgrims.'

'What a funny word,' said Maggie. 'It makes me think of

Thanksgiving. You know, Pilgrims and turkeys and all that. Musket-loaders with funnels on the end and friendly Indians bearing bundles of corn. In grammar school we used to draw pictures of them. Remember? I can still draw those turkeys—round bodies, a kind of fan for a tail, a little head joined to the body by a curving neck. We drew them on the blackboard with coloured chalk and left them there for a week or two. And sometimes on long strips of brown paper that we stuck together and pasted on the walls. Pilgrims! Plymouth Rock!'

'Yeah,' said Alex nostalgically. 'I always imagined it as a little rock, sort of black and pointed. And they would arrive in this gaudy old ship and pile out onto this rock, like seagulls or something and just sit there.'

William listened, looking from one to the other. 'And Chaucer,' he intruded.

They looked at him. 'Chaucer?' said Maggie.

'Whan that April with his shoures solte . . .'

'Oh,' she said.

'More pilgrims,' said Alex. 'Not to mention all those Mohammedans on their way to Mecca.'

William struck a professorial stance. 'So tell us, Mr. Pilgrim, why did you make this journey to Jerusalem?'

'Lourdes,' said Maggie.

'Yes, of course,' said William. 'Lourdes, I mean. I am doing a study, you see, of Pilgrim psychology. I want to know what makes a man come three thousand miles just to stare at a hole in a rock.'

'If you were serious, I'd tell you,' said Alex.

'I'm serious,' said William, his light tone fading into grimness. 'I'm dead serious.'

'Well, then you ought to know as well as I do, since you're also here, having travelled the same distance.'

'My role was to see that you got here.'

'Perhaps mine was to see that *you* got here.'

'Don't tell me now that it was all an elaborate scheme to convert me.'

'No, Doc, I don't want to convert you. You're having too much fun as you are.'

'Did you really come because of your eyes?' said Maggie.

Alex looked at her suspiciously and then at William. He sat up again stiffly and reached down for his shoes. 'For Christ's sake, what do you guys want me to say? What do you want anyway? I came for a lot of reasons. I couldn't even begin to name them all. I wanted to get away from where I was. I wanted to see Europe. I wanted to visit one of the great holy places in the Catholic world. I would have settled for Rome or Jerusalem, but I've always had a secret longing to see this place. That's all. It's always meant something special. I can't explain what. Perhaps I'm convinced that what happened here is true.'

'Do you really think it's true?' said William. 'I mean that a little girl saw the Virgin Mary?'

'One has to begin by believing in the Virgin Mary,' said Alex with a bitter smile.

They were all silent for a moment. 'And do you?' said Maggie quietly, gently, as though she were putting her naked foot down on broken glass.

Alex stared down at the dark rug for a minute and then looked up almost accusingly at Maggie. 'Do you?' he said.

She laughed. 'Who, me?'

'Yes, you.'

'No, I don't suppose I do. I mean, I've never even asked myself the question.'

William glanced out the window. 'It's beginning to clear up,' he said.

'It doesn't matter,' said Alex. 'It's already too late. I'll go tomorrow morning. Let's get something to drink and find a place to eat.'

Maggie stood up decisively, as though to put an end to the conversation. 'Good idea. As soon as I unpack and change into something less offensive. I feel like the original ugly American. Which room is mine?'

'The one down the hall is a double room,' said William. 'Why don't you take this one.'

'No,' said Alex, 'I'd rather keep this one. I'd like to be alone tonight.'

'What for?' said William.

'Because I'm tired of being asked stupid questions.'

'Well, I think you're out of luck, Mr. Pilgrim. We got the last two rooms in the whole town.'

'You two can have the big room. It's almost legal.'

'No, thanks.'

'All right, then, Maggie and I will take the other room. How about that? Or maybe we should all sleep in the same room. Head to feet.' He was smiling but his voice was angry. 'You know, like those garden of evil oil paintings in the middle ages, or whatever they were called. Varieties of sexual experience.'

'That's a fine and holy attitude for a guy who's about to fall on his knees before the Holy Virgin.'

'Come on, you two,' said Maggie. 'That's enough. What a pair of knights in shining armour. Don't you know there's a lady present?'

'Where?' said William.

'Look, each of you take a room and I'll go out and hunt up another one,' she said.

'No, no,' said Alex. 'We'll do it the right way; we'll toss a coin for the lady.'

'You'd make out better if you tossed it *at* her,' said William.

'Bastard,' she shouted, suddenly pale with rage.

'Miss truth-lover can't stand the truth.'

He saw her stoop and then ducked as a shoe sailed across the room towards his face. It glanced off his shoulder and smashed a small round mirror on the wall, which fell to the floor, frame and all. The noise echoed in the tense silence that followed. A door opened and closed near by. There were footsteps in the hallway and then a gentle knocking.

'Come in,' said Alex, and the doorknob turned.

A curious face appeared—the bleary-eyed, somewhat ravaged face of a priest, a youngish man of perhaps thirty-five. 'Is everything all right in here?' he said. 'I heard a noise. I thought perhaps . . .'

'Everything is fine, Father,' said Alex. 'Just fine.'

The priest laughed nervously. 'I'm—a—I'm Father Malloy.' He said it shyly, almost as though he were confessing a sin. 'I have the room next door. I couldn't help but overhear—I mean,

I hope there's nothing wrong.' He stepped into the room. William and Maggie studied him. He was a strange, embarrassed creature with straight blond hair plastered into place, and a red, lean Irish face. William was sure that he swayed as he stood there. Maggie, too, could see that he was drunk. 'I didn't mean to intrude, especially if it's a private—I mean—a—you know, domestic disagreement.'

Alex laughed. 'Yeah, a domestic disagreement. How did you guess? I'm trying to persuade this man, who was once married to this woman, that he should take her now as his mistress.'

'Uh, Oh, I see—I mean, that's very amusing.' He took another step into the room. 'It's good to hear some Americans again. I'm from Boston. My name is Joseph Malloy—I mean——a—Father.'

'How do you do,' said Maggie. William smiled politely but said nothing.

Alex shook hands with him and introduced the others while Father Malloy's face quivered and he nodded his head. 'Such a pleasure. Really. I suppose you've seen it all already.'

'No,' said Alex, 'we've just arrived today.'

'Oh, I see. I see. Well don't—a—don't—a . . .' He seemed to forget what he was saying. 'What I mean is, I hope you're not disappointed. Many people come here and then are disappointed. They think it's a kind of,' he laughed, 'pharmacy or hospital.'

'Well it is in a way, isn't it?' said William. He lit a cigarette and offered one to the priest, who accepted.

'Maybe. Maybe that's exactly what it is. But for sick souls, not for sick bodies. Though, psy-psy-psychosomatic ailments are—I mean, if one has faith perhaps. A whole mind and heart.'

'People have been cured of such things even by hypnosis,' said Maggie.

'Hypnosis,' echoed the priest. 'Hypnosis. It's not the same.' He rubbed his thin lips as though he were considering a profound point. 'Sci-sci-science can't explain everything. Some states of mind, I mean. There are s-s-some kinds of madness . . .'

He hesitated and blinked his eyes several times. Maggie studied him. His black suit was wrinkled, as though he had been sleeping in it. His collar was stained. 'Isn't it merely a matter of definition,' she said, more to relieve his embarrassment than to argue with him.

'Yes, definition,' he said. 'But even the devil—even the devil can quote scriptures. Words are funny things.'

William was forced to smile at the man's awkward intelligence. He was tempted to speak for him, sensing that behind his few sputtered, clumsy remarks there lurked elaborate and subtle ideas. But he held back.

'Well,' said Father Malloy. 'In-in any case, I'm here. I mean, if you need anything. Or perhaps we can get together later, another time. A drink perhaps. A pleasure to speak English again.' Nodding and backing up he found the door and slipped out, closing it quietly behind him.

'Have I had a vision, or was he for real?' said Maggie. 'What a funny creature.'

'Whatever he is,' said Alex, 'he arrived just in time.'

William brushed the broken pieces of the mirror into a corner with his foot. 'I guess we'll have to pay for it,' he said.

'I'm sorry,' said Maggie, 'But sometimes you can be wicked.'

William said nothing.

'Not sometimes, sweetie,' said Alex, lying down again on the rumpled bed. 'He was just born rotten.'

William put on his jacket and walked towards the door.

'Where are you going, Doc?' said Alex.

'I'm going out to carve my dirty initials in the bosom of the Holy Virgin. I'll see you later.' In the doorway he paused and added. 'I'm sleeping in the other room. You two can argue over this one.' And then he was gone.

'He's mad,' said Maggie. She threw her suitcase on the bed and snapped it open. 'Here,' she said, 'this is for you, Mr. Pilgrim.' She handed him the pint bottle of Scotch and looked around for a glass. 'I was saving it for a special occasion.'

'I guess this is special enough,' said Alex, squinting to read the label.

'There are no glasses. We'll have to be primitive.' She nudged his feet and he moved them so that she could sprawl at the foot of the bed. She lay on her belly and stared at the faded rug. 'Ding, dong, bell, William's in the well.'

'He's lost his sense of humour, that's what. And when a man loses his sense of humour he's in trouble. Especially this guy. He's been this way for months now.'

'Has he?'

'Almost since the end of the winter.'

'What happened?'

'Nothing special. He was seeing this broad Marianne all winter and then, for no reason at all, they broke up. It wasn't anything serious—just a girl. He's always got a girl or two tucked away for the cold weather. She was all right—young anyway, and pretty. Good enough to amuse him. He took her to New England for a little holiday between semesters.'

Maggie listened, one arm folded under her chin and the other dangling down to the floor, where, with a long finger, she traced invisible designs in the rug.

'Was she intelligent?'

'She wasn't stupid, but she wasn't exactly what you would call an intellectual. I mean, she didn't care one way or the other about the complicated things in life. She liked to ski and swim and—and I guess she liked to roll around in bed, which is big Bill's favourite sport. She was lively. Full of energy.'

'How old was she?'

'Oh, I don't know. About twenty-three or -four maybe. A teacher. She taught third grade in Freeport or Malverne somewhere and drove around in a little Triumph sports car. Very sharp.'

'Doesn't sound like William's taste at all.'

'Maybe his taste is changing,' said Alex. 'Maybe it's the kind of girl he needs, after all. You know—simple, straightforward.'

Maggie lifted her head and stared at him. 'You mean unlike me.'

He stared back at her and without answering took a long drink from the bottle. She waited for him to answer. 'What do you want me to say?'

'Nothing.'

'You're a great woman, Maggie, but I wouldn't want to be married to you. I don't mean that as an insult. It's just that some people are cut out for marriage and others aren't. You're not and neither is Bill. He's as bad as you are.'

'Bad?'

'I don't mean in the moral sense.' She reached out her arm and he handed her the bottle. He took a deep breath and sighed, as though he were trying to collect his thoughts. 'Bill is probably the most brilliant guy I know in the whole world. He knows all about people; he writes like an angel; he talks like a poet; and he drinks like an Irishman. But he's never committed himself to anything or anyone. He's the original loner, the stranger. If you love him he runs away; if you hate him, he hates you more intensely, or else he attacks you with indifference. He's tried almost everything and rejected almost everything. He could have had anything he wanted in this world, but there's nothing that he wants. He could have been anything, but there's nothing he wants to be. And now he's almost forty years old, he's burnt a lot of bridges behind him, he's broke, and he doesn't know what to do next. He knows something is wrong, but he doesn't know what. One of these days he'll put a bullet through his head just so that he won't have to drag himself through another rotten day of wondering. The existentialists have a word for it. He's discovered not that life is dull or painful or mysterious, but that life is absurd. He doesn't believe in anything.'

'And what did you expect him to do here? Find God in a souvenir shop?'

'I didn't expect anything, except . . .' He hesitated.

'Except what?'

'I don't know. It's very hard to explain. We're very different, but we understand each other. He's the other half.'

'The other half of what?'

'I don't know. Of me, perhaps.'

'I don't understand.'

'I've tried to explain it once or twice, but people look at me as though I'm queer for the guy. The minute two men show any real affection for each other in America they're accused of being homosexuals—and it's the women who accuse them. Are they all so damned twisted that they have to have men for rivals as well as lovers?' He snatched the bottle from her hand and leaned back against the pillow.

William felt the slippery, hard, still-wet stones of the cobbled street through the soft leather of his wrinkled shoes. Hard stones, polished smooth by generations of plodding peasants and pilgrims. *A pedestrian sense of history*, he thought, and smiled. Walking tours through the ancient capitals of Europe. Travel posters and brochures fluttered in his mind. Around the world in eighty days. The wonders of the Ancient World. Athens. The Acropolis—which no one ever reaches. And the Eternal City. Have you been to the Ufizzi? The Louvre? London Bridge in the rain. And oh, my dear, that charming little market place in Verona under all those umbrellas! The home of Romeo and Juliet, you know. It's so mediaeval—Chartres, I mean. Sun and fun on the Riviera. St. Bernadette in a bikini. The place to go now, of course, is Spain, where everything is so much cheaper. Buckingham Palace. Monte Carlo. If we hurry we can stop for a day in Istanbul. Or in Portugal where they don't kill the bull, even if it still doesn't matter about the horses. The sound of galloping hooves rumbled in his chest. His own feet slapped against the wet stones. Once more it was raining.

'Everybody wants something from other people,' said Alex.

'No,' said Maggie, 'I never wanted anything from him. I hated the idea of people clawing at one another, squeezing, pushing them, leaning on them, demanding pity and love.'

'You have no pity?'

'No. I don't feel sorry for anyone. Not even you. And certainly not him.'

'Call it compassion, then.'

'Call it what you please,' she said. 'Love should free us, not imprison us.'

'And passion?'

She looked at him with her wide, large eyes. Cat-like, they narrowed. 'We make love to escape our passion.'

He wet his thin lips meditatively. 'If you're so concerned

with your god-damned freedom, what are you doing here?'

'You don't understand. What I do for other people has nothing to do with pity. I'm not here as a missionary or a martyr.'

'Hardly!'

She hesitated. 'You were angry when I decided to come. I hope I haven't ruined it for you.'

'No,' he said. 'If it wasn't for you we would never have gotten here. He would have let me down.'

'I don't think so,' she said. 'It means too much to him.'

'It doesn't mean a damn thing to him. Any willing dame in the world could distract him in a minute. He's only here because he has nothing better to do.'

'I don't think that's true, Alex. He cares what happens to you. And I care too.'

'You know, I think you do and I don't understand why.'

'Because you're a rare and wonderful man,' she said. 'Because there is more life and feeling in you per square inch than in almost anyone I've ever met. Because you're not a coward.'

'That's what you think,' he said. 'I couldn't begin to name the things that scare me.'

'But I can name a few that don't,' she said.

The rain dampened William's shirt and warm skin. He felt it on his arms and face as he walked close to the walls and shop fronts of the winding street. He stopped in the doorway of a souvenir shop and stared at the clutter of ashtrays and pennants and plaster Christs in the window. It could have been a souvenir display in any of a hundred other cities in the world. The word *Lourdes* was stamped or carved on everything, and, though some of the details were different, the general effect was the same—sickening colours, shiny metal, carved wood, an internationally accepted and understood blandness and dullness in the style of everything, including the saints and madonnas and water-colour paintings of the grotto.

A sheep bell jangled as he pushed the door open, and then again as he closed it behind him. No one else was in the shop except a pretty, dark-haired girl who came towards him with a shy smile. She said something to him in German and he shook his head. 'Do you speak English?' he said.

'A little. You wish to find something.'

He smiled at her. 'That's fine,' he said. 'Your English is very good.'

She blushed and folded her hands across her breasts. She could not have been more than sixteen, and the pink smock she wore over her dress made her look like a little schoolgirl.

'I'll just look around, if you don't mind,' he said, turning away from her. She went to the back of the shop and started to unpack a box that seemed more filled with straw than anything else. He could hear her humming as he surveyed the shelves and counters of candles and jewellery and statues. He looked more closely at some of the things, and at the price-tags. There were rosary beads of all kinds, wood, stone, glass. There was a model of the basilica with an electric light inside that worked on a battery. It reminded him of the little houses and stations that went with electric train sets. At Christmas-time when he was a boy he would visit the elaborate displays in the department stores in New York. Miles of track wound through tunnels, across artificial meadows, past farms and mills and towns, and little men, caught for all of eternity in the act of waving or working or throwing a switch, decorated the unreal, motionless world through which the powerful little engine charged, the only living thing in the whole display, aside from an occasional blinking signal or a gate at a railway crossing that closed as if by magic when the train went roaring by.

There were hats and shawls and canes (but no crutches), and all marked with the word *Lourdes*. Hand-made silver jewellery from the Basque country, wood-carvings in bas-relief of the Last Supper, the Crucifixion, and, of course, St. Bernadette kneeling before the grotto. That young girl, that dark-haired young girl, with naked feet and asthma in the dead of winter!

On a table in the centre of the shop there stood hundreds of madonnas. They came in all sizes, but each one, no matter what her size, smiled with loving kindness and outspread hands towards an invisible kneeling Bernadette. Perhaps it was she, thought William, who had the vision, and not the other way around. In the centre of the crowd of plaster madonnas there was one enormous statue, similar to all the others except for her size. She was perhaps three feet high and seemed to dominate the others. Her features were somewhat more distinct and her look of rosy-cheeked sweetness was a bit sickening. William's jaw tightened and he felt his teeth grinding. How stupid can people be, he thought. How utterly stupid!

At the back of the shop the girl kneeled beside the crate that she was unpacking. William glanced at her and noticed that her knees were slightly parted. He could catch a glimpse of her white thigh. How easy it would be, he thought, just to fall on her—right there in the shop, right on the floor, just to lay her down and part her legs. He forced himself to look away.

A rack of walking-sticks caught his attention. Some had curved handles, others had metal or stone or ivory knobs. He felt the weight of one or two. Then he took one down that was made of olive wood. It was smooth and heavy and quite beautiful. Perhaps he would buy it, he thought, and saw himself striding across open green country or poking his way along a mountain path. He was alone. Armies of birds played in the underbrush and a cold, clear stream ran soothingly over the smooth rocks. He sat by the stream in a shower of sunlight and wondered away the afternoon. Perhaps that's how he should do it? Perhaps that's how he should write his books, alone, embraced by nature and silence. There would be no people, no intrusions, not even a dog to sniff at his ankles. He wouldn't smoke or drink. His simple meals would come from the forest—fruits and nuts and cool water. He could see himself, bearded and brown and lean, his eyes glowing with special purity and wisdom, his hand firm and sure on the olive-wood stick.

'Six months. They always say six months, which only means that it can happen at any time or that they just don't know enough about it.'

Maggie now was stretched out on the bed and Alex sat beside her. 'And there's nothing they can do?'

'No. The retina is almost gone and there's no way to replace it. They know what's happening, but they don't know why. It never gets better; it only gets worse, though sometimes it seems to be arrested at a certain stage. It's been the same for a while now.'

'Perhaps it'll stay that way.'

'No. Sooner or later it has to give out.'

'And then?'

He shrugged and took another sip from the bottle. 'And then nothing. That's it.'

'I mean what will you do?'

'I don't know. I really don't know.' He felt her hand move to his and then along his wrist.

'There will be something, I'm sure,' she said. 'There are many things . . .'

'Oh, that part of it doesn't bother me. There's something else; something even worse.'

Her hand tightened as though she was afraid to hear what it was, but she waited for him to say it.

'I've never mentioned it to anyone, not even Bill. Not even my wife.' He hesitated and looked away from her. 'It's the kids. The damned thing may be inherited. I took them all in for a check-up not long ago and the doctor said he couldn't be sure but he didn't like what he saw in at least two of them. I told Helen that everything was all right.'

'Oh, my God,' said Maggie, forcing back the warm tears that rushed to her eyes. She sat up and took him by the shoulders to pull him towards her. He let his head fall against her shoulder and he felt her long gentle hands stroking his neck and back. 'It's not fair,' she whispered. 'It's just not fair to kick you that way when you're down already.' Her voice quivered and the tears clouded her eyes.

The constant tension in his whole body that caused Alex to tremble and ache suddenly subsided and he leaned more heavily against her. He closed his eyes and listened to his own heavy breathing. He put his arms around her and she held him as though he were a child, rocking him back and forth to comfort him.

William lingered in the shop, glancing now and again at the rain that beat against the windows and at the girl who hummed quietly to herself as she worked. The heaps of gaudy souvenirs that filled the tiny place made him dizzy. He felt enormous and clumsy, as though any minute he was going to turn round and break something. The shelves mounted to the ceiling, racks protruded, plastic saints and grottoes dangled above him. He closed his eyes for a moment to blot it all out and thought suddenly of Alex in his darkness. Like a child playing blind man he tapped cautiously with his stick and tried to take a few steps. Something blocked his way. He opened his eyes and stared down at the hundred plaster madonnas. They smiled at him with their painted kindness. Or were they merely laughing. His head tightened. He tried to focus on one face in the sea of similar faces, but his eyes swam around amongst them, settling at last on the tallest of the figures. His heart pounded in his chest, and then stopped for a second as he imagined that the statue moved. She bowed her head towards him and a breeze seemed to ripple through her veil. Before he knew what he was doing he had raised his stick over his head and brought it down like a sword. The decapitated Virgin toppled into the lesser madonnas and half a dozen of them crashed to the floor.

The startled young girl ran towards him wringing her hands and crying, 'Monsieur, monsieur.' With wide eyes and a pale, puzzled face she looked at the broken statues and then at William.

'An accident,' he muttered. 'It was an accident.' He held the stick out to her. 'It was the stick,' he said. She shook her head and backed away from him. From his wallet, with trembling hands, he took a hundred-franc note and threw it towards her. It fluttered to the floor on the broken bits of plaster. 'There,' he said. 'That will pay for everything.' And then he too backed away. Before he turned to leave he took another hundred-franc note from his wallet and put it down on the table. Without another word he rushed out of the shop, still carrying the olive-wood stick.

The half-sleep that descended on Alex as he lay on the bed, still comforted by Maggie's warm embrace and fondling hands, was threatened with the beginnings of a hundred dreams that his half-waking state interrupted and drove off. He was weeping in a garden beside a lemon tree. He was back in high school, shifting from foot to foot as Helen came down the echoing stony hall, laughing girlishly with her friends. His wife groaned in the hot August night as her belly ripened into another child. He could smell the perspiration in the stuffy room and hear his son Andy breathing through a summer cold. She whispered to him and he groped in the darkness. In the stench of McGrogan's rat-ridden bar William, breathing smoke and leaning over his tenth bloody Mary, muttered his drunken lecture. 'The poet is a distillery. He has no life of his own. He is gravel through which life like water seeps and is purified, but for others, who drink at the cool clear stream and are refreshed, not by goodness but by truth, by something as necessary as water.' And on he droned, his tie undone, the sweat, like grease, smeared across his forehead and running down his temples to his unshaven cheeks. But nothing would hold together in his dreams. Nothing would stand still. He was neither awake nor asleep. Memories mingled with fantasies and he could feel the warmth of Maggie's breast against his face.

'You mustn't give in,' she whispered. 'You mustn't let it destroy you.' Her voice came to him across the canal and from beyond the bay and over the wide rough sea. The seagulls sailed on the wind, circled, dipped, circled again and glided silently shoreward. He felt the crude, lovely texture of the sails of his first boat and the force they captured as the sun twinkled on the rippling bay. How excited he was. How young. How free. The world was a feast and he came to it with his invitation clutched in his trembling hand.

'Everything will be all right,' she said, leaning beside him and caressing his cheek. 'Don't let your anger destroy you. Don't weaken. You're too tired now to know.' His breathing was more even. He remembered the old Buick he used to drive, a ludicrous, ancient, rattling machine, stuffed with children and baskets of food and balloons. They howled and sang as they rumbled and squeaked the few miles over clogged highways to the state park for a Sunday picnic. He drove in open defiance of the law, that said he could not see well enough, even in those days, to be issued a licence.

He stirred in Maggie's arms and sighed. She felt him slipping into a deeper sleep. Her words melted into music, a distant song, tender and nostalgic, fading away and returning, like the breathing of a calm surf.

William lurked outside the door, pale and uncertain. He carried several bottles and the deadly olive stick. For some reason the number on the door did not look familiar. There had been so many hotels, so many numbers. He stared and hesitated for another moment and then turned the knob.

Maggie raised herself up half-way, but the drowsing Alex rested heavily on her arm and hand. She looked at William but said nothing. Her blonde hair was wild and her clothes were twisted and dishevelled. William slammed the door loudly behind him and Alex stirred, lifting his head and coughing. 'A touching scene,' said William. 'Florence Nightingale and the fallen angel.' He put the bottles down on the bureau and waited for her to say something or for Alex to notice that he was back.

'Tell him to go away,' mumbled Alex. 'Tell him I'm busy.'

'He was asleep,' said Maggie, standing up and straightening her clothes.

'After you got through with him, I'm sure he was.'

'What's he talking about?' said Alex, now sitting up in the bed and rubbing his face. William noticed the empty pint of Scotch on the night table.

'He thinks we've been making love,' said Maggie with quiet anger. She found her bag and searched for a comb.

'Oh, is that all,' said Alex. 'Sure. Sure, Doc, we've been making love, all right, but what's that got to do with you? I mean, the lady's not your wife by any chance, is she?' He squinted towards the empty bottle and rubbed his chest through his half-unbuttoned shirt.

'You're not amusing, Mr. Pilgrim, so just knock it off, will you.'

'I didn't intend to be amusing, Professor Mariner,' said Alex, his tone sharper and more angry than ever. 'I'm a grown-up man, just a trifle older than you, in fact, and I'll do what I damn please. You're neither my brother nor my priest. If I want to make love, or throw myself off a cliff, or spend all my money on booze, that's my business. Just because you were big-hearted enough to come along on this trip, it doesn't mean I hired you as a nurse-maid or a travelling companion for a gibbering idiot.'

'You didn't hire me at all,' said William. 'I came for reasons of my own.'

'That's been clear since we started out,' said Alex. 'You haven't been concerned in the slightest about my reasons for coming. You're never concerned about other people's reasons—for anything. You don't even know other people exist.' He lit a cigarette, his hand shaking visibly as he snapped open his lighter.

'We haven't been doing anything,' said Maggie, combing her hair with her back to the window. 'But he's right; it's none of your business.'

William looked from one to the other. He nodded his head slowly and laughed. 'I begin to understand now. St. Maggie's murderous wedge of kindness, driven like a spike into the poor cripple's heart.'

Alex pointed a threatening finger in William's direction. 'Look, Doc, you may be a professor of something or other, but there are a few things you'll never understand. For one thing, I could have made this miserable trip all alone. I'm not that inept, and I'm not that blind. There are ways to get around. But I thought if I gave you the impression that you were helping me, it might make you feel a little more human. That's right, old buddy. I was doing you a favour, and you rose to the occasion like a rock in water. You can't stand being tied to anyone that closely. It's not that you don't know how to do it—God knows you're efficient enough. It's just that you don't know what to feel. Real human contact embarrasses you and annoys you, like a fly on your nose. You prefer to be left alone. Well, I wouldn't leave you alone. For years I wouldn't leave you alone—not only for your sake, but for mine. Yes, for mine, too, damn it, because I need you as a live friend, not as an emotional corpse. But I can see that I've been wasting my time. It's just no good.' He hesitated. 'So, you know what, Doc? I'm going to let you have it your own way, after all. I'll make it alone from here to wherever I go.' His voice trailed off, and he leaned forward on the edge of the bed as though he were looking for his shoes.

'What you really mean,' said William, 'is that you've found yourself another crutch, one who's a little better looking. And, besides, she's a woman, which means that you can sleep with her occasionally, if you ever get up the courage to do it.'

'Oh, for Christ's sake,' shouted Alex, rising abruptly to his feet.

'Let me finish,' said William. 'You made your pretty speech; now I've got one to make to both of you. Not only have you been taken in by this saintly siren here, but she's been taken in by you. You're both a pair of con-men when it comes to other people. You both see yourselves as towers of virtue, suffering, sacrificing geniuses of the human heart. She crusades for truth and beauty, shoving people's noses into their own weaknesses, destroying them while she urges them towards some impossible ideal of themselves. And all in the name of self-awareness and spiritual perfection. She thrives on cripples because it gives her the upper hand. She waves her magic wand of sex and kindness and watches them perform. You must be better than you are, she says. You must have hope. You must fight. You must pursue the wild goose of truth even into the dark and terrible night. And it all sounds so grand, so convincing, so benevolent and saintly, until you realize that it is only her way of playing God. It is her brand of overweening pride. But, worse even than that, it is her brand of cruelty, because at any moment she can raise the standards and trip you up. She sets herself up as judge and watches you perform. She rewards you with kisses and caresses and *bravos*, but she's never in awe of you, never really afraid, never inferior. She is always in complete control, not only of you, but also of herself.

'She's poised. Look at her. Tall, blonde, arrogant. She's never yet been put down by a man, though she's allowed a few dozen of them to imagine that they have overwhelmed her with their passion and virility. She doesn't know what it means to be overwhelmed. Every time she's come within a mile of a real man, either she's avoided him or he's avoided her. So, Mr. Weary Traveller, even if you did sleep with her, you can stop congratulating yourself. It's no big deal, and no proof of manhood or anything else, except maybe, from her point of view, that you're an easy mark. On the other hand, I have to give you credit for being just as good at your trade as she is at hers.

'*Your* power madness takes another form. You get people to do your bidding and to amuse you by giving them the impression that you need them. But you're subtle. Very subtle. You seem to reject pity. You do, in fact, reject the pity, because you're playing for higher stakes. You don't want pity, you want love. You demand love. It's your privilege and due, and if you don't get it from the people you choose, you will be furious with them. You will find a way to destroy them or punish them. That includes, unfortunately, your children. I've seen you turn on them. Yes, your own kids. Because they pull away from you or disagree with you, you find them insolent little bastards. It is their duty to love you, and not only because you're their father, but because you're Alexander Morgan, and because you suffer more than anyone else in the world suffers.

'With a helping hand from Fate, or whoever blinded you, you've committed an act of self-crucifixion, and now you want the world to admire you and love you for it. You're up there on the cross, smiling and drunk half the time, just to demonstrate to the compassionate world that you're good-natured and brave, and to give them the impression that you will demand nothing of them. You suck them in and once you latch on to someone, there's no clear way out. You do not allow people to dislike you, though sometimes you can't stop them.

'Well, I fell into your little trap, buddy. That's how clever you are. I had myself convinced for a long time that you needed me—not my arm to drag you through crowded streets, or my eyes to describe the world for you, but me. And I fell into hers, too.' He glared at Maggie. 'But now you can go to hell. You can both just go to hell, together or separately. I couldn't care less.'

Maggie stood pale and statue-like, the comb still in her hand.

Alex stumbled towards him, his fists clenched. 'You rotten bastard. You egotistical, cold-hearted bastard.'

'At least I'm honest about it, which is more than I can say about either one of you.' Alex came closer, knocked over a chair stumbled, cursed, and lunged at him with a roundhouse swing. William's heart leapt, not with fear or anger, but with sudden compassion as he realized what was happening. This clumsy, pathetic, half-man was going to hit him. He saw the doubled fist, the grimacing, trembling face, as though the pirate were weeping already. It was such a ludicrous, awkward gesture of violence or bravery, such a flailing, almost comic attack. He wanted to laugh and cry and playfully step out of the way to allow this slapstick Don Quixote clown to fall on his face. But in that moment he could not move. He could not let him do it, could not let him swing and miss and fall—he could not rob him of this last shred of manliness in him. He closed his eyes and waited for a split second that seemed infinitely long before he felt the crashing sting of flesh and bone against his jaw.

He staggered back. A blot of darkness jolted his brain, so that he did not feel himself hit the floor. But he was not unconscious as he lay there. He sat up and shook his head. When he looked up he could see Maggie holding Alex around the shoulders and forcing him back towards the bed.

He got up slowly, rubbing his aching jaw, partly to ease the pain, but more to cover his smile. He went out without another word and closed the door gently behind him.

26

THE LAST HINTS of cloudy light faded from the thickening sky over Lourdes. The mountains merged with the air and lost their identity in the darkness. But still the singing, hopeful pilgrims paraded, across the esplanade, up to the basilica, and down to the grotto, anonymous and invisible now except for their voices and torches. William watched from a distance. Their shielded candles bobbed like fiery corks on a dark sea. Sometimes a face was caught in the slanting light, a ghastly, shadow-ridden face. Sometimes the torches sagged precariously to one side or went out altogether, or fell, like falling stars, so that one could imagine the bearer dying right there, crumpling to the damp ground, or perhaps even being swallowed up by the darkness, with only the falling spark to mark the place where once he stood. The shuffling motion of their slow steps was echoed in the floating torches, and in the simple rhythm of their song. *Laudate, Laudate, Laudate, Maria.*

Though the rain had finally stopped, William did not follow the procession to the grotto. He went back to his room at the pension to write the letter to Edith that he had been rehearsing all day in the back of his mind.

He sat at a small, bare table and wrote it in longhand on unlined sheets of typing paper. Before he could even begin, however, before he could insult that white, empty space with his magic words, there were half a dozen cigarette butts in the ashtray near his right hand. The dizziness and nausea that held him back reminded him of those hundred occasions on which he sat this way before his typewriter, waiting for the courage or the strength to hammer out the first word. Often it did not come and the blank sheet sat there for days, until, when he finally removed it, it curled of its own accord, having taken on permanently the shape of the roller.

He forced himself now to think about what he wanted to say to Edith. If his mind wandered he drove it back to the subject. He asked himself questions and searched for the answers. Did he want to marry her? Is that what he wanted to say? Or did he merely want to come to Paris to live with her for a while? How should he put it? He needed her. She was good and simple and true. She was kind. Or perhaps what he meant to say was that she needed him, that his satisfaction would come from amusing her and soothing her. But no. It was neither. The truth lay elsewhere, and was much more complicated than that. Nevertheless, he could do it with romantic high-school language. He could get his way with such over-simplication. Surely he knew how to get his way. Hadn't he always been able to persuade everyone? Wasn't he, after all, William the Voice, William the shaper of words, a kind of magician? The drunken priest's stuttering voice echoed in his spinning head. 'Even the devil can quote scriptures.'

He grew impatient with himself. Perhaps there was no truth to announce after all. All he wanted was a place to rest and Edith would provide it. Time to think. He mocked himself with the phrase. Time to think. There will be time. There will be time. But when? Time was running out. He felt it slipping away—a thin cushion now between him and some oppressively solid wall against which he would soon be crushed. Did it matter, then, whether he lied or told the truth? Or was that now the whole point at last? Was it finally time to say something honest. His hand trembled over the blank sheet.

For a salutation he wrote her name only. And then, in that painful, erratic, grammar-school penmanship of his, he said: 'Perhaps you will understand all this better than I do. Women have a way of sensing the truth about people and life long before men, with their clumsy intellectual approach, begin to put the pieces together. And you, more so than any other woman I have ever known, have had this patience and insight. I can hope, then, that none of this will confuse you or offend you.

'I will tell you first what I want, and then why you should not accept, and finally why you should. There, is that professorial enough? It's like that old basic principle for teachers: tell them what you're going to tell them, then tell them, then tell them what you've told them. Perhaps teaching was my real trade, after all. I should have stuck to it. It was always much easier than writing. But why do we distrust the things that come easy?

'What I want to do is to come to Paris and marry you. There, I've dropped my rock into the still pool and the circles widen from the broken centre. (Not a bad sentence, that, for an ex-writer!) I'm sitting in a hotel room in Lourdes, cold sober—or almost—and the offer is serious. I've decided that it would be a worth-while gamble for both of us. But let me tell you first why you shouldn't do it.

'The main thing you have to know is that I don't love you in the ordinary, romantic sense. And what's more I'm not sure I know what love is all about. If I wanted to be sweet and persuasive, I'm sure I could justify using the word *love* to describe my feeling for you, but, for a change, I'd like to be more accurate and more honest. I don't think you, yourself, would call it love, though you might. I respect you and I trust you. I even admire you. Those are mighty powerful words for a guy who has spent half his life proving that women are no damn good.

'Not only would you have to put up with the fact that I have no high-school palpitations about the whole thing, but the fact that I'm writing to you partly because I've got my back to the wall. (Not very flattering to you, is it?) My little ball of string has about run out and I don't know what to do next. Nothing seems to work. Maggie's been here, and for a while I thought we might get together, but it hasn't happened, and is not likely to at this point. All we do is fight. And I can't even remember what the fight is all about. So, I'm turning to you, Edith, somewhat out of desperation, which is why you should turn me down.

'On the other hand, I'm playing it straight with you, which is a good beginning. I don't think I've ever been able to do that before with anyone, including Maggie. That's a good reason for accepting this funny, formal offer of mine. The other reasons I leave to your good instincts. Think about it. I'll call you as soon as I get to Paris.'

He read the letter over several times and then folded it twice like a piece of business correspondence. He glanced at his watch. The crystal was broken and it was stopped at ten minutes past ten. He shook it and held it to his ear, but heard nothing. 'Damn,' he muttered aloud in the empty room, and tried to recall exactly what happened when he fell. He remembered Alex stumbling towards him, the wild look of rage and frustration on his face. He remembered that slow-motion roundhouse blow, the clenched fist moving towards him until he could no longer focus on it. But he could not remember the impact or what happened afterwards until he was lying or sitting on the floor. His face throbbed with pain, but he was too pleased or relieved to feel it. Alex had negotiated a tightrope across a profound ravine. He had risked his dignity and self-respect when he struck that blow. And it was an odd pleasure to feel him connect.

He took the watch off and laid it on the table beside the folded letter. Then he took off all his clothes, which he dropped haphazardly on the floor, turned off the light, and climbed into the bed, feeling the nakedness of his body between the cool clean sheets.

After a while, he could not tell how long, the door opened cautiously and someone came into the dark room. He could not see her at first, but he could tell it was Maggie by the sound of her movements. She stood by the window for a while, a tall, dark silhouette against the dim and cloudy moonlight. When she turned to look at him he allowed himself to breathe more heavily, as though he were asleep. She seemed to be waiting for something to happen. Then she undressed slowly, draping her clothes across the foot of the other bed. She went to the window once more and looked out at the sky. She stretched her nude body wearily, her long arms reaching towards the ceiling or the clouded moon, and sighed. As he lay there, William felt the pain and despair and loneliness of that sigh in his chest and in the pit of his stomach. He wanted to comfort her, as once he was able to do. He wanted to use his gift with words, his lies, to soothe her, to tell her that all would be well, so that she would close her eyes, and, with her body pressed against his, slip into drowsiness and finally into sleep. But he said nothing, and she got into the other bed and drew the covers up to her chin like a child.

They lay there for almost half an hour that way, each believing that the other was asleep, and, therefore, as good as dead or indifferent. Then Maggie, without moving, whispered, 'Are you asleep?'

'No,' he said, and that simple exchange conjured up those hundreds of nights when they had spoken the same way to each other, lying in bed, exhausted sometimes but unable or unwilling to sleep. 'Are you asleep?' How similar the tone was. And when she would discover that he was not sleeping, she would raise herself up on her elbow and talk to him. Certainly, now she would do the same. Certainly, she had something to say. And it would be cruel of him not to listen. He remembered how sometimes half drunk with liquor and fatigue, his head leaning to one side, his eyelids like lead, he would hold himself awake to hear her. He would grunt or nod to show that he was listening. And she would say something wonderful or awful, something that she had to put into words before she could sleep. 'I was thinking of my father,' or 'I've been unfaithful,' or 'It's so terrible about George's accident.'

He waited now, but she did not say anything. Then he helped her. 'Is Alex all right?' he said.

'Yes. He drank himself to sleep.'

William forced a laugh to make it still easier. 'Mr. Pilgrim on the rocks,' he said, and he could imagine Maggie's half-smile in the darkness.

'You have to forgive him, Bill. He's very upset.'

'Who am I to forgive anybody?' he said. 'I take Alex as he is.'

'But it's worse than you think,' she said. 'He didn't tell you about the children, did he?'

'What about them?'

'They may have the same trouble with their eyes.'

There was a pause. She heard him make a peculiar noise, somewhere between a sigh and a moan. 'All of them?'

'I don't know. He saw a doctor who told him that two of them showed some signs already.'

'Which two?'

'He didn't say.'

The army of Alex's children paraded before him in William's mind, laughing, devilish boys with crew-cuts; pretty girls with sparkling eyes and long hair. Which two?

'It's so sad,' she said. 'So terribly sad.'

'He finds it hard to hang on to his faith,' said William. 'How can he believe in a benevolent God?'

'How can anyone?' she said.

'I don't know,' he said, and they lapsed again into silence for a while.

After about ten minutes she said it again: 'Are you asleep?' This time she lifted herself up and leaned on her elbow, facing towards him.

'No,' he said.

'Are you angry?'

'No,' he said. 'I'm not angry. Not any more.'

He sat up and put on the light. He saw her huddled in her blankets like a frightened little girl. He rubbed his eyes and shook his head. 'Do you know what I've been doing in here—I mean before you came in?' He pointed to the table. 'Take a look for yourself. That letter there.'

She got up slowly, and, unaware of her nudity, went to the table and read the letter. She refolded it carefully and put it back. She tried to laugh, but it was a feeble effort. Then she climbed back into her bed, pulled the covers once more up to her chin, and closed her eyes.

Neither one said anything further, and after a long time they fell asleep.

27

THE MORNING BLOOMED with flaming red and ocean blue over the restless town, like a giant celestial flower. Dispersing clouds caught the earliest rays of sunlight and heralded a perfect summer day. The still-damp streets began to dry. Shutters opened. The persistent pilgrims were already gathering at the basilica and the grotto.

When William opened his eyes he could not remember for a moment where he was. He looked blankly at the other bed in the room, which was empty, and at the window, through which sunlight poured, filling the place with colours which could not have been seen in the greyness of the day before. Even the rug proved to be more than the solid, muddy grey that it had seemed. It was a worn, deep, oriental pattern, in which the faded red and blues were now visible.

He sat up in bed and looked about the room. He saw the yellow-white walls, the framed photograph of the esplanade, the heavy but simple furniture, and, on the table, the folded letter. He rubbed his unshaven face and frowned as he remembered the events of the evening before. And, then, as if to drive them away again, he got out of bed, dressed quickly and washed his face with cold water. When, he wondered, did Maggie get up? Surely she had gone to see Alex. Unless she was walking, as she sometimes did in the early morning hours. 'It helps me to sort things out,' she used to say. He opened his suitcase and searched for his razor.

His face was still half full of soap when Maggie appeared in the doorway, pale and weary-looking. 'I think you'd better come and talk to Alex,' she said, 'He's in bad shape.'

His hand froze in mid-air and his heart tightened. 'What is it?' he said.

'He got at the bottles you left there last night and he's dead drunk and raving like a madman.'

'All right,' said William, with the sudden coldness of a surgeon. He finished shaving and tucked his shirt into his trousers.

'Jesus Christ,' said William, as they walked into the room. 'What the hell has been going on in here?' Chairs were overturned, drawers pulled out of the bureau, the bedclothes stripped from the bed. The curtains were torn, as though someone were trying to claw his way out through them, and a split pillow oozed feathers over the wrinkled rug. Alex lay sprawled on his stomach, fully clothed, on the bare mattress.

William walked over and poked him in the shoulder, as though to wake him. 'Go to hell, you bastard!' shouted Alex, without looking up.

'Come on,' said William, like a scolding schoolmaster. 'Get up!'

'Go away, I don't want to talk to you. You're a rotten bastard.' He lifted his swaying head and seemed to be looking at William from under his eye-patch, which was shoved back out of its normal position.

'Pull yourself together and listen to me,' insisted William. He had him firmly by the arm now.

Alex allowed himself to be dragged into a sitting position, but he sagged precariously and could not quite keep his balance. 'Enough god-damned shit,' spluttered Alex. 'I've had enough. I won't stand for it anymore—God or no God.' William steadied him. 'Who's that?' bellowed Alex, trying to pull away.

'That you, Doc? Come to give me your Sunday morning lecture on fornication? Come on, Professor, tell me all about it. How to fuck your way to heaven. How to be a lousy bastard without going blind. Article by William Mariner, Professor Mariner, Ph.D. Professor of nothing! Another god-damned phoney.'

'Take it easy, buddy,' said William. 'There are other people in this hotel and it's early in the morning.'

'I don't care. Bunch of phoney pilgrims. Come to hang up their god-damned crutches. What do they know? What do they care about anything? What does anybody care about anything?'

'About you, you mean.'

He looked up as though he was searching for William's face. His uncovered eye was a squinting bloodshot mess. There was a bruise on his cheek where he had fallen against something. 'Yeah,' he shouted. 'Me! What's wrong with that? I have a right to live, don't I? I worked for it. I earned it. I broke my ass to build a family. And I loved them. I'm no god-damned saint like you. Or like her either.'

'Please,' said Maggie. 'You're all upset over nothing.'

'Nothing? Nothing?' He jerked his arm away from William. 'That's right, nothing. Nothing to you or to him. Nothing to anybody except me. And now I don't give a damn anymore. To hell with it. To hell with the whole stupid mess.'

'See if you can get some black coffee,' said William to Maggie.

'All right,' she whispered, and went out.

'That's right, Doc,' said Alex. 'Coffee. That'll fix everything. Right? Black coffee for the old drunk. Well I got news for you, old friend; it ain't going to fix anything. I'm through. I'm not going down to that damned rock. I'm not going to crawl to him anymore. If there's a God, he'll have to come and get me. I'm finished. Through. I don't believe in him anymore, and I hate him. God's a bastard!' He raised his voice again 'Do you hear what I'm saying? I said God's a bastard.' His voice broke and tears spilled from his eyes. His head fell forward between his knees and he shook with sobbing.

William went into the bathroom and soaked a towel with

cold water. He dropped it without warning on the back of Alex's neck. Alex stiffened up. 'Jesus Christ,' he cried. 'What are you doing?' He tried to shove William aside and to brush away the towel. Water dripped down his back and he shivered. 'Get that damn thing off me. Get away from me. Just leave me alone.'

'You'll be all right in a little while,' said William.

'That's what everyone keeps telling me. You'll be all right. You'll be all right. Well, I won't. I know it, and they know it. Even you know it. Why doesn't somebody tell me the truth for a change. Lies. Everybody tells me lies. Even you. You, who I loved more than a brother. You lie to me, Doc.'

'Come on! You've got a lot to do today.'

'I have nothing to do. I'm not going out there, I tell you. Didn't you hear me?'

'You're going if I have to carry you.'

'Look, Doc, I knocked you on your ass once; I can do it again. Surprised you, didn't I?' He laughed bitterly. 'You didn't think I could still do it, did you? Well, I'm not dead yet, fella. I still have my hands.' He held them out towards William. 'I did a lot with these hands. Remember? I built houses. I sailed boats. I held my children. I worked. I made things. They're good hands. Strong hands.' His voice grew quiet, almost meditative. 'With these hard, dirty hands I made love to that young girl who was my wife. It was winter and I was shovelling sand and mixing concrete all week. She was pregnant for the first time, and bloomed like a rose. I'd come home with these leather, animal paws of mine and try to feel the softness of her skin and flesh through the callouses. I was almost afraid to touch her. No matter how much I scrubbed them I couldn't get them clean. The cement hardened in the creases and under my nails. But then later, in bed, she took my hand and held it against her naked breast. And that was all I needed, Doc. That was all.'

William put his hand on his shoulder and Alex moved away, but not violently this time. 'I'll run a bath for you. You can soak for a while.'

Alex shook his head but said nothing.

'You'll feel a lot better.'

'You don't understand, Doc,' said Alex. 'I'm giving it all up.'

'Giving up what?'

'Everything! God. Love. You. Everything. Hope. That most of all. I don't believe in this place. We came all the way here from across the ocean and I don't believe in it. I should have found out sooner. You must have known that I didn't believe in it. Why didn't you tell me? Would have saved us both a lot of trouble. The whole thing is a stupid circus. Souvenir shops full of saints. What a laugh. And all those jerks out there on their knees praying to a rock, where some hysterical little girl thought she saw something. Stupid. The whole thing is incredibly stupid.'

'Maybe not for those who believe in it,' said William, sitting down now beside him.

'Well, I'm not one of them. I don't believe in it. I don't believe in anything.'

'You may feel different later on,' said William, getting up again and going into the bathroom to fill the tub. He turned on only the cold water.

When he came back Alex was lying back on the bed and seemed to be falling asleep again. 'Come on,' he said firmly. 'Take off your clothes.' He sat him up and started to unbutton his shirt. Alex's protests were drunkenly feeble, as if his outburst had completely exhausted him.

When Maggie returned with the coffee she found William dragging a naked and flailing Alex towards the bathroom. She made no attempt to turn away. She set the metal pot down on the bureau and unstacked the three cups. She heard them fumbling and wrestling in the bathroom. Somebody slipped and William cursed. Finally, there was a splashing of water and Alex's plaintive moan.

William turned on the shower and let it pour down on Alex's head. 'That's enough. Enough,' he protested through streams of water that ran over his face.

'Just sit there a while,' said William. He came out and looked at Maggie. 'He'll be all right in a little while.'

She sat down on the bed with a sigh of relief. 'Thank God.

When I first came in I thought he had gone completely off his head.'

William poured himself a cup of coffee and lit a cigarette. Then he offered some to Maggie. She accepted and they smoked and drank for a while in embarrassed silence. Finally she said, 'I'm sorry I couldn't tell you last night. It was a good letter. I didn't know—'

'How could you know,' he said. 'I just made up my mind yesterday.'

'Well,' she said, getting up and walking towards the window, 'I guess that's that.' She stared down into the sun-drenched street, where people passed like puppets in a toy village.

Before he could say anything, Alex's moans and curses intruded.

An hour or so later Alex was sane again. He was dressed and shaved and full of coffee. But the more sober he became the more silent he was. His lips grew thinner and his jaw tighter.

'Are you about ready to go?' said William.

He nodded. 'But alone,' he said. 'From here on in I'd rather be alone. I mean all the way—all the way back home.'

'All right,' said William. 'If that's the way you want it.'

Maggie looked at him and frowned, as though she was about to object or was puzzled by William's easy agreement.

'That's the way I want it, Doc,' said Alex. He got up, and with reasonable firmness, found his way to the door.

28

THE LAST CLOUDS melted from the morning sky. The sun grew smaller and whiter as it rose higher, threatening a day of mid-summer heat and blinding light. Sunlight caught the rising stone spire of the Basilica of the Immaculate Conception, a slender, decorated tower topped by what seemed, from a distance, a lace-like metal cross. Smaller spires stood like sentinels at the head of the enormous curving ramps that rose over the crypt where Bernadette was buried. Inside, the body of the saint, her hands and face idealized with wax, lay in a state of obvious composure and purity in a highly decorated, glass-panelled coffin, her head resting on a lace-covered pillow, and the rest of her, except for those waxen hands and face, shrouded in her black nun's habit.

Saint Maggie, too, lay silently on her back. Her face, unlined and pale, might also have been made of wax. And her long fingers were gently intertwined, as though she had died in the act of praying. But her crypt was only the small, battered hotel room in which Alex had spent the night. Sunlight poured through the torn curtains and the air was stale with the smell of burnt tobacco.

She was alone. Bells sounded in the distance and small birds chirped in the gutters. She thought of the birds that sang in the ivy at college. How long ago it seemed, and how young she was, even then writing her play, painting, planning to go to Europe for the first time, in love, not only with men, but, in a different way, with women, with Louisa, the sparrow of a dark-haired French girl with whom she played and laughed, and who she watched flutter and fall into madness before she was twenty-one years old, a beautiful bird with a fiery heart and a broken wing. Her nervous, smiling face leapt into the oddness of the moment, a fleeting meteor of reality that faded as fast as it came, to be replaced by the dampness of the old graveyard where she and Charlie Walsh made love, both delighted at their daring, both charged with animal youth and youthful wondering. She was already notorious, already admired and feared, not only because of her height and physical prowess, but because of her articulate flaunting of all the middle-class absurdities from which her less imposing, pimple-faced classmates so desperately wanted to free themselves.

She helped them. She preached. She painted outrageous pictures and failed courses in Chemistry and Mathematics with the bravado of a gambler tossing away hundred-dollar bills. Of course she never graduated, never, in fact, finished anything, but what was it she had in mind out there in those carefree, hopeful days? What secret secured her against Louisa's kind of chaos? Surely there was something, some vision, some goal, some confidence in her own joy and strength. She could never say that she wanted to be specifically this or that. She could never envision her future. There was marriage, of course. They all talked about that, and she, too, dreamed and idealized and wondered. Eventually, yes, but not for a long, long time. There were too many other things to consider, to feel, to roll around in one's young heart.

She was alone in the ruined crypt. William had gone out—partly to see the town, but more, she was convinced, to get away from her, to whom now he seemed unable to speak. He avoided her eyes. He spoke in the coldly polite way that he used towards students or shopkeepers or deans of universities.

She heard him close the door. She heard him walk down the hallway, and, then, from the window, she saw him stroll heavily away, a slightly slouching brute of a man, unable to lose himself in the crowd of shuffling sightseers and pilgrims.

Her hands tightened against each other and against her chest. But she could not draw herself in and away from that sudden chill of loneliness. He had let her come to him again, but only to slam the door in her face, only to remind her that she was a fraud and a failure. Was that all he ever wanted from her, she wondered. To beat her and beat her with the stick of his own guilt and anger. To mock her as Saint Maggie. To mock all women, all goodness, all hope. Or was he, in some way, right? Was it possible, after all, that she had played the devil in this rambling drama, though she recited only the lines of prophets and virgins and saints?

In the dampness of doubt her body ached. Rain swept like a hail of bullets across the lake near the old farm. Her father winced in stubborn silence as the pain drummed endlessly in his wasted body. He told her with his hand that he wanted her there until the very end. She gave him her hand, and, without tears, waited through the long night for a dawn that he would never see—a dawn so ordinary that one might have expected to wake to the reassuring fragrance of frying bacon and eggs and the sound of slippered feet in the kitchen. She would row across the lake to the shack on the other side that she was fixing for herself as a studio. She would cut a few boards, dab on some paint, read a while on the sloping bank, and then come back for lunch, having also, perhaps, taken a swim to sharpen her appetite. But none of those things could happen any more. Nothing would ever be the same. The dome of her little girl's world had fallen in and a cold black sky showed through.

Bells rang again. The birds sang. A gentle breeze lifted the torn curtains for a moment and then let them settle against the window frame.

Alex sorted out the confusing world of Lourdes through a crack of light and with a whirling, trembling mind that, for a long time, could create no order out of the chaos of slanting and sliding fragments. He walked slowly, looking for the corners and edges that would betray the shape of things about him. He saw cobble-stones and granite walls. Iron railings guarded roadways and paths. Where did they all lead? Some curved up towards the basilica; others dipped down only to be lost in the trees and shrubs, or in the darkness of his peripheral blindness. He could smell the nearness of water before he actually saw the river. He imagined, too, that he could hear it, though it flowed by silently, somewhere far below the road on which he wandered towards a complex of buildings. He stopped often to feel the cool iron of the railings and to study the many-levelled scene. He had missed the entrance to the esplanade, and now he could see it below him, inaccessible from where he stood.

People passed him. He heard their footsteps and the rustling of their clothes. They spoke mostly French, but at times he heard other languages—Italian, German, Spanish, and some that he could not identify. A child was shouting and crying somewhere. Two priests in long gowns brushed past him. They laughed, or someone laughed. Strips of red and black material flashed for a split second across his narrow field. He tried to follow them with his eyes, but he saw only a blur of faces beside him, a family apparently, gathered for a moment at the same railing, a man with a bald head and bulging eyes, three or four children, a young woman and an older woman. The older one was dressed completely in black. Her face was collapsing into ruddy rolls of fat. The man herded his flock together and pointed a camera at them. Alex stepped aside to avoid being included in the picture. A body wrapped in blankets floated by a few feet from the ground. He could not see the wheels that supported the stretcher, but he caught a glimpse of an old woman's agony-stained face. Her lipless, sunken mouth was pressed together. Her eyes pleaded with him and the world. For what? he wondered. For what? Did she think she would ever be a girl again? Did she think the Blessed Virgin would rescue her from the humiliation and pain of old age? Only Death could do that for her, and perhaps she was already beginning to see that he was no enemy after all.

He turned back to the puzzle of avenues, trees, and lawns

below. He saw that the curving ramps led up to the basilica and remembered pictures of the place he had seen. Before making the trip with William he had talked with a priest in Seaville, who had given him a pamphlet with illustrations. He knew, therefore, something of the rituals and the buildings in Lourdes. Somewhere, he knew, there was a huge confessional centre, where one could make his confession in his own language to a priest who understood him. He would go there first and try to prepare himself for the visit to the grotto. But he would not ask for information or directions. He would study the numerous signs and find his own way. Nothing, he was sure, could be very far from the basilica. He would keep circling and exploring until the place felt more familiar.

William enjoyed wandering in new places, especially crowded places. And he enjoyed doing it anonymously and alone, not for any particular purpose, not because he was a notebook novelist or an amateur sociologist or a greedy tourist, but only because he was fascinated by people in the process of living. He liked market-places and busy avenues and cafés, subways and buses. Air terminals, too, were filled with people in the midst of something, coming or going, with a dozen little pieces of business to attend to: their luggage, their tickets, their wandering, wailing children. He liked the crowds at baseball games and football games. But, even more, he enjoyed the wide-eyed worried gamblers at the racetrack, each one lost in a private world of calculation and hope, each one trying to predict the future, laying not only money on the line, but ego and intelligence and judgement. And each time he failed one could see in his face a lifetime of disappointment, hurt, or feigned indifference. Sometimes, even, a faint smile of satisfaction. And each winner beamed or howled with sudden joy, his self-respect and confidence restored for a few hours at least. *Poor Man, poor Mankind!*

The whispered echo haunted him now in this haunted holy place. They lay on stretchers along paths and on lawns, lined up like wounded soldiers waiting to be evacuated, or victims of a great disaster, a flood, perhaps. Attendants rushed here and there to help them, to move them towards the grotto or the baths or wherever they chose to go. They were the *invalids*, the chosen ones, their bidding must be done. How much closer to God they were, after all, being diseased or crippled. They lay there in their stretchers, pleased for the chance to appear this way in public, to dramatize with saintly looks of agony and hope whatever tragedy, however mundane, brought them to this holy and infirm state.

There were many more women than men, William noticed. Why? was it simply the male sense of dignity that kept some men from displaying their weakness this way? He tried to imagine himself lying there on the damp grass under the morning sun, or being wheeled about in one of the wheelchairs provided by the volunteers. But that wasn't fair; that wasn't enough. To capture the feeling he also had to imagine himself the victim of some deadly disease or accident—cancer, paralysis, a failing heart, blindness. Perhaps then fear would drive him to try everything. Would he then pray? Would he come with this kind of humility and self-pity to bow his head before the Virgin on the outside chance that she really existed, really appeared before a fourteen-year-old child?

He didn't know. The possibility made him angry, not because people are frightened in the face of death (he, too, was frightened in the war), but because their fear obscures the truth. How can one trust the faith of a dying man? The time to discover God, if, indeed, there was a God to discover, was when one needed him least—in the midst of joy or contentment, not out of desperation. Then, perhaps, he might wonder more seriously about the possibility. But *poor mankind* did not seem to work that way. Men turned to God only when they were convinced that no mortal hand could save them. Children turn to their mothers and fathers only as long as they can think of them as god-like. After the disenchantment they need something else to fill the terrible vacuum. So the Blessed Virgin is everybody's mother, and God himself, not Christ, sits back, remote in his maleness and authority, a universal father.

Images of the limp and naked Christ figure passed through his mind. And what is *he* in all this? The son! And, therefore, the victim; therefore, slight of build in many of the portrayals, almost a boy. He thought of Michelangelo's *Pieta*—the Christ child, now a full-grown man, still a child in the arms of the young Virgin, now a woman, still a girl. And, of course, it is he with whom we must identify. It is Christ who took on a human form, who died a human death, who cried out, 'Oh my God, why hast thou forsaken me,' as we might all cry out to that remote father, 'Why oh why hast thou forsaken me?' How difficult it is to believe that his arbitrary punishment of the entire race is all a form of divine justice. The guilt of our fathers! No wonder Alex was shaken over and over again in his faith. And no wonder he kept running back to it.

William found himself staring at a sturdy, middle-aged man in a wheelchair. He was carrying a colourful banner, a flag for one of the groups of pilgrims. His air was almost militant, though his legs were withered and limp. He wore a sweater under his ill-fitting old jacket and a tie with a soft large knot. One could imagine him with his impressive belly and his broad shoulders as the boisterous but lovable mayor of a small village somewhere in a farming district of France. In his thick hand he clutched a rosary. It was that, more than anything else about the man, that touched William. It was that thick, powerful hand, too awkward and swollen with work to handle those delicate beads. What those hands needed was rocks to smash and trees to tear apart and ploughs and hammers, and enemies to subdue in the name of simple, muscular justice. He was a healthy bull of a peasant from the waist up and a corpse from the waist down. Perhaps, like Alex, he had come to avenge himself on God. Perhaps that accounted for his frown and his huge, clenched fist.

William walked away, but the image of the crippled peasant stayed with him. How could such a man ever accept the justice and benevolence of such an attack on his body? And, yet, sometimes people do. Sometimes they put aside their defiance and anger—their pride. He remembered football players who were built like this peasant, hulking and strong and quick. They moved through the world with such a physical sureness that one might imagine they had solved all human problems.

But the sureness was only physical.

He had felt it, too, when his body was young and hard and he could move with force and grace over the green carpet of the playing field. But even then he knew it was only an animal achievement, even as his feet tore into the ground, even as his legs hurled him through space or against the equally hard chest and shoulders of the opposition, he knew that this mere exercise, this mere enjoyment of flesh and violence could do no more than amuse him for the moment. It solved nothing. Which is why he gave it up. But how ironic! How miserably ironic! He had given up attacking the world with his sweating, flying body, in order to attack it with his mind and his art. He had lowered his head in another way. The opposition was invincible, and now he sat there on the ground, dazed and exhausted, wondering if he had even the strength to go on playing the game or the courage to accept with dignity the fact that a victory was no longer possible.

Yes, he thought, this is what he had come to at last. He was the peasant in the wheelchair. Half of him was still driven by youth and sheer physical strength; and the other half was crippled and dead. He was driven forward by hope and backward by despair. He knew the game was lost, but he could not stop playing it. That was the impasse, the contradiction. One had to accept the inevitable defeat, but go on acting as if victory were still possible. He shook his head, as though to free himself from the paradox.

The sun grew warmer and the crowd grew thicker. He could see the gentle river and the rolling hills beyond. He allowed himself to be soothed by the freshness of the green hills and the reassuring warmth of the sun. The path to the grotto was not crowded for the moment, but then he heard the singing of a shuffling parade of pilgrims. They came towards him, four abreast, their banners flying, their priests leading the way, their voices echoing through the summer stillness of the valley—*Laudate, Laudate, Laudate, Maria!* He watched them pass by, unmoved either by compassion or anger, yet impressed by the spectacle, the sheer drama. Huddled together this way they achieved a certain nobility and dignity that, individually, they did not have. Their song clouded his mind—but pleasantly. Silently his lips formed the words that they sang, and his foot tapped the slow rhythm.

Maggie drifted. She was afloat on an endless sea, warm, naked, and alone. She remembered the sunlight and the soothing uniformity of the blue sky. What a comfort it was—that day on a deserted stretch of beach somewhere below Chioggia, the Adriatic, ancient and calm, like a wise old man recalling a hundred million years of nostalgic memories. And then the dream-like week at Castiglioncello, the old hotel, empty in the off-season, except for them, the gardens, the rocks, and the catamaran from which they dived into the clear deep water, splashing each other, laughing, forgetting for a while the old battle.

She longed to be somewhere else again, somewhere warm and unreal, another land, another beach. But there could not always be another country, another sea, another dream of perfect peace and love. The pieces never held together. All her life she had tried, holding her breath, shutting her eyes, to hang on to the vision. But always something went wrong and her soaring sea-gull flight was turned into a spiralling plunge. Out of the past came the screeching tyres of the speeding Jaguar. The wild-eyed young Greek beside her pushed his foot to the floor and sent the roaring machine hurtling off the road into the rocky, sunbaked desolation of that dry land.

He had pleaded with her to marry him and she had refused, but so kindly, so generously, that all his passion turned to rage, to something worse than humiliation. After the nightmare of the collision there was the drugged dream of the hospital, the white uniforms, the masks, the blue eyes of the nurse, the tinkling of metal instruments and the smell of ether. It was four days later that someone told her that Nicolas was dead, and more than another month before she believed it. By that time she was home, recuperating, her body stitched and inevitably to be scarred in half a dozen places. The realization came to her as she sat by the lake, pretending to read a novel by Virginia Woolf. She let the book slip from her hand and wept quietly —for him, for herself, for the whole world.

Alex circled. He discovered signs. He translated. Paths and buildings grew familiar, more to his feet than to his eyes. The slanting of the sunlight told him much, as did the breeze. After wandering for half the morning he even had a sense of the whole place, a vague shape, rising land, the river, the valley, an old town, a new church. He knew where the confessional was, but he hesitated, waiting for the exploded pieces of himself to settle into place. The air cleared his head, and the coughing that left him breathless disappeared.

He found a winding path that led up a hill towards a huge cross on which hung the crucified figure of Christ. Along the way the stations of the cross were depicted with life-size painted statues. The wooded hill was quiet, except for an old man making his way towards the cross on his knees. The noisy town receded behind him. He lingered here and there to study the groupings of statues. The story of Christ unfolded. He remembered with boyish sentimentality his Sunday school lessons, old Father Prentice, who had long ago died, and some of his childhood friends, dispersed now, gone, somewhere into the world, or dead. And his cousin who was so much taller, so much more handsome, even as a young boy—that promising, carefree lad, whom he could not see to save.

At the top he tried to kneel and pray, but his legs would not bend and his mouth grew tight, as though to prevent the words from coming out. He did not stay there long at the foot of the cross. And when he came down the hill again he went directly to the place of confession, without hesitating or faltering.

What was it, thought William, that he had set out to write, so eager, even in college, to put it all down. There was the story of a young boy, wandering in the streets of a big city. He was ten years old and he had been driven from his home by his father's drunken violence. But why was it so important to say it? Why did it have to be re-created, selected, shaped? And the story of Martin, the rebel. And later, a hero named Christopher who died in the war. Men, women, young girls, Negroes, students, mothers and fathers. His characters. His creations.

They haunted a ghostly stage and he did not understand them. Wasn't he, after all, the creator? Didn't he shape them for some purpose? Surely he had something to say, but what? What was it? That life is sad? No. That love lurks in a thorny garden? No. That mankind is deathless and noble? That the world is absurd? That logic is a lie? That meaning can only be discovered in life through the experience of living? That anger and contempt are the weapons of heroes? That all men are always and for ever alone? Identity? Empathy? Pity and compassion? No. No. No.

There was something else. Something more important. Not a proposition from a philosophy text. Not a mere statement. Something. Some feeling of roundness. Some feeling of a perfect thrust with a perfect dagger, to kill something and create something, to resolve, to untie the strangling knot inside, to bleed, to weep. But no, not quite that. The old vision slipped through his net of words. He flung it wide, then wider, but still he could not say what it was. A boy, a man, a woman with blonde hair, an eighty-year-old peasant, a young girl in white tennis shoes skipping among the rocks along the sea, her thin arms flying, her hair blown wild by the threatening storm. Hands reaching to touch something. Long fingers brushing away a child's tears.

Maggie lingered in the ruined room, walking towards the window and then away again, lighting a cigarette, putting it out. Splinters of broken glass glistened in the fuzz of the rug. The array of bottles on the bureau wavered before her. She had wandered out onto this neck of sand and the tide had washed in behind her. She could go neither forward nor backward. He had slammed the door between them. It was finished. What series of dreary adventures awaited her now she did not know, but her girlhood dreams of sailing ships and islands and lovers could no longer sustain her.

She felt old and dirty, a long way from the innocence that all these years she imagined she clutched to her heart, the innocence preserved, she thought, through endless violations of ordinary virtue and goodness. That was her secret and her strength. Her innocence. Her peculiar sensation of innocence. And now it was gone. Not only gone, but possibly never there. She felt naked and unprotected. She folded her arms across her belly and closed her eyes, trying not to remember the child that she almost had, trying not to recall the reasons why she knew at the time that it was all right not to have it, afraid that those reasons would melt into lies—broken glass in the romantic food on which, for so long, she had fed herself. She shook away the memory and lit another cigarette. And then, as if to escape further from it, she opened the door and wandered into the hallway. She walked back and forth for a moment or two, unable to decide where to go or what to do. The door next to Alex's room opened slowly, and she saw, peering through the crack, the shy face of the drunken priest, Father Malloy.

Alex whispered in the womb-like confessional. A deep, kindly voice answered, urging him to go on. He hesitated, still trying to find the right words to describe the sinful state of mind and heart into which he had fallen. 'I want to say it in my own way.'

'Yes,' said the voice. 'Say it in whatever way you can.'

'I have denied my God. I have put myself before Him. I have been angry with God because I am losing my sight.' Alex heard himself talking and wondered if, after all, these were his own words, if these were really the things for which he was sorry. Wasn't there more to it than that? Wasn't there something else, some twist or warp so fundamental that it absolved him from the responsibility and therefore from the sin? 'But there are things that I don't understand. Perhaps it is humility I lack, but I cannot be humble without submitting, and I cannot submit without resigning myself like a fatalist to whatever happens. And I cannot resign myself. My instinct is to hope and to fight and to preserve my dignity as a man. But my anger destroys my dignity and my hope destroys my faith. I go around in circles.'

'It's the oldest sin,' said the voice.

'Pride?' said Alex, and he heard for a moment William's

sleepy, lecturing voice. They were sitting out on the bulkhead behind Alex's house, drinking beer one summer night about twelve or one o'clock. William talked about King Lear, about that raving old man on the moors, and about Job and Oedipus and Hamlet. His mind knitted things together like the quick hands of a peasant woman. He borrowed bits and pieces from everywhere to make his point, his pattern. But what was it that night he started out to say? The old man raving, Oedipus at the crossroads, Ahab and the white whale, Hamlet, who could accuse himself of such things that it were better his mother had not borne him. What did he mean? What was the point? Is the fault in us or in our stars, dear Brutus? Was he trying to locate responsibility? The grinding wheels. Billiard balls. Determinism. Free will. Absolute justice. It was all in the sleepy, serpentine talk, one of William's endless monologues, spoken as much to the moon or the sea as to the half-listening Alex. And he, lulled by the sheer music of his friend's voice listened to the gentle lapping of the waves, and fixed his eye on the blur of light that came from the bedroom window of the house across the canal.

William was at the grotto. A priest conducted a mass for the people of his village who had made the pilgrimage to Lourdes. They kneeled at the railing. Behind them were stretchers, and behind those were wheelchairs. Some people sat on wooden benches in the rear of a marked-off area before the grotto; others stood or kneeled or walked about. The grotto contained a small altar, many flowers and an elaborate candle-holder. In a small niche above the grotto, where Bernadette first saw her vision, there was a statue of the Virgin. Her hands were pressed together as if in prayer; her eyes were fixed on heaven. A large rosary dangled from her wrist. On a stone slab under her feet were the words: *Que soy era Immaculada Concepción.*

A priest passed among the invalids and administered the holy communion. William watched as they offered their tongues for the wafer which was the body of Christ. It struck him as oddly indecent—these corpse-like people, lying there wrapped in blankets, conjuring up hospitals and the stale air of sickrooms, sticking out their tongues, as though they were about to be examined by a doctor, and then to have, instead, a symbolic piece of the body of Christ dropped into their mouths. He could not reconcile the biological and spiritual aspects of the scene, and for a moment he wanted to laugh.

Not far from where he stood, two nuns knelt and prayed. He could not see their faces under their protective hoods. The soles of their plain black shoes protruded from their black robes that collapsed in folds on the ground about them. Many of the women, old and young, wore kerchiefs or shawls over their heads. A well-dressed man with horn-rimmed glasses and a checkered jacket tried to look pious as he surreptitiously raised his camera.

The crowd was quiet, except for the mumbling of those who prayed aloud. The priest at the altar had his back to the gathering, his neckless, rounded form robed in white and red. Because the morning sun was so bright, the grotto seemed immersed in shadows. William tried to imagine the original incident, the little girl kneeling and trembling before that massive stone with its mysterious cave-like openings. But he could not scrape away all the encrustations, all the people and structures that had accumulated at that same spot. Surely, he thought, it was very different then, very lonely and frightening. He was startled out of his speculation by a tall blond young man who suddenly fell to his knees not five feet from where he was standing. His hands were pressed together and his head was bowed. He looked like a university student—German perhaps, or Dutch. William heard him moaning or sighing quietly, but he could not make out his language.

He looked about at the other kneeling figures. Unembarrassed and unnoticed, they humbled themselves there on that stone ground in the midst of the preoccupied crowd. He tried to imagine himself doing the same, but the effort sent a peculiar chill through his chest and stomach. No, he thought, he could not do that, could not address words to a God he did not believe existed. But how would he do it if he did believe in Him? What would he say? Please. Please. No, not even that. God's will be done. Perhaps. Do what thou wilt. But no, God needs no permission. Even one's acceptance of His will is part of His will. No, there could be no prayer that made any sense. Only perhaps complete submission in absolute silence. And for a moment he was alone by the sea, kneeling on the wet sand and staring out across the endless stretch of water. But only for a moment. He woke himself from his reverie thinking, 'Since I am unworthy, I can ask for nothing.'

'I've lost my f-f-faith,' said Father Malloy, punctuating his confession with a nervous laugh. He sat stiffly in an armless chair, his perpetually blushing face veiled in clouds of smoke. 'I was on my way to R-R-Rome. A very nice assignment for three months. I had permission to stop here, and,' he laughed again, 'this is where it finally happened. F-f-funny, isn't it? I mean ironic.' He raised his glass as though he were drinking to the irony that he just described, and then, with one gulp, emptied it. 'And that's wh-wh-why I can't hear your confession,' he said, his face still tightened from the sharpness of the whisky.

'But you're still a priest,' said Maggie. 'You still have all the official privileges and the authority.' She sat on the edge of the dishevelled bed, her bare legs crossed, her hair still uncombed. She was wearing a white sweater and a summery white skirt that revealed the shape of her thighs and hips. Father Malloy looked distractedly, his eyes blinking constantly, from her to the floor, to the mirror on the wall and then to the window and back to her.

'I s-s-suppose I am,' he said. When he smiled he looked boyish. His blond hair was short and straight, plastered to one side just as it might have been when he was eight or ten years old. 'But it wouldn't be f-f-fair.'

'To whom? Me or you?'

'Either one of us.' He offered to refill her glass, but she held back his hand.

'I only wanted to ask you how it's done. You see, I'm not even a Catholic.'

He stared at her for a moment and then he looked away and shrugged his shoulders. 'I can't grant you absolution.'

'It doesn't matter.' She stared into her glass and then took a sip.

'W-w-was it something terrible?' he said.

'I don't know,' she said. 'I think I want to die.' Her voice was flat and distant and she looked away from him.

'Oh,' he said, and then waited for her to go on.

'That's all,' she said. 'I think I'm a bad woman, but I don't know what my sin is.'

'P-p-perhaps you can describe the feeling.'

She shook her head. 'My whole life is a lie. Don't you have something in your religion for that?'

'I don't know,' he said. 'You have a very s-s-strange way of putting things. You're very nice. I mean you s-s-seem to be sincere.' He tugged at his stiff white collar.

'I'm sorry,' she said. 'I didn't mean to embarrass you or to take up your time.'

'Oh, no! No. Don't say that.' His nervous grunting laugh escaped again. 'Time? I have all the time in the world now. I was just thinking before you c-c-came in—I was just wondering what I was g-g-going to do now. I mean there's no sense in going back, is there?'

'Will you go to Rome?' she said.

'No. No, I can't do that. I mustn't. I think I will just go somewhere else. Tangier maybe. I have a sister in Tangier. She owns a café. They tell me she has lots of money. Catharine her name is—Catharine Malloy. She was always the wild one.' His gaze floated away, as though he were recalling childhood incidents.

'Tangier,' echoed Maggie.

He stood up and walked back and forth without saying anything. Then he stopped in front of her and pointed as though he were scolding her. 'You musn't f-f-feel that way.'

She frowned, brushing from the shadowy afternoon of her mind visions of narrow streets and Arabs with leather faces. 'I can't help it,' she said.

'There is always something that one can do.'

'Yes,' she said abruptly, standing up as if to prove that she was taller than he, 'one can always go to Tangier.'

'Wh-wh-why not?' he said. 'You think it's disgraceful to run away? To hide?'

'Yes.'

'W-w-well, it's not.' They stood there facing each other, no more than a foot apart. How easy it would be, thought Maggie, to put her arms around him and kiss him. Perhaps it would shock him out of his awkwardness and stammering shyness. 'It's better to go to Tangier, or to the end of the world somewhere, s-s-so long as one can f-f-find a way to live.' He took a deep breath and sighed. 'My sister is a whore in Tangier. Sh-sh-she told me so herself. And what's more she's proud of it.'

Maggie looked at him differently all of a sudden. A kind of intelligence that escaped her at first now shone in his blue eyes. And then she realized that he reminded her oddly enough of William. That curious discovery forced her to smile—she didn't know why. His hand reached out and touched her shoulder. 'Are you all right?' he said.

'Yes, yes, I'm fine,' she said, and leaned forward to kiss him lightly on the mouth. He turned away and coughed.

'You mustn't do that,' he said.

'I only meant to thank you,' she said.

'For what?'

She shrugged. 'I don't know. I really don't know, but thank you anyway.'

They both smiled and he poured them each another drink.

The grotto would come last, thought Alex. By this time he had been to the basilica and to the crypt, where, after about ten minutes of darkness, he could finally make out the waxen face of the dead saint. But he saw only her face, as one might see a mask-like apparition at a seance. It floated there, a blur of beauty in a throbbing black field. Surreptitiously he fingered the beads of the rosary that he had not yet taken from his pocket.

Now he was on his way to the baths, where he would be totally immersed in the healing waters of Massabielle. The details of his confession ran through his mind. He was not satisfied with it. Why hadn't he been able to force into words exactly what he felt about himself? Why had it finally disintegrated into a ritual performance, a ritual recital of specific sins, with the priest saying over and over again, 'Is there anything else?' like a clerk in a grocery store. He wondered whether or not the priest was even listening, whether or not he was aware of the complexity of the situation. Or was it simply that his case, especially here at Lourdes, was only ordinary. He wondered how many people came to this same priest in the course of a day and told him, with tears of despair or with tired bravery, that they were dying, that they were given only six months or three or two more at the most. And the priest would answer, in that same flat but tender voice, 'Is there anything else? Is there anything else?'

But surely it was not the priest's fault. He had been granted absolution for everything he could name. The rest was too vague, perhaps even unnamable. And, besides, he could not hope, should not hope, to reduce that anonymous, invisible priest to the level of a compassionate friend. It was William who could have served him that way. But William, too, had refused, and, without the privilege of the priest, had been more priest than friend.

William wandered away from the grotto and away from the town. He wanted to be alone and quiet for a while. Following a path into the hills, he rose above the spectacle and noise, above even the endless song that echoed in the haunted valley. He looked back and saw the church and the old village, and the river, beyond which, in green fields, cows grazed dreamily, unaware of him or the pilgrims or Lourdes or even the simple perfection of the summer sky.

'I decided to become a priest one night while I was r-r-running a two-mile race in Madison Square Garden in New York,' said Father Malloy. 'I was a sophomore in c-c-college and quite a good runner. It was the New York Athletic Club meet, or maybe the M-M-Melrose Games. I forget. But I remember the big crowd lost in the shadows, buzzing and cheering, and I remember the lights and the sound of the boards as we thumped around—twenty-two laps. There was s-s-something in the rhythm, s-s-something in the discipline, the triumph over the flesh. In m-m-many ways it's like flying. And then the loneliness. Those nine minutes or so stretch out into an e-e-eternity of pain and concentration. It's like having a f-f-fever. And then the desperation. W-w-win or die. Give everything. Heart pounding and b-b-breaking; head spinning for lack of air; legs turning to w-w-water, melting out from under you.' He panted and his eyes bulged with intensity as he relived the experience. Maggie watched him, fascinated. She too felt the shortness of breath, the pain and desperation. 'And then the final thrust,' he said. 'The impossible, insane effort at the very end.'

Someone took Alex gently by the arm and led him into the darkness of the bathhouse. He tried to explain to him in French that he should remove all his clothes and then wrap a towel around his waist. 'Yes,' said Alex. 'Yes, I understand.' He heard other people moving in the damp stony room. And he could smell them as they took off their clothes. It was the locker-room smell from high school. In his mind he heard the slamming of metal doors and the sound of bare feet on wet tiles. Voices echoed in the shower room—the playful, arrogant voices of boys growing into young men.

The attendant returned and took his arm again. He saw patches of light by this time, but still could not make out any forms. The man guided him to a line of naked men and told him to wait. Then he was gone again. Alex shifted nervously from foot to foot on the cool stone floor. Some of the men in the line mumbled prayers. He wondered what they looked like, whether they were old or young. Perhaps the man in front of him was also blind. Perhaps he was dying. He wanted to talk to someone, but he didn't dare. He heard the man in front of him move forward and he took a few cautious steps in the same direction, afraid not of falling, but of touching the man's naked body.

When the attendant returned again he warned him to be careful and then led him to a sloping ramp, down which he had to walk alone into a pool of water. He hesitated, his hand feeling the air in front of him. In a moment someone reached out and took his hand. It was the priest who presided over this ritual. He led him into the water, turned him around and, with his arm supporting his shoulders, helped him to lie back so that the water could cover him completely. He whispered to him rapidly and solemnly in a language that he did not understand. Then he took hold of Alex's hand and helped him to make the sign of the cross. He could feel his hand and arm trembling in the priest's firm grasp and for a moment he could not catch his breath. He wanted to ask, now, at this very moment, in a silent prayer, that the miracle be done, but even in his mind the words stuck in his throat. In a moment he was being lifted out of the water and ushered back into the crowded dressing-room.

The full heat of the afternoon sun burned on William's face. He sat among the rocks by the side of the winding dirt road, high above the swarming village. In his pocket he found the still unmailed letter to Edith. He read it through again, thinking of that dark-haired girl with the sad Jewish eyes, who only wanted, all her life, to be a woman, a mother, to comfort someone with her abundant warmth and love. He shut his eyes and tried to imagine them living together again. Did it matter, he wondered, that he did not love her in that painful and ludicrous romantic way? Or was it even better that he didn't? She had something that she had to give away, some generous sacrifice that she had to make. Wouldn't it also be an act of generosity and affection on his part to accept it? It was not unfair, he told himself—not unfair at all to take her this way. She needed him. She needed even his confusion and helplessness. And right now, at this peculiar time in his life, he needed her. Right now!

The future stretched out before him like a lengthening shadow. How many years made up of how many days? Food scraped from plates, wine gurgling deliciously into clear glasses, cigarette butts heaped in overflowing ashtrays. He would go on shaving and reading and coughing in the morning. Perhaps he would have some children. Perhaps some day he would write another book. About what? His half-conjured characters had already dissolved, like a sprinkling of snow on barren rock. About Alex, perhaps, who, like his characters, had found him out and abandoned him. It was too true, what his blind pirate had told him back there in the hotel—too remarkably true.

But why did he have to say it? It was their secret, something they had both known for a long time, the very keystone, in fact, of their whole relationship. When he kicked it out of place the whole beautiful, balanced arch of their friendship came tumbling down. It could never be the same again. Never. Like lovers who had dared to talk too bluntly about the act of making love.

'L-l-love is more important than l-l-life,' said Father Malloy. 'Have you ever been in love?'

'Yes,' said Maggie. 'Just once.'

'Once is enough.'

'And you?'

'Y-y-yes. But she never knew it.'

'You never told her?'

'N-n-no. I never even spoke to her.'

'Were you afraid?'

'Y-y-yes, I was afraid. I don't know of what, b-b-but I was afraid.'

'Was she pretty?'

'I don't know. In my eyes she was a s-s-saint.'

Maggie winced and then smiled.

'D-d-do you understand?' he pleaded, leaning forward in his chair.

'Yes,' she said, 'I think I do.'

It was late in the afternoon by the time Alex arrived at the grotto. He was exhausted, but his heart was pounding with excitement that he could not quell, no matter what reassurances or lies he used. He had kept this visit for the very end. It was here that he knew he would make his request, kneeling like a boy before the statue of the Virgin. How much easier it was to talk to her, he thought, than to that great white whale of a god. She was an almost human intermediary, kind and sympathetic. As a young lad he had read the story of the famous juggler of Notre Dame and he had been moved to tears by it, though he could never say why. And he came, like that humble man, to lay his tattered gift at her feet. He had nothing to offer her but his often-damaged, often-repaired faith and affection.

He added his candle to the crowded, dripping rack and crossed himself as he knelt to pray at the railing in front of the empty altar. No service was being conducted at the moment, but a large crowd was still gathered in the marked off area in front of the grotto. Through squinting eyes he could see the stone life-size statue above him. He stared at it for a long time, waiting for his heart to stop pounding in his chest. At last he bowed his head, closed his eyes, and whispered, 'Dear Mother of God, listen to me. I've come all this way to ask one thing only of you. Intervene for us. Help us to escape this killing darkness. And if for some reason I am beyond all help, earthly or divine, then think, at least, of them, of my children, whose innocence and goodness should protect them. Please. I ask you from my crippled heart and torn soul. Please spare them. Please protect them. Please.' His whispering voice trailed off into silence, but he stayed there for a long time, his eyes still closed, as though he were afraid to open them, afraid even to move.

We are all alone now, thought William. All of us—alone. He tossed pebbles into the dusty road and listened to the breeze. What an ancient sound that must be, he thought. That sleepy wind whispering its secrets in all the forests of the world for all of time.

When Alex finally opened his eyes he found that nothing was different. The stone statue had not moved, the altar was still half swallowed up in the deepening shadows of the cave, the throbbing in his temples was still there, the blurs of light, the crack of clear vision, like a door that someone failed to close all the way. The noises of the shuffling crowd behind him, which for a while he had blotted out, now intruded again. A new procession of pilgrims was moving towards the grotto from the direction of the basilica, their song ringing already in the stony green foothills and rising to the deepening blue sky.

Alex wandered away, relieved and disappointed. In the final minutes he had not known what to expect. He was as prepared to accept the recovery of his sight as he was to be struck totally blind. For some reason that ironic possibility had haunted him for days, and now as he walked away he was relieved to discover that no such cruel joke would be played on him.

He walked along the slow-moving river, still feeling, in the back of his mind, that something might happen, that perhaps it was only a matter of time, that perhaps miracles, like medicine, had to be absorbed by the body before they could do their work. He sat down on a wooden bench along the path that followed the river and smoked a cigarette.

But no, he thought, nothing would happen. The minutes slipped away. The birds played in the underbrush behind him. They were excited and busy. Surely nothing would happen now. Nothing. But if it did, he wondered, how would it feel? How would it begin? Perhaps he would be sitting there on that bench, smoking a cigarette and staring out across the river, as though he were at the theatre and the curtain was still closed, except for a crack of light that was more tantalizing than revealing. He would be waiting, a bit restless and impatient, for the drama to begin. Suddenly there would be a slight change in the light, as even now there was as an isolated cloud drifted across the sun. A rumbling of satisfaction would ripple through the audience, and the curtain would begin to part.

And, indeed, the curtain before him did seem to part, opening not on a luxurious drawing-room or a romantically dilapidated shack, but on the broad spectacle of green fields and mountains and blue skies. Light crashed in on him, forms exploded into visibility, colours rang in his mind like sirens. His cigarette fell from his hand and the flesh on his face quivered. The simplest sights were like bolts of lightning to behold—trees drenched in sunlight, cows grazing, a scattering of yellow flowers in a field, a stone wall with its riot of cracks and thrilling hardness, birds swooping and gliding like angels.

The whole world opened before him and he allowed himself to remember all the things that had gradually died into darkness for him—stretches of heavy, breathing sea, horizons that showed him where the sky began, Sunday crowds of people dressed for church in festivals of colours and materials, little girls with stiff skirts and long blonde hair, boys running, falling, tumbling, their ill-fitting shirts half out of their pants, their pants slipping below the roundness of their bellies, the row of happy-sad faces at a bar, the dinner table spread with roasts and fruit and flowers and wine, the expanse of stars on a clear night, the first streaks of light at dawn, the faded façades of buildings, bright labels, signs, patterns in a rug, paintings and words. Yes, above all, words. Giant pages of deep, black, beautiful words fluttered before him. What a feast! What an orgy, after the stingy ration of one or two at a time.

He sat entranced, leaning forward on the bench and holding on to it with both hands. A smile of youthful excitement illuminated his weary face. But even as he wallowed in the lush valleys and forests of the landscape across the river darkness threatened from the wings. His smile was slowly withdrawn. The curtain inched from both sides towards the centre, hesitated, and then closed completely. He shut his eyes and waited for a full minute, his breath short and shallow, his hands trembling. Then he opened them, but the world was still dark. A bolt of fear cracked in his chest and shook his whole body. He stood up and then sat down quickly. He opened and closed his eyes several times, rubbed them, adjusted his patch. He could feel the clammy coldness of his own hands against his flushed face. But still he saw nothing.

'No, no, no,' he muttered aloud, rejecting wildly and stubbornly what was already obvious. No, he thought. It's a warning; just a warning. God is trying to scare me. I know him. It'll pass. In another minute it will all pass. Things will be the same again. I'll find William. Everything will be all right. We'll have a drink and laugh. Maggie too. Everything will be the same. Nothing changes. Nothing ever happens.

He kept his eyes closed and held on to the bench so tightly that the bones in his sweating hands ached. His heart beat more fiercely and he was dizzy. No, he insisted again. No. I'll wait. I'll wait for a long time. Everything will be all right. He felt for the rosary beads in his pocket. They were warm in his cold hand. He took them out but he did not use them; he just sat there by the river in that blinding sunlight and held the beads in his clenched fist as though he were trying to squeeze something from them—blood, water, pity, pain, compassion. What did he want to do? What did he want to say? He could not stop trembling. He stood up suddenly, fury boiling inside of him, bursting his chest. And at the top of his breaking voice he shouted to the gentle hills, the innocent green fields, and the patient, indifferent river, 'Damn! Damn! Damn you!' And flung the beads into the endless darkness. The breeze wafted across his damp and empty hand and the hot or cold sensation in his palm was like the scorching of a fiery iron or the icy stab of a driven spike.

It was already early evening by the time William returned to the hotel. He found no one in either of the two rooms. The smaller room had been put in order again. There were no signs, in fact, of any violence or confusion. He packed his bag, slowly, methodically, and then found two sheets of paper on which he wrote identical notes:

Since I do not believe that it will do any of us any good to stay together, I am taking the train to Paris tonight. I'm not angry or disappointed; just weary of this many-sided war. Should either of you also decide to take that train, you can find me in one of the second-class compartments. We were all right in our own way about everything—but each of us only in our own way.

29

THE MYSTIQUE OF the *chemin de fer.* A good title, perhaps, thought William. But for what? Certainly there was something mysterious about railroads. He remembered a story he wrote as a boy, his very first attempt at a real story. He was twelve, or perhaps thirteen years old. Everything in the tale was vague and suggestive. The characters had no names, the places were not specific. Perhaps he had not yet learned how to use particular events and people; or possibly he had already discovered that there is a similarity between dreams and fiction.

The story was a kind of nightmare. Had he even dreamt it himself once? He could not remember. A man was riding on a train. The world went by outside the window. He was lulled into a trance-like state, as one often is, by the regular, clicking motion and by the telephone poles that flashed by with silent sameness. Houses, trees, towns, and cities floated by. Through lighted windows he could see people moving and talking. They came closer and the train moved more slowly. He could recognize their faces, familiar faces, which at first he could not place, then, finally, people he knew. A woman, a boy, an old man, other children. A disconnected series of events on a kind of horizontal film-strip.

It began to rain as the train pulled into the station. There were many tracks and switches and signals. On another track another train moved slowly out of the mist towards the platform. A man in a raincoat tried to hurry across the tracks, but he did not see the oncoming train. The man who was watching was overcome with confusion and terror. He pounded on the dripping glass through which he looked, but he could not make any noise at all, either with his fists or his voice. A huge cloud of steam issued from the train and suddenly obscured the almost certain tragedy.

He looked around and, seeing that no one else was at all concerned, he began to think that he was imagining things. When the train finally stopped, he took down his raincoat, got off, and hurried through the mist. As he stepped cautiously across the tracks and switches, he was too preoccupied with his dream to notice the iron beast that slid, ghost-like towards him.

What an odd story it was, thought William. And how long it had lingered with him—almost haunted him. He could even recall his boyish attempts at what he thought must be literary language. He had been fascinated with such words as *dreary* and *ominous*, and could not seem to use them often enough.

Now, twenty-five years later, he sat in a half-empty train, waiting for something to happen, as the darkness gathered (not ominously) over the world outside. He was the only one in the compartment. His single suitcase looked lonely on the long rack.

Through his window he saw the lights of the station and shadowy people moving with anxious steps towards the train. An old bundle of a woman went by beneath him, dragging behind her a stumbling idiot of a young man, his thick tongue filling his drooling mouth. A real challenge for the little saint of Lourdes, he said to himself. And she, herself, a little asthmatic.

Faces passed the doors of his compartment, glanced in and then moved on. He looked back at them as if to warn them that they could not enter. How strange it was to see them appear there, framed in wood, silenced behind glass—a toothless, unshaven old man with a stiff new hat, a plump woman with a baby in her arms and two other children hanging on to her black sweater, a handsome young woman with dark glasses, a wide-eyed boy darting away like a frightened bird, a middle-aged man with eyes full of caution and awkward dignity. Their faces appeared and then disappeared, lingering for a moment in his mind. Voices mumbled in the corridor. A whistle sounded in the distance.

His broken watch could not tell him what time it was. He expected any moment to feel that first horrible and wonderful lurch of the train, that motion that saved one from haunting indecision or condemned one to a crushing sense of the irrevocable. But it did not come and he grew uneasy. Up to this moment he had not allowed himself to reconsider anything, but now, looking again at his broken watch, he wondered whether or not there was still time to change everything. He could leap from the train, rush back to the hotel and—and what? What did he have to say to them, after all? It was not even a matter of forgiveness. Apologies, explanations, tears, anger—nothing would do any good. Nothing would be resolved between any of them. Nothing. The impasse was too perfectly contrived. This was his detour, his way of going roundabout. But only in order to survive, only in order to go on living. And still he was tempted, still he fingered the unmailed letter in his pocket.

He looked towards the platform again. Perhaps Alex was rushing to catch the train. Perhaps he was merely lost in the dark narrow streets of the town, stumbling around with his suitcase in one hand while his other groped for strangers who might tell him how to get to where he wanted to go. And if he came, would she come with him? He could not even guess. He had been more cruel to her than he wanted to be. He had only wanted her to see herself more clearly. He had only wanted her to understand why he could not stay with her any more. But all she could do was to talk and act as though their reconciliation was inevitable—or at least her choice and not his. What presumption! What stubborn pride! Or did she, after all, know something that he did not know? He longed to have another look at her face, a final look, just to be sure that he was doing, not the *right* thing, but the only possible thing.

Doubts, like invisible rats, scurried through the walls and under the floorboards of his now whirling mind. He started to get up, without even deciding that he wanted to get off the train, when that awful lurch came, the springing of the trap on the gallows, and he was pushed back again onto the musty grey seat. He closed his eyes for a moment and felt the train gather speed. So it was done, now, he thought—done for him or by him. It didn't matter. His choices were gone, and with them went his joy and pain. He would give himself now to the rhythmic motion of the train and to the dull luxury of being in no fixed place for a long long night.

His cheek was pressed against the cool glass of the window. Occasional lights and dark silhouettes oozed by in the thickening night. His body relaxed with fatigue and drowsiness. He would have fallen asleep that way, leaning against the window, had it not been for a loud tapping and scratching at the door. Two faces, leaning together, peered in at him through the now misty partition.

The door slid open and Maggie and Father Malloy staggered in. His face was redder than ever and his eyes were unfocused. He supported himself with an arm around Maggie's neck, and she helped him with an arm around his waist. 'I'm looking for the home for wayward priests,' she said.

'F-f-forgive our intrusion,' said Father Malloy. 'But we decided not to g-g-go to Tangier after all.' Maggie lowered him into a seat. He blinked his eyes several times and looked around him slowly as if to discover where he was. 'Are we m-m-moving by any chance?' he said.

'Yes,' said William.

'Why?'

'Because we're on a train.'

Maggie and William stared at one another for a moment, neither one of them able to suppress a smile of satisfaction. Then suddenly William frowned. 'Where's Alex?'

'I don't know,' said Maggie. 'I was hoping he was with you.'

William shook his head. 'And I was assuming *you* would look after him.'

'The poor man,' she said, 'stumbling around Lourdes in the dark. I hope he's all right.'

'He's all right,' said William. 'I'm sure he'll find his way home somehow. The world looks after him. Somebody will tell him what to do or where to go.'

The train rumbled through the darkness, carrying them further and further away from Lourdes, hurtling them back into reality. It was all over, thought William. The pilgrimage was over.

Suddenly Father Malloy leapt to his feet, hit his head on the luggage rack, and moaned, 'W-w-where are we going? We're moving.' There was a look of confusion and terror on his face.

'We're on our way to Paris,' said Maggie quietly, sensing his sudden panic.

'Paris? Paris? What am I going to do in Paris?' he said. He glanced about nervously. 'No, no, I better g-g-get off. I b-b-better get off right away.'

'You can't,' said William, and Father Malloy glanced at him for a long moment as though it was William's fault that he could not get off. Then he sighed and sat down again.'

'I r-r-really wanted to go,' he said. 'Honest. I really w-w-wanted to go to Tangier with this woman. I wanted to see my sister.' He looked up at William. 'She's a whore, you know.' His tone was matter-of-fact. 'In Tangier, I mean.' His chin slowly sank towards his chest again. 'We would all have been safe there—absolutely safe.'

'What's all this about?' said William to Maggie.

'He wanted me to run away with him to Tangier,' she said. 'To live with him in what he calls a state of horrible innocence.'

'Yes,' muttered Father Malloy. 'Horrible! Flesh is horrible. Human f-flesh. Human m-m-meat. I can't even stand to eat animal meat—dead flesh cooked, once alive.' His hands made fluttering shapes. 'Birds flying, goats leaping, galloping horses, and fat breathing cows munching grass in God's lovely fields.' His voice faded into dreaminess and they thought he might be falling asleep. But suddenly he straightened up again, his eyes wide open. 'The supplies,' he said. 'Where are the supplies?'

Maggie put a hand on his arm to steady him. 'Right here,' she said, pointing to a straw basket from which she then took a bottle of Scotch and a bottle of water.

'Ah,' he said. 'The magic ingredients.'

William smiled and watched patiently as the priest mixed the Scotch and water in a plastic cup. 'The water,' said Maggie, 'is from the holy rock, the spring in Lourdes. It's blessed or miraculous or something.'

'Angel water?' said William.

'Yes,' said Father Malloy. 'Angel water and S-Scotch.'

'Isn't that a sin of some kind?' said William. 'I mean, misusing holy water.'

'I'm not misusing it,' said the priest. 'I have s-s-something wrong inside of me that I'm trying to cure. The devil is there and I'm going to drown him.'

'I'll take mine straight,' said William, 'if you don't mind.'

'Coward,' said Maggie. 'It's just good spring water.'

'Y-y-yes,' said Father Malloy. 'But on the other hand. That is to say—w-what we r-r-really need is a higher ruling, a bishop or a c-cardinal. Maybe even the Pope himself. How I remember those beautiful scholastic arguments! How many angels can dance on the head of a pin? It all comes back. Magnificent words, sentences without meaning. Luscious constructs.'

They raised their cups in a toast. 'To what shall we drink?' said Maggie.

'To you,' said Father Malloy.

'Yes,' said William, 'to Maggie St. Claire, the patron saint of Tangier.'

'No,' she said, 'to you. To William Mariner, ex-writer, ex-everything.'

'Such a clever girl,' said William.

'I'm sorry,' she said. 'We should not be drinking to ourselves at all. We should be drinking to the pilgrimage, the journey.'

'Yes,' he said, 'and the end of the journey.'

'The journey never ends,' mumbled Father Malloy.

'And to him, to Alex, the pilgrim, the pirate,' she said.

They drank and sadly, silently, put down their cups.

'Will he be all right?' said Maggie.

'Yes,' said William, 'he'll be all right.' He became conscious of the dull rushing sound of the train. In his mind he saw the narrow track stretching out behind them, fading into the darkness. The whistle of the train wailed its warning, a long shrill message to the sleeping world. And then, as though it were an echo of the whistle, there was the anguished bellow of some man or beast. 'William,' called the voice. 'William Mariner. Where are you? Where the hell are you?'

There was a commotion in the passageway. Other voices complained. Doors opened and closed. The disturbance came closer and then Alex was framed in the glass door of their compartment. His face was grey and wild. His whole body trembled. His cheeks glistened with tears and sweat. Like a frantic insect he searched for the handle and then pounded and tugged and bellowed again. 'Hey, Doc. Hey, William Mariner. Where are you? For the love of Christ, where are you?'

William pulled open the door and Alex fell forward into the compartment. His tie was gone and his shirt open all the way to his waist.

William put his arms around him and helped him to a seat. 'It's all right, Alex. It's all right. It's me. It's William.'

Alex hugged him and could not speak. His sobbing choked off his words, though his mouth kept trying to form them. Maggie wet a handkerchief with the water from Lourdes and wiped his face and neck. Father Malloy poured some Scotch into a cup and put it in Alex's hand.

'Yes,' said William. 'Drink this, Alex. You'll feel better.' He steadied his hand and guided it towards his mouth. Alex turned away once or twice and shook his head. But then he drank.

'We're all here now,' said William. 'Don't worry. Don't worry about anything.' And then his own voice broke and he felt his eyes fill with tears.

Maggie held one of Alex's hands in both of hers until his trembling began to subside. 'We'll take care of you, Alex. It's all right. You're going home now.'

In a few minutes he could get out a word or two. He kept

swallowing, as though to drive back the tears. 'Home,' he said. 'Home!'

They gave him some more whisky and waited. He became calmer. He sat there between Maggie and William, rocking slightly with the rhythm of the train, staring at the floor. Once more the whistle sounded in the darkness outside. Once more William heard the dull roar of the train.

'What happened?' said Maggie gently. She looked at William as though for approval, but she saw in his face the shocked expression of a man who has just been shot. She did not have to wait for his answer to know that Alex was blind.

'I can't see, Doc,' said Alex. 'I can't see anything.'

Maggie lit a cigarette and put it in Alex's hand.

'God made me blind.' He breathed in the smoke and then sighed, his face trembling again. 'I went to the grotto and pleaded with him to let me see again. But instead he took away everything. I was sitting by the river. I thought I could see—the hills and fields, the faces of people; but then it stopped; everything went dark.' He hesitated. 'Something happened inside. I could feel it, like blood behind my eye. The curtain closed. It got narrower and narrower and then it closed.'

'God's vengeance,' muttered Father Malloy.

Alex turned suddenly to William and grabbed him by the arm. 'What did I do wrong, Doc? What did I do to deserve this?'

'Nothing,' said William. 'Nothing at all.' A score of comforting lies rushed through his mind, but he could say none of them.

'I need you, Doc. I was scared. I thought I wouldn't find you. At the hotel they told me you were going to Paris. Somebody took me to the station. I don't even know who. A child, I think, a girl with small hands. She kept talking to me in French.' He paused and then laughed bitterly as though to keep himself from crying. 'How god-damned ironic. How stupid.'

'It was coming for a long time,' said William.

'I know,' said Alex. 'I know, but I never believed it. All these years I never believed it would finally happen. I thought I could just go on seeing, just by sheer will, just because I wanted to.'

'I never believed it either,' said William.

Maggie reached over and touched William's hand.

'People n-n-never believe anything until it happens,' said Father Malloy, pouring out Scotch and handing around cups. Then he took a long drink from the bottle. 'B-but you'll go on living. W-w-we all go on living.'

'Yes,' said William. 'You'll be all right.'

'Will you come back with me?' said Alex.

'Yes, I'll come back,' He looked at Maggie. 'And so will she. We'll both come back with you.'

Alex smiled. 'And we'll get the island, Doc?'

'Yes,' he said. 'We'll get the island.'

'And we'll make it work, won't we? We'll build a bulkhead. You and me and Maggie. We'll make the island work.'

'Yes,' she said. 'It will be a beautiful place.'

Alex drank his Scotch. 'Paradise Island, Incorporated.'

'Me too,' muttered the drunken priest. 'Me too. Take me with you. Take me to your island.'

'Sure,' said Alex. 'Sure! We'll all go. We'll go home and work. We'll go home and make our island. We'll have everything there. Everything. Gardens and flowers and—everything. Won't we, Doc?'

'We'll have gardens,' said William. 'Hyacinths and roses, tulips and irises. Houses with slate roofs and maybe white stucco. Paths winding. Water lapping at the dock. A breakwater. A dry-dock. A place for the kids. Fields and streams and waterfalls. Windmills and towers. Bonfires burning into the night on the white beach. We'll sing away the hot summer.'

Alex's head fell slowly back against the seat. William got up and he and Maggie helped to make Alex comfortable. They stood over him for a moment, looking down at his sleeping smiling face.

'Did you mean that, Bill,' she said. 'About our going back with him?'

William took an envelope from his pocket and held it towards her for a second. 'I couldn't mail it,' he said, and then tore the letter in half and let it fall to the floor.

The priest was asleep now. They went out of the compartment into the passageway and stood before a large window. They stood very close and watched the vast dark world sail by. Lights like stars dotted the blackness, or streaked by near the window like meteors.

'Is it a comedy or a tragedy?' said Maggie.

'I don't know,' he said. 'There are some things we will never know.'

'Are they important?' said Maggie.

'No,' he said, and felt her long gentle hand on his arm. 'They're not important.' He let his forehead lean against the cool glass and closed his eyes for a moment as though to savour his friend's blindness. 'It's what we can know that matters, and we have all been so ignorant and so unkind.'

She moved closer to him and held his arm more tightly. 'Is it too late?' she said. She felt him shrug his shoulders, but he said nothing. He was back in Assisi again. They were standing under the giant gentle sky, holding one another, waiting, longing, wondering. They were lovers then, and for those few rare moments they knew exactly what that meant.

He turned to her now and kissed her. She whispered something to him, but the wailing whistle of the swift train drowned her words.

9 780967 333403